TEACHABLE MOMENTS

ROBERT GRAEF

outskirts press

Outskirts Press, Inc.
http://www.outskirtspress.com

ISBN: 978-1-9772-1468-3

PRINTED IN THE UNITED STATES OF AMERICA

CHAPTER 1

Tuesday, 7:15 a.m. Tom Clausen and his athletic director, Billy Keyes, stood at Keyes's desk studying three calendars; one from the district office, Northbridge High's version, and the Wesco Athletics calendar that set game schedules for the league. Oblivious of din from the gymnasium and the tire-shop odor of the weight room's new rubber flooring, they had eliminated all conflicts but one: a prior booking for the main gym that left a three-way wrestling meet homeless. Still to resolve were a parent's charge that his daughter was being denied playing time, the chronic shortage of registered game officials, a state-mandated change for players' physicals, and whether two varsity baseball players picked up by sheriff's deputies at a kegger should be eligible to play next year. First period was underway when Clausen arrived at the office.

The day at Northbridge High started without incident, leaving the office staff to chase down missing first-period attendance reports. Office assistants scurried to distribute counseling appointments and FYI memos to teachers. The faculty room was evacuated, overheated copy machines quiet, and the office staff settled into another day of updating records for 1,822 students. Behind a door at the end of a stub of corridor, Clausen draped his jacket on the back of his chair and settled in to check the contents of the folder that Alice, the school's head secretary, prepared for him each morning. He was still reading the first page when the blinker on his intercom signaled the first of what would become a normal day's overload of interruptions.

"Mr. C," Alice whispered into her headset, "we have a situation."

"Where's Darrel?" he asked.

Darrel Van Horn, Northbridge High's no-nonsense vice-principal in charge of discipline, was ex-Air Force, a retired colonel turned educator. Two frustrating years of classroom teaching convinced him that if he were to contribute, his efforts would be better spent on changing negative behaviors than trying to teach history. He enrolled in a night-school program and two years later left the classroom to become one of Northbridge High's two vice-principals. Well-versed in Air Force bureaucracy, Van Horn expected to be fired when policy enforcers demanded a more politically correct form of discipline, but until that time he was determined to give it his natural best. Van Horn moved into the enforcer's office when Clausen moved up from vice-principal to principal, completing a round of adjustments intended to put people where they belong. At first, Clausen cringed at his uncompromising tactics, but that was until he made clear that he was fair, tough, and man enough to handle any heat his style generated.

Alice said, "He's covering for a sub who checked out sick. Part of the situation, it seems."

"What do we have, boys or girls?"

"Boy. Just one."

"I'll take it." Clausen closed the folder and stepped into the reception area. Alice nodded toward a lanky, round-shouldered youngster sitting hunched with his elbows on his knees, chin cradled in his palms, his gothic-druggie costume decorated with rips and chains. Clausen pointed to his office and said, "In there."

With the door left open for Alice to witness what might not go right, Clausen pointed at a chair and said, "Sit." The boy dropped into the chair, slumped into his chin-in-hands posture, and shut his eyes. Clausen shrugged and turned to check a textbook inventory that had required opening every cabinet and locker on campus during winter break. He was penning a marginal note about a find of fifty-four second-year French texts for an enrollment of twenty-five when the boy opened an eye.

Clausen leaned back and said, "You're Scott Riddle. You wrestled varsity, won some bouts. How did you do at District?"

No response.

Clausen tried again. "According to this note"—he held it up—"you were so hard on a substitute that she abandoned her classroom. Is that a fair picture?"

Scott jumped to his feet. "The bitch came down on my mother, said she shoulda taught me to dress better. Like she picks what I wear?"

With Riddle's file up, Clausen scrolled down to find that, aside from a pattern of Monday morning tardies, his record was clean. He picked up his phone. "I'm going to have to call your parents."

"Don't bother. Mom's out of town working, and my dad's a total fucking asshole."

Clausen cradled the phone and stared the boy down. "The rule here is no rough talk, so you're done with that. About your father, the law says I have to try. For the time being, we're going to find a space for you to cool down. Then we'll talk. Come with me."

When Clausen rose, his weight inclined toward Scott, startling him. He banged his chair against a wall, bumping a sports photo askew. More frightened than defiant, he warbled, "Don't touch me!"

Clausen stepped back and put his hands in his pockets. He studied the boy, careful not to engage him in another stare-down. "I wasn't going to touch you. Nobody here wants to hurt you. Do you want to let me in on what's going on?"

Scott shuffled from foot to foot. "It's nobody's business. I need to go to the can. I gotta take a leak. I gotta go real bad."

Unless he was on drugs, which was always a possibility, the boy was as agitated as any Clausen had worked with. The door they had entered would funnel them back through a busy office, where passage would turn every head and ratchet up his emotional state.

"Okay," Clausen said, "hold it for a minute. I'll be right back." He ducked out to Alice's desk and leaned to her ear. "Get hold of Fred Imhoff. Tell him to drop whatever he's doing and get over here."

Alice raised her eyebrows. "You hear that?"

Clausen looked up to see that his door had been swung shut. He tapped twice and entered to find Scott Riddle urinating noisily into his resonant metal wastebasket.

To Clausen, it was one more in a career of incidents that would have been made worse by reacting. He looked to see if a stain was spreading on the carpet before checking his desk to see if it was as he left it. Without looking directly at Scott, he said, "Follow me."

Cringing with embarrassment, the boy took the long way around the wastebasket to follow the principal to a conference room off the library.

"Wait here," Clausen said. "Whatever's troubling you is going to grow or shrink depending on what you do next. You have the room to yourself. Stay here." Clausen figured odds were high that he would bolt during the twenty or more minutes it would take the district's go-to counselor to reach the building.

Clausen stuck his head in the counseling center to alert Trudi Fenstra about the boy in her conference room before joining a swelling flow of students in the A-wing corridor. He fell into step with an upper classman. "What do you have first period, Bruce?" Bruce had come from Mr. Cowley's World History class that just disgorged students before the bell. One more item for the overcrowded faculty meeting agenda. What's so difficult, he wondered, about holding students until the end of the period? You wait for the bell, a simple concept. Yet that and a dozen other persistent breaches of policy kept him struggling to run a tight ship with a light hand.

Alice waved a folded sheet at him as he passed her desk. "Note from Mick Ostrander about the Riddle boy."

By the end of third period, the day had turned into another of putting out brushfires. Each time Clausen settled in to work at clearing his desk, another crisis erupted—the last being afternoon car-prowls in the student lot that resulted in three broken windows and a stolen sound system. Van Horn identified one of the two culprits caught on security tape as a dropout. At five o'clock he stuffed the overdue textbook inventory into his briefcase and left his desk. He let himself out of the west exit, tried the door behind him, and walked to his car where he punched the preset of his favorite PBS station.

Clausen was four cars from crossing the Burlington Northern tracks that bisected Northbridge when a southbound freight triggered the crossing barrier. The tracks, a civic asset during the glory days of rail, had become a hindrance to local commerce and an annoyance to anyone entering or leaving town at certain hours. For Clausen and the drivers queued up behind him, stoppages were an accepted nuisance that locals had to plan around. He switched his engine off and leaned back and closed his eyes, half hearing, half feeling the rhythmic clacking of freight car wheels hammering through the crossing. The next thing he knew the train was gone and a toot from behind urged him into motion.

He drove slowly, never exceeding thirty. Leaving the sterile sidewalks and pavement of Commerce Street, he swung onto Walnut, which bisected three blocks of well-tended cottages built for mill workers during the twenties and thirties. Turning left where Walnut bent right, he entered Dogwood Lane where, seventy and more years ago, Northbridge's merchants and professionals settled on generous lots affording views over the waterway. Over time, all of the waterfront homes but the mansion across the street from the Clausens' classic Cape Cod underwent renovation at the hands of new owners. He drove under mature maples that arched from both sides to cut the street off from all but a spotty ribbon of sky. Rounding into his driveway, he eased over root-buckled concrete to park his Subaru over an oil spot that testified to the impossibility of squeezing a car into the semi organized clutter of the Clausens' detached double garage.

Jane Clausen made a point of leaving her math classroom at Port Gardner's Stevens Middle School at four fifteen, exactly one hour after school let out. Her thought was that, with her husband captive to the million and one things that could and did happen at his school, someone had to keep home life in balance. Even with stops for groceries, she invariably beat him home. The day was no different except that he looked more drawn when he dropped his briefcase for their ritual hug. He gave her a squeeze and a pat and said, "I'm going to take five. Don't let me sleep long."

He loosened his tie and dropped into his recliner. It was 5:40, thanks to the delay at the tracks, but still near his regular homecoming time. Feeling that gravity had firmed its grip on him, he levered his chair into a semi recumbent position and clicked on Channel 7 News before shutting his eyes.

With groceries stowed and dinner preps underway, Jane looked in to watch him breathe. Anyone who did not know him well might not have detected any change. He was scarcely heavier than the 170-pound man she married. His hair was cut considerably shorter than when they met. Though never an outstanding athlete, he had at least looked like one and had played C-Division racquetball in his thirties. In high school, he was a benchwarmer in football and fifth on the cross-country roster. It was only in the last year that he had begun walking flatfooted as though carrying an invisible load. Jane blamed the change on his work schedule—the nonscheduled times he was called out, the night functions, the endless reports, the demanding parents, and the teachers who didn't understand what rules were for. Predinner naps, she thought, were good and necessary therapy. Before turning to set out plates and cutlery, she watched his right hand flutter as though grasping for an object in a dream.

Her homecoming routine began with changing from her no-frills work outfits to her off-duty uniform of jeans, sandals, and a boy's plaid flannel shirt. The change was more than just for physical comfort because with it she shed her teaching persona. Jane Clausen was an exemplary teacher but often felt she was an imposter in the classroom. Though her mind for numbers and command of detail were better suited to accounting or research, her inability to carry a child full-term left her with maternal urgings that she gave vent to by teaching kindergarten. Every few years she applied for and received transfers that let her progress through the grades as though she was nurturing growing children of her own. By eighth grade, some almost caught her in size. Petite, with an athlete's sinewy build, Jane was scaled so similarly to her more mature students that, aside from dress, she melted into their midst.

Tom Clausen's late afternoon naps were a new thing. Quick snoozes as short as ten minutes helped to recharge his batteries, but they were not enough to regularly fan the spark that, until recently, drew them to bed at the same hour. Through most of their childless years, they found completion in holding and loving each other, but lately he had taken to dozing in front of the television before trudging half-asleep to bed where he dropped off immediately. Mornings were better. On workdays, Jane showered first, dressed, brushed her short salt-and-pepper hair and sat briefly for the Clausens' standard breakfast of oatmeal, juice, and half-caff coffee while swapping sections of the *Tribune*. Tom found opportunity to touch and hold her during breakfast cleanup that, were it not for the clock and call of duty, might have led to more. Stepping over Buster, who napped as close to her busy feet as possible, she moved to the living room to watch her husband sleep, smiling at the thought of how often he said she never looked sexier than when in her flannel shirt and jeans.

Silently calculating his respiration rate, Jane recalled the last time he commented on her mind for numbers—Mrs. Mathemagician he'd called her—and said that she'd be making more than he did if she'd opted for technology. "Yes, that may be," she'd said, "but what about you, Mr. Investigator, Mr. Gotta-Know-Why, always digging under the surface? This principal gig of yours—in anybody else's hands, it'd be a whole lot easier, right?" He acknowledged without argument. They talked on about the events that led them to where they were and agreed that, for a couple of misfits, they were pretty good at what they did.

Tom felt more alive when the issues that filled his time were rich in stories and backstories. The rest he dismissed as "been there, done that" issues better suited for vice-principals. His pick of the action at Northbridge High was managing change, and when it came his way he probed for the why of it, the story behind it. He couldn't help it. It was his way, and it was using him up.

Tom's active hazel eyes were set under sandy brows, underscoring a forehead that was pushing his hairline back. His red-tinged brown hair was touched with gray at the temples and worn long enough to fall onto his ears. The white scar that once connected his right eyebrow to his boyhood hairline now dead-ended on his brow like an underfunded road project. Its cause, a tumble from a rope swing onto a brush pile, also explained the bend in Clausen's nose.

His accident-skewed boyish features misled some into taking him for an average person capable of no more than average insights. And what some took as a distracted air was the private working of a busy mind that Jane sometimes had to call him away from to make room for people. As one who cherished thoughtful solitude, Clausen often wondered how he had come to be surrounded by hordes of young people and a rambunctious faculty of individualists. He took whatever success he enjoyed as proof that people can and do contribute to society by overcoming their natures.

Clausen's normal expression was neutral. His narrow-lipped mouth might have seemed severe but for its ends turning up when he set his jaw, disguising determination with a suggestion of a smile. Family photos linked him to his Norwegian father while his red-brown hair and freckles were gifts from his Scottish mother. With no one feature calling attention to itself, his face was easily lost in crowds. New to wearing glasses, his were on, off, or perched on his forehead, and perpetually smudged. The round-rimmed tortoise frame, a plain gold wedding band, and a thirty-five-dollar Timex were his only accessories. His clothes, like him, were free of pretense.

Jane picked up his glasses from where they had slipped into his lap and thanked God it was a free night—no meeting, no evening activity to supervise, and no public scrutiny. No need, as the school board advised, to keep their beaks dry. A glass of wine before dinner—the Clausens were a red-wine-only household—would help set the pace for a mellow evening. The evening off would sustain him, she hoped, until the upcoming three-day weekend. She whipped up a salad and dressed a sockeye filet before wrestling the cork from an Australian Syrah. Tom's request for five minutes had stretched to twenty when she carried the bottle and glasses to the coffee table and settled on the arm of his chair to let the soft pressure of her body wake him.

When his eyes popped open, she murmured, "Tell me about your day." She sat up to make room for him to right his chair and stretch before handing him his glass.

He sniffed at the wine. "My day? Oh, boy. Well, I logged another first but not one for my résumé."

"Mm-hmm. Will it make you famous?"

He extricated himself from his chair to stand and stretch again. "Only if my public finds something ennobling about a kid peeing in my wastebasket."

"No!"

"No kidding. And, believe it or not, there were extenuating circumstances, including me telling him to hold it when he couldn't. The kid's mother called—she's a National Guard officer meeting with FEMA in DC—to tell him she's stuck in hearings for another week. And then he found out his dad is shacking up with one of his mom's friends, even sneaking her into their house, and that sent his little sister into hiding, which he said she's really good at. The kid's out-of-his-mind angry. When his dad discovered he'd left home, he didn't even try to find him—even after he was gone for a week."

"Did he tell you this?"

"No, Imhoff got him to open up. When he asked him if he wanted to go home or to Child Protective Services, he chose CPS. After CPS contacted the father, the jerk descended on us as though righteously offended."

"To see Van Horn, I hope."

"Nope, me. With blood in his eye, so I called the police." Tom savored his first sip of the wine and nodded approval.

"Good for you. I hope that settled it."

"There was more to it. The nurse has him on file for a spastic bladder problem—like he has to go at every class break, or else. His teachers knew about it, but I didn't. And then Trish Ostrander's son, Mick, sent a note asking if he could talk with me about the boy, so I called him in; Mick knew him from wrestling. He suspects, and I think he could be right, that he could do something to harm his dad, maybe himself, too. The kid's so unhinged that nothing would surprise me."

"Like Columbine?"

"No. He has friends, and school's the best thing in his life. His dad's the worst. Sure, he's mad at Bush and the National Guard for calling his mom away, but his dad's the lightning rod for his anger."

Jane slipped off the arm of the chair to reach her glass, slid back against him, and whispered, "You want to tell me more, or should I start the fish?"

"Good morning, Alice. All quiet on the western front?" Tom scooped out the contents of his box and scanned the morning bulletin. "Who's Dr. Della Dujardin?"

Alice Michaelson would know, her desk being the school's crossroads for information on attendance, scheduling, appointments, purchase orders, agendas, paper clips, dry-erase pens, and rumors. With all aspects of school business under her scrutiny, she was Northbridge High's undisputed best source of information on whatever might be going on or about to happen. She was also Tom's gatekeeper and, being seated on a sight line to his desk, his witness should a witness be needed. Though Van Horn was foremost of the two vice-principals, Alice was Tom's de facto second officer. She once described her work as a supremely exhilarating and draining paradox.

Alice Michaelson was a substantial woman. While many women of her height and weight fret about cellulite and sagging arms, her roundly plump limbs and torso appeared as evenly inflated as heated sausages, giving a pleasant impression of substance without distracting wrinkles or bulges. She had earned a fabled reputation for multitasking by doling out information right and left while her chubby fingers danced out reports on her keyboard. At forty-seven, Alice's hair had gone prematurely silver, which accentuated her overly large deep-brown eyes. She embellished her elegant Nordstrom wardrobe with bold accessories collected as travel mementos from far places. Alice's two-door BMW testified that it was something other than her secretary's salary that held her to her job.

Alice's husband, Jerome, an overage extreme sports enthusiast, was spending a year away from his office to heal from injuries incurred from flying over the handlebars of his mountain bike. As one of Microsoft's early hires, the loss of a year or two's wages wasn't a concern, and, as it turned out, he was handling his workload from home. His big issue was how to occupy his mind while his damaged back and shoulder healed. Bereft of the fast tempo demands of work and wit permeating Microsoft's campus, Jerome became bored and peevish. All too often, Alice found him spoiling for an argument when she arrived home in Mill Creek.

She took to monitoring his moods by phone each afternoon, and if she found him sounding owly, as she put it, she would work late and dine alone in one of the few Port Gardner restaurants with enough light to read while lingering over coffee. When she called to test his mood, usually before seven o'clock, he was unfailingly contrite and begged her to hurry home. His extra hours of solitude, while confirming that absence *does* make the heart grow fonder, also let him focus on PBS's *Jim Lehrer News Hour* without wifely interruptions. Meanwhile, Alice enjoyed the guilty pleasure of nibbling at off-diet desserts that would have drawn Jerome's disapproval. Another satisfaction was letting the evening commute sort itself out while she relaxed with her coffee and her book.

Alice handed Tom a promotional brochure. "You might know our visitor as Della Dujardin, aka Dr. Della Garden. She writes young-adult fiction. She has a head-office pass to set up in our library."

"To do what?"

"The good news is they said that's up to you. You'll find her having coffee in the faculty room. Might be an interesting start for your day."

"Anything new on our young friend from yesterday?"

"Darrel's on it. I don't know how they worked it, but Scott was released from CPS into the custody of Mel and Trish Ostrander, Mick's parents. After Imhoff's nose-to-nose session with the father, it appears that he doesn't care to be anywhere near his son. Oh yes, on the upside, Darrel talked Del Johnson into accepting Scott for sixth period at the school farm. Darrel calls it animal therapy. I call it shoveling poop."

"Don't knock it. It works. We'll need to get his teachers to meet with Imhoff to see if there've been classroom incidents that shed some light."

"Imhoff's already requested it, but for now you'd better see what Dr. Della is up to." When she swung back to her screen to puzzle over why second-period attendance came in lower than first, Alice pulled a sticky note from her monitor. "One more thing, Claudia McPhaiden called. She wouldn't leave a message but said she'd call again."

CHAPTER 2

Claudia McPhaiden called back Wednesday to ask Clausen if he had attended the Northbridge girls' Friday afternoon softball game with archrival, Roosevelt High. He hadn't, but he had heard about it, a squeaker victory that Northbridge claimed in the final inning. Northbridge, down by two in the top of the seventh, found hope when shortstop Hannah Terry punched a crisp shot into the right field gap. After stretching her hit into a double, the next two at bat followed with a single and a double to send Terry and another base runner across the plate. When a fielder's error allowed one more to score, the Viking team leaped off their bench for a celebration that spilled across the third-base path until officials ordered the diamond cleared. Roosevelt's last chance at bat started with a single before their next three batters went down swinging to leave the Vikings with the win. Interviewed by the *Port Gardner Tribune*, Coach Dale Runyon had said, "All credit goes to the girls. They love the game, and they love to win."

Clausen hung up after ten minutes of listening to Mrs. McPhaiden and scribbled a summons to Coach Runyon. His next hours were filled with an inspection by Northbridge's fire marshal followed by a visit from a county health inspector who shooed the food service staff out to search for what might have caused three students to vomit in the lunchroom the day before. That settled, he listened to a parent's demand to know why her daughter, who forgot to bring her permission slip, wasn't allowed to go on a class field trip to an art exhibit at Seattle's Volunteer Park Museum. After she left, a traveling pastor who requested time to debate creation versus evolution with the principal was blocked by Alice who sent him to the district office for permission to visit that wouldn't be granted. By holing up in his office between interruptions, Clausen managed to make progress on reviewing the textbook inventory.

Dale Runyon tapped on his doorjamb. "Hi, you wanted to see me?" Runyon's signature ensemble of turtleneck, slacks, and loafers spoke to his conviction that the less variation in his visible persona, the less confusion about what he expected of students. If his success was an indicator, it worked.

Clausen and Runyon's history began with three years of study at Washington State University together, the last two as roommates. Their bond ripened from frequenting the same taverns, fishing nearby Idaho streams, learning tennis and racquetball together, and even dating the same girl at different times. Their family homes in Washington's Skagit and Whatcom Counties were close enough that they carpooled across the state for holidays, and one summer, thanks to the Coast Guard, they survived a Puget Sound squall after the mast was blown out of their borrowed sailing dinghy.

Dale was taller than Tom by five inches, and with his mother's Mediterranean coloring and wavy black hair, he had been considered one of the campus's more desirable hunks. His father, Charles Runyon, was a Bellingham restaurateur who married and divorced young. When in his thirties, Charles married Dale's mother, Marta Manos, a Greek-American waitress in his restaurant. Between children, Marta moved up from waitress to management. Vivacious, intelligent, and, aside from a wide-eyed cast to her features that caused her to appear startled, she was dramatically pretty. Item by item, she added Greek cuisine to the menu until, on their tenth wedding anniversary, Charles and Marta announced a grand reopening of Runyon's Grill under its new name, Athens West.

Clausen was drawn to the social sciences. His pleasure reading leaned heavily toward biography and historical nonfiction. Runyon was a more passionate learner whose sputtering enthusiasms focused on breakthrough technologies. He loved his environmental studies and computer classes but suffered other required courses as donkey work. Both were able students with busy extracurricular interests that limited their grade-point averages to the B range. Neither developed a lasting love interest during those years. Instead, both graduated with warm memories of fun-loving coeds who drifted into and out of their social circle.

Tom's first teaching job was with Tacoma's public schools where he fell in with another first-year teacher, Jane Reichelt. Jane, a petite brunette, impressed him when she dribbled through his defense during a faculty coed soccer game. That she could, despite her size, demolish him at tennis was even more impressive. But it was the laughter that really hooked him. When they were together, anything could be hilarious. The slightest trigger set them to giggling, snorting, and spouting happy tears until they collapsed into each other's arms gasping for breath. Onlookers took them to be more insane than lost in the delirium and wonder of discovering their love for each other.

Dale signed on with the Spokane School District where Paulsen High School's principal, Myron Krumm, saw him as the man to keep his school's computers online. On the surface, Dale's job called for four periods of computer education and one of biology, a good fit. But Krumm also looked at him as Paulson High's in-house computer tech and summoned him at any hour to fix whatever problems befell the school's computers.

Predictably, his oft-interrupted teaching was a disappointment to Dale and his evaluators. Needing something to keep his mind off his job situation, he turned to Betty Wahlstrom, a tall, beautiful, and provocatively remote English teacher. Betty had been on the faculty two years when Dale arrived to find her playing the princess among peasants. Betty wasn't connected with any of Paulson's male staff because she considered herself to be of such worth that if one dared to woo her, he had better be without fault. When Dale met her, no one had yet measured up to her moral and intellectual standards. Having a high opinion of her abilities and ranking teachers in general as her intellectual inferiors, she would have opted for a different career but for her devout family's tradition for mission work that, by their measure, included teaching. Though friendless, she found it impossible to relax in others' company without judging them or loosening up enough to forgive their unfamiliar behaviors. Betty became an island in her faculty's social sea.

Dale hadn't tumbled for college girls, partly because they were too easy. Handsome, intelligent, dark, rangy, and witty, he was the perfect package coeds hoped to land. So he found himself, aside from fleeting relationships, brushing attractive girls away. Friends who failed with the same girls he shrugged off invented sour jokes about him and cursed him for squandering what to their hormone-driven fantasies were wasted opportunities. He amused them by pursuing interesting but unattainable females—one, a young assistant professor of mathematics, and the other, a brilliant graduate student in physics from Finland. He failed with both.

Two things pushed him toward a visible relationship with a woman. One was that Betty Wahlstrom brushed him off. The second was Loren Mortenson, an art teacher whose interest in college sports paralleled Dale's. Loren was a nice guy and the faculty comedian. He was Dale's buddy right up to when he begged Dale to visit his apartment for "a quiet evening together," and once he'd declared himself, he couldn't keep his conversations free of inuendo. Dale reasoned that if Loren suspected his orientation, he needed to make a clear statement that he preferred girls.

As with the math professor and the Finnish physicist, Betty Wahlstrom became a cause to pursue. Dale was relentless. He made himself such an inescapable part of her landscape that she was stumbling over him at every turn. At the same time, he found himself less upset by Mr. Krumm's claims on his time which, in fact, had slacked off. Mulling this shift made him wonder if Betty's reluctant presence in his life might be playing a part in it, not suspecting that his interest in pursuing her might be overshadowing his grudge against Krumm.

In time he made progress, if progress could be measured by the number of hours they spent together. Betty thawed degree by degree, having dinner and attending plays with him, which the faculty rumor mill accepted as an engagement of sorts. Still, not having moved Betty beyond companionship, he was disappointed that he'd drawn so little warmth from her until the night of the Romanian wedding.

Dale and his Romanian landlord, Georghe Tomic, had become close friends through their shared fascination with new developments in computers, and through Tomic, Dale was introduced to the Ionescu family. The Ionescus' daughter, Viorica, was engaged to another Romanian Dale had met, and when their wedding was announced, he was surprised to receive an invitation. Needing a date, he asked Betty. Both were understandably wary, wedding dates being minefields that blast uncountable dating couples into matrimony. Nevertheless, she agreed to accompany him.

Following the Orthodox wedding that Betty found foreign but interesting, a feast was held in an Odd Fellows hall on Spokane's east side where the Romanians would teach their rental agent that one Romanian wedding feast adds years to the age of a hall. Dale and Betty arrived to find platters of cold cuts set out on long tables arranged to seat two hundred. Placed among the platters were carafes of homemade plum brandy. An accordion and drums duo squeezed and thumped out lively folk music as latecomers, intent on catching up, swooped down on the brandy before greeting the bride and groom.

The Orthodox church, the ceremony, the raucous crowd, the drinking—all of it was so foreign to Betty's upbringing that she sat stiff as a mannequin until Dale's burly but dignified-appearing landlord hoisted her out of her chair and towed her onto the dance floor. Once he taught her the steps, Georghe traded her with another couple. Dale watched, unbelieving, while a glow bloomed in her cheeks as she whirled from partner to partner. Georghe returned her, breathless and wearing a smile he'd never seen before. Before seating her, Georghe filled two glasses, handed one to Betty, locked arms with her, and bellowed, "Salud!" Amazingly, they both tipped their glasses, leaving Betty gasping and wide-eyed as the unaccustomed shock of seventy-proof homemade schnapps seared her esophagus.

The cold cuts were cleared away and replaced by soup, and the soup left to be replaced by salad, and that by chicken and chops. Then came cabbage rolls and schnitzel. At each change, servers saw that the carafes were topped off. And at each refilling, another Romanian would escort Betty onto the floor, and before or after each episode, she let herself be talked into quaffing another toast to the bride and groom. She laughed like a schoolgirl, learned how to deliver European air-kisses to the cheeks of dance partners, and ate like a farmhand. From all appearances, Betty was having the time of her life until she woke up the next morning lying with Dale on his bed, not in bed with him but with her skirt askew and a blouse button undone.

With no Romanians around to jolly her out of her guilt, she slipped out of bed, gathered her sweater and shoes, and locked herself in the bathroom where she cursed her weakness while sobbing over lost virtue. She emerged red-eyed but committed to taking the necessary steps to make an honest woman of herself. When she announced that she would accept his proposal, she was not so much agreeing to marry him as confessing her sin and accepting penance. She had been guilty of weakness, guilty of yielding to the flesh, and guilty of abandoning her standards of behavior. For his part, Dale couldn't remember uttering the proposal Betty insisted he bestowed on her, which left him a bit dazed and more than a little wary of Romanian brandy while Betty's public behavior became that of a bride-to-be.

Confident in her beauty, Betty enjoyed being admired and was delighted that she turned even more heads when seen with Dale. They were a handsome couple. Smiling and vivacious, she covered her grim determination to marry with a front that kept him on the hook. Unlike the unattainable women of his college years, she reminded him with small intimacies that she was his, especially when suspecting that his attention might be wandering. Her little displays of affection, being more public than private, made them the focus of faculty gossip. She was lovely, bright, and unpredictable. He wanted her. Dale and Betty wed in June with Tom serving as best man.

Eight years after Dale and Betty's wedding, Tom moved from teaching in the Tacoma School District to a vice-principal's office in Northbridge, a fast-growing bedroom community where sprawling new subdivisions guaranteed that schools there would grow for years to come. To cope with the influx, the district's brick-and-mortar buildings became surrounded with portables like hens with chicks while openings for teaching positions were broadcast to placement offices at every college of education in the state.

It was during Tom's second year as a Northbridge High vice-principal that a position tailor-made for Dale's talents opened. Calling for three periods of computers and two of biology, it was a long-shot combination that, if no one with Dale's qualifications applied, would be pieced together from two new hires, a complication that would require painful juggling of teachers' schedules. If Dale took it, it would be a win-win situation. Not only was he a perfect fit for Northbridge High's needs, but it could be his chance to break free from Krumm's extracurricular demands. Tom mailed the listing at a time when escape from Spokane seemed heaven-sent. The rub turned out to be Betty's reluctance to trade sunny Spokane for Puget Sound drizzle. Dale won her over by promising to replace their two-bedroom duplex unit with a three-bedroom home with separate rooms for Roger and Ellen, then ages five and six.

In the years following the Runyons' move to Northbridge, Dale developed a professional home at Northbridge High School where he built an exemplary computer-education program, while Betty found her niche teaching English at North Counties Christian Academy. They decorated and landscaped the promised three-bedroom rambler while Roger and Ellen grew to high school age. Tom, known to the Runyon children as Uncle Tom, moved up from vice-principal to the principal's office. Though on track for a superintendency, he and Jane would have traded it all in an instant for children like Roger and Ellen, but by then they knew that wasn't to be.

Tom rose from his desk and shut the office door. "Have a seat. I just got a call from Claudia McPhaiden. Her granddaughter, Hannah Terry, plays softball, right?"

"Right. One of our better hitters."

"And in yesterday's game after she crossed the plate there was a celebration. Right again?"

"Well, yes. What of it?"

"And instead of giving her an atta-girl, you slapped her on the butt. Is that true?"

"I might have. No big deal."

"Claudia McPhaiden was in the stands when you placed your

hand on her seventeen-year-old granddaughter's ass. She's considering bringing charges against you for inappropriate touching."

Dale jumped to his feet. "Inappropriate touching! You've got be kidding. Did she say anything about the mob scene after the game? Ask anybody. Girls were crawling all over me, her granddaughter, too. I can't believe you're taking this seriously."

"Buddy, I don't expect you to like this any more than I do, but until it's settled, you and I go by the book. Unless Claudia drops it, I have no choice. She's not listening to reason. Sorry, but until we find out how far she wants to take it, you're going to have step back from coaching."

Runyon did take a step backward, widening the distance that had suddenly sprung up between them. "Isn't that a little extreme, sir?"

"Don't start with the sir stuff, and no, it isn't extreme when complaints for less than this have ended teaching careers. Not when the complaint comes from the chairperson of the school board. No, the best thing you can do is keep a low profile while I figure out what she intends to do. Teach your classes, and don't touch a female unless she's bleeding to death. And if anybody brings up the incident, act surprised."

"Ask Hannah; she'll tell you. I didn't do anything wrong."

"She probably would, but that doesn't matter. Claudia's take on what happened has hit the fan. It's her perception of what you did that matters, and if you think I'm being hard-nosed about it, stop to consider that this was dropped on my desk, not yours. To put it bluntly, it's my job now to save as much of your sorry ass as possible while you stay in the background. Now what do you have left, two games?"

"If we don't qualify for playoffs."

"Okay, help Kristi with the rosters and whatever, then back away and hope Claudia cools off. I'll have a talk with her."

"When?"

"When she calls, and she will. If I call her, she'll take it as a biased move to help a friend, which wouldn't help. I'm sorry, very sorry, but you're just going to have to wait." Dale was stalking toward the door when Tom said, "Hold up a minute. We can't let this get between you and me. We're still on for golf Saturday. No backing out."

Dale raised a hand in acknowledgment and walked out of his office.

"Mrs. McPhaiden on two." Alice noted the hesitation before a bead of red light popped on when Tom picked up. He hadn't been looking forward to the call. It was Thursday morning, almost a week since Dale patted her granddaughter's bottom, plenty of time for her to cool off—more than enough to come to a full boil.

"Tom Clausen speaking."

"Mr. Clausen, I need to meet with you this afternoon."

"Okay. I'm pretty jammed up until after today's faculty meeting. Would a quarter to five be convenient?" Though he could have offered four fifteen, Tom knew that Claudia would take the earlier time as confirmation that he and his staff didn't work full days.

"That will be satisfactory. I'll come to your office. Goodbye, Mr. Clausen."

Not much cordiality there, he thought. She's after blood. He reviewed his prickly history with Claudia McPhaiden, wondering how he might minimize the damage she seemed intent on causing. Claudia had two approaches to school issues: the uncompromising critic and the self-proclaimed expert on most things. But they didn't always work for her. When posing as an expert, she often was caught delivering a flawed statement on an issue she knew little about. He hoped the memory of having to apologize might cause her to think before wading into Dale's areas of school sports and the subjects he taught. But he sensed from watching her at school board meetings that the doors of her mind just might open a bit if given room to listen. If he moved carefully, he might make use of that.

Tom returned at four twenty from inspecting a line of leaks in the auditorium roof to find Mrs. McPhaiden interrogating Alice, whose late stay at her desk suggested that her husband was in one of his moods. He broke in with "No calls for a while" and motioned toward his door. "Go right in and have a seat." He followed and shut the door.

Claudia McPhaiden arranged herself symmetrically with her purse squared on her thighs. Prim, freshly styled, and tinted, she wore a perfectly tailored charcoal suit and an ivory turtleneck that corralled the loose tissues of her aging neck. She straightened her spine and said, "After our talk yesterday, you must appreciate my concern."

Tom hesitated. "I think I have a fair understanding of what happened. Maybe you should explain what you saw."

"Then I'll get right to it. As I explained over the phone, you have a coach, your girls' softball coach, who has caused my family a great deal of anguish. Try to imagine my shock when this person, in full view of at least a hundred witnesses, improperly put his hand on my granddaughter's body. You read in newspapers about lecherous teachers carrying on with young girls, but I never thought it would happen here, yet it's obvious that your faculty is infected. Your Mr. Runyon had the nerve to act out his impropriety in public, humiliating a teenage girl in front of her friends and parents. Action must be taken."

"How did Hannah react?"

"Once I explained to her what happened, she stopped speaking to me. The poor dear is traumatized."

"Well, the first step would be to get her parents in for a conference. I'm not doubting your concern, but you and I both know that school policy limits me to dealing with parents, no one else. In fact, you and I are out of order discussing this until I've met with them."

"You do what you must then, but you won't find them much help."

"How so?"

"Let's just say that their lifestyle is permissive enough that I refuse to stand by and defer to their judgment. If I can't protect Hannah as her grandmother, I certainly can bring suit for improper touching as a concerned citizen."

"I'm sorry to hear that. If this went public, there's no way to predict the kind of publicity Hannah would have to deal with. The whole school would suffer." Claudia stiffened and was about to speak when Tom swiveled his chair to point to photos of Northbridge athletes. "Maybe I'm being too open-minded, but it's normal to see more touching between coaches and players than between teachers and students. Another thing, with girls' sports now competing with boys' sports for audiences, a lot of the boys' sports culture crosses the line into girls' sports. Some of that's okay, some isn't. I think the congratulatory fanny slap is part of this. Most male coaches refrain from touching girl athletes in any way, even to being standoffish. Unfortunately, Mr. Runyon has what you might call a spontaneous personality—which is a long way from lechery. I agree with you that he may have acted wrongly and should be brought up to date on what's unacceptable. What I don't want to happen is for him to lose his job over an impulsive but innocent congratulatory slap. What I propose is this: You and I drop in on one of Mr. Runyon's classes so you can get a more complete read on who he is and what he does. I also need to get Hannah's parents to bring her in to give her version of what went on between her and Mr. Runyon."

"No, Mr. Clausen, I'll oppose subjecting my granddaughter to any further humiliation. Have I made myself clear? However, I'll consider your offer for an observation of Mr. Runyon. You may expect a call from me in a day or two."

Mrs. McPhaiden accepted Clausen's proposal that she visit one of Dale's classes, calling the next afternoon to agree to observe him in action. When Tom suggested second period, she agreed to that, too. When he proposed the following Thursday morning, she said she'd be there and asked for a specific time. Things seemed to be going well. Not too well, he hoped.

Dale's teaching schedule required three preps, Biology II and first and second year Computers. Since the quiet intensity of computer work can appear boringly empty of classroom drama, Tom scheduled Claudia for Runyon's second-period Biology II. Sandwiched between first and third periods, second was most teachers' best period of the day. Whenever citizens asked for permission to visit a class in session, Tom tried to book them into second period. First period can be shot full of holes by tardies and start-of-the-day interruptions. Third can be almost as good, but it is a rare afternoon class that measures up to second period. He recalled a planning session when Karl Munson, a history teacher with thirty years behind him, quipped, "I don't care what you give me to teach. Just make it all second periods."

Runyon's classroom arrangement had no single pattern. When

Clausen and Mrs. McPhaiden entered and took seats at the rear, students were seated in neat rows. That arrangement dissolved when a student assistant with a laptop projected a room arrangement titled "Discussion Groups" onto a wall screen. Desk chairs were pushed into a semblance of the diagram as the student assistant pulled up a page titled "The Power of Thinking." Tom leaned toward Claudia to whisper, "About the boy on the computer, Runyon requires that his lab assistants learn PowerPoint and Excel so they can pipe his planning charts onto the screen."

When the last chair scraped into place, Runyon lifted a forefinger toward the ceiling and stared at his watch. The noise level diminished to a whisper as his finger came down. When it touched his watch, he looked up. "Eighteen seconds. Not bad."

He asked, "Ready for note-taking? David, how do you take notes?"

David said, "Yeah, we know the drill. You can't listen and write at the same time, so you jot down the important bits and flesh them out as soon as possible."

"Right, so here we go. We've been studying descriptions of organisms and related data up till now and are ready for the next step. The next thing scientists do is use that kind of knowledge as a foundation for discovering new knowledge that won't be as neatly structured. We all know what an echinoderm is, and that bit of knowledge isn't likely to change much. But it wouldn't be wise to try to write a live-forever definition of what happens to an echinoderm if its habitat changes because...anybody?"

"Different impacts have different outcomes." The boy who spoke wore a letterman's jacket.

"Exactly. Futures aren't as easy to predict as life-forms are to classify. You've all discovered that the body of knowledge you've touched on is way too big to memorize. No mind can contain it. We use computers to store it and access it, computers to trace relationships within it, and computers to extrapolate beyond the here and now. Mikki, what's the problem with extrapolations?"

Mikki could have been a poster girl for nonachievement: spare tire lopping over low-rider jeans, spiky bleached hair, nose stud, and variously decorated nails. She said, "They're based on history. Unless the past becomes the future, like nothing changes—and we know that's not gonna happen. Every life-form, including us, is in for surprises. But maybe not totally surprising since we think we can see some of the things coming up. Anyway, looking backward you can be a lot more accurate than looking forward."

"Good job, Mikki." Runyon called for the next visual on the screen. "We've been using reliable sources of biological information, and that's all well and good. But now that we're heading into unexplored territory, we won't have that to fall back on. Think about it this way: if you discover a new species, how careful do you have to be in describing it? You've seen that you have to follow the rules or your work isn't trustworthy. There are special rules for looking into the future, and we're going to talk about the first of them. Anyone, what's the first thing you do when confronted by a new problem? C'mon, c'mon. This ought to be a slam dunk for you guys." No hands went up.

"You plead ignorance; you embrace your ignorance. Anybody here qualified?" A low chuckle rippled. "That's what the world's best minds do when approaching new problems. They think, 'We really don't know what's going on here.'" He lowered his voice. "You won't hear me deliver this next great truth more than once, so listen up: Recognizing and respecting your own ignorance is essential, but if any of you go home and say, 'Today I learned that it's important to be ignorant,' I'll flunk you so flat that you'll have to look up to tie your shoes. Liviu, what did I say about ignorance?" A typed line scrolled onto the screen: *Rekonition of ones igorance is essential.* Runyon grimaced and said, "Close enough. Everybody got that?"

He continued, "Let's pool our ignorance and start from scratch. Here we are, not knowing what to do, and we have a problem to solve. The problem is right outside our window: the poor quality of water in our river. Even dummies can assume that healthy fish don't float belly up and that children shouldn't get sick from swimming in it. What else might a dummy observe about our river?"

A half-dozen hands went up. "The water stinks some days." "It's not very clear." "It smells like cow pies." "A lot of litter washes downstream."

"Some of the places people used to fish aren't fished anymore." "There's a lot of bark floating around, maybe from mills."

Runyon held up a warning hand. "Whoa, you went too far. You're supposed to be making simple observations, not linking effects with causes. In the beginning it's important to not let observations lead to conclusions. That step can begin only after all observations and measurements are taken because if you jump to conclusions too early, you'll run the chance of missing important connections. Connecting dots is a lot easier if you have all the dots, so you need to get everything on the table before trying to establish relationships. You got that?" Half the class looked up to signal understanding. Runyon continued. "So far so good. What do we do next?"

A single hand went up. "Try to draw meaning from the observations."

Runyon countered, "How are you going to start that?"

A girl squeaked and threw her hand in the air. "I know, Mr. Runyon; I absolutely know. You form-u-late ques-tions."

"Right. The irrepressible Stephanie has it. We'd better get hot on this because our ecosystem that hadn't changed for almost ten thousand years has changed dangerously over the past hundred. While we sit here discussing how to solve problems, things affect our world in ways that aren't very nice. What we need to do is choose the best way to enter the problem, and it will be your questions that get us to that entry point. Here we go. Somebody ask a question about our river. Any question. Okay, Damon, you're up."

Damon offered, "How has the river been changed from its natural state?"

"You reached a little too far there," Runyon said. "Your question asked about processes over time. Try again, but limit your thoughts to observations about the river itself."

The class fell stony silent and watched Damon. He said, "How about this? What, besides natural stuff, is in the river?"

Runyon called out, "That'll do. Work groups!" In the ensuing shuffle, students from each discussion group shifted to other groups, helping to spread each discussion group's insights across the class. When the shuffling settled down, Runyon said, "You heard Damon's question,

'What, besides natural stuff, is in the river?' Your job is to answer that question with a second question, and then answer the second question with a third. Keep it going until you run out of insights. Go to it!" Runyon wandered the classroom, hunkering down for quiet chats with each group.

With his students on task, he pulled a chair next to Claudia McPhaiden. With no trace of tension or animosity, he asked, "Anything I can explain about what we're doing today?"

She studied him for a time. "Yes. What's it all about? I saw no textbooks. Is this within the curriculum?"

Runyon chuckled. "These are bright kids. They've covered the curriculum and then some, so we moved on to practice in thinking. Today was the beginning of a unit that teaches them how to measure and evaluate change in an environment. As it progresses, I get to watch them discover how wonderful their minds can be. With some, it's a slow awakening; with others, it's a big aha! Those are a real kick to watch. The boy on the computer had no English three years ago. Then there's Vu." Runyon pointed to a small dark-skinned boy. "He's our pacesetter. He came to America five years ago with no English. Watch how the other kids wait for his cues and see how he works his group. That's natural leadership, and it bloomed just this year.

"It's impossible to see progress in a single period, but you're welcome to come back. Another thing: don't let this angelic behavior fool you. They can be truly unruly but not today, not with the principal and a guest aboard." A bell ending the period sounded. Runyon's voice rose over the shuffling of chairs. "Remember to read chapter eleven in Rosen. It has to do with where your questions might take you. Scram now."

When the three adults stood, Mrs. McPhaiden held out her hand. "It was enlightening, Mr. Runyon. Your teaching is most impressive, but to be frank, I wish I was as impressed by your coaching behavior."

"Mrs. McPhaiden, let me explain something. I am not a slave to the kind of unhealthy passions you have in mind. I might be a bit impetuous at times, but the worst damage I'm capable of is embarrassing myself. If you think whacking your granddaughter's behind betrayed some pattern of sinister sexual appetite, well, what can I say except that it's not in me.

"When Hannah hit her double and later when she crossed the plate, the whole team went wild. Thinking back, I remember giving her a high-five. There was some confusion while her teammates danced around her celebrating. Play had to resume for the bottom of the last inning, but we were still off the bench celebrating until a yell from the ump told me to get the girls settled. I pushed the nearest girls toward the bench, and the rest followed, except for Hannah. You were there. You saw it. The swat was half in recognition of her score and half to pull her back to the here and now and off the field, like an attention-diverting swat on a diaper when a toddler reaches for a no-no. What you saw was ordinary sports behavior. If you want, I can apologize. What I can't do is feel that I wronged your granddaughter. Can you accept that?"

Claudia made a small ceremony of adjusting the balance of her head on her spine as she did whenever she rose from a chair. She said, "It has been an interesting visit. I'll be talking with Mr. Clausen about this later. Goodbye, Mr. Runyon."

Tom opened the classroom door for Mrs. McPhaiden. As he followed her out, he reached back to give Runyon a thumbs-up.

CHAPTER 3

"Tom, get the door, will you? I'm all sticky with cookie dough."

"I didn't hear the bell. You sure it wasn't the TV?"

"Of course, silly. It was a knock so it has to be Garnie."

Tom set a pen and yellow pad aside and yelled, "What's the password?"

After a few-second pause, Garnie called out, "Don't do this to me, Thomas. I'm not accustomed to being put off."

Tom opened the door. "Come on in. We'll sit in the living room." He called to Jane, "Hon, when you get your hands free, put the pot on, would you?"

Tom and Garnie's get-togethers were always one-on-one, unscheduled, and from Tom's perspective, unpredictable. Garnie would call or drop over out of the blue, supposedly to discuss neighbors' pets or other trivial issues but always with a question about one of his interests. Tom tolerated them as windows into the remains of the Pittman empire. Their talks, sometimes coupled with Tom lending him a hand, had worn a trail that angled across the Clausens' front lawn to pick up on the other side of the street between the overgrown junipers and leggy azaleas that screened Garnie's aging mansion from the street. Whether at Garnie's house or Tom's, tea lubricated their discussions.

Tom disappeared into the kitchen to select a tea while Garnie inspected his reading tastes by rummaging through his stack of magazines. He leaned to scan the pad Tom had been writing on. Tom felt offended the first time he caught him at it, but as time passed he accepted his neighbor's snoopiness as being as much a part of Garnie's nature as a dog's need to sniff at fire hydrants.

Tom returned from the kitchen and set two steaming mugs of mint tea between them. "Find anything interesting?"

Garnie blustered, "If you're touchy about personal papers, I suggest you stop leaving them lying around, and no, I did not find anything interesting."

"Well then, old buddy, let's figure out what fiendishly clever notion brought you over today."

Garnie opened his arms. "Thomas, Thomas, Thomas. Is it too much for you to accept that I might simply desire your company?"

"No. As a matter of fact, I feel honored that you choose me to afflict with your wit and wisdom, such as they are. Now out with it."

Garnie smacked his hands together. "All right, you've found me out. I'd like to have your opinion on whether it might be a wise investment, considering the age of my house, to have gutter guards installed."

Tom chuckled and shook his head. "Buy the stupid gutter guards so we can get down to what's really on your mind."

"Sometimes you hurt me to the quick, Thomas. You may not realize it, but I am actually a very sensitive person." He glanced over his half frames with a comical flash of petulance. "But since you seem disinclined to discuss gutter issues, let me pose a different situation." He launched into a detailed description of a piece of land with commercial potential, one that Tom had often driven past. It lay to the east on the northeast corner of the intersection that connected Moraine with the Stevens Pass Highway. Garnie explained that an investment group wanted to buy it and that he wanted Tom's input on how to approach the issue. He folded his arms and arranged his jowly face into a cherubic smile while Tom regarded him suspiciously.

Tom had no doubt that Garnie was up to something but had no idea what it was. Yet his neighbor's devious games were fascinating enough to keep him on the hook. And while Garnie rode roughshod over most people's sensitivities, he was, in his way, careful around Tom and Jane. An odd chemistry was at work that made Tom the only person in Northbridge to take and match Garnie's conversational barbs. Tom also sensed that, since he was one of the few to think generously about Garnie, he might be the only one who gave a damn about what his cantankerous neighbor was up to or feel that being around Garnie could be fun at times. But not now, not yet, not until he'd pried his purpose open. He said, "Garnie, if you want advice on land deals, go to an expert. I know nothing about real estate or investment strategy. You know that."

"Precisely, Thomas. Once again you've hit the nail on the head. How do you suppose I'm to evaluate my consultants unless I compare their expertise against that of the average man on the street? I've posed a problem to you to see if your unlearned erudition might be equal to that of my advisors. If it is, I should fire the lot of them. There, you see what you can do for me? Come now, Thomas, shall I restate the situation for you?"

Tom hopped up to skim the thoughts from his mind while pacing from the fireplace to the door. "Okay, okay, I'll play your game. Off the top of my head, I'd like to know what the developer was going to do with it, and that leads to questions about how that would affect surrounding property values or usages. If I had personal connections with it, I'd ask if the developer's scheme might conflict with some pet vision I had for the property's future." Tom halted in midstride to say, "Excuse me, I got carried away with the first-person pronoun. This is your property, right? If you sold it now, you're wondering how sure you could be that it would be put to the highest and best use. Of course there'd be zoning issues to settle. Is the offer in line with what that highest and best use might be? What have similar properties sold for?" Tom sat again and sipped at his tea, which was still too hot.

"Obviously, that wasn't too difficult for you, was it, Thomas?"

"Don't interrupt. I'm not through yet." Tom enumerated points on his fingers. "Then there would be strategy issues: Would the sale adversely affect your tax situation? Do you need the money, or would it be better to keep that part of your net worth in land? What about leasing it? Over the long pull, might it be in your interest to be an owner-developer so you could control who your tenants would be?" He wrapped his hands around the warmth of his cup, waiting for another thought to occur. When nothing surfaced, he said, "There you have it. My erudition in a nutshell."

"Bravo, my boy!" Garnie's shout caused Jane to look up from her reading. "Bravo, you've just talked me into renewing my consultants' contracts."

Jane, an intuitive cook and approximate measurer, tossed a few handfuls of oats into a microwave bowl and said, "Before we forget about it, add oatmeal to the list." She sprinkled in salt. "Why does Garnie have to be so rude?"

"What do you mean, rude?"

"Well, last night he asked you for your opinion, and after you gave it to him, he said it wasn't any good. I'd call that rude." She uncapped a carton of orange juice and poured two glasses. "But then, maybe it's just payback."

"Explain." Tom brought brown sugar and milk to the table.

"You weren't being Mr. Tact when you said, 'Buy the stupid guards so we can get down to it.'"

Tom trailed a hand around her waist as their paths crossed. "Garnie and I regard each other as pet porcupines—prickly, by nature. Besides that, we were having a guy talk, the kind girls don't relate to. Now, Mrs. Big Ears, is there anything else that needs explaining?"

Claudia McPhaiden's son, Roy, a graduate of Northbridge High, had settled on a career reading meters for Puget Sound Gas and Electric after failing to gain entrance to any of Washington State's public universities. Marci, Claudia's second daughter and Hannah Terry's mother, remained doggedly married to Jamie Terry, one-time star midfielder for Northbridge High's 1988 soccer team. Jamie was a senior when he impregnated Marci during the spring of her sophomore year. Any confusion about her future was settled by Jamie's parents, Joe and Marijke Terry, who sat the two lovers down for a reading of Exodus 22:16 that says, "And if a man entice a maid that is not betrothed, and lie with her, he shall surely endow her to be his wife." With Jamie's parents' unswerving commitment to live by faith looming over Claudia's secular disillusionment, it was game, set, and match. Marci and Jamie were married during her sixteenth year.

Claudia saw her children mired in mediocrity. Roy, an avid

supporter of Northbridge High's sports teams and a now-and-then participant in fun runs, had become a fan of body art. He treated himself on birthdays to new tattoos he concealed under long-sleeved shirts with cuffs and collars for the rare times he was called upon to appear conventional. Marci lived for her soaps, recording them to replay when doing household chores or when Jamie was out on training runs. Their reading leaned toward sci-fi fantasies and bodice-rippers.

Claudia bemoaned the ordinariness of Roy and Marci's lives, especially when the local weekly, *The World*, published test results from the region's schools. Historically, Northbridge's tests ran lower than surrounding school districts, and though results had improved dramatically over the past three years, so had the results from Buchanan, Aldergrove, Moraine, and other nearby school systems, leaving Northbridge still below the county median.

For years, Claudia had vented about the lower-than-average scores in letters to the editor of *The World*, a paper that specialized in lauding Northbridge High's sports while condemning its academics. An opportunity to do something opened when school board member Ada Hornstein's cancer took a turn for the worse, causing her to resign her seat in midterm. Claudia ran unopposed for her seat in the 1992 general election to become a thorn in the backside of the district's professional staff.

It became Claudia's mission to see that her town's schools would give her grandchildren a better education than that which, in her opinion, condemned her own children to small-town ambitions. Her goal was to place Northbridge's schools over a refiner's fire to drive off every vestige of mediocrity. And she would become that fire. She lorded her superior outlook over the community through dress and grooming—silver hair cropped short and half-rim readers dangling from a sterling chain onto the breasts of conservatively tailored business suits.

Claudia operated a small tax and accounting service that she took as qualification to serve as watchdog over district finances. She took it upon herself to ferret out waste and faulty prioritization of spending. She dug into accounting audits to study the motivations behind each expenditure, micromanaging the district's budget, line item by line item, which turned board meetings into such droning bores that the public all but stopped attending.

Her sense of mission grew after hearing Northbridge's superintendent, Dr. Philip Krause, comment on the district's challenges. Sensitive to her children's plight, she reacted when he said, "Our schools are challenged with having not only to teach subject matter but also how to learn," as though Northbridge's children were a bunch of dummies. He even implied that one of the reasons for lack-luster test scores might be that children from some Northbridge homes weren't as ready for learning as children from certain neighboring towns, using lower preschool enrollments as his excuse. That was so weak, blaming parents for his poor performance rather than holding Northbridge's schools to higher standards. She found that she wasn't the only board member who thought that way.

Runyon and Clausen were no better. And Clausen had disobeyed her by having her daughter bring Hannah in to relive the experience of Runyon's hand on her body. On Monday, April 3, Claudia brought the issue of dismissal for cause before the school board. She asked her fellow board members, hypothetically, what the district's obligation would be if it was faced with a situation in which a staff member's behavior reflected adversely on the reputation of a school in particular and on the district in general. Her friend, board member Harry Morgan, asked the chair, which Claudia occupied, to entertain a motion to refer the issue to district counsel for specific language of state code and an opinion on board responsibility in response to state code. The motion was seconded and passed.

"I'm telling you, Martin, we're not going to change anything as long as we accommodate every whim or voice in the district." Claudia McPhaiden and Martin Koutac were strolling through the park-like grounds of Semiahmoo Resort, site of the Northbridge school directors' annual retreat. "If we're serious about raising standards," Claudia continued, "we can't go begging for cooperation. We must demand it and expect results. It does no good to expect results if our schools, for known reasons, are incapable of producing them. If I had to pick two reasons for the mediocrity of Northbridge schools, I'd put the teachers' union first and wishy-washy administrators second. If we could bring the two of them into line, you'd see results." When Martin failed to respond, Claudia confirmed the rightness of her statement. "Yes, yes. That's exactly what needs to be done. What about you, Martin? If you were asked to identify two barriers to excellence, what would they be?"

Martin hoped to plant a seed of reason that might germinate in the thicket of her prejudices. He searched his vocabulary for words that Claudia might actually hear, words that would stir alternatives to her hard-edged convictions. Having worked with her for almost two years, he knew he would have to phrase them not as criticism but as sidelights or alternatives. "What you say may be true, Claudia, but we can't forget that teachers and administrators have to work with those who enroll. Seen in that light, they're not doing all that badly. When we tried to identify key issues at last year's retreat, we were all on the same page; our kids are just as smart as kids elsewhere. It's just that a lot of them aren't as academically motivated, and the ones who are get just as good an education as they'd get in other districts. We agreed most of that reflects what they bring to school, not what they get in school."

Claudia replied, "And when Kirsten left, leaving us without an assistant superintendent, and I told you that I might know someone who experienced issues just like ours, you were happy to welcome Dr. Wainwright. Remember that?"

"Not exactly. What I said was bring him around and we'll listen to him, not hire him—certainly not if I had known he would split the administrative team. Wainwright's way of fixing things would be great if he were an architect, but we're not working with building materials. He doesn't listen to the buzz. He refuses to know the staff he wants to remold, so please, please, you and Wainwright need to lighten up. Don't push things so fast. For now, he's no more than the district's special-projects person and not our superintendent. Until you and your friends announce that you're canning Phil, Phil's still our superintendent."

Claudia snorted. "Change is necessary." She put her balled fists on her hips and raised her chin to look the tall man in the eye. "What you fail to appreciate is that Charles Wainwright assumes that every teacher can perform, and if they can't, he'll see to it that they're history. Anyway, that's not our business. Our responsibility is to see that district policy charts a path for improving performance. Once that's in place, employees who can't or won't follow it can certainly be replaced."

They walked in silence, aware of the distance between them. Koutac went personal for his next try. "Look, Claudia, I'm as gung-ho for improvement as you are. It's just that my daughters taught me some valuable lessons about situations like this. Trish taught me that I should have been better at assessing the good in her, just as Wainwright ought to be doing with the staff he's tasked to work with. Dana taught me that all the planning and expectations in the world might miss the mark. What I see in Wainwright's scheme is a potential for riding roughshod over good things that are already happening. Too much planning, too little understanding. Too much telling, not enough listening."

Claudia shook her head. "Really, Martin, we can't run a school district based on family anecdotes. Dr. Wainwright offers scientific studies to back his agenda. We can't let ourselves be swayed by personal views, can we? You ought to be pleased that we finally have someone on board who has what it takes to whip the district into shape."

Martin fixed his gaze on the haze-shrouded straits masking Canada. He had no more to say. They walked to the point to watch a purse seiner idle through the no-wake channel on its way to the town of Blaine's fishing piers. While Claudia talked on about drawing lines and demanding results, Martin retreated into memories of his daughters and the well-meaning mistakes he and his wife made on their behalf, mistakes that brought him to temper his expectations and advice for others.

Martin and Marie Koutac's daughters, Patricia and Dana, were fraternal twins. The fact that they shared the same womb proved to have little to do with their characters or inclinations, Trish being extroverted and Dana shy. It might have had something to do with their parents' expectations since the couple had planned to have both boys and girls. But Marie's first pregnancy produced twin girls whose birthing so upset her reproductive equipment that her doctors advised her to be content with her two healthy girls.

The parents compromised as best they could. The larger and firstborn daughter they named Patricia. Number two was dubbed Dana, a gender-neutral name that captured a shadow of their lost hope for a boy. Marie could not have known when she launched her daughters into the world that they came factory-wired to be different and unconventional in disturbing ways. Though she and Martin showered attention evenly on the girls, they grew in such different directions that it seemed to the bewildered parents that they might as well have fallen from different planets.

Patricia became Trish, brash, impudent, sassy, uncontrollable, and beautiful. Martin and Marie didn't know what to do with her. Dana, though, practiced the piano. By doggedly plugging away for hours each day at her Schaum exercises, she mastered enough technique that, by the age of fourteen, she provided relief for the United Methodist children's choir's accompanist. But while her technique improved, Dana remained slave to whatever spots and symbols filled her pages of music. She could barely play "Happy Birthday" in the key of C without the music in front of her.

Trish was spontaneous and unpredictable, so much so that in the summer of her junior year at Northbridge High, she and a friend were caught skinny-dipping in Dr. Hanson's backyard swimming pool at two in the morning. There were originally three, but one chickened out. The dentist woke to sounds in his backyard and rose to switch on the lights that illuminated the pool. While one girl stayed in the water with her bare self pressed against the side of the pool, Trish climbed out naked to pick up her T-shirt, toweling herself with it and holding it before her as a gesture of modesty as she padded toward Dr. Hanson to apologize. "Sorry, I know, we shouldn't be here." Hanson could hardly breathe. Beautiful, well-formed, and wet and sleek as a seal, Trish Koutac appeared unperturbed and unashamed, which terrified him into stumbling backward. She turned to collect the rest of her clothes and called to her friend, "You'd better split, Suzie. See you later." Dr. Hanson stood helpless as Trish's well-rounded bottom disappeared between arborvitae, leaving an image that wet footprints on concrete or swimming pools in the dark would awaken to stir him.

Of course, Dr. Hanson told Martin and Marie, who had a serious heart-to-heart with Trish that failed to dent her independent spirit—a quality that, aside from animal cravings, led Mel Ostrander to fall captive to her. Beyond her beauty and grace, he found her full of surprises, such as discovering once he had her in his arms that, after hearing she knew her way around, she was a wonderfully inexperienced lover. Otherwise, her high-spirited independence helped to loft her own children's achievements above Northbridge's par.

Trish had been simply too much for high school suitors and a mystery to her frustrated parents. Every healthy heterosexual boy and more than a few of Northbridge High's younger male teachers fantasized about her, but each time a date fumbled to get under her clothing, she torpedoed the planned seductions by turning chillingly clinical about what they were up to. Using her precocious understanding that the brain is the most important sex organ, Trish became so adept at messing up the libidos of male schoolmates that the boys she dated would long remember suffering her legendary dosings of arousal and intimidation. Through those years, she somehow managed to pick companions with enough care to avoid brutes who wouldn't have played by her rules.

Mel Ostrander was twenty-seven and Trish was eighteen when their paths crossed. A stint in the Army, two years of community college, and infrequent affairs had left him unmarried and uncommitted. Martin and Marie Koutac had contracted with Mel to build them a house, his third as an independent contractor. When Trish first appeared as a blip on his screen, Mel addressed her as an adult, looked her in the eye (not at her boobs), and was apparently undistracted by her megawatt presence while discussing house issues with her parents. Until Mel, Trish assumed there had to be something lacking in males who ignored her, but Mel Ostrander appeared to be all man—handsome, strong, independent, and not slave to her presence. For the first time, she found herself tingling with what she assumed normally horny men felt for her: desire.

She invented reasons to spend time at the new house, measuring and jotting notes as though she had business there. Mel sawed and nailed as though she was invisible, brushing her aside with a muscular forearm when he needed space. Trish rushed to special vantage points to better appreciate how his powerful body strained at his shirt and jeans when he climbed ladders, never suspecting that Mel's remoteness might be an act or that his posturing on ladders was bait. For Mel's part, though her nearness did erode his concentration, he was determined to suppress his volcanic urge to snatch her into his arms until her father signed off on the contract as completed. No sense complicating things, he reasoned.

A time came when Dana discovered that, though she had trained her fingers to dance across piano keyboards as she followed written music, she would never be a musician. She took no real joy from music, there being no compelling connection between music and her soul. Her disenchantment was sealed during an evening rehearsal when she was called upon to strike notes the church orchestra would use for tuning. All along, she had thought that her reluctance to sing had been because of a poor voice, but when she had to confess that she had no idea whether a flute was sharp or flat against her piano's concert A, she rightly suspected that she might be tone-deaf. Dispirited, she quit music.

Martin and Maria Koutac were crushed. From their vantage point, the steadier of their two daughters had given up her life's goal, had abandoned the music that, in recorded form, filled the Koutac home. Dana's decision dropped the value of her parents' investment in expensive piano lessons to zero and left them with a question mark in place of a hopeful vision for their daughter's future.

But from Dana's perspective, once liberated from piano practice, her heart was lightened. She filled what had been practice hours with running and soccer and used the time she'd spent in rehearsals and recitals for dates. While the design of her old life had been drawn by her parents, Dana claimed her new life for herself. Martin and Maria, whose experiences with Trish left them feeling powerless as parents, could only watch as Dana, having cast her childhood shyness aside, stumbled through seamy social misadventures, the worst being her relationship with, and marriage to, Gus Gustafson at the age of eighteen. Gus, like Dana's brother-in-law-to-be, was older. His education at Northbridge High had ended during his junior year when he took a job with Klein Timber and Milling, a local producer of studs.

Gus Gustafson was only months out of the Army when he spotted Dana. Though Gus blamed his erratic behavior on combat-related PTSD, he spent his tour of duty in relative safety, running a forklift at a supply depot. Nevertheless, he joined the more heroic but unfortunate derelicts of the Vietnam War on society's fringe.

After his stint in the Army, Gus returned to his prewar job at the Klein mill. The work was healthy, and the pay was good until a collapse in the building industry caused the mill to close. Two weeks of severance pay kept him in beer while he applied for work at the handful of mills still in operation. With the timber industry widely depressed, however, he found the remaining mills either shutting down or laying off entire shifts. His problem wasn't that jobs were scarce but that his beer and marijuana-addled mind couldn't see opportunities outside mill work. Six months after wedding Dana, he settled into the ranks of the unemployed. Meanwhile, Dana worked for the Northbridge School District as a bus driver to pay the couple's most pressing bills.

Gus and his new friends figured that unemployment was the thanks they got for fighting for their nation. They were stuck on the dole because fat-cat mill owners took their profits and ran. Look at the houses they live in—gated communities, four-car garages stuffed with Beamers and Benzes. Hell, they wouldn't even let the workers they dumped mow their lawns. Meanwhile, the goddamned tree huggers tied up the woods to save owls while trainloads of lumber flowed south from British Columbia. Meanwhile, politicians sat back on their fat asses figuring new ways to screw the working man. Bartender, another pitcher!

Gus and Dana were into their sixth year of marriage with a seven-year-old daughter, Pip—short for Pipsqueak, a.k.a. Eleanor Marie Gustafson. Gus's mornings were his own, as were the rest of his hours. By the time he rose, Dana had dropped off Pip at her sister Trish's house and had clocked in at the bus garage. His life settled into rituals, an hour or two of soaps followed by now-and-then stops at the Unemployment Security Office. He gave up regular meals, preferring to graze through cupboards and the refrigerator. The day was prelude to evenings of rough-and-tumble fellowship at the Green Chain Tavern where he and his friends drank up their unemployment checks.

Having been abandoned by the System, they felt no obligation to play by its rules. As beer flowed, plots hatched that would have earned years of hard time had they all been attempted. Some of their schemes actually were carried out, which accounted for four outboard motors lifted from boats moored at Middle Slough Marina and six obsolete computers stolen from the junior high library. The computers were Gus's idea, payback, he thought, for the teachers who made him want to quit. He didn't like teachers, but the coaches who stopped at the Green Chain after games were okay. Gus and friends reasoned that their thefts weren't hurting anybody, just milking the fat cats of the insurance industry.

Their life of leisure left time to dream. Theft was too simple. What they needed was enterprise, something to drain off backlogs of time and energy. So it was that the Green Chain Gang, the name they adopted, went to work but not on the terms of the society and industry that had abandoned them. Their business plan flaunted the rules of the system that cast them aside. They became cannabis farmers and distributors.

Having watched raids on high-tech operations on TV, they settled on taking seasonal profits from plantings on land owned by other people, especially the timber companies that had cast them aside. Aerial searches able to spot patches of marijuana couldn't detect their scattered plantings in replanted clear-cuts. Their plan worked. In two growing seasons, Gus made enough to cover the payments on his new pickup and take an occasional run at the tribal casino's quarter machines.

Gus was out harvesting when a trio of woods-wise twelve-year-olds spotted him. The three were upslope working on their secret camp when they heard his truck come to a stop. They sneaked closer to see what he might be up to. He skirted a stand of third-growth fir to enter a tract of shoulder-high fir saplings. When he moved from plant to plant to clip the sticky buds and wad bagfuls of them into his pack, they understood what was going on. After he finished harvesting and drove away, they began a search for more of those plants.

One whiff was enough to alarm their parents, who, by chance, had come across the odor before. Their children reeked of smoke from roasting whole marijuana branches over their fire after attempts to roll cigarettes from green marijuana and toilet paper failed. After grounding the boys for starting a fire in the woods, the outraged parents grilled them, and once they put their stories together, they had a fair description of the secret farmer and his truck. Together, they took their account to the sheriff's office.

It was during the television phase of Gus's day that two sheriff's cars pulled up in front of the Gustafsons' duplex. He had no doubt that they had come for him, only about which operation had gone sour. He sprinted out the back door and leaped into his pickup with barely enough time to pull his revolver from under the seat before an officer rounded the building. Gun in hand, Gus played the role he had been building toward for months. He fired a warning shot into the air and shouted, "Git the fuck offa my property!"

The deputies' call for backup brought a raucous symphony of sirens converging on the scene. Gus sobered at the clack and clash of cartridges being chambered and dropped his gun to stand charges for armed assault, discharging a firearm in the city, resisting arrest, and trafficking in a controlled substance. He was cuffed and remained docile until he learned that his pickup, having been used for transport of a controlled substance, was confiscated. It took four officers to get him loaded for transport.

Locked up and stripped of personal belongings, Gus wanted to tell Dana to post bail but couldn't until she got home from her last bus run. Meanwhile, Pip, whose bus dropped her within eyesight of the flashing lights surrounding her house, holed up in the neighbor's laurel hedge and didn't budge until her mother's car turned in from the street. While neighbors stood clustered, staring and pointing, Dana hugged

Pip to her and brushed past uniforms to get into the house where a female officer had questions. Gus's call came while Dana was in shock from watching drug agents toss her home. With the policewoman's ear close, she answered the phone, listened, made up her mind, and wordlessly lowered the handset into its cradle. Dana couldn't bear the sound of Gus's voice—ever again.

After viewing her backyard on the ten o'clock news, Dana began a new life for the second time by separating everything of Gus's from the house. She heaped clothing, back copies of *Guns and Ammo*, scales, and empty plastic packets in the center of the carport. She resolved that whatever money she might scrape up would go not toward bail or a defense lawyer but for a divorce attorney. She went to bed, slept soundly, rose early, and delivered Pip to Grandma Marie, her sister being out of town, and reported to the School Transportation Office for work as usual. A public defender was appointed to defend Gus.

For the second time in her life, Dana felt lightened by change. As a lover, Gus had shown all the tenderness of a rutting rhinoceros. As a father, he lavished more attention on Rocky, his Rottweiler, than Pip. As a provider, he had cajoled, threatened, and twice beaten her out of the contents of her purse, and Dana was sure it would have happened again had Rocky not taken her side so forcefully that a month passed before Gus peeled the last bandage from his forearm.

There would be no more Gus Gustafsons for Dana. She would begin a march up the social ladder, and should anyone question her credentials, she could still play the piano, tone-deaf or not. No more brainless braggarts, no heavy drinkers, no uneducated know-it-alls. Her parents, Martin and Marie, had seen to her grammar and manners, and though few would call her beautiful, enough men had come on to her to confirm a muted sexiness. Five-two, good teeth, strong legs more sinewy than sleek, Mediterranean skin, small breasts, large brown eyes, and a tangle of honey-toned curls. Though the package wasn't perfect, she hoped it was good enough to help boost her into a better social circle. What she needed was to log social time with guys from a better cut of society—people like her dad.

"Garnie's at it again." Tom passed the Letters to the Editors page to Jane, lofting it narrowly over the butter.

Jane shook the page flat and furrowed her brow as she did when reading without glasses. She surfaced after a moment to say, "This is soooo typical of your oddball friend. Listen: 'Who is responsible for Northbridge schools' abysmal test results? Who is responsible for improving them? Can the staff that presided over failing grades be expected to bring about success? What are the most important questions to ask our schools before the next election?' When he gets on his high horse, there's no horse higher. More coffee?"

Tom pushed his cup forward. "What's his point? I've heard him out enough times to suspect that he's fishing, but for what?"

Jane topped off Tom's cup. "Maybe, but for what? Anyway you already have enough irons in the fire. Pass it off to L. H. Since he can't figure out which he likes less, the schools or Garnie, he'd love it." Jane referred to L. H. Terhune, crusty publisher-editor of the weekly *Northbridge World*. Terhune had taken to double-initialing his given name, Lionheart, a gift from overly romantic parents.

"Garnie likes to stir up debates and then sit back and criticize the debaters. This," he tapped the newspaper, "is how he does it. But whatever he says is usually aimed at getting something done, not undone, so what's his story here?" He pulled the page back. "I want to read that again." He looked at the letter again and set it aside. "You remember when he took on the school board for the price they paid for the Jefferson Elementary site? Turned out he'd offered them a better site for less money, but they turned him down. Call me crazy, but no matter how it looks, he always supports schools."

Jane said, "Maybe so, but that doesn't make up for his weirdness. Mary Margaret said he buys his suits at thrift stores, and when they get to smelling bad, he has Aunt Sigi wash them in their machine. She says they come out looking like the wrath of God. Sigi presses them as well as she can, but—well, you know what he looks like. It's a wonder anyone takes him seriously."

"Some don't, and that's a mistake. He's sharp, maybe too sharp for his own good. If he reads everything he carries out of the library he has to be the best-read man in town. Did Mary Margaret tell you about his 'personal' newspapers?"

"You mean how he expects to lay hands on the *New York Times* at ten o'clock every morning? Can you imagine the scene if somebody else has it? Honestly, I don't know how she puts up with him. And then there's the way he treats the library staff."

"I guess tolerance is what he gets for casting such a large shadow. He was born here, you know, right across the street. L. H. said his family was deep into the timber business. They made some money and sent Garnie and his sister to college, but it seems he wasn't wired to fit the family business. He took a degree in Eastern European history instead of business, which upset his dad so much he up and died."

"You said sister?"

"Mm-hmm. He had a brother, too, a flier, but he was killed in Korea."

Jane put the paper aside. "What does he do with his time?"

"As far as he'd like the world to know, nothing, except for polishing his image as Northbridge's number-one weirdo."

Jane asked, "Do you know how he supports himself?"

"That's not a problem. If he and his sister still hold title to even a corner of the family's interests, they're sitting pretty. There's an office suite for an outfit called Pittman Pacific in the Port Gardner Savings Bank building, and it's possible he has an interest in that, too. Pittman used to be a big name around these parts."

"Like really big money?"

"Apparently, but he doesn't talk with me about that. But I do know that he's left his fingerprints on some of the area's big developments."

"Well, if he's that big a man, why does he allow you to challenge him like you do? Honestly, sometimes I think you deliberately try to aggravate him. And how is it that you come to know so much about him?"

"He interests me. He lets little things drop, and I dig up some stuff on my own." Tom looked at the kitchen clock. Six forty-five. He cinched his tie and pushed away from the table. "I don't try to aggravate him. Like I said, it's a guy thing, a style we pick up in locker rooms, except that wouldn't apply to Garnie. Lots of guys are small thinkers, short on self-confidence, can't take ribbing or criticism. The ones with healthy doses of self-confidence, like Garnie, soak up hard-edged banter with a smile and fire right back. If you're well matched, and he and I seem to be, nobody gets their feelings hurt."

Jane shook her head as she carried dishes to the sink. "This is just too weird, you and Garnie—as though you two have anything in common." She gave him a peck on the cheek as he shrugged into his jacket. "Spaghetti tonight."

It was Monday, and only two substitutes were available to cover three late call-ins from flu sufferers. Having no appointments, Tom was able to leave his desk to cover a ninth grade Algebra class. A sub came puffing in at the end of the period to release him back to his office where his intercom was blinking. He opened the circuit to Alice. "Mrs. Cobb is waiting to see you. Says you'd know what it's about," which scuttled his plan to sit in on a first-year teacher's US History session.

He left Alice hanging while he leaned back to rub his eyes. She knew to expect a delay when he was cut out of subbing or observing, the special treats in his days. "Send her in, but make sure she understands she has no more than five minutes."

Marian Cobb stepped into Tom's office to find him hovering over a sheaf of papers, hoping that she might one day come to understand that her unannounced visits interfered with his work. Mrs. Cobb was an enthusiastic critic of public schools and a prolific writer of letters to editors. Her self-righteousness was legend in Northbridge, where she vented considerable energy against the ungodly. For a time she had been a stalwart of the Church of the Nazarene until, as with public schools, she discovered what she took to be flaws there. When Mrs. Cobb cornered Pastor Emerson to straighten him out about his mistaken interpretation of the third chapter of Paul's Epistle to the Romans, she found him not only unapologetic but suggesting that it might be she who was in error.

Underlying Mrs. Cobb's many dissatisfactions was her unhappiness with herself. Plain, with a limited worldview from never traveling outside the state, her only handle on happiness was a faint hope that she could pull the world down to her level of misery. Steeled for the meeting, Tom looked up from his work and said, "Marian, always a pleasure to see you. Come in and have a seat. What's on your mind today?"

Mrs. Cobb sniffed. "It's good of you to grant me all of five minutes out of your day. You got my email, I presume."

"Sorry about the time limit. You'd want to get the most out of the tax dollars that pay my salary, wouldn't you?" His attempt at wit drew a flat stare. "Well, as I recall you had some questions about Mark Twain." Tom managed to keep his smile in place though it did seem that Mrs. Cobb might be a bit more ill-humored than usual.

"No, that is not what I said. I do not have *questions* about Mark Twain; I have *knowledge* of Mark Twain and how the lying and disobedience and disrespect for authority in his stories set terrible examples for young readers and run contrary to good parenting. That is what I said."

"Well then, if you feel that strongly, let's walk over to the library and put a stop on your son's library account to keep him from checking out Twain's titles. Will that take care of it for you?"

"Mr. Clausen, you are avoiding the point. If Mark Twain's books are not fit reading for my son, they are not fit reading for anyone's children. If you allow other students to read them, they become just like sexual predators. Just because they don't harm certain people is no sign that they aren't dangerous for others. I am not some radical; I am just careful. And it is not just my Byron I am concerned about. It is the whole school, your school. In case you don't know it, one of your English teachers actually requires children to read Twain."

"'The Celebrated Jumping Frog of Calaveras County.' It's been in literature books in public and church schools for most of a century without complaint. I'm sorry, but we can't go along with you if you're suggesting that we censor it."

"With a whole world of literature to pick from, when you have hundreds of good Christian authors to choose from, why on earth would you cling to literature that, at best, is morally flawed? This is not just my opinion, you know. I've heard that the entire Christian Voter's League agrees with me. As the principal of this school, you, of all people, should understand that Mark Twain is one of the reasons your schools don't pass bond levies. You think about that, Mr. Clausen." Mrs. Cobb stood and tugged creases from her skirt. "Thank you for your time. You'll likely be hearing more about this."

As soon as Marian Cobb's broad form disappeared from view, Tom signaled Alice. "How'd she look on the way out?"

Alice whispered, "Full head of steam."

"On the bright side, she got it all out in less than five minutes. See if you can fend off interruptions for a while. I need solitude." When he touched the button turning off the intercom, it popped back on again.

Alice again: "No way, Jose. You've got fifteen minutes until you're due in the lunchroom at eleven twenty."

"Alice, your organizational skills are an inspiration to us all, but leave it to me to sort what I'm supposed to do from what I have to do. No, let me put it this way: I'm not surfacing until I've checked the science lab safety reports. Got that?"

"Okay, I haven't seen you—which will be true if you keep your door shut, but should anyone ask me, you *are* in the building this afternoon, which, I hope, will be true. I'm serving notice, Mr. Clausen; some of your excuses for going into hiding push the envelope, so keep in mind that I won't fib for you."

"Thanks, I guess. If you order me a tray for the beginning of second lunch, I can be back on schedule by twelve fifteen. Promise."

"Got it. At the risk of sounding like your mommy, if you plan to go incommunicado for the rest of the morning, you might consider a potty stop about now."

"I thank God constantly for your comprehensive advice. Goodbye, Alice." Tom clicked off and ducked down the office corridor to the staff lavatory.

Fifteen minutes later, Clausen's intercom light flashed again. He slammed his highlighter down and said, "Alice, please. Whatever it is, pass it to Darrell."

"Dr. Krause to see you, Mr. C. Shall I tell him to go away?"

The superintendent of Northbridge schools was one of the few Tom welcomed at any time. He and Phil Krause had developed an easy working relationship from wrestling with issues such as the school board's decision to limit the transportation budget to busing students to and from school, a change that required rewriting budgets for special education, athletics, and departmental field trips. Krause tapped at Clausen's door and entered.

Tom loosened his tie and said, "Nice to see a friendly face. What's the occasion? Please, sit." He settled back into his chair while the superintendent remained on his feet, looking about the office as though checking for out-of-plumb pictures. He stepped back to shut the door and turned to face Tom's gallery of school photos. Speaking to the wall, he said, "Have you been hearing rumors?"

"All the time. It's how news travels. Some are credible, some incredible. Why do you ask? Is there something I should know?"

"Well, as you know, sometimes the school board takes positions that aren't entered into their minutes."

Tom said, "I'd expect so. It's not right, but I suppose it's necessary. Sometimes. Of course you have something in particular in mind. Dare I ask what it is and why you're here to talk about it?"

The superintendent sprawled into a chair and crossed his ankles, his size-thirteen shoes reaching half the height of Tom's desk. He said, "You and I work well together. You know what I mean; we approach problems pretty much the same way. I like to think that we're both good listeners and try to keep our pet biases out of problem-solving arenas. I just wanted you to know how much I've appreciated that."

Tom's apprehension grew as Krause danced around his purpose. "Should I be saying thanks for the kind words and support; it's been nice knowing you? What's going on, Phil? Am I in trouble?"

Krause drew a deep breath and exhaled. "The board hasn't made it public yet, but I'm being replaced. Nonrenewed. You might know that my continuing contract has been up for renewal since the first of the year. Well, when I pressed the board for commitment, Claudia told me I was being replaced. Not, sorry, you'll be missed. Just that I no longer fit in with their plans. No other reason given. It seems that when Koutac pushed the board to end the delay on my contract, they took it into executive session, which was illegal, and voted three to two to terminate me. Claudia's camp had one more backer than Koutac's. What's important now is that you understand that for all practical purposes I've already been replaced. As of the first of the month, all business with the superintendent's office bypasses my desk, if I have one. A word to the wise: If you need to say anything to me, do not go through district channels, and watch your language. Any expression of support for me will identify you as one of the enemies."

Tom was stunned. His respect for the Lincolnesque superintendent put Claudia and her supporters on the wrong side of whatever issues were at stake. Tom had known leaders, and he knew education, and he had never before worked with anyone who blended leadership and educational know-how as well as Phil Krause. His ability to function under pressure was showcased during a meeting when a critic of a building plan fired a question intended to sabotage the design. Krause heard him out before saying, "I can't say I'm on the same page with you, but I'd like to know more about where you're coming from. Keep talking." It was the smoothest defusing of a heckler Tom had ever witnessed. He knew that dumping Phil Krause could not be good for the district.

As the many ways Krause's departure might affect his school took root, Tom said, "Phil, I think what's happening may be akin to what happens before general elections. Kingmakers figure they need to freshen up leadership and let people know who runs the show. They're wrong. Claudia's wrong. I know you, and I know the board. The way I see it, Claudia's people are unhappy because you can see what they're too blind to see. Worse for them is remembering the times you cleaned up the damage they caused. You'll always be a class act. They can't take that from you." When Krause didn't reply, Tom added, "If you're out, when does the board start interviewing?"

"They're not going to interview; they've gone in-house. The pick hasn't been announced yet, but everything addressed to superintendent already goes to his desk."

Tom exhaled heavily. "Wainwright? Then you're here to advise me to keep a low profile and hope to survive. Right?"

"That's about it. Stay alert and don't discount rumors. Make sure that you aren't seen as disloyal. He expects all-for-one support from the staff but don't look for a reciprocal one for all. He's using disloyalty as grounds for dismissal, cleaning house, or whatever it is he's doing." Krause stood and repositioned his chair. "That said, I'm here to visit Mr. Palmer's class. I want to congratulate him and his band for their showing at the Northwest Jazz Band Festival, which, by the way, is my official reason for visiting." He looked at his watch. "Yes, they'll still be in class. You coming with me?"

Tom stepped from behind his desk to clasp Krause's hand. Krause, who had been a reliable source of pleasant surprises, gave him another, a hug, breaking to say, "You've taught me a lot. Don't worry; you'll weather this. You remember the story about the king who offered a great reward to anyone who could, in five words or less, give him comfort against the thousand and one things that besieged his reign?"

"And this, too, shall pass."

Krause opened the door. "And it will. Let's go."

After their stop in the band room, Tom walked Krause to his car. Instead of returning to his office, he detoured to the cafeteria. Krause's bombshell left him in no condition to concentrate on a safety report so it would be more night work. Seeking respite from fears about what the board and Wainwright were up to, he entered the Viking lunchroom. The hall reverberated with teen spirit that echoed the energy of the Viking caricatures on the walls dribbling soccer balls, flying over pole-vault bars, swatting tennis balls, and standing menacingly at bat.

The upsurge in sack lunches following the cafeteria's switch to healthy cuisine had faded as most adapted to the new choices. Where pop machines once stood, new coin-op dispensers served up bottled water, iced tea, juices, and yogurt. Snack machines remained, but instead of potato chips and candy, they dispensed granola bars, nuts, and fresh or dried fruits. The day's over-the-counter offering was lasagna with green beans on the side.

The cafeteria was prime testing ground for giving mischief-makers the eye. Over his years in education, Tom, like others, came to believe that teachers, like sheep dogs that depend on eye contact to throw fear into flocks, can do the same with students. The belief was that staring could focus a beam of psychic energy to interrupt mischief. Tom focused on a boy who was sinuously bellying onto his table to reach the lunch of a girl whose attention was distracted. Within seconds, the boy looked over his shoulder into Tom's laser-like stare. Tom motioned him over.

Pants low on his hips, the boy shambled over and mumbled, "Sorry, Mr. Clausen."

Tom replied, "Sorry doesn't cut it. Look, Richard, if you value her friendship, stealing her food is about the dumbest thing you could do. Now get back there and do or say something nice." The boy opened his mouth but nothing came out. Tom turned him around and said, "Go on, scat."

Still in the lunchroom when his scheduled lunch supervision time began, the cafeteria's din rinsed away enough of Wainwright's effect to allow hope of keeping his school relatively untouched by the paranoia sweeping the district. The lunchroom's energy was a quick-acting tonic. Even better had been helping students gain insights into the relationships and mechanisms of their world and, most satisfying of all, witnessing their amazement when they found themselves thinking bigger thoughts than ever before. But he had to admit that those delights had become all too rare since he left the classroom for administration.

With nothing on the school board's agenda that affected his school, Tom had the night off, and Jane had wine glasses ready for a bit of freedom from the townspeople's expectations that educators hold themselves to lives of 24/7 saintly abstinence. With shoes kicked off, he and Jane settled in with a bottle of middle-shelf Tempranillo. Noticing motion, he glanced through open front curtains to see Garnie's Chevrolet swing out of his driveway and disappear up Dogwood Drive. "Garnie's headed out," he said. "How much you want to bet he's headed for the board meeting?"

Jane called from the pass-through to the kitchen, "Forget the school board, Mr. Workaholic. No shop-talk tonight, remember?"

At five before seven, Garnet Pittman was settled in his usual seat when the board filed in. Aside from the superintendent, who was expected to appear pressed and groomed in suit and tie, Pittman was the only attendee to be in semiformal attire, the difference being that Pittman's outfit looked as though it had been pulled from the bottom of a laundry basket.

Pittman watched for Northbridge's superintendent, Dr. Krause, to enter. He enjoyed Krause's style—how he kept the board straightened out when, as often happened, it misunderstood school law or district policy, or didn't understand issues within the district. He and Krause, though not friends, had locked horns in spirited discussion a few times. A dapper stranger took Krause's chair. He was solidly built with dark wavy hair that reached his collar. To Pittman, his precisely folded pocket hanky was a misdemeanor he elevated to a capital crime when he shook his cuffs free to display jeweled gold cuff links. Pittman didn't hold with affectations. The stranger looked out into the nearly empty room to find a man in a rumpled suit staring balefully back at him.

Garnet Pittman's history with the Northbridge schools began in first grade. Twelve years later, the 1952 Northbridge High yearbook listed Garnet Franklin Pittman as having graduated with honors, performed in school plays, and played viola in the school's string ensemble. His picture showed a somber, round-faced boy with short hair parted in the middle. The Longfellow verse he'd chosen to accompany his picture contrasted with humorous quips from his classmates: "The love of learning, the sequestered nooks, and all the sweet serenity of books."

A socially insecure oddball during his school years, Garnet didn't find friends until he attended the University of Washington where he and other brilliant social misfits gravitated toward each other. They developed long-term friendships that gave Garnet his best sense of belonging, though contacts with those intimates over the years were infrequent. They were an odd mix ranging from super achievers of academia to penniless artists, all too bright to fit any mold. One would be delivered to Garnet's home by a limo service, the next on foot. In the days following one of their visits, he appeared energized as he went about his daily rounds, surprising fellow humans by offering greetings instead of plowing along cocooned with private thoughts.

Garnet lived simply. He considered his inheritance of tens of thousands of acres of timberland and assorted commercial interests a trust to help beneficiaries of his choosing. The Pittman estate's roots were planted in Northbridge when Garnet's grandfather, Joseph Pittman, settled there. Then, the village was known as Broward's Ferry. In 1897, Joseph was clearing stumps and logging debris to start a farm when reports that gold was for the taking in the Yukon seized his attention. He returned in 1901 after two good years in the goldfields, carrying letters of credit, a considerable weight in gold, and the profit from selling his worked-out claim to a latecomer.

Joseph soon married a young widow, Astrid Olafson, and invested part of his war chest in three sections of timberland. In time he observed that while his trees grew, his remaining gold didn't. He began to worry that sitting on his treasure might invite the wrath of God, as happened in Luke 19:20 to the servant who was too timid to put the money his Lord had entrusted to him to work. Having been raised by strong Calvinist parents, the doctrine of salvation through works lurked in his subconscious, spurring Garnet's Grandpa Pittman to buy more timberland.

In the early 1930s, the Great Depression undercut small timber companies, rendering them as ravaged as the stump-strewn clear-cuts that marked their wakes. Grandpa's first son, Waldo, who by then had picked up the reins of his father's vision, tapped Joseph's gold reserves to buy out a number of destitute landowners, expanding the family holdings from tens of thousands of acres to parts of counties. He courted and married Mildred Weston, daughter of Northbridge's banker and hardware merchant, and within a span of twelve years, she delivered four children, the first of whom died in infancy.

Grandpa and Waldo watched their logging operation progress from oxen and corduroy skid roads to diesel yarders and trucks, and from axes and misery whips to the first chain saws. Following Grandpa Pittman's death in 1944, Waldo bought a tidewater mill that generated handsome profits from processing Pittman logs until it burned in 1956. Waldo and Mildred's three surviving children, Charles Winston, Alicia Marie, and Garnet Franklin, graduated from Northbridge High and went on to the University of Washington. In 1951, with the Korean Conflict's military draft breathing down his neck, Charles dropped out of the university to enlist in the Air Force, which fast-tracked him though officer's candidate school and flight training. Garnet was in his freshman year at the University of Washington when, on a crisp morning in January 1952, two formally uniformed military officers stood at the door of the Pittman mansion to deliver the news that Charles's plane had been shot down over North Korea. Charles had been Garnet's hero.

Both Waldo and Mildred became unhinged by the loss of their oldest child. After some months of trying to carry on, Waldo recognized that he could no longer function as before. Charles was to be the future of the Pittman timber empire, which by that time was known as Pittman Pacific Timber, Inc. Without Charles to take over, toiling for the family's businesses and their employees lost all meaning. He gave little thought to his second son, Garnet, who had always been an enigma and not the sort of man's man needed to rule a logging empire. He did keep a keen eye on the value of his empire and set about organizing it as a trust to be operated within specific latitudes and restrictions by whomever might become its administrator. Just as the arrangements were being finalized, Waldo dropped dead of a stroke at the age of sixty-one. Alicia had married well and invited her mother to live with her near Tacoma's Brown's Point where she spent the last twelve years of her life. Garnet, who was waiting for some kind of delayed reaction to his father's death, received the first of many formal contacts from lawyers. His signature was needed, his presence was requested, and he was required to appear. There seemed to be no end to it, nor any way to fend it off. When he asked his mother what he was supposed to do, she replied, "I'm sure you'll do the right thing, dear."

William Dodge, Waldo's attorney, read the will to Mildred, Alicia, and Garnet during a meeting in Dodge's law office where Mildred and Alicia, as though by agreement, took seats behind Garnet. Dodge had drafted a plan for insinuating himself into Pittman Pacific's management which, as he explained, was a necessary precaution to protect the Pittman heirs' interests against unscrupulous opportunists.

He proposed a management team with him at the helm, detailing a grand plan that Garnet and Alicia heard there for the first time. Garnet asked for a second reading of the will through which he scribbled notes. That completed, the lawyer again led him through the logic and advantages of his proposal, thus fulfilling what he took to be his obligation to the Pittman estate under the law. When Dodge concluded by saying, "and I will dedicate myself to seeing that Pittman Pacific continues in its role of far-sighted and profitable business leadership," Garnet fired him on the spot and dismissed the meeting.

Dodge was the first of many who would underestimate Garnet Pittman's steel and intelligence. Within days, Garnet redrew the trust agreement; rehired Chet Tovson, who had managed the fire-destroyed Pittman Mill, to supervise timber operations; engaged a firm of certified public accountants to audit Tovson's books; and appointed a trust officer at Port Gardner Savings Bank to audit the accountant's work. He and Alicia agreed on allowances for themselves and their mother, agreeing that profits from Pittman enterprises should be donated to charities focusing on education, charities they would select during annual meetings.

With his burgeoning involvement in Pittman Pacific, Garnet found himself at a crossroads. He was in his third year of teaching history at Portland's Lewis and Clark College while finishing his doctorate. The few academic papers he had published on "Commercial Bases for American Involvement in Latin American Elections" showed a flair for historical research, but his teaching was so mind-numbingly dull that several students had complained to the dean of instruction. The dean, in turn, passed the complaints on to the Committee for Review of Untenured Professors, which, sent Garnet an uncomplimentary summary of his effect on the college's reputation. Tipped away from teaching and toward Northbridge, he resigned effective the end of the term and moved home to the Pittman mansion on Dogwood Drive.

Garnet's makeup didn't allow him to live up to the scale of his mansion. He slept, read, and ate no differently there than when living in a duplex on Portland's east side. Though owners of the other grand homes along Dogwood Lane employed gardeners, Garnet chose to do his own mowing, a task that grew lighter with the years as aggressive shrubbery encroached on what had once been broad expanses of grass. Rhododendrons and other uncontrolled shrubs rose to obscure the handsome building from the street, and deciduous trees, once planted to provide patches of shade, expanded their umbrellas to provide perfect shelter for algae and moss to take hold on masonry, walkways, steps, the roof, and the birdbath. Though the home's neglected grounds underscored Garnet's opinion of fussy gardening, he was quick to hire skilled craftsmen when something broke or needed replacing.

Northbridge citizens snickered at Pittman behind his back. Though not grossly overweight, his doughy body lacked muscle definition. His half-rim glasses rode low on a potato nose that served as a hanger for folds of cheek that sagged into jowls. His active gray eyes were set wide below sprouting brows and a tousle of sandy-gray hair that fell from his balding crown. It was rumored that he cultivated his unkempt and disagreeable persona to keep people at a distance when, in fact, he simply had no concern for public opinion. Some made the mistake of judging his mind by his appearance, but they had never sat across from him at a chessboard, engaged him in an argument, or let him catch them voicing a poorly founded opinion. Few suspected that he was, in fact, capable of buying the entire town.

Garnet Pittman, known to his few intimates as Garnie, drove his Chevrolet to the Northbridge library each day to read the front pages, financial sections, and editorials in the *Seattle Times*, *New York Times*, and *Wall Street Journal*. He arrived about ten thirty, a half hour after it opened, at which time he expected his choice of those papers to be available. The library's clerks clearly remembered times when he alienated patrons who, if they held a section of a newspaper he wanted, found him perched uncomfortably close, staring, glancing repeatedly at his watch, and fidgeting until he drove them away. His behavior could have cost him his library privileges were it not for his annual donation of $50,000 to the library's operating fund.

Garnet didn't live alone. In 1935, during the depth of the Great Depression, impoverished parents commonly sought help by placing their children in homes that could feed them. Fifteen-year-old Sigrid

Halvorson's parents offered her to Waldo and Mildred as a house servant in exchange for food, clothing, and a bed. The Pittmans were moved to pity at the sight of the undernourished moppet and responded generously, not only taking in Sigrid but also giving her father a job in the woods.

Sixty-five years later, Sigrid, long known as Aunt Sigi, was still there. Her father, who survived World War II in the Pacific, returned to Pittman Pacific as yard foreman at the mill. He and his wife, Gert, built a retirement home on the beach at Utsalady on Camano Island, a property they eventually sold for enough to buy a retirement condo in Seattle's Scandinavian enclave of Ballard. Sigi cloistered herself in the Pittman house and never married, though her three brothers and an older sister did to produce a teeming pack of nieces and nephews for her to dote on.

In a very real way, the Pittman mansion was more hers than Garnet's. Her entire investment of self and most of her personal history were embedded in its rooms and corridors. Echoes of stages of her life resounded from its walls, and when she counted her most cherished memories, few lay outside its perimeter. Her early childhood, small ventures out into Northbridge society—everything outside her years in the Pittman home—amounted to no more than footnotes to her life in The House. Across her years of service to the family, she witnessed the deaths of generations while "The House" remained her one constant. When she was away square-dancing at the Nordic Hall or shopping or running errands, and Sigi finally had to return home, she would say, "It's time for me to get back to The House." Something of the awe she felt when she first entered the Pittman home never left her, though she had lived and worked within its shelter and protection for more than six decades.

Sigi's closest friend, Inger Matthiesen, lost her husband to a shake mill accident before they were able to start a family. Over the years of their friendship, they came to spend every Tuesday afternoon together at Port Gardner's Nordic Hall where the club's Norwegian sponsors laughed at well-worn Ole and Lena jokes and good-naturedly ribbed the Swedes, Finns, and Danes who joined their company.

The Tuesday afternoon attraction at the hall was dancing to a trio of ancient musicians. Holding forth on accordion, drums, and bass fiddle, they shed years when belting out foot-stomping polkas to a hall loosely crowded with aging immigrants. There had been times when Sigi and Inger had to deal with dance partners who longed to become suitors, but the ladies were content to live out their years without the complications of husbands. Sigi, though, couldn't bring herself to break entirely from Karl Steffanson. Karl, a lanky ex-lumberjack with an infectious smile, was everything the single ladies of the Nordic center craved: a gentleman, a marvelous dancer, and he still drove at night. Karl persisted in his pursuit until Aunt Sigi accepted him as "her special friend," a relationship that generated enough phone calls to irritate Garnet into installing a private line for her.

With Waldo and Mildred Pittman long deceased, Garnet and Aunt Sigi were left to lay claim to whichever of the big house's rooms met their needs. Because each was independent in his or her own way, disagreements arose. Garnet would not lower toilet seats, nor did he think locking the house at night was of importance, though he refused to pass that responsibility off to Aunt Sigi. So she trembled in her bed until fear of intruders drove her to pad down in her slippers each night to see that the locks were set—front, back, and patio. They often were not. The tone of their relationship was colored by Aunt Sigi's style of dealing with Garnet when he was a boy attending grade school in Northbridge.

Aunt Sigi was a long-time member of the Lutheran Ladies Guild, an organization of rabid quilters. Her passion for outdoing other quilters was displayed in the fabric cuttings that, from time to time, decorated most flat surfaces in the home's dining room and den, where working light from the rooms' high windows was best. The dining room and den were also Garnet's spaces, where he stacked newspapers, left books splayed open, and spread sticky notes and pages from writing pads about. As housekeeper, Aunt Sigi took it upon herself to tidy Garnet's spaces with deliberate disregard for whatever order he might have been working toward. Her forays into what he took to be his domain set him to muttering unpleasant things about her while slamming out of the house to drive off to one of his haunts. Page markers and specially placed notes denoted the progress of Garnie's thoughts as surely as dribbles of a wolf's urine marked its territory. And like a wolf, intrusions into his literary markings triggered primal outrage. Epic clashes arose from Garnet's refusal to recognize that he sometimes mislaid things without Aunt Sigi's help.

Each came to think of their spaces as private domains they claimed without discussion. Aunt Sigi's impoverished childhood had left her with an abiding hunger for plenty, and in Garnet's deceased parents' suite, she saw opportunity to bask in queenly luxury that topped every dream of her childhood. Her explanation for moving her belongings into the master suite was "You complain so much about my quilts that I had to move their frames into your grandpa's bedroom. No other place was big enough."

CHAPTER 4

Garnet's private domain consisted of two connecting bedrooms, one to sleep in and one he converted into an office. He also claimed the den but was unable to hold back the spread of Aunt Sigi's scraps and cuttings there when she was stitching a major project together.

It was during one of their more difficult times that Garnet and Aunt Sigi agreed that it would be a good thing to spend some time apart. The event that brought the matter to a head was Aunt Sigi's blowup after finding her carefully color-sorted clippings jumbled together in a laundry basket where Garnet had chucked them to reclaim table-top space. On the morning after her eruption, they agreed they would be less likely to kill each other if they separated for a time, but when it came to deciding where Aunt Sigi might travel to, she was unable to think beyond the horizons of The House. In a fit of frustration, Garnet sat her down and told her that he was sending her to Hawaii for two weeks. Aunt Sigi had never flown, was afraid to fly, and wouldn't think of flying anywhere alone. She broke down in tears. When she sobbed out Garnet's ultimatum to Inger, her friend recognized potential in the conflict. Having suspicions about how deep the man's pockets were, she advised Aunt Sigi to tell him that she simply could not go anywhere unless accompanied by her friend, Inger. So it was that over the next eleven years, Garnet's travel agent arranged for Aunt Sigi and Inger Matthiesen to spend the first two weeks of every February at the Four Seasons Resort in Wailea on the island of Maui.

Fixing the upstairs bath's leaky sink faucet was at the top of Jane's Saturday honey-do list. Tom was tightening the valve with its new washer onto a freshly buffed valve seat when she called up the stairwell, "Phone. It's Garnie."

"Ask him to call back or take a message." Ten more minutes, he thought. What was supposed to have been a simple project had already cost him half the morning and a trip to the hardware store.

"He says he needs to talk to you now."

"Well, I'm not available for twenty minutes so that's as close to now as he's going to get," Tom shouted back.

"He wants you to come over."

"All right, all right. Tell him I'll be there. Twenty minutes." With everything cinched into place, he reached under the sink and turned on the supply line. The faucet's running leak had stopped, but still dripped. Tom grasped the valve handle and wrenched, slowing the leak to a swelling droplet that took a half minute to grow heavy enough to fall. "Close enough," he muttered and gathered his tools.

Still grumbling about his wasted morning, Tom dropped his wrenches on the garage bench and stopped. He was in no mood to match wits with his manipulative neighbor. It had been a difficult week that left him feeling too unsettled to deal with anyone's guff, and Garnie wasn't just anyone. He stared out the garage window at the overgrown Pittman estate and strode back into his house where Jane said, "Twenty-five minutes. You forget something?"

"Please, I need a little help." He stepped toward her with his arms out.

She said, "Like this?" and raised on tiptoe to melt against him.

He gave her a squeeze and broke loose. "Thanks, Mrs. Sweet Britches. I needed that." He glanced back as he cut across the lawn to catch her following him from the dining room window.

Tom climbed time-stained marble steps, pausing on the colonnaded porch to admire the tall iron-strapped doors. A clicking of latches settled the need to ring. Garnie, glowering, pulled the right-hand door open. "How many times have I told you, Thomas, to come to the side door? No one I care to see comes in this way. By the way, whatever were you doing just standing there? Had you planned to ring the bell, or were you testing my powers of perception? For heaven's sake, do come in now that the door's open. You're letting all the heat out." Garnie was tented in a paisley silk robe over baggy gray sweats that went poorly with his brown dress shoes.

"The reason I requested your presence posthaste was that there is something you must hear. Come with me." He set off across the living room to a door near the far corner that opened into a solarium. "This way, please." He crossed the solarium to open a door to a patio that faced his neighbor's fence. He stepped to the rail and whispered, "Listen!"

Tom listened. The far-away freeway hiss and roar laid the background for the putt-putting of a neighbor's single-cylinder engine struggling under periodic loads as though powering a pressure washer or paint sprayer. Other than the motor and a flicker knocking on a tree, he heard nothing out of the ordinary. He turned to Garnie and shrugged. "Well, what am I supposed to be listening for?"

Garnie pointed toward his neighbor's fence and whispered, "Do be patient. It will start up again any moment now."

Tom's patience was already worn thin. "I really don't have time for this. Just tell me what's going on."

"Ardis Swenson's dog, that's what's going on. Every time I open a book or pick up the phone—it doesn't really matter what I'm doing—the beast starts baying. It can't even bark like a normal dog. I tell you, Thomas, the dog can sense when I need quiet. Take this moment right now. It knows we're talking about it, so it's over there biding its time. As soon as you return to the quiet of your home and I settle down to concentrate on something, it will start up again. You can count on it. The beast is loud, evil, and prescient." Garnie lowered his voice to a conspiratorial hush. "Now here is what I'd like you to do. You may know that my relations with the Swensons are a bit strained, so what I'd like you to do is speak to Ardis about her dog. I'm sure you can handle it without ruffling her feathers."

Tom suppressed a laugh. "Garnie, you've outdone yourself this time. Jane and I aren't bothered in the least by Ardis's dog. For all we know, he's mute. How can you expect me to complain to a neighbor, one I get along with just fine, about a problem that, as far as I know, doesn't exist?"

"If you trusted me you would believe me. But since you assume I prevaricate, there's no need in carrying this any further." Garnie suspected that Tom was lying because the other neighbors he'd talked with agreed that there was a problem. The animal, a mixed-breed hound named Digger, bayed mournfully for periods that would wear out most voices. It chose odd daylight hours to wail in a clear tenor, pausing only to top off its lungs with breath enough to howl another stanza of complaint about being confined.

Tom knew Digger from the many times he had dropped by to visit Buster in past years. Digger was a congenial beast that greeted humans by presenting an itchy spot above his tail for scratching. Now that Buster, Tom and Jane's eleven-year-old beagle-retriever mix, slept through the day—except for midmorning escapes through his doggie door to decorate the side yard—Digger didn't visit anymore.

Because Northbridge's leash laws were enforced only when dogless neighbors complained about loose dogs, the canines of Dogwood Drive had enjoyed perfect freedom until the cat-loving Mackeys moved in. The Mackeys felt that cats had equal rights to roam without being chased by dogs, so after the local dog society joined in treeing the Mackeys' Siamese in their own front yard, they had the police ask the dogs' owners to keep their animals confined, gaining the half-hearted type of compliance that erodes with time.

Ardis Swenson never forgave Cindi Mackey for bringing in the law. Before Cindi called in Northbridge's animal control officer, Digger, Buster, and two other mutts met each morning in front of Garnie's mansion to watch the neighborhood drive off to work. The foursome sat in a circle to work up plans for their day before trotting off nose to tail, not necessarily with chasing the Mackeys' cats in mind—cats, like squirrels, being momentary fun. It was after Cindi's orange-striped tabby went missing and she jumped to the conclusion that Buster, Digger, and friends had done it in, that their freedom came to a crashing halt. Ardis and Tom and other owners received official letters from the city detailing their options. Tom installed an invisible fence. Ardis opted to keep Digger on her fenced deck that he tolerated by sleeping until she left for work, at which time, according to Garnie, Digger howled out his loneliness and frustration. In truth, Tom and Jane had heard and smiled at its mournful melodies. Buster simply took long naps.

Ardis bought a cat trap that she set out in her roadside azaleas. After each of the few times she scored, she made a show of loading the trapped cat into her car and hauling it off to the animal shelter. To her credit, Cindi did try to turn her two remaining cats into house cats, but having savored the delights of hunting small creatures along the slough's brushy banks, they took every opportunity to escape.

With the issue of Ardis's dog shelved, Tom put a finger on Garnie's chest and looked him in the eye. "Not prevaricate, manipulate. Now come down off your high horse so we can get to the meat of why you called me over."

Garnie assumed a pout. "Why is it that whenever I come to you with a simple request, you become testy? You can go if you wish. If you don't care to help a neighbor in distress, you can go." Having played the scene before, Tom moved toward the door on Garnie's cue and Garnie, as expected, followed in his footsteps to tap him on his back. "Just one thing more. Aren't you even a little bit curious about why I was interested in the property adjoining the Moraine intersection? I would love to know what you told Jane about our discussion the other night. You do talk about me behind my back, don't you?"

Tom turned to lap an arm around Garnie's shoulders. "Okay, my friend, so you did have something meatier than a howling dog on your mind. Where do we sit?"

Garnie led Tom into his den where three chairs surrounded one end of an antique table scattered with books, some sprouting colored bookmarks. A quilting frame sat propped against a wall of bookcases. Back copies of the *Economist*, *Mother Jones*, *The Nation*, and regional newspapers were stacked in order of date.

Garnie was miffed that he hadn't been able to draw Tom into his complaint about the Swenson dog. Though he respected and enjoyed Tom's independence of mind, he tended to turn peevish when his scheming lost traction. He said, "Sit there," and Tom sat, wondering how much more of his day he would spend prying Garnie's agenda into the open.

"Thomas, as your friend and neighbor, I'm going to overlook your disregard for my need for peace and quiet. In return, I want you to hear me out while I bring you up to date on your input regarding the commercial property near Moraine."

Tom burst out laughing. "Input! You asked me for my two bits worth and then told me it was useless."

"You wrong me as you always do. I said no such thing. If you use your memory, you'll recall that I said only that I intended to renew the contracts of certain corporate snakes I called consultants. If you chose to take that as a personal affront, well, what can I say?" Garnie held his gaze intently on Tom to gauge the effect of his needling. Disappointed, he continued, "Now, please, do pay attention. I'd not like it if you should misinterpret what I'm about to say—again."

Tom sprawled back with his hands laced behind his head. "Say away."

"Well then, as you may know, I fancy myself as somewhat of a historian. Take Northbridge for instance. Because of my ancestors' involvement, I inherited a grasp on how past events wove to make our present and how our present may influence the future. Native Americans, settlers, merchants, farmers, schools, politics—every little bit of the past conspiring to influence the evolutionary progression from its beginnings to who knows where it will all end. Everyone who made a difference along the way is woven into the tapestry that depicts local culture."

At that moment, Aunt Sigi limped in with a tea tray, set out mismatched English china cups, and poured, causing Tom to suspect that his visit had been so prescripted that she had been hovering out of sight awaiting her cue.

He said, "Sigi, you're limping. What happened?"

"It's nothing. I stepped down off a ladder wrong."

Tom threw an accusing glare at Garnie.

"Thank you, Aunt Sigi; that will be all," Garnie said. He waited until she had left the room to whisper, "Don't blame me. She took it upon herself to drag a stepladder through the house so she could vacuum the tops of curtains. I've told her a million times, no ladders, but the woman doesn't take direction well. Never has. She wouldn't even see a doctor."

Sigi's head popped around the corner. "Just how was I supposed to get to a doctor when I couldn't walk to the car? And before you do anything else, check your blood, Mr. Garnet."

Tom said, "Blood?"

"Oh, yes. Have to keep track of my blood sugar, you know." He looked in the direction of Aunt Sigi's last appearance and said, "That woman has magnificently keen hearing, wouldn't you say?"

"Did you offer to drive her to the clinic?"

"Well, no, but—"

Tom cut him off. "I rest my case. You deserve each other."

Garnie lifted his chin imperiously. "I'll not waste time wondering what you meant by that. Instead, let's return to the issue of Moraine. I'm quite sure that you, not being as deeply rooted in this town as I am, can't have much of a sense of historical continuity. You relative newcomers move into new developments with made-up names, like Moraine, and dream up your annual festivals as though one could invent tradition. There's no history there, nothing I'd call an accumulated culture, yet Moraine continues to grow by leaps and bounds. Their software industry is building a false culture! Taken together, it seems Moraine's residents have all the money in the world to flaunt, but they don't know how to use it. Consumerism appears to be key to what they mistakenly call culture."

Tom asked, "Did you own the townsite?"

"Well, not personally, not directly."

"Close enough. And now you're concerned that selling more land near Moraine…" Tom jerked upright to level an index finger at Garnie. "That's it. All that new money, all that financial power has moved onto what was once Pittman land, and you can't know where it will lead to and can't do anything about it. That business of using me as a whipping boy for Moraine's cheeky nouveau riche—you're spooked. You're upset because the unpredictable course or destiny or whatever's going on there has slipped beyond your influence. No wonder it's got under your skin. Your family has been the only mover and shaker on that parcel for generations."

"Balderdash! If you think I'm one to be buffeted about by who owns this or who owns that, you've severely misjudged me, Thomas. I had thought you to be a better judge of character. Drink your tea; it's cooling."

"What I'm warming to, Garnie Pittman, is that in addition to other aspects of your endearing nature, you have a conscience that stands revealed as rooted in the empire you claim you have nothing to do with. You worry about that land like a father whose daughter has just run off with a gigolo. The fact is, she's gone. It's not going to do you any good to stew about it. You're stuck with figuring out how to make the best of a situation that's slipped beyond your control." Tom picked up his cup, balanced it precariously on the arm of his chair and sprawled back while Garnie nervously watched the cup teeter. Tom let the issue of the teacup's security escalate until, when Garnie lunged to secure it, he took it in both hands and asked, "Tell me, did you order the gutter guards?"

Had his free time been a welcome gift, Dale Runyon might have enjoyed it by fishing or playing racquetball. But his release from coaching, coming as it did, was a bitter pill that darkened his moods and refused to flush from his system. Beginning when Roger and Ellen grew big enough to swing bats until they entered school sports, he'd coached little league teams, and after that he'd seized an opening to coach high school softball. Not coaching, not being buoyed up by predinner hours amid active children soured his disposition. On the Thursday of his first week of empty afternoons, Betty found him distant and out of sorts when she came home to ready herself for their weekly dinner out. She said, "I don't care what made you so disagreeable; just keep your black cloud out of the house. Now, are we going to dinner or not?"

She disappeared into the "girls" bathroom she shared with Ellen. Along with a change of clothes, leisurely early evening showers had long been part of her transition from work to home. She locked the door and bent to gather her dress, lift it over her shoulders, and in a flowing motion like a dancer, gracefully extended her arm to hang it from a hook on the door. She lowered herself as though bowing at a curtain call and rose smoothly, her hands rising above her head to carry her slip away. She unhooked her bra and lowered it with the finesse of a Tai Chi master. She slid her panties down slowly, stepping out with one foot and then the other in perfect balance, never breaking the flow, all the time following her performance in the mirror.

Taking up a hand mirror from the counter, she stepped away from the vanity mirror to where she could view her backside. Squaring her shoulders and breathing deeply, she rose onto her toes, flexing the muscles of her bottom. She turned to expose the reflected profile of her left breast, raising her free arm to counteract age and gravity. She carefully palpated each breast, kneading tissue as though searching for something lost, and when satisfied that there was nothing to find, her relief was nearly matched by her disappointed need for anxiety.

She bent to the shower control to adjust the water temperature and stepped in to lose herself under the sprayer's thrumming massage. In time, she reached for soap and washed and washed, moving through cleanliness to pleasure. Such times sometimes set her to wondering whether enjoying her body so naturally when alone was a special blessing or a sin.

Conversation was sporadic during the drive to a waterfront restaurant. A question. An answer. Then silence, followed by another question and answer. Once seated, Betty ordered an iced tea, and Dale, a "special" martini. Both strained to break the conversational impasse by stretching their questions and adding sidelights to their answers. Still, their conversational serves crossed the net no more than twice, making for a lackluster game.

Dale fished the olive from his drink and munched pensively. Questions about her day, her classes, and the latest book she'd read failed to stir a spark. He tried going personal, always chancy given Betty's tendency to react. "I need something to fill the void. After coaching for—what's it been, twelve, fourteen years? It's been better than something to fill time. Not bragging, but I'm good for the kids and they're good for me, which is why it was so tough to quit cold turkey, especially when quitting wasn't my idea."

"Well, you coached Little League before you took on the high school job. Why not see if you can get back into that? From what I hear, they always need coaches, qualified or not."

"It's a thought. I don't know; the season's close to starting so they probably have a full roster by now."

Betty snapped, "Listen to you, all gloom and doom. If there's a chance it might put a smile on your face, why not make a few calls? See if you can get involved somehow. Maybe they'd let you be an umpire." She reached to pull Dale's plate toward her. "Let me try your fish; my prawns are absolutely flavorless." She wrinkled her nose at the salmon and said, "You'll find something. If you don't do softball, you'll find some other way to spend your time on a game."

His suspicion that Betty held little wifely affection for him had grown stronger in recent years. The familial obligations of establishing a home, raising children, and saving for their educations provided common purposes so long as they lasted, but as Roger and Ellen began to chart their own courses, Betty and Dale found themselves dancing around each other without touching, each carving out personal space and time while maintaining routines of household civility. Sometimes they'd catch themselves staring at each other, wondering how to bridge the chasm they knew was widening.

No Oedipal leanings colored family relationships. Dale and Roger were one team, Ellen and Betty another, though the children's choice of same-sex activities with their parents was soft edged. Dale and Roger tackled projects together, the most recent being a week of evenings overhauling Tom's outboard motor. Betty and Ellen were shoppers. Roger and Ellen's brother-sister bond and Dale and Betty's Thursday night dinners out kept communication open between the camps.

Roger and Ellen worried about the tortured civility of their parents' marriage and wondered to each other why they were the only ones in the house who had fun. Their visits to friends' homes exposed them to how other parents did it, strengthening their concern that their mother and father's relationship was, as Roger put it, really weird. Having learned that commitment is not the same as love and that not all marriages last, they worried about their parents as a couple.

Dale and Betty had what they accepted as good days with hand-holding walks downtown, where she proved she could still turn heads, and he enjoyed watching her turn on the charm. There had been a couple of memorable nights, both out of town, when she surprised Dale by responding with a passion that left them holding each other long afterward. However, he hungered for a bit of spontaneity to break the ritual of infrequent ten-thirty encounters. He recalled the odd places and times that seemed right but that Betty had rejected as "unnatural"—the night spent aboard a friend's sailboat, the grassy glade above Blanca Lake, the moonlit night on an air mattress on the lanai of a Hawaiian condo.

Because good times together were so predictably rare, they took refuge in personal interests. Betty became one of Grace Lutheran's most faithful volunteers. Dale's fulfillment came from working with youngsters on playfields. Though it had been years since he'd enrolled his children in parks departments' athletic leagues and coached, the idea of getting back into the game wasn't totally unattractive to him. It would get him out of the house.

Acting out their separate needs to be out of the house, whether to Betty's church or Dale's athletic fields, only widened the gap. Betty was comfortable filling time with regularly scheduled school or church committees and choir practices while Dale preferred to program his time loosely to allow spur-of-the-moment golf or fishing or skiing. Even their faith, something they took to be a common bond when getting to know each other, divided them once they compared the austerity of Betty's Wisconsin Synod brand of Lutheranism with the more tolerant Evangelical Lutheran tradition of Dale's past.

The Wisconsin Synod, a somewhat solemn splinter of Lutheranism, treasured its traditions, whereas Dale's Evangelical Lutheranism flexed to reconcile present-day living with Luther's Reformation beliefs. Right or wrong, Betty and her Wisconsin Synod maintained a higher level of certitude about what had to be believed and how to believe it than did the Evangelical Lutherans. Betty's church was heavily German while Evangelical congregations tipped toward Norwegians and Swedes. As with their Lutheranism, they found that it was areas where they were most closely matched stirred the most agonizing conflicts.

They handled most of their differences as manageable undercurrents until they returned from their first vacation without children. What was to be a dream vacation became a nightmare. During the planning stage, Betty found that Dale wasn't keen on museums, antiquities, and concerts. When he suggested the great outdoors, she said she'd rather stay home than be subjected to sleeping in a tent full of mosquitoes. After weeks of dickering, they settled on a package visit to New Orleans where Dale grumbled about tour guides who ignored his list of requests to stick to the city's list of top-ten attractions. They did agree, except for gumbo so spicy it was returned uneaten, that the food was excellent and their tour of quiet, mangrove-rimmed bayous, memorable. Nevertheless, after ten days of unrelieved togetherness, both were happy to escape into separate distractions when they returned home.

An argument between school custodians and organizers of Northbridge's invitational volleyball tournament forced Tom to cancel a Saturday golf date with Dale. Their rescheduled match for the following Saturday collapsed when an alarm from the high school's pool area required Tom to visit the site where he found that a technician had tripped the alarm while updating the school's security system. After two weeks of false starts, they met at Hemlock Hills Golf Course in time to test the putting green. At the call of "Clausen party of two, on deck," they moved to the tee to stretch while a foursome of Japanese golf-tourists ahead of them placed three of their drives tidily in the center of the fairway, all four within a seven iron of the green. Tom tossed a tee to see who would lead off while the Japanese carted away down the path. Dale won.

He teed his ball and stepped back. "Just to clear the air, I'm okay with how you handled it," Dale said. "It stung at the time, you know, me busting my butt for kids and getting beat up for it."

"Hey, it wasn't easy for me either; you know that. But please, no more shop talk." The foursome ahead moved beyond Dale's range. "You're up. Show the tourists how it's done."

Dale sent his ball straight and true, rolling ten yards short of a hazard, a 240-yard shot that turned the heads of the Japanese foursome when they heard it land.

With a wait ahead of them, Dale killed time by clipping dandelions with his four iron. "Sorry about bringing it up. I guess I'm a little uptight from other stuff on my plate. I could have done without McPhaiden right now." He stepped up and ripped a long shot down the left side of the fairway to put the Japanese on alert again.

After exiting the seventh green, Tom and Dale towed their bags up the steep approach to the eighth tee. Tom dropped onto a bench where the landscape leveled out beside the tee. "Whooof! Break time. Is that hill getting steeper, or am I getting older?"

"No to number one, yes to number two. You're a physical wreck going somewhere to happen. Come on, two more holes and we'll take a break at the turn."

Still puffing, Tom stripped the cover from his three wood and trudged to the tee. Dale looked him over. "You really shouldn't let yourself get so out of shape. You're flushed, short of breath, and generally look like hell. You quit racquetball, play almost no golf, work too much, and—oh, what the heck, you're not listening. The fairway's clear. Hit away."

Two and a half hours later, they sat over a late lunch in the clubhouse. A light squall had moved in to clear the course of fair-weather golfers, leaving Tom and Dale to play the back nine at their own pace. Midway through his burger, Tom commented, "So Claudia piled on top of other stuff?" Dale glanced up quickly and returned to his chili. "Okay, it's none of my business. New subject: how's the inquiry seminar shaping up?"

Two teaching interns had talked Dale into giving a seminar on the inquiry techniques he used in second-year biology. Their interest was sparked when they overheard a student say, "That's my one class where the action is, man, but you gotta think, gotta stay on your toes." One of the interns intruded to ask, "Whose class?"

"Runyon's. What do you want to know for?" one student said, as though suspicious of the question.

The interns requested and received permission to observe Dale in action, sat through two of his classes, and became disciples, enthusiastically shelving much of their university-taught methodology.

For Dale's part, he felt that having visitors shadow his teaching took the edge off his carefully orchestrated lessons, which he mentioned to Tom. Tom pulled the interns in to write up their observations but mainly to get them off his friend's back. Impressed with their report, he took the opportunity of the golf lunch to suggest that Dale organize his approaches into a seminar for an upcoming in-service training day.

Dale crumbled crackers into his bowl while chewing on the idea. "Two one-hour shots would work better. It's nothing more than simple role reversal. In traditional classrooms, teachers own questions they dose out to students who are then supposed to hunt down and take ownership of the answers. The problem with that is answers terminate curiosity while questions stimulate curiosity, so why not get kids involved at the questioning stage? I'll tell you why. Answers are fixed and manageable while questions can lead into unpredictable directions, and that spooks most teachers. There's more: Questions have longer shelf lives than answers. And it's possible that the same question will generate different answers from time to time. So if we want students to be lifelong learners, why not teach them to be better questioners? That's it in a nutshell. There's no way to stretch that into a full day."

Tom said, "I agree, but there's a big however. *However*, to earn public support, we have to show results like on test scores. If the district's bean counters don't get test scores, how do they know we're doing our jobs? Have you ever seen a test that measures students' questions? How would you go about scoring it if there's no one right answer? Where are the standards you measure questions against?"

Dale was unmoved. "If you're trying to aggravate me, you're doing great. As far as test scores go, that's more your problem than mine, at least until you convince me I shouldn't teach kids to think." He pushed his bowl away. "I think I have a good grip on what jump-starts kids' minds, and it isn't twelve years of unrelieved gorging on answers. Yeah, some of that's necessary but just some, not all. I'm no more wired to teach answers than kids are wired to learn that way. Not my style. Not their style. Infecting kids with good questions is the best thing I can do for the health of their minds. Look at it this way: after they leave school, shouldn't they be towing questions through life like fishing lures, snagging clues and answers wherever they happen to be?"

Tom grinned. "Use that passion to set the stage, and then put 'em through their paces just like you do with your classes. Model it. Use the faculty as your class. Leave the organizing to me, okay? Set it up so the teachers will have to question the issues that hold us back. Make them question their own questions like you do in Biology II."

"Ha! You really believe that if it works with kids, it'll work with teachers?" Seeing that Tom was unmoved, Dale said, "I can try, but teachers are adults. Too many of their brains are wasted. You'll see." He wiped his last French fry in ketchup and said, "Oh, what the heck, I'll work up a couple of one-hour lessons, but no full day. Will that make you happy?"

Tom called for the check. "They'll thank you for that. Now, the way my scorecard reads, you owe me sixty cents."

Instead of Marla Staehli, who had served Dr. Phil Krause and his predecessor, Dale found a new superintendent's secretary on duty. Fortyish and tall even when seated, she radiated a take-charge attitude. Gold dangled from her ears like wind chimes. Fingers and thumbs bore an assortment of rings. A doubled, gold-flecked bead necklace emitted enough color and flash to balance the rings, all of it effectively displayed against a black cable-knit sweater.

She touched a key. "Mr. Runyon is here." She listened for a moment. "Yes." Another pause. "I understand." The gate guard raised mascaraed eyes to focus on a point beyond Dale's left ear. "Dr. Wainwright will see you in a few minutes." The woman was evidently another in the rash of new hires, but no nameplate had yet replaced Marla's on the reception counter. When he leaned to read the name on her ID badge, she folded her arms across her breasts and said, "Please take a chair." Sheila, it said. The last name was short, beginning with O.

"The superintendent will see you now."

Dale rounded the corner that opened into the superintendent's office and found Wainwright's attention fixed on a computer monitor equipped with baffles to keep curious eyes from his screen. Without looking up, he said, "You're late. You were due here at three fifteen."

"Sorry, but I can't make three-fifteen meetings if they're off-site. My last class lets out at three."

"I can appreciate that. If it happens again, arrange with your principal to be released."

"I'm not sure I could get away with that. He's a stickler for following district rules, just like me. I know you're probably overburdened, being new and all, but it would truly help to keep us on task if you would book appointments for teachers that don't cut into class time. The policy against leaving the site during class hours is there for a purpose." Runyon, along with much of the district, was still simmering over the rumored dismissal of Dr. Krause. Since no public announcement of Krause's termination had been published yet, he took the plunge. "Excuse me, it's Wainwright, correct?"

"Dr. Wainwright."

"Yes, exactly. Well, I think I may be speaking to the wrong person. You see, I came here thinking I was going to be speaking with the superintendent. Where's Phil Krause?" Though not one for snap judgments, Dale took an instant dislike to Wainwright, which was mild compared with Wainwright's reaction to what he correctly took as needling from a subordinate. As Wainwright's color rose, Dale settled into bland unflappability that served to elevate Wainwright's blood pressure.

Wainwright shut his eyes and leaned back to compose himself. When he opened them, the impudent underling who had addressed him with an impertinence that implied he thought he was his equal, was smiling at him, actually smiling! He took Runyon's measure: taller, composed, darkly handsome, and seemingly relaxed in a navy turtleneck, suntans, and loafers, reflecting a casual dress standard he intended to do something about. Wainwright's disinterest in individual teachers left him ignorant of Dale's reputation as possibly the most effective and innovative teacher at Northbridge High. He would have been even less interested in his reputation for lightening dull faculty meetings with droll comments.

The de facto superintendent gazed over steepled fingers at Runyon's chest, over his shoulder, everywhere but into his eyes. He spoke through his teeth. "While Dr. Krause is on leave, you may consider that you are addressing the superintendent whenever you are in this office. Now, I'm hearing that you're deviating from the district scope and sequence plan for biology. Do you have anything to say to that?"

Wainwright's question shook Dale's composure. "Yes. Who's complaining?"

"That doesn't matter. What matters is that you follow the rules. Adhering to curriculum is a rule."

"Agreed. I have no problem following district curriculum for biology because I wrote it, and I teach it. The kids in my classes are in good hands when it comes to biology curriculum."

"That's not the issue. You are required to confine your teaching to the curriculum. This aimless probing and environmentalism and—"

Runyon cut in. "You're mistaken, Dr. Wainwright. Northbridge teachers are not confined to teaching the curriculum. That kind of academic confinement is something you're not going to find in any good school and certainly not here. As to what you call aimless probing, we do a short unit in learning to question the biological world as a way of opening students' minds to make lifelong learners of them. And environmentalism? Are you seriously suggesting that the environment shouldn't be a consideration in every classroom? I'm a good teacher, and I have classes filled with good learners. If we complete the required curriculum ahead of time, what would you suggest we do? Watch videos?"

Wainwright erupted, shouting through a spray of spittle that sent Dale sliding his chair backward. "Young man, you're out of line. When you step into this office, you show proper respect. Do you hear me?" Wainwright may have had a year or two on Dale, but addressing him as "young man" didn't win him any points. What tipped Wainwright over the edge was that a teacher, an ordinary district employee, had shown the effrontery to say to him, "You're mistaken." Worse was watching Runyon sit unimpressed through his tirade, studying him as though it was he who had been called onto the carpet. He made a mental note to check Runyon's file.

By seven o'clock on the morning of May 25th, the board room at Northbridge School District's administrative offices was filled in response to a May 20th bulletin announcing the official greeting of Dr. Charles Wainwright. Wainwright, who was hired the year before as special assistant to the superintendent, had acted as de facto superintendent for the past three months while Phil Krause, the popular superintendent who guided the district through twelve years of growth, was without an office. All principals, assistant principals, and supervisors had been instructed to attend. In case anyone was unclear about their status, a list was included in the bulletin.

At the stroke of seven, Claudia McPhaiden, school board chairperson, gaveled for attention. All eyes were on Wainwright, who occupied Krause's chair. Board members Harry Morgan, Nate McCollum, and Claudia McPhaiden took their seats, leaving two vacant chairs. Wainwright adjusted his cuffs, straightened his tie, and divided his attention between a sheaf of papers and quick glances into the audience.

Claudia leaned into her microphone and said, "Good morning to all of you. It's great to see you all back and ready to go after a weekend of rest. We're starting off with some great news, which probably isn't news by this time, but I'm going to announce it to you like it is anyway. Ladies and gentlemen, it is my great pleasure to present to you, Dr, Charles Wainwright, new superintendent of schools for Northbridge School District 508. Please give him a hearty welcome!"

A rattle of applause arose from parts of the audience where hands were most visible.

"Dr. Wainwright, as you know, has been with us for a year now. He came to us from Meade County, Kentucky, a school district that faced issues very like what we face here in Northbridge. Dr. Wainwright was responsible for pulling his county's schools together in troubled times and instituting programs that significantly elevated student achievement. As time passes, I'm sure you will all come to share my conviction that he is the right man for the job. Now, I turn the microphone and leadership of the Northbridge schools over to Dr. Charles Wainwright."

Again, zonal applause sputtered and died.

Wainwright rose and stepped to the microphone, straightening his jacket to flash his cuff links. "Good morning to all of you. Over the past three months, your school board has been meeting with me to bring me up to date on issues facing this district. As you know better than I, Northbridge is a district that continues to experience constant and rapid growth. With growth comes challenge, and that is why I am here, to guide you into new perspectives on how to manage growth." Wainwright spent the next quarter hour telling how, in Kentucky, he had built programs, solved problems, and provided leadership where it was lacking. All the time his gaze grazed heads and moved across pictures and charts that hung at the five-foot level about the room, insulating him from reading the confusion spreading throughout his audience.

Tom, like others, was puzzled. Wainwright's opening statements sounded fine on the surface, but they had a generic ring to them. The new man was committed to raising test scores, balancing the budget, and building the reputation of the district, but when he spoke of what happens in classrooms, it was the same gobbledygook that filled educational journals. He referred to new organization, new goals, and new programs as though the district's existing programs should be swept away. He avoided acknowledging support staff or the good work they did. Though he stopped short of stating it directly, he came close to telling his administrative staff that he wasn't so much interested in working with them as telling them what to do and how to do it.

"Now for the business at hand. Please make note of some target dates that will help you to get ready to end the year. Room inspections will be conducted in elementary schools on Monday and Tuesday, June twenty-first and twenty-second. Budget requests for the next year should be on my desk by the fifth of June to give us enough time to allocate funds. All final grades should be turned in no later than twenty-four hours after the students' last day. Oh yes, one more thing about budgets: Please be aware that with growth putting a serious strain on district finances, I'm sorry to say that we must trim eight percent from all account codes. I know it will be a challenge, but a policy of no exceptions makes it fair.

"Plan to be back here at the same time on Thursday when we'll discuss attendance issues, and if time permits, we'll get started on developing clear-cut standards for staff and student discipline and dress. I'm sure you'll have helpful input to offer. Now, if any of you feel you have issues you must discuss with me personally, my door is always open. Contact Sheila to arrange time on my calendar. Thank you for coming, and have a good day."

Trina Phillips, assistant to the curriculum director, stood and said, "Excuse me, excuse me."

Claudia reclaimed the microphone. "Yes, do you have a question?"

"Some of us would like to know when Dr. Krause's send-off party will be held. We'd sort of like to celebrate his years with us."

Board members Morgan and McCollum looked uncomfortably toward Claudia, who said, "I'm sure he would appreciate anything you plan on his behalf. Now, are there any other questions?"

Leaving the audience murmuring, Wainwright and the three board members filed out. Brad Koenitz from Spruce Elementary said, "Is there a little chill in here? If that was the good news, I can't wait to hear the bad."

Trina said, "Sheila, not Marla? Did he misspeak, or has he imported his own palace guard?"

Corrine Marx added, "A word to the wise, Trina. Things happened while you were away on behalf of the elementaries. Before you say anything more, you'd better check your office."

"Why?"

"Your stuff is boxed and sitting in the corridor. Looks like you have a different office or job. Maybe both. Maybe neither. Welcome back."

Trina mumbled, "Oh," and stalked off toward her office in the west wing of the old elementary building that served as district headquarters.

Tom signaled the junior high principal, Petra Nielsen, to meet him at the doorway. Petra whispered, "Can you believe the guy? He wants budgets in two weeks? The grades I can manage, but a budget? How does he figure we're going to supply more kids with less money?" Petra's lowered voice did little to disguise her agitated body language.

Tom put a finger to his lips. "Not here, wait until we're in my car."

Petra looked around and said, "That bad? Then the rumors are true?"

"You heard him. If he doesn't like what he hears, heads roll. My school's vocal music program was shot down when he squeezed out Turner. Runyon's on thin ice, and you just heard about Trina."

Once belted into Tom's Subaru, they exited the lot and drove to Conifer Junior High where he pulled into the no-parking bus zone. He pushed his seat back and said, "Okay, What's your take on him? From the gut."

Petra thought for a moment. "I was looking for the reason he was hired but so far, nada. This isn't right. Like have you heard one word from the board that justifies putting Dr. Doom into what, in my mind, should still be Phil's office? By the way, what do you think about two board members not showing?"

"Hard to say. Chesterton and Koutac are levelheaded. You think they had other commitments or that they didn't want to be part of it?"

"Most likely the latter. They both run their own businesses, so they'd have been there if they wanted to. I'm thinking that Wainwright was hired on a three-two vote, and the two no-shows are off somewhere being unhappy about it. Whatever happens, I'm giving the guy—listen to me; I can't even bring myself to speak his name—a wide berth."

Tom nodded. "Uh-huh, me too. It's going to be a contest of who keeps the lowest profile. I'm also thinking we'd better start taking steps to protect our teachers."

"Like how? What can we do?"

"Like making double sure that everybody understands that any and all contact with district offices be piped across our desks. And letting our people know that whatever we do to protect ourselves, it can't be seen as an anti-Wainwright conspiracy. So, I'm going to stiffen up my control to keep my 'more exuberant' people from making waves or venturing outside curriculum. That sort of thing."

"Mm-hmm. Here's another interesting thought: What do you think will happen if he crowds Denise Macklin? She's so scrappy on her good days that it won't be pretty if he gets snippy with her teachers' union. "

Tom started the engine. "We're going to need to communicate if anything newsworthy comes to either of us. Are you okay with that?"

Petra nodded and gave the top of his car a dismissal pat. "Righto. And if you do catch anything worth sharing, call me on my cell."

Tom drove back to the District Service Center lost in thoughts of how he might best protect his staff and programs.

At the time Claudia was introducing Dr. Wainwright, the two missing school board members, Mary Chesterton and Martin Koutac, were sipping cappuccinos at the Starbucks near the freeway interchange. Martin was a Northbridge native, his Serbian-immigrant father having logged for Pittman Pacific. Thanks to the GI Bill, Koutac finished three years of college before joining the Lynnwood insurance firm he now owned. Chesterton, a tough-talking New Yorker riffed during a Boeing cutback, operated three Subway franchises.

Martin said, "Nothing to do but accept it as water under the bridge, except I'd sure like to know what Claudia had on Nate to get his vote."

Chesterton mulled Nate McCollum's defection. "I thought he had more starch. Hard to believe he caved in after once leading the charge to advertise for candidates. Anyway, time will tell how tight he is with Claudia." She brushed biscotti crumbs from her ample breast and waved to an acquaintance. "Good idea to meet here. Outstanding visibility. Considering the Northbridge grapevine, us missing Wainwright's coming-out party might make page one of Terhune's fish wrapper. It's short of an apology, but what else could we do, other than quitting?" She pointed the stub of her biscotti at Martin. "You know, it's not gonna be a picnic dealing with that guy."

"Yep. But this is too good a town to suffer the likes of him. Somebody has to stick it out to rein him in. I guess that's us." Martin looked at his watch and rose. "Well, we either made a statement or we didn't. I'd better go earn a dollar. See you later."

Wainwright's call for reports on homeschooled children after they transferred into Northbridge's schools left Tom with nothing but questions. Who would do it? Who could? All he had was Alice and her assistants, Zoe and Candi, and their hours were booked full. He had past years' reports from the Home-School Alliance (HOSA), which tracked homeschooled students who supplemented their home studies with part-time attendance in public schools, but that was it. It was clear that neither he nor anyone else in the district was qualified to even hazard a guess about homeschooling. He buzzed Alice to ask for undisturbed time and went to work on his yellow pad:

Why do families opt for homeschooling?

How much do we know about the quality of Northbridge's homeschool programs?

How do homeschool curricula compare with public school curricula?

What public school issues bother homeschool parents and students?

How do standard test results for homeschooled students compare with those of public school students?

Should the results of that comparison be taken at face value or might there be qualifying factors?

Are there identifiable trends in homeschoolers' use of public school classes?

With a half page filled and his mind emptied, he googled an educational cooperative that dealt with homeschool performance. A few clicks convinced him that he might be on the right track. One site built a case for homeschooling Muslim children, speaking of support for a clearer moral base, fears about Columbine-type violence, fear of destructive peer-pressure issues, and insensitivity to other races or languages. Another gave undocumented figures linking homeschool success and family unity. Still another celebrated the greater breadth of curriculum available to homeschoolers. Tom scanned his calendar. After a four o'clock session with the head custodians from day and swing shifts, his evening was free. He would go where Google can't reach; a spawning ground for homeschooling.

Tom and Jane turned off Mill Road into a floodlit parking lot. The small lot in front of the church was filled with vehicles, mostly minivans. Bumper stickers advertised owners' convictions. "Save the Whales." "This vehicle will be unmanned in case of Rapture." "Honk if you love Jesus." Another touted Beulah, North Dakota, as the Lignite Capitol of the World. Following a graveled track, Tom was the first to park in the close-cropped pasture grass of the main lot.

The Riverside Gospel Assembly building was once a Grange Hall that had been expanded by a generous Sunday school wing over a full basement that served as the congregation's social hall. Inside the entrance to the old structure, Tom and Jane faced double doors leading to the chapel where a vocal group was rehearsing. To their left, a short corridor led to offices and classrooms. On the right, the top of a stairway ducted up a babble of voices punctuated by a piercing female laugh. The sound rode a current of warm air scented by a wood-fired heater somewhere below. Pungent little scents lurked behind coffee and wood-fire aromas, hinting at the soaps, polishes, onions, and spices of grandparents' kitchens.

A sign at the top of the stairs read "Accepting the Genesis Promise, downstairs." The double doors to the chapel bumped open, propelled by the hip of a young Hispanic woman carrying four clattering folding chairs toward the stairway. Spotting Tom and Jane, she changed course. "Here you go. Take these down, will you? If you're new, save a seat so I can be your meeting mate." Catching their confusion, she added, "Don't worry; it's a hospitality thing we do here."

They unfolded the chairs at a distance from a small woodstove that offered more show than glow and settled to watch a pair of musicians on digital keyboards. A man and woman, neither beyond their mid-twenties, noodled through chorus after chorus of ad lib schmaltz, their lush harmonies embellished with arpeggios that segued from key to key. An increase in tempo proved to be an intro for a guitar-bearing song leader who bounded onto center stage from the left. He introduced himself as Brother Dave, "here with a song on my soul." Dark and ponytailed, with a stout torso, he reminded Tom of his sister's ex who sold Buicks in Santa Barbara.

Dave smoothed his temples and began tapping a heel. Beaming, he threw his arms wide (still tapping) to embrace the universe and called out, "Brothers and sisters, let's open our hearts with a song!" The keyboard duo proved versatile. Picking up Brother Dave's tempo, they punched out a hard-driving soft-rock intro that brought the seventy or more attendees to their feet for chorus after chorus of a gospel verse.

Brother Dave introduced Pastor Berwick, a missionary, Bible scholar, and former pastor of Christian Alliance churches in the upper Midwest, adding that the pastor was committed to a new mission to make clear to all people how God intended for us to live in this world.

With his Bible open, Berwick pulled a hand back as though drawing a bow, paused for dramatic effect, and stabbed the Bible with a finger. "Tonight-uh, we let the twenty-sixth-uh verse of the first chapter of the Book of Genesis speak to us-uh. Tonight-uh, God's word-uh will guide our exploration of the his-to-ry of man as custodian of God's creation-uh. Tonight-uh, we seek to know the will of God-uh in our lives, to know how we might serve his will-uh in living according to His word-uh as revealed to us right here, brothers and sisters, right here-uh in the Book of Genesissss."

Tom felt Berwick's eyes homing in on him time and again. As a newcomer and overdressed by the congregation's standard, he smiled back as others' glances turned his way. As Berwick proceeded, Tom found himself listing flaws in his arguments that suggested the Bible might be the only book he ever opened and that he was over selective in his reading of it. His sense of apartness from other listeners wasn't helped by Jane's little elbow jabs that found the same rib each time Berwick threw in another "uh." She whispered, "I've got it. Uh, uh, uh. They're commas and periods, phonetic punctuation like Victor Borge."

Pink, bald, and beginning to perspire, Pastor Berwick intoned, "Then God said-uh, 'Let us make man in our image-uh after our likeness; and let him-uh have dominion over the fish of the sea-uh, and over the birds of the air-uh, and over the cattle, and over all the earth.' But God didn't leave it at that-uh. No sir, he didn't! He went on to tell us, 'Be fruitful and multiply-uh, and fill the earth and subdue it; and have dominion over the fish of the sea-uh and over the birds of the air-uh and over every living thing that moves upon the earth-uh.' And God said, 'Behold, I have given you every plant yielding seed-uh that is upon the face of all the earth-uh, and to everything that creeps on the earth-uh, everything that has the breath of life-uh, I have given every green plant for food-uh. And it was soooo!'"

Berwick demanded, "Who said these things?"

Strong voices shouted, "God. God the Father, the Creator God." Others sat silent.

"Who does he speak to?"

"Us! He speaks to me!"

Berwick accepted the spotty chorus as encouragement to move on. "How much of his creation does he want us to have mastery over-uh?"

"All of it! All of it!"

Pastor Berwick shut his eyes and held both arms out like a bird wondering if it might be a good time to take flight. It was a signal for silence. Holding the microphone against his lips, he lowered his voice to a rumble and continued, "God promised all of it. Because he has a plan-uh, God promised all of it to us-uh. And yet there are those who don't understand His word-uh, who work to pervert His word-uh, who make laws contrary to His word-uh, who train our children to disobey His word-uh.

"They don't understand that his plan for us includes not only salvation-uh, but supply. Just as His word is all powerful, his supply is all sufficient-uh. Yet there are those who would close off the children of God from His bounty in the name of environmentalism. I ask you, is there any more powerful protector of creation-uh than the creator himself-uh? In his omnipotence does he need man-made laws and restrictions to protect what is his to give-uh? Not our God-uh. Not the God who made all this and who promised that it should be our supply-uh."

Jane leaned close to whisper, "This bozo sure didn't pick up his stuff from the homeschool lessons I've seen. And"—she jabbed him again—"he better not be what you brought me here to hear."

"These meddlers in the divine scheme are of the same mind as those who claim that processes are at work to tinker with what God has made-uh. I speak of evolutionists. Read the great Book of Genesis again-uh. See how God defined all He created-uh. See if He said anything about tinkering with what He created-uh. Yes, they call this heresy evolution! I tell you truly, there can be no two ways about it-uh. Either God's word in the Holy Bible is true, and the plan he laid down in Genesis is true, and his promises to us are true-uh, or we can follow the strange teachings-uh and false prophets the Bible warns us about-uh.

"What can we do, brothers and sisterssss? There's nothing we can do about unbelievers who harden their hearts against the word of our Lord-uh. But we can do something about keeping the faith among ourselves-uh. It comes down to this: when faced with false teachings, do we choose the way of the world-uh, or do we choose to follow the word of God-uh?

"It will be difficult. Oh, yes, it will be difficult. You will find yourselves in conflict with politicians, with teachers, with neighbors-uh. You will be faced with difficult choices that will certainly impact your eternal souls at the final accounting-uh. In the name of Jesus Christ-uh, I ask that you do not fail in being true to your calling-uh. Amen."

Pastor Berwick wound up with a prayer excoriating science in general and environmentalists in particular. At the prayer's end, someone shouted, "We've heard the word. Amen to that, brother! The word of God! Praise the Lord! Thank you, Jesus!"

Brother Dave sprang into action again, setting a hand-clapping, body-swaying rhythm for the closing number. A projected image of a Bible verse set to music bloomed on a screen above the lectern as Dave crooned and strummed through the melody once before calling on all to join him.

"Hi." It was the young woman with the chairs. She settled next to Jane and whispered, "From watching you flinch, I bet you a donut you're an environmentalist."

Jane offered, "Let's say I get a different message from the Bible about our responsibility for God's creation."

"Amen to that. Me, too!" she said, her dark eyes sparkling. "Pastor Berwick is a visitor. We host a lot of traveling preachers here, but that doesn't mean we have to agree with them." She leaned around Jane to say, "Excuse me, but I know who you are. You're the principal of Northbridge High, right?"

"Guilty as charged. Tom Clausen, and this is my wife, Jane. And you?"

"Inez Montero. You've got me curious. How come you're here on Wednesday evening, not Sunday?"

"Do you have children, Inez?"

"Yes, two boys."

"Okay, it's possible that I came to see you if you could spare a few minutes. Here's the situation: I think the public schools need to know more about the motivations and needs of parents who opt for homeschooling. And we feel we need to become more sensitive to the issues that separate public schooling from homeschooling. Do you have any opinions along those lines?"

Inez giggled and took a deep breath. "Oh, my goodness. I hardly know where to start. Excuse me, I'd better call home. I'm pretty sure this is going to take more than a few minutes." She flipped her phone open and stepped away.

The congregation straggled upstairs, leaving Tom, Jane, and Inez to spend the next hour with their heads together.

Northbridge's board, like many boards of education, viewed computer education as a fiscal black hole. Dale worked to sidestep their tight-fisted budget pinching by scavenging hardware and software wherever he could. Among the sources he worked were Boeing's surplus sales and online distributors of applications that never managed to capture a market. One of his favorites was a site called Corgyn's Collection, a source he had tapped for free computer-aided design programs, accounting packages, and even music-writing software. One of the problems was that some of the best were such heavyweights that they ate up too much downloading time. This was why Dale was in his lab on a Saturday afternoon typing in www.corgynscollection.com. When he hit Enter, a window opened that said, "Sites containing the word ORGY will not be opened. Please enter a different search."

Alone in the room, he shouted at the walls, "Noooo. They wouldn't dare!"

Some months before, and after a newspaper report of smut being seen on a public library computer, a central office tech was sent to install new pornography filters for the school library's computers. Having seen no work order nor heard any complaints of blocking from his students, he hadn't considered that they might have tinkered with his system, too. The filters installed in the library had so crippled searches by screening out words such as *association* because they contain *ass*, that the library's computers had become a campus joke. One student reacted by writing, "Sweetness and Light Only" on a monitor's frame with a permanent marker. For Dale, there was no other answer than that the head office authorized and installed modifications to his systems behind his back. If they'd asked, he could have proved that his standard Microsoft filter functioned well as a porn blocker. Someone had better be ready to answer questions.

He entered his administrator's password and called up the list of district programs, finding only one he didn't recognize: MeritOnly. He backed out to run a Google search on it. On MeritOnly's home page he clicked Lists. The tabs for Churches, Schools, Children, and General led him to prepared lists of suspect words and terms that, according to each list's header, "often lead to morally repugnant content." Clicking on Customize, he found "Users may select from lists recommended for their special situations. Once a list is chosen and installed, users may easily add or delete terms as new improper words enter street language. Unlike many filters, MeritOnly puts you in control." Dale returned to the window that listed settings for filters and clicked Off. A moment later he was browsing through software titles on Corgyn's Collection.

Shortly after seven thirty on Monday morning and a half hour before first period, Northbridge High's corridors were filling with students and teachers readying themselves for the day. Dale Runyon unlocked his room at seven twenty to admit the early birds from his first-period Computers II class. Three drifted in to compete over a maze game. He opened web access to let a girl from biology run a search for her project and told her, "Keep an eye on things." Then he stepped out, confident that the early birds valued extra lab time enough to keep watch over the room while he dashed to the faculty room to down a quick cup of coffee while waiting for a turn at the copy machine. Back in the computer lab, another early arriver settled in at his station. Ignoring the gamers, he dropped his book bag and fired up his computer.

Though unrestricted web access was never available in Mr. Runyon's lab, it was Pete Kirschberger's habit to check whenever he touched a computer keyboard. It was also his habit when alone in his room at home, checking changes in his acne, to type in the search string, Hot Babes. This he did and was doubly surprised when a menu of porn sites popped into view. When he clicked the top item, his screen bloomed with a familiar collage of pink and brown feminine flesh. Another click exposed naked contortionists performing acts that turbocharged his already seething hormones. Eyes glued on the screen, he sat stunned as primal brainstem priorities overrode his cerebral cortex. Sweating lightly, he came to his senses. If caught in the act of accessing porn, he would lose access to the computer lab, or worse. Pete hit Exit, and the girls vanished from everything but his memory. He glanced guiltily left and right. Safe!

Pete chuckled at a private idea. He scanned the room. Straight-A, stuck-up Kari hadn't shown up yet. He shifted to her station and repeated the pathway to the hottest item on the Hot Babes menu. He selected a couple engaged in an athletically intimate act and used the computer's energy saver to put it to sleep until someone touched a key or moved the mouse. Perfect, he thought. That'll fix her. The stuck-up, know-it-all prissy nerd needs a little straightening out.

Dale rapped twice on the wall beside Tom's open office door. "I got your note. You have time to see me now?"

"Come in and sit." As Dale dropped into a chair, Tom moved to the door and shut it, drawing a quizzical glance from Alice as the door swung closed. "A Mrs. Olmstead called. Does the name ring a bell?"

"Sure. Kari Olmstead. First-period computers. A bright, self-contained kid. Will probably turn out to be an engineer or something of the sort. Why? Is there some problem with her?" Dale noticed the shadows under Tom's eyes, another indication that all was not well with him.

Tom arranged his elbows on the desk to rest his chin in his palms. "Here's how it came to me: Mrs. Olmstead says that yesterday her daughter came into your classroom, sat down at her computer, and when she was arranging her things on her desktop, a porn site popped onto her screen. After the shock of it, she looked around and found Pete Kirschberger smirking while doing a poor job of trying not to watch her. It seems we have two issues here: One, Kari believes Pete set her up, which we'll check into. The other, her mother wants to know how such stuff can be accessed on a classroom computer. I'm ready to hear what you have to say about it."

Tom had only begun to lay out the problem when the entire sequence of events came clear to Dale. He said, "What can I say? I disabled the filter. I forgot to restore it. Oh, man. Technology's going to be the end of me. Why didn't I stick with biology?" He rearranged himself in his chair and said, "Here's how it happened." He explained what he had discovered when he tried to access Corgyn's Collection and how he had disabled the filter. He talked about how the library's notorious filters had minimized the research potential of its computers and how the same software must have been installed in his lab, and though he didn't remember doing it, he must have deactivated Microsoft's filter, too. Either that or the district tech deleted it when he installed MeritOnly. "I didn't think to check the system afterward," he said. "Thinking back, I really can't see how I disabled anything but MeritOnly. Microsoft's filter should have still been functioning. Obviously, I made a mistake."

"Do you want to talk with her—the mother, that is? You do that, I'll handle the Kirschberger boy and we'll see how it works out. Can you do that?"

"I'll take care of it. Sorry, it seems I've screwed up again." On his way to the door, Dale turned and said, "You look worn. Tough day?"

"Routine stuff. Scott Thiessen's mom showed up with a lawyer who claims that drilling holes to peek into the girls' locker room—and getting caught at it—shouldn't be grounds for suspension. The inspectors who checked the portables for mold say they might have to shut three of them down. Then a bus with our High-Q team is sitting beside the freeway north of Tacoma. And Harry Compton brought me a bucket full of cigarette butts and trash our students threw over the fence into his garden." He rubbed his eyes and added, "Tell me, are we still educating kids here? I'm too buried in idiocy to know." Tom pulled his chair closer to his desk and made shooing motions. "Scram, I've got work to do."

CHAPTER 5

The barrier arm dropped in front of the big Dodge pickup ahead of Tom. He checked his watch. Six forty-six. He'd never been stopped by a train on the way to work before. Must be a special, he thought. The engine, less than two blocks south, approached slowly, passed the crossing with six lumber cars in tow and parked for a minute before reversing with a clashing of couplings. His watch read six fifty-two, eight minutes until he was supposed to be seated at administrative council. The engine dropped a single car, reversed again to pull out of the siding, stopped, and rumbled off southward. The barrier lifted at six fifty-eight. A glance at his side mirror showed that the morning commute had stacked up as far as he could see to choke off access to the freeway. He wouldn't be the only one reporting in late.

Most of a century before, Northbridge had been proud of the rail line that cut its western border. Before the advent of UPS and FedEx, it was Railway Express that moved parcels to towns like Northbridge. Rail passengers came and went from the depot, and incoming and outgoing mailbags were exchanged at mail cars' doors. Out-of-town newspapers and magazines and the Sears, Roebuck and Company and Montgomery Ward catalogs were dropped onto the Northbridge platform. With goods, news, and people funneling through the long-ago demolished station, the hours surrounding trains' arrivals once made it the most exciting place in town. The station was gone, and only two sidings survived to serve local lumber mills while everything else was transported on trucks. The main line bisecting Northbridge remained as one of the West's two rail connections with Canada while its impact on the town was that of a periodic barrier to east-west traffic.

When Tom hurried into the administrative council at seven ten, he threw his arms up as though about to be taken into custody. Dr. Wainwright made a show of studying the wall clock until he was seated. He said, “Before we were interrupted,” which prompted Tom to duck his head under the table, eliciting chuckles all around. Not amused, Wainwright cleared his throat and said, “Mr. Clausen, would you be so good as to join us? Time is wasting.”

Tom pulled himself erect again and said, “Sorry. Got held up by a switch engine at the crossing.”

Ninety minutes later Wainwright rose at the meeting’s end and said, “Mr. Clausen, in my office, please.” The administrative council was dispersing into chat groups when Wainwright’s summons to Clausen halted them in midstride. Conversations dropped to a hush as they watched Wainwright lead Tom from the room.

Wainwright took his seat on the other side of his new, oversized cherrywood desk. The new furniture made Tom wonder who had fallen heir to its oak predecessor, an executive workstation that had served three previous superintendents. The chair was new also, a high–backed model in red leather. How many years had it been, he wondered, since he had been called into an office for a tardy? Thirty-five? Tom recalled how he and his high school buddies squeezed in one last foosball game at the end of every second lunch. Miss Peltier hadn’t been a stickler for punctuality, but his repeated late entries had pushed her beyond her limits. Here I am again, he thought. Tardy.

Wainwright made a point of studying some marked-up pages while Tom inventoried his expensive desk fixtures, the copy of a Remington bronze, the oversized plasma monitor, and the ivory-handled letter opener.

Wainwright had chewed out so many staffers during his short reign that Tom wasn’t surprised that his turn had come. The week before, when an article appeared in the *Northbridge World* telling of a state-level award won by one of Terri Laughlin’s distributive education students, Wainwright called her on the carpet for not having the student’s entry approved by the district office before submitting it. He had found fault with Tom’s vocal music teacher for attending and winning too many competitions without prior approvals to apply and compete. And there were his threats against Dale. Since the superintendent's complaints centered on super achievers, Tom considered that being chewed out by Big Man would enroll him in good company. He was studying the ladder left beside newly bared windows to foretell new curtains when Wainwright cleared his throat and looked up.

"I took this opportunity so we could spend a few moments one-on-one. I understand you live on Dogwood Drive. Nice homes there, Mr. Clausen. My wife, Jeanne, and I were interested in a home on the cul-de-sac, but it sold before we made up our minds." He closed his smile. "Well, enough of that. Let's get to business. Mr. Clausen—"

Tom cut in. "Most superintendents have called me Tom."

"Mr. Clausen, this is a copy of your report on homeschooling. Would you be so good as to explain to me what you were attempting to accomplish with it?"

"I thought I made that clear. You asked for the impact of homeschooling on our program and how we've responded. The trouble is we haven't yet collected enough hard information to accurately respond to those questions. To deliver what you asked for, I had to dig into the local background of the issue; that is, I needed to check out the motivations of families that opt for homeschooling—"

Wainwright broke in. "Pardon me, but judging from your report, it seems that you put your own interpretation on your assignment instead of responding to what I asked you to provide. I appreciate your initiative, but the district is not so much interested in motivations as the effect of homeschooling on our program. What I have here"—he picked up Tom's report by a corner and quickly dropped it as though loathsome—"can be taken as a case for homeschooling that, judging from some of your comments here, puts your sympathies on the wrong side of the fence. Frankly, it's difficult for me to see how you can be an advocate for public schools when you find it so easy to side with the opposition."

Opposition? If that was how Wainwright saw it, his attempts to shed light on the situation meant nothing. Faced with an impasse, Tom sought to circumvent his superintendent's prickly nature by airing

Wainwright's charge as amiably as he could. "Dr. Wainwright, you've hit the target. An essential part of our problem with homeschooling is that we tend to view it not as competition but as opposition." He leaned forward, which, in spite of the breadth of the desk, caused Wainwright to roll his chair back a foot. "Since schools provide much of the glue that holds this town together, we can't afford to let relationships become adversarial. The more cooperation, the better it works for everyone. Wouldn't you agree?"

"That's what I would call an overly generous thought, Mr. Clausen. I certainly have no control over your private thoughts, but what I expect you to carry away from our talk is that loyalty to public education and especially to this district's policies is a requirement. It's required that you show an understanding of that the next time you offer personal opinions when specific data is requested. Are we clear on that?"

Tom's reach for amiability died. "Crystal clear, but before I go, clear up one other thing for me. As principal, shouldn't I be made aware of changes that district techs perform on computer systems in my school?"

"Why do you ask? Is there a problem?"

"Yes. Because we weren't informed that a filter had been installed in the high school's computer lab, we were subjected to an embarrassing situation that took quite a bit of sorting out."

"Of course you mean Mr. Runyon's mistake. Not his first, I understand."

"There wouldn't have been a problem if he or I had been informed. Make no mistake, Dr. Wainwright, you're talking about the best teacher on my staff, a teacher whose methods and effectiveness with students are nothing short of inspirational. You should see his classes in action before judging him."

Wainwright wondered where high school people thought they were coming from, first Runyon telling him he'd made a mistake and now Clausen's warning, make no mistake. He snapped, "Don't underestimate me, Mr. Clausen. Just because I'm new doesn't mean I don't know my way around. I've received a report on your Mr. Runyon's teaching that portrays his, shall we say, unconventional approach?" Wainwright stood to signal that Tom was excused. "Thank you for staying for this chat, and remember what I said: you should separate your personal opinions and actions from what district directives and policy require of you. Good day, Mr. Clausen."

Tom stalked out without a word. If Wainwright had called him in for being late, it would have been less offensive than the scoldings he'd given teachers of award-winning students for not including him in their loop of success. But this was worse. The man had put him on notice. What concerned him even more was that if Wainwright's top-down power plays continued, they would surely cost the district more key teachers. Two of his own had already resigned, one an advanced placement math teacher.

Tom beat Jane home in time for a tussle with Buster. By the time she nosed her Corolla into its spot, he was nearing the driveway to take charge of the grocery sacks with Buster orbiting. After a peck on her cheek, he said, "Had a chat with the new superintendent today. Got to know him a little better." Buster caught him hunkered down at the refrigerator stashing perishables in chiller trays and nosed his cheek.

"Oh? Sounds congenial. How did you two hit it off?"

"We understand each other. He understands that I'm not going to take any crap off him, and I understand that he's a sociopathic wrecking ball."

Jane, alarmed, bent to take his face in her hands.

"He trashed the report on homeschooling you helped me with, said the district has no interest in families' motivations. Then he threatened me. He as much as said that anyone with my attitude shouldn't be principal of Northbridge High. Then he told me that I should be working to separate my personal opinions from district directives. It's the kind of language you use to start a paper trail in case someone needs to be dumped. What he did was set me up for a negative evaluation. All he has to do is cite his instructions to me and claim I don't measure up against them. He'd be judge and jury, of course."

She patted his cheeks. "Sounds lovely. Did you respond in kind? Give him the finger, moon him, that sort of thing?"

Tom pushed Buster aside and levered himself upright. "It's a crazy situation. Outside his inner circle, and we're talking about three board members and a handful of new hires, nobody dares to disagree with him. He may be bad news through and through, but I'm even more upset with Claudia. She engineered his hiring. He's acting like her pet pit bull, and judging from what he's done so far, it looks like he'll go after anyone with the gumption to be noticed. You remember Phil Krause's advice?"

Jane stepped aside as Buster came skidding around the kitchen island one jump behind Phoebe, the striped gray cat that adopted the Clausens. She said, "Keep your head down and focus on survival. Something like that."

"Mm-hmm. So it stacks up like this: I like this house. I like the town and the people. I'd be happy in my job if Wainwright would move on, so it boils down to who's going to survive. If there's any justice in this world, Wainwright's days are numbered, so if you catch me acting all wimpy and submissive, it'll be because I'm trying to outlast him." He took her by the shoulders. "Sorry to dump on you, hon. Would you mind dining out with me? Maybe someplace where we can watch people being happy?"

Tom entered Northbridge's public library and slipped unnoticed past Pittman, who was busy berating a clerk. When she tried to answer him, he thrust his hands out, palms forward, to indicate he hadn't invited any back talk. She gave him a frigid smile and stepped to the far end of the counter, saying, "Next, please. I'll help you down here." Garnie turned to the person behind him and growled, "I hope you weren't expecting service," and stalked off to the periodical section.

Tom was there to check for complaints about kids accessing porn sites on library terminals. With nearly a third of his students' homes lacking computers, school kids were heavy users of the library's back-to-back banks of internet-access stations, and it was here, more than at homes or school, that they claimed to access pornography. He cornered a reference librarian, introduced himself, and laid out his problem. "Is it possible for minors to access pornography on library computers?"

The ebony-eyed Asian with a pageboy do measured Tom before responding to what was an ongoing issue for the library. "To be frank, yes. No minor's library card allows unfiltered access, so they 'borrow' their mothers' cards, and they're in. Nothing much we can do about it. They don't even need the card, just Mom's card number. You see, when a card is issued, the borrower's number is coded into the system as minor or adult, and the adults opt for filtration only if they wish. It's a touchy issue for us, too, as you can imagine."

"Nothing you can do about it?"

"No, sir, not a thing. Not when doing more would bring the ACLU down on us for violation of the First Amendment. Anything else I can help you with?"

Tom was counting student-age computer users when raised voices at the counter signaled that Garnie was abusing the stiff-faced staff again. He waited for tempers to settle before following Garnie to the periodical section, where he was rustling noisily through a back issue of the *Wall Street Journal*. Though Tom loomed over him, Garnie feigned being unaware of his presence. "Oh, Garnie, Garnie. Earth to Garnie. Come in, Garnie."

"In case you didn't notice, I was reading. And for your information, reading is a solitary endeavor. Now go away."

"Still worked up about not getting your way at the counter, I see. What did they do to arouse your ire?"

Pittman glared over his glasses. "Hmm. Well, what was I to do? Two weeks. Two entire weeks to procure a copy of one small book, and they failed. Peasants, indeed."

"Why not buy it?"

"What for? I'd read it only once. I buy books I plan to read until the pages fall out. Anyway, finding documents for patrons is what librarians supposedly do. I gave them an author, George Lakoff. Their job is to get me the book. What could be more simple?"

"Lakoff, huh? Did you ask how many requests are queued up ahead of you? I assume you were after *Don't Think of an Elephant*."

"You've read it? Incredible. Well, if even schoolteachers read such things, they should have more copies."

"That wasn't at all nice, but I'll tell you what. I picked up a copy of it at Barnes and Noble, so if you promise to be nice to the girls at the counter for the rest of the week, I'll let you borrow it."

Pittman laid his newspaper aside. "You actually read Lakoff?"

"Yes, but being a peasant I was rather disappointed to find there were no pictures to color. What's it going to be? Would you like to borrow it? All you have to do is promise to be nice."

Pittman startled readers near him by noisily shaking his pages straight. "You have a lot of nerve to think you can negotiate with me, Thomas."

"I have the book. You want it. Is it a deal?"

Garnie allowed Tom a corner of a smile as he said, "You win. Now sit down. I have a question for you."

"Shhh, not here, we're disturbing readers. Walk with me. Don't you just hate it when someone chatters in your ear when you're trying to read? Why, it's almost as bad as a dog howling next door."

Tom led Garnie into a vacant activity room and said, "Does your question have anything to do with the article you tore from the library's newspaper? They have copy machines, you know."

"Yes, it does, and no, I didn't have a dime. Now I understand the school district was negotiating for a site near the intersection of 155th and Market Road. Is it still interested?"

Tom said, "About part B, the machine takes dollar bills and makes change. About the school site, I'd say they wrote it off when OmniMart took an interest in it."

"Is it possible that you're privy to the district's alternatives?"

"Forty-six acres at the corner of Hansen and Airport Roads. It's not perfect, but no site is." He looked squarely at Garnie who avoided his eyes. "Garnie, what's going on here? What's your interest in this?"

"Hmm, well, I make it my business to know that's happening to Northbridge, for better or for worse. For instance, if OmniMart should plan to invade, mm-hmm, yes, I'd call that my business."

"And you enjoy applying your considerable leverage."

"In the case of OmniMart, as much as it takes, as much as it takes," he said airily, enjoying the feel of the phrase.

"Which takes me out of my depth. But while we're on the subject, do you know anything about the piece at the city's limit, the acreage just short of Nelson Road on the west side of the old highway? As far as I can see, it's the next-best piece that's big enough to accommodate another high school."

Garnie shook his jowls. "Forget that. Too many drawbacks. Poor drainage, and I believe a good part of it is too steep for development. You'd do better to keep looking at the acreage at 155th and Market Road."

Tom shook his head. "No thanks, we already discussed that. Schools don't fare well bidding against OmniMart."

Garnie flapped his jowls negatively. "Hmmph. Once again you weren't listening. I said that *you would do better to look at the site* on Market Road. That's all I have to say on the subject."

Tom contained his excitement. Pittman had let his power show through, saying with undisguised authority that the site would be available to Northbridge schools. He said, "Okay, I'll see that someone follows up on it." An afterthought hit him. "If you know all this stuff, why do you want the article?"

"Hmm, keeping track, keeping track. It always pays to keep track of things. We have what people do, what they say they do, and reports of what they did. It's not all the same, you know." Pittman patted the pocket with the clipping.

With the Steamboat Days festival coming up, Garnie turned to reminiscing about bygone days when the festival drew hobbyists' steam launches from up and down Puget Sound and British Columbia. The current issue was that in recent years, so few hobbyists' steamers remained afloat that the festival's central event had moved from the waterfront to become a parade down Commerce Street. The year before, the parade's grand marshal rode in a real Stanley Steamer.

Dale arrived home at five thirty to find two notes under ladybug magnets. "Meeting with Pastor. Have dinner ready by 7:00." The other said, "Dad: Try disk P-3. Softball stats program ready to run." Roger, now a senior, had dodged his dad's computer classes, picking up a level of programming expertise on his own that few of Dale's students could match. He explained his avoidance of Dale's classes with "Dad, your classes are great for herd animals, but that's not the way I learn. Too slow."

Roger announced his growing independence with terse answers to Betty and Dale's questions. Because their bright, superachieving, and popular son seldom gave them reason for concern, his teen male secrecy left them no more than mildly bemused.

Betty: "Where are you going, dear?"

Roger: "Out."

"What are you going to do?"

"Don't know yet. We'll figure it out."

"Who is 'we'?"

"Some of the guys."

"When will you be back?"

"After a while."

Dale: "Let's run through that again. This time, try to fill in the blanks."

At six-two and one-hundred-sixty-five pounds, Roger was too gawky and loose jointed for most sports, but there was nothing awkward about his mind or hands. While he was quiet about many of his interests, nothing could mask his love for music that manifested itself in surprising abilities on keyboard, guitar, and reed instruments. But it was Roger's understanding of mechanical systems that kept friends hauling inoperative hulks to the Runyons' driveway for high-decibel repairs until a neighbor complained about his boom box. Dale was forced to put his foot down. No more than one vehicle at a time, work would be done under the fiberglass shelter beside the garage, and music would be delivered through earphones. Roger, half expecting a complete shutdown, said, "Okay, Dad."

Dale fanned through the mail—National Geographic's latest travel offer, a promotion from a new pizza parlor, and one marked "urgent" and addressed to box holder that fell into the trash unopened. Another was addressed to Roger Runyon. It, too, was marked "urgent," and Dale was weighing the ethics of trashing his son's junk mail when he noticed that it was from Port Gardner Savings Bank, the oldest bank in the area and not one given to mass advertising. He knew Roger collected fees for small programming jobs that a store-front accountant sent his way and that he picked up a few more dollars charging friends small fees for car repairs. Dale also knew he maintained a bank account but chose not to try to find out how big it might be.

He popped a Diet Pepsi open and moved to the living room to sit in semidarkness and stare out at the end of the day. The second-growth firs that filled the greenbelt at the end of the Runyons' property stood silhouetted against the twilight glow. The dimming sky pulsated where flashing aircraft lights aligned with the approach to Northsound International before dropping behind the trees. The silence broke when the furnace blower cycled on, its first breath forcing complaints from expanding ducts.

He held his untouched Pepsi while he thought, puzzled about the turns in his life and the difficulty of balancing responsibility with desire. He had tried to live his life according to one rule: do the right thing. Focusing on shaping better approaches to teaching and coaching had made difficult years with Betty possible. But now what? He knew the angst eating at him was rooted in losing his coaching job, and he knew he was the only one who could lever himself out of that pit. He made some phone calls that within twenty-four hours resulted in agreeing to take over for a coach who found he couldn't spare the hours. He wondered if two practices and a game each week with little kids might be disappointing for lack of high school-level competition.

On Saturday morning, Dale, along with two other coaches and four parents, manned sign-up tables for the league. Contractor's Concrete sponsored his team, the Olympics. Dana Gustafson, who shared the table with Dale, coached Buckley Truck Stop's Red Rockets. Dana coached to spend quality time with her ten-year-old tomboy, Pip, who spent the sign-up hours running errands for both. The table had only one stapler they shuttled back and forth.

Four teams practiced on Tuesday and Thursday afternoons at the corners of the junior high athletic field. Coaches with their own kids on their teams worked deals with other parents to drive their kids home while they bagged gear and checked for litter the kids missed. In truth, they stuck around to get to know each other over pitchers of beer at the Riverside Tavern. Phil Curnutt of the Green Dragons and Del Countryman, coach of the Penguins, completed the foursome to play liars' dice, loser buys. They introduced themselves as Phil the barber, Del the fireman, Dana the school bus driver, and when Dale identified himself as a teacher, Phil said, "Sorry about your situation. The story is you got screwed."

Not ready for his situation to become table talk, he shut his eyes and held his hands up as in surrender. "No comment."

Del nodded. "Understood. A lot of us guys follow Viking sports close enough to figure your people upstairs must have their heads where the sun never shines."

"One more time, no comment. Those people upstairs also sign my checks." He drained his glass. "See you later, time to head home."

Following the second practice, Del, the fireman, was on duty, which meant no beer stop. Dale, Phil, and Dana carried on without him. The next Tuesday, when both Phil and Del begged off, Dana, having found a ride for Pip, jumped into Dale's car. With no one else at the table, their conversation took new turns, beginning with tales from Dana's bus garage that would have driven Betty out the door. It became such fun that they threw themselves into it, turns of subject generating heat as they discovered each other's sensitive areas. They progressed through giggles and tantalizing innuendo to hands lingering on each other's forearms. When Dana returned from the girls' room to plop down to get a better line on the TV, her hand found his knee, his knee found her leg, and her hip moved against his, stirring Dale with thoughts about what might come next. He gave her arm a squeeze and said, "I'd better get you home." In the car, she curled sideways under her seat belt to watch him. Better looking than Gus, a whole lot better looking, she thought. And he smelled better. And he held up his end of banter while keeping it gentlemanly, but not so gentlemanly that he hadn't turned her on. And he hadn't used one word of her ex's disgustingly coarse language. All in all, she thought of it as a memorable afternoon.

When Phil and Del begged off again after their fourth practice,

Dale and Dana drove separate cars to the tavern where they took a table on the patio overlooking the river. They clinked glasses. She asked about his day. He asked about her husband. She sighed and said it was a long story that she proceeded to tell in detail:

Aside from his sullen expression, Gus had been reasonably good-looking and had presented himself as a battle-weary warrior returned to an ungrateful nation and in need of loving. Like misguided do-gooders who marry death-row killers, Dana took pity on him. She managed to find a small but endearing corner of rough humor in him that she claimed as base camp for the project of restoring him to mint condition. Where she erred, she said, was that her concept of mint condition could only have applied to someone more evolved than Gus. During her account, they worked their way through an entire pitcher of lager while her tale of old wounds found a sympathetic ear with Dale. They drank to fill awkward pauses. Dale's hand found her arm halfway through the telling, caressing it slowly to the end.

She closed her story by assuring him that her ex was so out of the picture that she never thought of him anymore, which led them to clink glasses again and gift each other with meaning-laden leers that left Dale squirming to find comfort. The pitcher and glasses were empty. It was time to go, but instead of turning right to her Hyundai two-door, Dana knocked at the passenger's window of Dale's Acura. He clicked the lock, and she slid in against him, took his face between her hands, and kissed him long and deep, breaking to say, "It's been a lovely afternoon, Coach." To which Dale said unsteadily, "Watch it, you're stirring improper thoughts."

She snapped back, "Not a problem. It's been way too long since I've been improper with anyone." She patted his cheek and slid out of the car. "Be seeing you again soon, right?"

Betty had two and a half hours between arriving home and her vestry meeting at church. Dale was due home near six after logging unpaid hours revamping the computer lab to accommodate two new students. Roger, who had undertaken a rebuild of a neighbor's outboard, was about to clamp a test hose to its water intake at five thirty. With Dale and Roger squeezed for time and Ellen, who turned up her nose at pizza as "greasy carbos," miles away in her college dorm room, it was an ideal evening to forget cooking and order in Betty's favorite, vegetarian with added sausage.

Dale scooped a first slice for Betty, trailing webbed strands of molten cheese toward her plate. Roger's fork shot out to intercept the cords of cheese before they touched her tablecloth, a small thing, but typical of the Runyon men backing each other up. Roger twirled the strands onto his fork and settled to eat as conversation yielded to munching. When he came up for air, Dale asked, "Rog, the envelope from the bank the other day, are they pushing credit cards?"

"No."

Dale separated more slices and offered another to Betty. "Sorry. The fault lies in my question. I'll try again." He pulled the box from Roger's reach and said, "Roger, unless your letter's contents were personal and private, your mother and father request that you share the nature of the bank's communication with you in more than one syllable, if you please."

"It's nothing if I don't make the cut. Please pass the pizza."

"Not yet. If you don't make what cut? Keep talking."

"The CWP Scholarship."

Dale shoved the pizza toward Roger and said, "Betty, our son is referring to the biggest annual local scholarship. It's worth ten-thousand a year, renewable."

"Uh-uh, Dad. It's up to twelve now." Mumbling through a mouthful of pizza, he added, "Jen Koutac and Thong Phan are the other finalists, and they're super-brainy. Anyway, interviews are on the twenty-sixth from seven till nine."

"That's great, Rog. Win or lose, you're in the top three of six-hundred thirty. That's way better than I did. What about you, Betty?"

"Me? Seventh place in a class of less than two hundred doesn't come close. We're so proud of you, but tell me, you were thinking of sharing this with us, weren't you?"

"Yeah, I was gonna, but I didn't want you two to go off the deep end like buying a time-share at Sun Valley or whatever."

"Going off the deep end?" Dale queried.

"Yeah. I called Ellen and told her about being a finalist. She said that if I nailed the CWP Scholarship or she married rich, you'd be off the hook for financing at least one education. She figured you guys might do something to celebrate, like, how long has it been since you went anywhere? I mean like travel. How long ago was it that you went to New Orleans?"

"Where did you get the silly idea that we might enjoy Sun Valley? Your father knows I don't care for skiing."

"Mom, I'm concerned that you *won't* do anything, not that you will."

"Nonsense. We just prefer the pleasures we find close to home, you and Ellen being at the top of our list."

Roger mumbled around the crust of his fourth slice. "Which means you're tied down by your kids, your two greatest pleasures. That makes Sis and me feel like you're pet owners who don't travel because you can't bear to put us in kennels. You guys gotta shake loose and break up your routine. Dad, you've been uptight ever since Uncle Tom kicked you out of coaching."

"For the last time, Roger, *it was not* Tom!"

When he reached for the last slice, Roger said, "Split it with you."

After Betty drove off to church, Dale stepped out to the garage to find Roger fitting the cover to the 9.9 horsepower Mercury. "Everything check out okay?"

"Yep, runs like new." He cinched the last cowling screw and said, "Is coaching peewees filling the void?"

Dale pondered. "You know, I try not to think of it that way. Varsity softball was one thing; this is another. One thing's the same though. Being around kids of any age, classroom or athletic field—I don't care what—just being with young people floats my boat. The good thing now is I get to give every one of them their minutes while a varsity team has its benchwarmers. But, yes, I do miss the competition. What about you? How are you going to get ready for the scholarship interview?"

"Not let myself get uptight. I can't afford to be anxious, so no all-nighters. If I put myself in the examiners' shoes, I'd be looking for the right person, not a bag of answers. You know, aware and well-rounded. So about the only extra thing I'll be boning up on is the month's news magazines. And then maybe figure out what's happening with local and state issues. I've got the night before reserved for a no-brainer DVD. You're invited."

Dana and Pip stuffed bases and catcher's gear into the last duffel. It was past five thirty, and her team had policed the field and grandstand and disappeared, some on bikes, some with parents. Dale, lugging his team's bags, veered toward Dana and the Red Rockets' diamond where he tugged the bill of Pip's cap down and said, "Nice game, slugger."

Dana tipped a bat bag toward Pip. "Take this to the car, hon. Just prop it against the door." Pip looked back and forth between her mother and Dale until Dana fixed her with a sharp stare and said, "Just go. I'll be along in a minute." She shrugged and trudged away, dragging the bag. Dana watched until Pip neared her car and shouted, "No, no. How many times do I have to tell you? No climbing the fence!"

With Pip out of earshot, Dale said, "I need to check out a friend's cabin at Big Lake. Care to ride along?"

"When?"

"Wednesday, as soon as you can make it after you turn your bus in."

"What's to do up there?"

"It's quiet, the kind of place where you make your own entertainment."

Dana's eyes widened in mock surprise. "Oooh. What should I bring or wear?"

"Clothing isn't a concern." Before the words had slipped out, a blush rose from his collar. "What I meant to say was …"

Dana shouldered her duffel and threw him a kiss. "Read you loud and clear, big fella. You can pick me up in front of the Salish Library at six thirty. Gotta scoot now." She walked away shouting, "What did I tell you about climbing fences!"

"I don't trust him." Wainwright had asked Claudia to remain after the board meeting ended at ten fifteen. He dropped Clausen's personnel file in front of her. "He's not a team player. What's more, he encourages radical approaches among his staff. It's come to this: either the high school's program is a direct reflection of district curriculum policy, or it isn't, and if what I heard from Runyon is typical of what Clausen allows, then he and that choir teacher are the tip of the iceberg."

Claudia pushed the file away. "He's a handful, all right, but you'd better think about the outcry if you replace him. He has a following, you know. Unless he does something illegal or some dirt shows up in his background, he stays."

"That's exactly what I wanted to talk with you about. Unless I miss my guess, Thomas Clausen is hiding something. Did you know that he has more friends in Moraine than Northbridge? Don't you think that's strange? And have you seen how cozy he is with that obnoxious toad, Pittman? It seems that his connections are outside our system, and that means that at the least, he's guilty of divided loyalty. From the things he's said, I wouldn't be surprised if he'd quit if Moraine offered him a job. Wouldn't that leave us in a mess? And he seems to enjoy keeping his intentions private, and as long as he does, I don't see how we can plan for the future."

"What do you propose?"

"I'll call him in. I need to be sure of his loyalty to the district, how willing he is to bring his faculty in line with district objectives, and how he's handling my suggestion to keep personal feelings separate from district goals. No harm in that."

"What if you're not satisfied with his answers?"

"You mean if he admits to being a problem? Either we deal with him or accept him on his terms. There's no way he can be managed if he insists on operating according to his own agenda. I don't like it, but we may have to conduct a discreet investigation, not because we want to but because he runs with that Pittman character. Thanks to what he told your board about the OmniMart site, we may have to go back to the original plan for the new high school. No matter how I look at it, it appears that Pittman and Clausen are working land deals that involve the district. We knew that Pittman had an interest in that piece, but it was Clausen who pushed the board to reconsider their choice. Think about that. They're neighbors, buddies.

"Outside of that, we just can't allow our high school principal to ignore district directives. That business of the men's chorus running all over the map was preposterous. First, they accepted invitations, and then they brought their travel plans to me as though it was my duty to rubber-stamp them. The whole attitude at the high school is out of control."

Claudia lifted her glasses from her breast to her nose and opened Clausen's file. "Martin Koutac won't go for it."

"Does he have to? What I propose is an exercise in district security. Any costs would be within latitude given me to protect the district. I'm just saying that we need to know more about Clausen than what's in that file. His behavior and interests impact our programs. All I need from you is a go-ahead. From then on, I'll take care of everything, keeping you posted, of course."

"I appreciate where you're going with this, but I'm going to have to think it over. We'll talk about it again."

CHAPTER 6

Gary Lightfoot had been a number of people with an equal number of names. Born to Gerard and Lucy Lightfoot of Ann Arbor, Michigan, and later Palm Springs, he fell heir to a portion of their mutual funds that, with dividends and interest reinvested throughout two good decades, provided an income of nearly sixty thousand dollars per year, enough to meet household expenses but not enough to support his fantasies. The inheritance came to him when he was in his early twenties, a time when his parents were experimenting with adventure travel. They were in Chile for a week of high-country trekking followed by a week of whitewater rafting. All went well until their raft nosed onto a boulder in a way that spun the stern onto another boulder, rolling the craft and dumping its passengers into the foaming current. Though the guide survived, both Lightfoots and another hapless adventurer tumbled through a bouldered stretch of canyon, past the quiet water of their planned take-up point, and on for another half mile before plunging down a Class V cataract. To Gary's knowledge, their bodies were never recovered.

Through Col. Gerard Lightfoot's twenty-seven years in the Air Force, he dragged his family from base to base where his son, Gary, and two daughters attended nine different schools in three nations. While other military brats took change in stride, Gary, who delighted family friends with his role-playing, reinvented himself to start fresh at each new school. By the time he graduated from high school in Germany, his preoccupation with planning who he might be next overshadowed his parents' plans for his future. He valued the people in new settings for endorsing the new beings he became. Locking the door to his past at each rebirth, he used the breaks from each previous identity to shed the dead weight of dead personas All that mattered was that he could and would become whoever and whatever he chose to be.

Gary's father retired and moved to a two-bedroom condo in Palm Springs where the colonel's exercise equipment and computer desk filled the guest room. While Gary's sisters were settled in nearby Glendale and Solvang, he was adrift, crashing with acquaintances until he wore out his welcomes.

Small brushes with the law culminated with a breaking-and-entering charge that grew to include petty theft. According to his statement to the police, Gary planned to crash in the home of acquaintances, but when they ignored his pounding and shouting, he pried a basement window open and bedded down on a couch in their recreation room. According to the homeowners' statement, Gary broke in, snoozed, used the toilet but didn't flush, and exited through the same window, carrying away a spotting scope he pawned. The judge gave him two years in Mule Creek State Prison at Ione, California. There, for the first time in his life, he found friends who, having tried fake names to dodge responsibilities, admired his stories about who he had been.

With time off for good behavior, Gary was out in little more than nine months. He drifted to San Jose where he clerked in a Radio Shack under the name Ian McCall. It was during a pickup soccer game in San Jose that a blindside tackle hyperextended his right knee, requiring three weeks of physical therapy. He studied Raul, his therapist, inspected the clinic's equipment, memorized the paperwork, and decided that he could do what Raul did and earn what Raul earned. Step one was getting a janitor to let him in after hours to copy the diplomas and certificates that hung on the clinic's walls. Rogelio Jimenez countered his offer of thirty dollars for access with a demand for fifty. Gary paid the fifty but exacted revenge by leaving the diplomas in disorder. He enjoyed the thought of Jimenez trying to explain that away.

Gary Lightfoot accepted that impersonating a physical therapist would require a period of intense study. He taught himself to talk a good line of myofascial and Mulligan techniques and cryotherapy. He read about ultrasound, phonophoresis, iontophoresis, massage, and the range of treatments for tendonitis, lower back pain, headaches, scoliosis, stenosis, and herniated discs. If he could just get some hands-on time, he thought he could be handling patients in a few months.

He practiced on soccer buddies and friends from work, claiming he worked at Radio Shack only to save enough to finish his physical therapy degree. Dropping comments about his PT classes at the University of Oregon helped to work him deeper into his new role. With fake records in order, he talked his way into a stint as a volunteer intern with an alternative medicine clinic in Fresno, finally landing a job with the Redding Rehabilitative Clinic. The only rough spot was the time he beat up a suspicious acquaintance who, after chatting with Gary about campus life in Eugene, said, "Bullshit. You've never set foot on the U of O campus." The incident illustrated the duality that distanced him from his sisters and friends in the past. The roles he chose were his turf and not subject to inspection, interference, or criticism.

Gary's hypersensitivity to criticism cost him his job as a physical therapist. Trouble arose when the senior therapist who mentored Gary through his first weeks on the job in Redding kept suggesting corrections to his procedures, even after he had graduated to caring for patients independently. He responded by shouting, "This is my patient!" His mentor, a partner in the practice, told him that one more outburst in front of a patient would result in termination. He held his temper for almost a month before a patient recovering from knee replacement called him a ham-handed sadist and demanded another therapist. Gary told the patient to shut up and stop whining and gave his knee a punitive twist. He emptied his locker and left.

Gary didn't like Redding, anyway. He packed his car and left his apartment at night to drive south to San Jose. His goal was Jeanne Holton, who had been an assistant manager at the San Jose Radio Shack where Gary worked as Ian McCall. He first dated her when she was thirty-six, one year older than Gary. Kind-eyed and pillow-breasted, Jeanne offered sanctuary during his bouts of insecurity. A reasonably attractive, full-figured divorcee with two daughters and a weakness for abusive lovers, Jeanne had given up battling the domineering males she attracted. When he told her what they would do when together, she said, "Okay." When he told her that it would be a good idea for them to marry, she said, "If you think so." She was attracted to his income, the source of which she knew nothing about and didn't question. Gary needed a wife and family for his résumés, and Jeanne was desperate to break from the two-job captivity of an underemployed single mom. It was a win-win situation.

Gary and Jeanne wed in Reno on April 22, 1981. He put a down payment on a 1970s rambler on East Curry Avenue in Cottage Grove, Oregon, where he installed Jeanne and her girls. The arrangement he set up was that he would meet the mortgage payments, taxes, and utilities, and Jeanne would find work that would cover food and household expenses. Jeanne proved to be a quick learner. The two episodes in which she questioned Gary about why he wasn't still Ian McCall and why his work called for prolonged absences taught her that it probably wasn't safe to make that mistake a third time.

While Jeanne kept house, Gary did a twenty-two-month gig in hotel management in Salem, followed by three pleasant years selling fine jewelry in a shop in Sacramento. Jeanne was living her dream, and Gary, or William Remus as he was known at the jewelry shop, was mixing with an educated clientele that spoke well and read the right books. The pleasure he found in talking with them nudged him toward considering another path, one that would take advantage of his knack for learning. The feeling he got when speaking with educated customers made him wonder if he wasn't so much a physical therapist or a hotel manager or a jewelry expert, but a student. That bit of enlightenment made him wonder if a career in education might be more rewarding. He took to hobnobbing with young profs from Sacramento State, American River College, and Los Rios Community College to glean what he could about their lives. Aside from the few who had inherited, their unifying theme was poverty, entry-level pay for college instructors being lower than that for beginning kindergarten teachers. Free to do whatever beckoned, Gary, now William, gave up on genteel campus poverty to survey other fields.

Gary and Jeanne awoke in a Comfort Inn in Pasco, Washington, having signed on to a Columbia Valley wine-tasting tour to celebrate their fifth anniversary. They arrived in Pasco on Friday night under the impression that the tour would begin early Saturday instead of its actual four o'clock kickoff. With time to spare, Gary and Jeanne found the public library on Hopkins Street, where he left her goggling at a colorful display of local Hispanic art while he browsed through the library's collection as he did in every town he visited. Still under the spell of education, he took a scribbled request for documents to the reference counter. A librarian led him to a multivolume resource titled *Revised Code of Washington* and pulled a volume for him that detailed how the state's system of public education was organized and controlled. It listed qualifications for every kind of work in education, citing the certificates educators were required to hold. Then he came upon a passage on superintendents saying, in effect, that a school board could hire a donkey for superintendent if it so chose. A smile grew on Lightfoot's face as he copied RCW 28A.400.010: "In all districts the board of directors shall elect a superintendent who shall have such qualification as the board alone shall determine."

Gary Lightfoot's knowledge of what motivates people was based on what he knew of himself, which left him suspicious of society at large, especially anyone with questions about what he was up to. It had been three years since he, now Dr. Charles Wainwright, had taken the short trek along Highway 99 to SeaTac's Red Lion Hotel and Conference Center. His mildewed room at the Athenian Motel was half the cost of a single at the conference center, a saving that allowed him to invite the right person for a drink, a coffee, or whatever might help to establish contact.

He breezed into the Red Lion in a gray suit, ivory shirt, and red paisley tie, shoes buffed to patent leather brilliance. Ahead, the lettering on an inflated eight-foot phallic symbol—meant to resemble an arrow—said, "Regional Meeting, Washington State School Directors Association." Lightfoot settled onto an upholstered bench to study the action at the WSSDA registration table where a bow-tied elder was clearly the person with the answers. When sure of his approach, he stepped up to the blue-skirted table and said, "Hello. I'm Charles

Wainwright. I'm considering running for a school board position but have concerns about what I might be getting into. Do you think I might be permitted to sit in on a few sessions?"

Finding Wainwright's name and history had been a stroke of luck. He and Wainwright were nearly the same age and hair color, but any resemblance beyond that was less than striking. What mattered was that Wainwright had left his position as superintendent of Kentucky's Meade County Schools for health reasons and dropped out of sight. It had taken some digging to find his obit in an Omaha paper. "Donations may be made to the American Cancer Society." From querying people in Meade County Schools headquarters, he found only that Dr. Wainwright had left, and they had had no idea where he might be. It wasn't perfect, but then nothing was. Gary Lightfoot stood at the registration table thinking, Okay, Dr. Wainwright, let's see if we can put you back to work.

The bow-tied gentleman said, "Absolutely, I admire your foresight. I take it you're not registered?"

"No, there's been no reason for me to be on your mailing list."

"No problem. We can fix you up for the sessions. Can't help you with meals or the keynote address, though. Sorry."

"Understandable. May I talk you out of a name tag? It would help with introductions, you know."

"Sure. Your name, please."

"Wainwright, Dr. Charles Wainwright."

Step one in assuming another's identity required the right search strings: superintendent retires, superintendent resigns, district loses superintendent, district replaces superintendent. Day after day he printed and tossed accounts of educators who were of no use because they were too prominent or too frequently photographed. When a hot possibility surfaced, he ran searches on that person's name. "No information available" was the ideal result. "Address unknown" was good. Yet each promising identity had a fatal flaw. Anyone less than a serial imposter would have given up, but with Lightfoot's entire history built on becoming what he wasn't, he persevered. He was seeking a big score, for the distance separating who he was from the man he might become was fuel for his drive to pull off a greater deception than any in his past. He asked himself why a superintendent might leave a job and drop from sight, which gave birth to one more search string: superintendent-health-personal-reasons, and that led to Dr. Charles E. Wainwright, formerly of Meade County, Kentucky.

Lightfoot, now Wainwright, had chosen the SeaTac conference after three failed interviews. His first try had been in Norfolk, Nebraska, where a perceptive school board cut through his lack of experience in short order. He took the bitter pill as a learning experience and studied educational journals for recent trends in education for three months before testing himself again in Allamakee, Iowa, where he was rejected for a résumé that listed only overseas military schools. Again, he went back to the drawing board before interviewing with Churchill, Nevada, a high-plains town experiencing new growth. He ranked fourth of five interviewees, which was better than he'd done before. He came out of the Churchill interviews feeling almost confident, but again, there was the issue of experience. He had found the right identity, one that wouldn't come after him. And he was offering to work, not tap anyone's bank account or run up credit charges in their name. All he wanted was to ride on a dead man's credentials and track record. In Wainwright's book, that wasn't dishonest because he intended to work for his pay.

After the Churchill interview, he called Jeanne at their home in Cottage Grove, Oregon. Jeanne answered, "Oh hi, Gary." He replied, "Charles, call me Charles." Jeanne had trouble adjusting to her husband's reincarnations, once making the mistake of complaining that she wanted to go back to being who they were when first married. Without laying a hand on her, he capitalized on his wife's dread of conflict, reducing her to tears by charging her with disloyalty for attempting to cripple his mission to become the man God intended him to be.

Tom was in the driveway putting new wipers on Jane's car when she called from the back porch. "Call for you, dear. It's Garnie."

Tom wiped his feet and stepped over Buster to reach the phone. "Hi, Garnie. What's happening?"

"Can you stop over for a moment? I'd like your opinion on something."

"Ten minutes okay?"

"Hmm, fine. I'll have tea on."

Tom hung up and said, "Here we go again. The Great Garnie says he wants my opinion. I wonder what's on his mind this time."

Jane eased against him as he stood with a hand still on the phone. "Well, Mr. Schmoozer, you probably know the old bear better than most. Better go see what he's up to." She gave him a squeeze. "I hate to admit it, but he's got me on the hook, too. Now scoot over there and bring me a report on his latest weirdness. Go on now."

Tom angled across the puddled street to the Pittman home, aiming for the gate to avoid a soaking from his usual route between wet shrubs. The never-closed gate opened onto a stone driveway and walk of European design that took him to a flagstone apron that met algae-stained stairs where Tom paused, as usual, to admire the faded splendor of the home. Its designer, having ignored the Victorian gimcrack embellishments of his era, had created a timeless masterpiece. The curved steps and arcade framed his favorite feature, double iron-bound doors curved at their tops to fill a brownstone Roman arch.

The front door creaked open to reveal an obviously peeved Garnie. "Thomas, Thomas, Thomas, how many times do I have to tell you to use the side door?" Pittman turned and walked across the foyer motioning for Tom to follow. "Oh, never mind, you never listen. Pull the door shut and come with me."

Tom followed. "You've got to get over the door thing. They are fine doors that speak of wealth and taste. You and your spectacular doors are about as close to rubbing shoulders with the rich and famous as I'll ever get, so if you expect me to keep visiting, that'll be my door."

"Humph. No matter how poverty-stricken you think you might be, fawning blue-collar pretension doesn't suit you. Now come and sit; Sigi will serve." He led Tom into the cluttered den where he mumbled at surfaces newly covered with stacks of quilt-cuttings arranged by color.

"Drat that woman! Sometimes I think I live here only at her sufferance. If I upset her precious quilting, there'll be hell to pay. Come, she will serve us in the dining room."

Tom had every reason to believe he was the only one, other than Garnie and Aunt Sigi, who knew his way around the old house well enough to appreciate it. Even Garnie's sister, Alicia, hadn't set foot in the place for a year or more. He couldn't help but admire the carved gumwood doors and trim, the excellent oriental carpets, and the period furniture that harmonized perfectly. The whole of it was clean and dustless, testimony to Aunt Sigi's dedication to housekeeping, up to a point. While she kept the house spotless, evidence of her handcrafts lay everywhere.

"Aunt Sigi, we're ready!"

"I'm right here; you needn't shout!" Sigi, in a chenille housecoat and slippers, shuffled from the kitchen carrying a tray. As she poured from an ornate pot that was likely a souvenir of Waldo and Mildred Pittman's travels in Europe, she said, "You should visit more often, Mr. Clausen. Aside from you we don't have many visitors." Only after she retreated did Garnie add a few ounces of half-and-half and two spoons of sugar. One sip and Tom knew why. It was Lapsang souchong, a tea he thought tasted like wood preservative.

He said, "Why don't you and Sigi get married? After living together for…how long has it been? Sixty years? You might as well, the way you two carry on, acting like an old married couple."

"Hmm, well, I choose not to recognize your improper conjecture other than to say that it doesn't dignify you, Thomas. Not at all. From now on, you may keep your shameful speculations to yourself." With his back to the corridor leading to the pantry, Garnie couldn't see Aunt Sigi pop her head out, pressing fingers against her lips as though suppressing a giggle.

Tom knew that under his sour comments, Garnie loved to be teased, stirred, challenged, or whatever it took to spice up the days that had become too routine for his active mind. He had little patience for the banalities of polite conversation, cutting townspeople off in midsentence if he found lack of depth in their words. Reportedly, he once told a chatty grocery clerk, "If you can't improve on silence, please hold your tongue." Beyond notoriously bad manners, Garnie's mental reach separated him from most people. While his sport was to push his intellectual horizons outward, most people he dealt with were content to live within limited frontiers. Tom took a sniff of his tea and said, "What's on your mind?"

"Mrs. Swenson's cats, Thomas. They leave muddy footprints on my windshield and wet on my back porch. Something has to be done."

"But after the issue with her dog, you can't talk with her, right? What is it you would have me say to Mrs. Swenson? Or would you like to leave that to my sense of diplomacy?"

"Oh, never mind. It's clear that you want no part of it."

"True. Now that we've got the Swensons' cats out of the way, what's bothering you?"

"Hmm, well, since it is obvious that you know nothing of the depredations wrought by semi-feral cats, you wouldn't care anyway. So let us move on. Assume that you had commercial interests here in Northbridge, say on the east side of the freeway. How would you contend with the new tribal developments on the Reservation west of the freeway?"

"You're asking for a generalization, not how I would compete with a casino or an OmniMart or an outlet mall, right?"

"Whatever springs from your fertile imagination, my boy. Skip the details. I'm not interested in specifics of how the uninformed man on the street might approach the issue. Of course any real solution may have to be as political as economic."

"I'm your uninformed man on the street, right? And once again you're asking my opinion on a situation I know nothing about. Am I missing something?"

"Please, Thomas, just answer the question to the best to your ability." Garnie leaned back with his hands cupped over his belly and waited.

"Okay, I'll play your game. The first thing I'd do is figure out what the Tribes are doing or planning to do. Once that's cleared up, I'd set my course by choosing from different directions. The Tribes have the natural advantages; visibility from the freeway, freedom from county zoning, no railroad to contend with, and plenty of level acreage for big-box developers. If planners want to pump new life into Northbridge, they should forget competing for big boxes and work on developing a new identity that'll attract combinations or groupings of specialty shops or services. How about music? Or crafts? Maybe alternative medicine."

"You'd concede?"

"Why call it conceding when it's a done-deal? The horse is out of the barn. It wouldn't hurt to survey marketing patterns in towns to the south and north to see what's already being done well and what needs to be done better."

"Theory and generalities. Try to put a sharper point on it. In your mind, what would be the best thing that could happen to Northbridge?"

"I can't see it happening for a number of reasons, but if I ran the zoo, I'd make the state such a sweet offer of a site that they'd have to accept Northbridge as home for a new four-year college." Tom sipped and grimaced. "This stuff is terrible."

"Don't be such a pessimist. Why can't you see it happening? Oh, well, well, well. Whatever, whad-wudever. Hmm."

"Traffic. Forget growth for the moment. If the existing population struggles to get in or out of town, no state planner will want to add to gridlock that's not…Garnie?" Tom had written off Garnie's slurred speech to sneaking an early snifter of Courvoisier, but when he slumped with his head lolling forward, he shouted, "Aunt Sigi!" and jumped to catch him before he toppled from his chair.

Jane was at the dining room window when Tom hopped a gutter running with rainwater and jogged to the back door. "Well, what was he after this time?"

Tom met her quizzical look with a shrug. "He said he wants me to complain to Emily about her cats, if you can believe it. Then he probed me about the best ways to put some life into Northbridge's business community—at least I think that's what he was after. You never know."

"The silly man. If he wants that kind of advice, he can hire it. But what does he have to do with Northbridge businesses, anyway? He doesn't care; he's managed to offend almost everyone in town."

"Who knows? It's strange. Sometimes I think he actually wants to understand how much or how little people like me know about local issues. Other times he just uses me as a sounding board, and as we well know, there's always his hidden agendas. It might be that he just enjoys hearing his ideas aired and has nobody but me to float them by. And, of course, he might just be lonely."

Jane poked him in the ribs and said, "Oh, come on, Mr. Reticent; that takes care of the first ten minutes. What else did you do?"

"Caught him as he was falling out of his chair. Yelled for Aunt Sigi. Watched her pull his mouth open to give him a squirt from a honey bear. You should have heard her: 'Stupid man! Won't check his blood. If it weren't for me, he'd be dead a hundred times over.' You wouldn't believe how she carries on when he can't hear her."

"Oh, my goodness. Is he all right?"

"Oh sure. The first thing he did when he came out of it was scold her for not reminding him to check his blood. They're quite a pair. He couldn't survive without her, and she wouldn't survive without his house."

CHAPTER 7

The waiting room at Northbridge Doctors' Clinic was quiet, even for a Wednesday afternoon. Tom leafed through a *People* magazine, marveling that a reading audience could care who Ben or Jen might be sleeping with. He was swapping it for a back issue of *Parenting* when a nurse called his name. She led him down a corridor to a windowless room where he slid out of his jacket to have his blood pressure read. One fifty-five over ninety-five. And then he was alone, feet dangling from his perch on the end of an examination table.

To put an end to Jane's nagging, he agreed to see Dr. Peter Castella, a general practitioner friend from Kiwanis. It wasn't that Tom lacked faith in medicine. He believed doctors' services should be reserved for emergencies, as when he chopped his leg while splitting firewood, or the time Castella sewed up his brow where it had been nicked by a racquetball racquet. Aside from seasonal sniffles, he was never sick. Dr. Castella breezed in and greeted him, opened Tom's thin file, and said, "About time we checked you out." He set about listening to his chest, quizzed him about lifestyle, and double-checked his blood pressure. He authorized blood tests and booked him for a return visit. "We'll talk more about the state of your health after the lab work comes back."

Ten days later, Tom was back to search the waiting room for reading matter with more depth than *People.* Two preschoolers chased and screamed while their harried mother sat as though in a daze. His turn came. A nurse led him to the same examination room and instructed him to strip to the waist. She cuffed his left arm and pumped. One fifty-two over ninety-seven.

Dr. Castella reviewed the test results with Tom, focusing on his blood pressure and a total cholesterol of two forty-five. He asked about diet, exercise, and stimulants. He paged back into Tom's file, pointing out that his blood pressure had risen markedly since he was last in. He discussed risk factors, medications, and necessary adjustments to diet and physical activity, and he suggested that Tom was most likely suffering from job-related stress and that cutting caffeine would be a best first step. But to be sure there wasn't a hidden bomb waiting to go off, he insisted on referring him for a full cardio workup.

Tom's next stop was a cardiology clinic in Port Gardner where, shirtless and in shorts and joggers, he stepped onto a treadmill. Adele, his cardio tech, decorated his torso with adhesive sensors and explained the gas-monitoring mouthpiece he would be using. The supervising doctor arrived, introduced himself as Dr. Rudy Myers, and gave Adele the go-ahead. The belt started and held at a relaxed three miles per hour while she fiddled with controls that adjusted the trace of his sixty-five per minute pulse on a monitor.

Myers asked, "How do you feel?"

"Fine."

The speed increased, eighty-two beats per minute.

"How do you feel?"

"Fine."

More speed.

"Are you still all right?"

"Still okay."

More speed. The monitor showed a heart rate of 124 per minute, about the demand of a fast game of racquetball.

Myers said again, "How are you doing?"

"Okay." Puff. "Okay."

More speed.

"Hey, this is getting to be work." Tom's pulse wavered at 141. "Hey, Doc, how high are you taking this?" Pant, pant.

"One fifty-five for three minutes, then you can rest."

More speed. Tom struggled to keep up, sucking air in great gulps, wondering if he had ever pushed his pulse that high. The thought hit him that if he were to give it up—let go of the bar and stop running—the belt, running at its mad pace, would catapult him off the back and across the room. No safety net.

Myers said, "We're almost there. Good work, good work. Keep it up for another minute and a half. Keep going, keep going. Attaboy, you're almost there. Go, go, go! Okay, that's it."

No matter that it was covered by insurance. Tom was stunned by the bill—more than two thousand dollars for imaging, blood-flow studies, and the stress test, all to satisfy Jane's concerns. But even then she wasn't content. She cut him back to decaf at breakfast and banned dietary luxuries, such as ice cream and Danish pastries. When he caught her casting worried looks at him, he asked, "What's that all about?" She said, "Oh, nothing."

But he did recognize that, when comparing good days with bad days, good days were scarcer, and the effects of bad days tended to carry over to affect what might otherwise be good days. Especially bad times left him feeling wrung out for hours. He tried eating lighter meals, drinking more water, cutting bedtime snacks, and walking more. At fifty-two he was far from an old man, but knowing that different people age at different rates made him wonder if his physical age might have passed up his chronological age. If so, it was becoming painfully obvious that aging isn't for sissies.

Getting through workdays became a daunting challenge. He found himself passing off tasks he would have taken in stride a year before, and there were times, usually toward the end of the day, when he closed himself in his office where, assailed by weariness, he lowered his forehead against his folded arms to doze for a few minutes. It helped. Each time he emerged, Alice checked his forehead for telltale creases. He would never know that she and Jane were in daily contact about his condition.

Dale spotted Dana standing in the late-day shade of the public library. She wore shorts, sandals, and a lime-green polo shirt and carried a beige travel purse over her shoulder. He double-parked while she trotted to the passenger's door to slide in. He inspected her. "No jacket? It might get cool."

"Got a cashmere sweater in here," she said, indicating her bag. "Swing by an espresso stand. I could use a coffee."

He pulled into a drive-through and picked up two lattes. Minutes later he was being entertained with anecdotes from her school bus runs. Dana teased, "You're too much of a pansy. You couldn't deal with it—like the third-grade boy who wet his pants and was too embarrassed to get off when we got to school, or the girl who broke down in tears because boys stole homemade sweets from her lunch, or the notebook somebody tossed down the aisle, scattering a kid's papers all over the place, and the girl who helped gather them up. But they're not all jerks; I've got my heroes, too. There's a boy on the secondary morning run who sees to it that nobody hassles our one handicapped student. You should have seen how upset he was when Lucas, that's the handicapped boy, wasn't at the bus stop yesterday."

Recalling how he had taken drivers for granted during his school-bus-riding years, Dale was surprised to hear her speak of her riders with the same regard he felt for his first-period class. She had up to two classrooms of students to mold into brief societies with rules and responsibilities four times each day, and it was obvious that she took her job seriously.

He said, "You drive early and late. What do you do in between?"

"Read. And I take a class every term at the community college so the midday break's good for study time. Poly Sci 102 this quarter. You want to know anything about evil-doing in high places? I'm your girl."

"What for? What's your goal?"

"Upward and onward. I told you about Gus. Well, even with him behind me I'm stuck in kinda like, you know, arrested development. I want to mix it up with people who do things with their lives." She poked him. "Like if you and I happened to be in the same room with somebody interesting, you might introduce me—all according to Hoyle, of course. You'd say, 'I'd like you to meet Dana, uh, what's your last name, young lady?' like we'd just met. I want to schmooze with people who've been to school. You think you could do that for me?"

"If we're in the same room with the right people, sure." They slowed to follow a tractor with a mower bar locked in the vertical position like an industrial-strength antenna. When it turned right at the next intersection, they resumed speed. Dale had been chewing on her request. "About connecting with interesting people, the world's full of them. No problem. But it'll take more than that. You need to start putting yourself forward. Put the credits you're earning together with your work experience in a résumé—driving a school bus sure won't hurt—and apply for work as a teacher's aide. Get recognized for what you can do—and what you are. You're a Koutac!"

She looked intently at him. "And make less money. Are you putting me off or giving good advice?" He ran a finger down her cheek and said, "Good advice. Trust me."

The sun was dropping behind the hills that loomed over the west side of Big Lake by the time Dale eased down a curving driveway that ended at a flat-roofed single carport, its far end invaded by brambles. The cabin appeared to be in better repair. The key, retrieved from under a blue flowerpot, turned easily in the lock, but it took a shove to break the bind of the door in its jamb. She brushed by him, dropped her bag on a counter, and disappeared into the living room. "Come here," she called back.

He set the bag he'd brought beside her purse and stepped into the living room to find her testing an orange slip-covered chair, "Isn't it a kick? It's like we're sucked into a time warp." The kitchen and living room remained as originally equipped and decorated, vintage 1960, and were cluttered with family memorabilia from summers at the lake. Aside from shelves of dated books and games that needed a good dusting it appeared ready for use. Dana hopped out of the chair to poke through the bookshelves. She blew dust from a book and said, "Hey, Louis L'Amour. I read everything he wrote." She disappeared into a hallway and called back, "What are you supposed to check out?"

"See if there's been a break-in. You know how vagrants use these places for crash pads. Make sure no water's running, look for leaks, and check the door and window locks. Stuff like that."

"Who owns it?"

"Neil Bassett, a teacher at the community college. It's been in his family since his dad built it." He took her by the arm and guided her back into the kitchen where he pulled a bottle from his bag. "Sorry, I didn't ask. Would you like some wine?"

"Yeah, so long as it doesn't have a screw cap." She took the bottle, an Oregon Merlot, from him and studied the label. "No, on second thought I'll pass. Not tonight. Alcohol never did much for my relationships. You go ahead." She set the bottle down, drew a squiggle on the dusty counter, and returned to the shadowy living room, now illuminated only by the sky's violet glow silhouetting the western hills. The lake was a darkening mirror, its far side reflecting the lights of waterfront homes where after-dinner cleanups were finishing and children were being readied for bed. She felt the heat of his body when he moved close behind her and turned, leaning into him to encircle his chest with her arms. "What next?"

"Follow me; I'll give you the grand tour." He led her to a dark stairway they descended without touching a light switch and entered a dim basement room stacked with stored patio furniture and gardening tools. Outside, fading light revealed a weedy veranda bounded by shrubs that obscured views of the lake. They stopped at the window wall to embrace again, clinging as he danced her into another room where one wall was heaped with storage boxes. A metal-framed double bunk bed with bare mattresses stood against the opposite wall. Dale squeezed her and said, "Not exactly inviting."

They started upstairs with Dana in the lead, Dale's overly helpful hands boosting her at each stair. She turned halfway up where her one-step lead brought their eyes closer and her lips just under his chin. Their faces touched, one side, then the other. Their lips and bodies brushed lightly, hands roaming freely. Dizzy with desire, he stumbled against the stairwell wall. He righted himself and put his lips to her ear and whispered, "Move it, girl. There are places for this kind of thing, and this is not one of them."

They returned to the shadowy living room where the renewed difference in their height hampered kisses. They gave way to pent-up hunger—searching and consuming until she felt his body go rigid. She pushed him to arm's length and asked, "What's the matter? Did I do something wrong?"

"No, it's me. Sorry, I guess I have a problem."

She pulled him close again and asked, "Something I can help you with?"

"I hope so. All of a sudden I'm nervous as a virgin. I've been a one-woman man for so long that, well, you'd think with two degrees in biology and knowing all about the mating dances of—"

"Hush!" She put her hand on his mouth. "You talk too much. Think of it like riding a bicycle. Like they say, once you get the hang of it, you never forget how. Now just relax; it'll all come back." She pulled his shirt loose. "For the moment, I'll lead; you follow."

Grasping and clutching, they staggered to a couch and tumbled onto it. Dale's elbow slammed against a wooden arm that did nothing to stem his passion. Her hands worked at his belt while he pawed beneath her polo shirt to get at her bra fastener. Possessed by primal momentum, he kept the presence of mind to recognize that what was happening was wilder and more primitive and unconstrained than anything he had ever experienced with Betty. Shoes and clothing flew. He lifted her against him, and together they staggered into a dim bedroom where they stirred a small dust storm by falling onto the bed. Deep kisses and bold caresses hurried them to where they knew they were going.

Later, they lay quietly against each other letting intimate touches and soft words fill what passionate coupling had failed to express. The room was dark, the only illumination a trace of purple sky glow outlining the western hills. In the stillness they communicated careful intimacies with fingertips and lips, while the rolling of the planet took the last vestiges of day with it. When he sensed tiny spasms carrying her toward sleep, he suppressed renewed arousal that she might rest in his arms. He felt overfilled with the joy of holding and loving this small woman who had given herself to him and was savoring that revelation when headlight beams raked across the kitchen and living room ceilings to illuminate their nakedness and trail of strewn clothing. "Who?" Dale grunted, jarring Dana awake. The lights had come to rest squarely on the kitchen window. He slipped off the bed, growling, "What the hell. Oh, shit, shit, shit! Oh, damn it to hell!" Dana jerked awake and stared at the light spilling into the bedroom. They crawled about retrieving clothes, Dale cursing while Dana whimpered softly. Outside, car doors slammed.

"Hey, Randy, does Neal drive a Toyota? This one's got a North Sound Toyota license frame." Inside, Dale pulled his pants on and limped toward his shoes.

"Get serious, he won't be back in the States for another month. Lift that flowerpot and see if there's a key."

Inside, fingers fumbled at buttons as they hastened to cover themselves. Dana had her shorts and shirt on and was stuffing her bra into a pocket when a voice from the kitchen porch called out, "It ain't here. Must be somebody inside." She thought to retrieve her purse from the kitchen but was unable to face the lights and whoever might be behind them.

A deep voice called out, "I'll find out. Stay with the car, and keep the lights on." The one called Randy tried the door before knocking. He called out, "Anybody in there?"

Dana grabbed the front of Dale's shirt. "What do we do?"

"It's probably innocent enough. Just to be on the safe side, you go downstairs and work your way around the house to the car. I'll meet you there." As an afterthought, he turned on a floor lamp in the living room and the bathroom lights, hoping light from windows on opposite sides of the house might illuminate whichever route she took.

He switched on the kitchen light and unlocked and opened the door. Swallowing his agitation, he said, "Hello. Something I can do for you?"

The caller was nearly Dale's height but florid and heavy around the middle. Folding his arms to display tattooed biceps, he growled, "I'm Randy Bassett. My brother owns this place. Who are you, and what're you doing here?"

Dale extended a hand. "Dale Runyon. Neal and I go way back. He's mentioned you to me. About what I'm doing here, he likes to have me check the place when he's away. You know, with vagrants holing up in recreational homes and all. Nice view from here so I usually end up hanging out for a while before taking off. Give me a minute to straighten up and it's all yours. I was about to leave anyway."

Randy's hostility melted at Dale's mention of his brother's name. "Hey, that's cool, friend." He swallowed Dale's hand in a meaty grasp and shouted to his car, "It's okay, Jamie. Our friend here's just leavin.' Irene, hold on to your damn dog, would you?" He turned back to Dale. "Got a little coed poker game going tonight. There's an empty chair if you wanna sit in for a while." He studied Dale and said, "Hey, you must be the teacher, right?"

"Guilty as charged, but no poker for me tonight. Excuse me while I gather my stuff. I won't be a minute." He grabbed the sack containing deli sandwiches and the Merlot, tucked Dana's bag under his arm and prowled the living room for left items. Running a hand around couch cushions, he turned up Dana's panties and his other sock. A glint in the shag carpet led to an earring, its backing lost in the deep pile. He stuffed his finds into the food sack before straightening cushions and plumping pillows and resquaring the couch. He knew he didn't have it all, but with Dana frightened and waiting, it was no time to hang around searching for it.

Dana eased the basement door shut behind her. With the back of the house as a guide, she stepped off into the dark. Rounding the corner in dew-damp grass, a bramble trailer hooked the strap of her sandal. A few steps more and another higher one pulled at her shorts, one thorn catching on flesh above her knee. She lifted them away cautiously. Light from a small window passed high above her to lose itself in brush some yards to her left. Working upslope, she found the going easiest if she kept her back to the wall so she only had to fend off thorny creepers from one side. But as she inched uphill, she came into the glare of headlights and lost her night vision. It took her full measure of self-control to crouch low and pick her way onward where the thicket seemed less dense. She straightened when her legs cramped, driving a thorn painfully into her scalp. Reflex drove her down, but that move caught a shirt sleeve on more thorns. She pressed her oozing scalp with a free hand and sobbed. Choked by fear and pain, the sob narrowed to a thin wail. Now there was only one goal. A patch of light from the kitchen penetrated the foliage ahead. Like a moth, oblivious of blood or pain, she struck out toward it.

She crawled into the back seat from the passenger side. Thorns and panic behind her, pain took over. She whimpered and quaked. The trembling wrist from which she sucked blood bumped spastically against her lips. Pain from different wounds took their turn. A pulsing ache sprang from her scalp to join a wave of stings from her left forearm. She grimaced, spreading a gash in her lower lip. Flinching one way threw her against other sources of pain. Like an animal, she lapped blood from her damaged forearms and reached to shake a forelock from her eye, only to loose blood-stained tears onto her snagged shirt. Mastered by pain and fear, she curled into herself as her blood seeped into the back seat's fabric upholstery.

She recoiled when Dale jerked his door open to slide behind the wheel. After glancing back to see that she was with him, he muttered an unintelligible complaint and started the engine. He spun the car around to face uphill, slammed the shift lever into low, and accelerated over potholes and through the widening triangle where the lane and highway met. Without stopping, he careened onto the road and accelerated southward.

"Of all the crummy luck," he grumbled. "A million-to-one chance of somebody showing up and look what happens! And he knows who I am. I'm so sorry. I don't know how, but I'm going to make it up to you."

In a voice he'd never heard, she snapped, "Don't even try."

He looked back at her silhouette and tossed her purse over the seat toward where she was curled in the far corner of the passenger's side. "Hey, I'm sorry. I'm probably the sorriest guy around so say something, will you? I'm sorry, I'm sorry, I'm sorry. Look, let's find a place where we can shake this off. Maybe have a couple of drinks, maybe just hold on to each other." When he reached over the seat to touch her, she batted his hand away, which didn't surprise him. He said, "I'll pull over so you can come up front."

"Just drive. I need help." She winced as if a finger was shut in a door.

"Me, too. Look in the bag. I got as much of your stuff as I could find. We'll find a place where you can finish dressing." Dale caught a change in sound from the back, hiccupping gasps and whines, that alarmed him, and he punched the emergency flashers and pulled onto the shoulder. He turned to her as an oncoming car flicked its lights on bright to illuminate her face, her scalp wound leaking fresh blood, her forearms bloody, her hair in disarray, and her blood-stained shirt snagged and pulled by thorns. Stunned wordless, he moaned, "Oooh, oh. Ooh no. Oh, oh, my God, what? Dana, Dana, whatever happened?" Shock so engulfed him that for the moment he was incapable of speech. When the headlights of a string of three cars held on her condition for harsh seconds, he had to shut his eyes.

"I'll tell you what happened." Her voice was shrill. "I picked the wrong man again. Shit! All you had to do was walk me out the door like you thought I was worth something, but no, once you got what you wanted, you told me to go out the back door, and I got this!" She thrust her bloody arms at him and fell back, sobbing and rummaging in her bag.

"What are you doing?"

"What do you care? I'm calling nine-one-one. I need help."

"I do care, more than ever, and I'm going to get you to help faster than an aid car. Belt up and hang on." He drove like a madman, tailgating, passing on the shoulder, and never looking at the speedometer. With tires screeching, he careened up to General Hospital's emergency entrance and jerked to a stop in a slot marked Physicians Only. He leaped out, pulled her out, and propelled her through automatic doors. A passing nurse spotted the blood and took charge, steering them to a treatment room. She said, "Talk, what happened?"

Dana pointed to Dale. "He happened."

Dale said, "Blackberry brambles happened, but yes, I guess I'm responsible."

"Out. You can wait by reception." The nurse pushed him out and pulled the curtain.

"Wait, don't go. Don't leave me." Her voice followed him to reception where another nurse said to him, "You're bleeding; let me take a look."

"No, it's not my blood." His explanation, meant to minimize her interest in him, had the opposite effect. She nodded to a security officer and directed his attention to Dale with another nod toward him. When the officer moved in his direction while speaking into his handset, Dale made for the door, leaped into his car, and put distance between him and the hospital without knowing where he was going.

He walked into his house at 11:30 p.m. to find Betty waiting up. She took in the blood on his shirt and said, "Oh, dear, what happened? I knew it had to be something. Are you hurt? Why didn't you call?"

"I drove a woman to the hospital. She was cut up pretty bad from blackberry thorns. She's a bus driver for the schools."

"Well, then, we ought to pause for a moment to give thanks that you were put on the scene. Where did you find her? Was she alone? Is she all right?" Dale headed for the shower, knowing that there would be more to deal with than Betty's questions. Much more. She called after him, "You were chosen to help someone in need. Isn't that wonderful? Can you feel the joy?"

He was in his pajamas when the doorbell rang. Two police cruisers were at the curb with lights flashing. Two officers were at the door, two more by the cars for backup. His heart sank when he checked them through the peephole and opened the door. "Are you Dale Runyon? Is that your car in the driveway? Did you drop a woman off at the hospital tonight?" He was Mirandized and cuffed.

He asked, "May I get dressed?" They followed him into the walk-in closet off the bathroom and uncuffed him. He dressed while Betty, in the hallway, tried to convince them that it was a godly home and that they had the wrong address. Cuffed again, Dale was escorted to the street and stuffed in the back of a cruiser. He accepted the discomfort of sitting in a car's back seat with his hands cuffed behind him as the beginning of what couldn't help but become much worse.

At the police station, he was searched, photographed, and printed. He gave his personal information; dropped his watch, penknife, billfold, and belt in a tray; and was informed that he had been brought in on suspicion of aggravated assault. He was locked in a holding cell with two others—a tearful hit-and-run driver who looked like the average mom next-door and a transient pulled in for petty theft. With nothing else to do, they got to know each other.

Dale plodded through the motions of teaching his morning classes, his mind trapped in the headlights of that night. Off campus, café prattle about people whose antics contrasted with ordinary life found a focus in Dale and Dana. By midday of the morning after, styling salons and coffee shops were abuzz with spectacularly inaccurate accounts of Dana's trip to General Hospital—that she had lost pints of blood due to multiple gashes or stabs, that it was not known whether she'd survive; that she was brought to the hospital by Dale Runyon of Northbridge High School in a blood-soaked car, and that Runyon had posted bail. Without facts, they were left to conjecture about the charges he would face should Dana not survive.

Tom's day began with Alice taking him aside. "Stories about Mr. Runyon are circulating. Since you're usually the last to know, you might not know that he got into a situation you really should know about. Shall I send for him?"

"Yes, during his conference period." What now, he wondered, cursing the barrier that insulates principals from faculty buzz. By not passing stories up the ladder, teachers left him as last to pick up on rumors. Alice's carefully worded heads-up told him that whatever it was, it would be best to hear it from the horse's mouth than secondhand.

Alice continued, "Hold on to your hat; there's more. Claudia McPhaiden called to say she'd be here directly, and if you were busy, she would wait for the first opportunity to speak with you."

After Claudia's visit, during which she charged Runyon with attempted murder and adultery, charges she embellished with details from the more lurid rumors, his day took a needed turn for the better during fourth period. He was headed for the sprinkler control closet in the south wing when the corridor's air thickened with cooking odors. The source was Room 126, home of Liz Crawford's ELL classes. Formerly ESL, for English as a Second Language, the name was changed to recognize that immigrant students most often arrived with two or more languages, hence the change to ELL for English Language Learners.

Crawford's job was to fast-track immigrants into the regular curriculum, which meant not only teaching them English but also motivating them to use it. The size of her task would have been reasonable if all her students had come from Mexico or Russia, but she had to deal with the various needs of Sudanese, Guatemalans, Southeast Asians, Russians, Poles, Iraqis, and others in a constantly changing mix. Her other challenge was while certain nationalities tended to be assertive, others were shy. It took unusual techniques to protect and bring out the shy while capitalizing on others' forthrightness, all the while working to develop mutual respect. The word had been leaked that it was one of Crawford's ethnic food-fest days when one group—today's odors indicated Middle Eastern cookery—showcased their people's cuisine. Since the student cooks always whipped up enough to share, the aromas made a magnet of "Crawford's kitchen."

As curious faculty and students with trumped-up passes dropped by for tasting and introductions, her Middle Eastern students were drawn another step closer to integration with the student body. Because the program worked, Clausen turned a blind eye to the half-dozen regulations it overstepped, and both Liz and Tom knew it was only a matter of time until the county health department would cite the school for breach of food handling and preparation standards. Her argument had been "Come on, Tom. This is one of those situations where it's a lot easier to get forgiveness than permission." Before Crawford took over, Northbridge High graduated three or four immigrants per year. At the end of her first year, that number climbed to eight, and last year it had risen to thirteen, a number that was attracting attention at state level. Tom turned the knob and stepped in to find out what was cooking.

Over the four days following the escapade at Big Lake, comments from other emergency patients, loose-lipped police, Randy Bassett and friends, an anonymous emergency room staffer, and Dana herself lent enough accuracy to cool the wilder versions that had Claudia crowing about her capacity for judging character—how she had known all along that there was something deviant about that Runyon person. She lectured Clausen on how he was fortunate that his friend hadn't acted out his perversion with a student and spoke of the wheels she had set in motion to rid his school of the problem. She was taken aback when he responded, "You'll find we have policies for dealing with such issues."

It took three overheard comments to drive Dale deep into his shell. Normally outgoing and spontaneous, he underwent a transformation to maintain remnants of control, not over what might happen to him—he was resigned to accept that, whatever it might be—but over how he would react. It was during predawn, only ten hours before, that he came to understand that the only ground he had left to protect was a narrowing sense of balance. It was a matter of whether he could preserve enough of himself to keep outside forces from reducing him to helplessness. Sleepless, he accepted that little of what he had been could be part of his future.

The first comment to hit him came from Betty the first evening after his return to work. "Well, I hope you're proud of yourself," which, aside from "Put that plate down, I'll do my own dishes," was the last he heard from her. The second undermining comment was a jibe from a friend and fellow teacher with a habit of dishing out good-natured ribbing. He punched Dale on the shoulder and said, "I heard you had quite a night." Dale walked away and made a point of avoiding him thereafter. He heard the third while placing an order at Starbucks when a young woman turned from her cell phone to say to her companion, "They say she looked like she'd been stuck with a thousand knives." He decided against coffee and took a slow drive toward the pass and back. He returned hardened to accept whatever came his way. The note asking him to stop by Tom's office came the next morning.

Tom found himself facing a stranger. Dale glanced at Tom and then anchored his gaze on a bookcase. "Are you sure you want to know?" Sitting across the desk from Tom, he displayed no frown, no wry smile, no tears, and no nervous tics.

Tom said, "I have to know. Claudia's been here. I expect your version's different from hers."

Dale shrugged. "It wouldn't make much difference, but yeah, you have to know." He clasped his hands, leaned forward to look at his shoes, and began. "You must know that Betty and I never had the kind of marriage you and Jane have. We tried, but there's never been much chemistry to work with. I don't think there ever was. I respect her and admire her beauty, but we don't relate. I'm not trying to hang any responsibility on her. In fact, I really think I screwed her up by marrying her, but that cuts two ways. When we tied the knot, we did each other out of finding real companionship. Anyway, it was my doing, not hers.

"When I bumped into Dana Gustafson we just clicked. No strain, no pain, we simply got along easily and enjoyed each other's company. If Betty was my anchor, Dana was my wings. What's more, I enjoyed doing things for her, and I don't mean sexually, just doing or saying little considerate things. I got to looking forward more to seeing her at softball practices than going home to Betty. Then things started to get out of control. Half of me was still married; the other half wanted Dana. She made no secret about being available, which, as you can imagine, planted thoughts in my head. It was Wednesday night when we tossed inhibitions aside." He shut his eyes and monotoned a brief description of the ill-fated evening.

Tom said, "I once heard a radio pop-psychologist say that fantasies are fine. You just don't want to let them cross over into your reality. This must be what she meant."

"I suppose so. Betty didn't know the whole story when two police cars pulled up in front of the house. I answered the door. Two cops on the porch, two by the cars, watching. One asked if I was Dale Runyon and then asked me to step outside. They went through the whole arrest thing like in the movies. As far as I knew, Betty was still back in the den with the TV, but you can bet the police cars had the neighbors at their windows. Roger was sleeping like a log, thank God."

"What did they charge you with?"

"It never got to that. They thought they had me for aggravated assault, but it didn't hold. They hauled me in because the cop at the emergency ward asked Dana about who she was with, not if I had anything to do with her condition, which to be honest, I suppose I did. I told the whole story to the cops who took me in, which had them rolling their eyeballs and shaking their heads. Before they stuck me in a cell with some quite interesting people, I suggested they check with the hospital to find out what caused Dana's wounds. I guess they did. When they got back to me, they were enjoying it like it was a joke. They actually laughed at me when they released me. Can you believe it?"

Tom nodded. "Well, looked at from the cops' perspective, you have to admit it has all the elements of a comedy of errors."

"That's easy for you to say," Dale quipped, which Tom took as a sign that his old nature might still be accessible. "There's going to be hell to pay. I can see the fallout coming, but that's the way it goes. The best I can do is try to land on my feet. Our marriage has been a sham, and it's over, which is just as well except for what it'll do to Roger and Ellen. Betty and I aren't talking yet, but I'd like her to understand that we'll be setting each other free and that the kids might get two better adjusted parents out of the deal, just not under the same roof.

"Here's my new reality: Claudia, the board, and Wainwright know that I took a woman, not my wife, to a cabin on Big Lake. Betty charged me with lying to her about that night, though everything I told her was the truth, just not all of it. She and I are calling it quits. I'm carrying an ache inside for what Dana's gone through, and though you and everyone else might advise against it, I need to keep trying to patch things up with her."

"How does Betty feel?"

"Totally humiliated, of course. But once out from under that, I think she'll find that having me out of the house will be a plus."

Tom said, "You should know that Claudia's after your hide. She and Wainwright figure they're above procedure so you can look for them to push for a summary firing. They're not going to like it when I hold them to policy."

Dale waved that off. "Let Martin Koutac handle it. He's Dana's dad. You don't want to tangle with McPhaiden and Wainwright over me. They're going to do whatever they want, and I'm resigned to accept it."

"What are you going to do about Dana Gustafson?"

Dales's starchy defense crumbled. "Tom, that's the part that weighs on me more than losing my job or parting with Betty. She's hurt so badly that she may never speak to me again. I really, truly need to do everything I can to make amends."

Tom shook his head. "That may be where your heart is, but you'd better start listening to your head. Working out whatever it is with Betty must be your top priority for now—for Roger and Ellen's sake. About your contract with the district, that's out of my hands. Check the fine print and you'll see a provision that allows them to fire you before the end of the term. If that happens, you'll be a hard man to replace."

"You'll find a way."

"Only because I have to." Tom glanced at his watch. "You'd better get back to your room. Class break's in two minutes. See what you can do to preserve some normalcy in your classes, okay?"

On his way out, Dale turned and said, "Thanks. Are you all right?"

"Just tired. Very tired. Thanks for asking." He reached into a drawer for a bottle of antacid tablets, but before he had the top off, the accursed box on his desk beeped, and its light went on. He tapped a button and growled, "What is it?"

"Sorry, but Petra Nielsen's here. Says she has to talk with you."

"Send her in."

Petra threw her jacket over the back of a chair and said, "You said we ought to keep each other informed. By the way, you look terrible."

"So they say. What's up?"

"It seems the man's got me in his sights, too. It was pretty much the same as you got, not following policy."

Tom said, "What did you do?"

"It was more a matter of what I didn't do. By suspending and not expelling a seventh grader, I broke his zero-tolerance policy for drug use. His teacher said, and I agreed, that the boy 'reeked' of marijuana so I sent him home to clean up—and informed the parents that we had taken notice of pot use, possibly in the home. Then I called the police and suggested that it would be a good time to have a heart-to-heart with the parents while the boy was home—that's where kids that young usually get the stuff. Instead, Chief Tuininga showed up at my office to fill me in on what he called one of the more colorful arrests his troops ever made. It turned out that the boy and his friends were instrumental in putting a grower and distributor out of business. But because he reeked, I was supposed to expel him? Tell me, how do you tell Wainwright that he's wrong?"

CHAPTER 8

Tim Lapointe veered into a left-turn lane on Highway 2 to wait for an opening in oncoming traffic. Three years earlier, the property behind the northeast corner of the intersection was filled with aging mobile homes, their soon-to-be-evicted residents making the most of a grace period that ended with the arrival of earthmovers. Two years earlier, the Municipality of Moraine annexed the mile-long corridor connecting the town with Highway 2, a move that attracted the interest of PSD Associates, a Puget Sound mall developer. Skiers bound for Stevens Pass in January 1999 whizzed past new piles of raw earth at the Moraine turnoff. By the 2000 ski season, they were dumbfounded to find a completed commercial center there.

When a gap opened between a bakery truck and a tractor-trailer rig, Lapointe wheeled his Jetta across to a Chevron gas and convenience store. While paying for coffee and a pack of M&Ms, he asked how many minutes it took to get to Northbridge. The clerk, a turbaned newcomer from the southern margins of Asia, said, "Now, fifteen to twenty minute. Morning commute, half hour." Lapointe pocketed his change, taking note of a pyramid of coffee mugs decorated with frogs sitting in rain-splashed puddles. A caption under the puddles read, "More Rain, Washington." Sports fans picked up the local joke about the town's name and microclimate to propose two names for the new high school's mascot: Frogs or Ducks. The Frogs won.

Twenty-five minutes later, Lapointe swung his Jetta into a visitor's stall in front of the Northbridge School District's offices. It was 9:55 a.m. A tall receptionist with gold and black earrings the size of Christmas ornaments directed him to sign in, handed him a clip-on pass, and pointed to a cove of waiting-room chairs. For reading materials, he had his choice of a binder containing certificated and noncertificated job openings and stacks of public information blurbs. By 10:45 a.m., he had exhausted it all. It was nearing eleven o'clock when the tall one said, "Mr. Lapointe, you may go in now."

Lapointe entered an oversized office where a spit-polished dandy he took to be Wainwright stood by a desk that could seat ten for dinner. A conference table made of the same wood as the desk filled the space to the right. A private entrance behind the conference table shared the wall with tall windows that backed the big desk, leaving visitors squinting into their light. Wainwright greeted him without introducing himself and settled into a leather chair suitable for a Fortune 500 CEO. While the desk accessories—a brass cowboy sculpture, a for-show-only marble and brass desk pen set, and a huge monitor—were meant to impress, the superintendent's furtive eyes didn't match the show. He left Lapointe standing.

A woman of upper-middle age sat across from Wainwright. She shifted her seating angle toward the chair reserved for Lapointe, all the time appraising him from head to toe. The superintendent's shifty glances and the woman's bold appraisal had Lapointe wishing he had drawn another assignment. The odd couple, he thought. Before a word was uttered, he understood how important it was to his hosts that he grovel a bit. The woman started things off. "Timothy Lapointe, is that correct?"

"Yes, ma'am. Representing Dern McComber and Sessions. Here's my card. May I sit?"

"Oh yes, please do. You're rather young."

"I believe it's qualification, not age, you're after. You'll find all you need to know about me in my personal file." He placed a folder on the big desk. "Our investigations are sometimes rather sensitive, so as a matter of policy we try to make our clients comfortable with the investigators on the case. I hope you find my qualifications satisfactory."

The woman said, "Young man, this is Dr. Charles Wainwright, district superintendent, and I am Claudia McPhaiden, chair of the Northbridge School Board." Lapointe was amused at how quickly Ms. McPhaiden pecked him to the bottom of her order with her "young man" designation. She continued, "Have you been informed of the particulars that caused us to engage an investigator?"

"Not really. The information that came to my desk spoke of a need to discreetly determine certain backgrounds within the district staff. Discreet fact-finding can fit anything from cheating spouses to embezzlement. Would you like to fill me in?"

Wainwright spoke up. "We, that is the school district, are suffering a rash of behaviors among critical personnel that impact the image and performance of the district. Given the protections professional educators enjoy, termination isn't an option without documented evidence of disloyalty, and you may take disloyalty as a behavior that negatively impacts the mission of the district. Are you following me?"

"Yes, but you're painting a pretty generalized picture without offering specifics. To be honest, I won't be of much use if what you want is a workup on subtleties of behavior. Normally, clients provide us with specific charges to follow up on, such as embezzlement or theft. Without knowing how it's acted out, disloyalty could be no more than a state of mind. Records, specific actions, habits, contacts, associates, finances—we handle that sort of thing." Lapointe's notebook lay open on his lap, but he had entered nothing more than McPhaiden and Wainwright's names and positions. "Frankly, unless you can offer specifics, I don't think we can do anything for you." He closed his notebook and sat back while they exchanged glances.

Again Ms. McPhaiden took charge. "Specifically, we're dealing with two issues and two people whose insubordination and disloyalty can't continue. It also involves others who have been terminated or reassigned. It also seems that one of the people may have made himself vulnerable by profiting from the sale of real estate to the school district. What we need is specific evidence that will help build a case for his dismissal."

Lapointe said, "That's better. Of course I'd need a list of the employees who were let go or moved. How many are we talking about?"

Wainwright said, "All told, no more than twenty."

Lapointe whistled softly. "Then here are your issues: First, if an investigator checks out twenty or so people in one school district, your investigation is out in the open. But maybe you don't see that as a problem. Next, you should understand that with schools being public entities, an investigation could cause more issues than it solves."

McPhaiden cut in. "You let us worry about that. A bad apple in the barrel must be dealt with. Please understand that we are addressing a situation that, because of its nature, is more important to this district than anything else. Now, I (Lapointe jotted a note about her choice of pronoun) want you to start with a short list of reassigned employees that we'll provide. We know that some are resentful and spreading disloyalty because of their transfers. It is essential to identify the individuals who are beating the drum, and since the teachers' union is a hotbed of discontent, you might start there. The fact that so many of them enjoy drinking might be of use to you."

"Okay. But I can't emphasize enough that the project you propose has upsides and downsides. We always advise clients to weigh costs against benefits, and by costs we include downside results like resentment and loss of trust among employees. I need to make that clear to you."

"You've made your point. Now, what else do you need?" she said.

Wainwright seemed content to let McPhaiden carry the ball.

Lapointe took the lead. "Two things: I need the legal description of the property and the identity of the person in question. Does he or she have a name?"

"Yes, everything you need to know to begin is in here." She slid an envelope to Lapointe.

"The twenty or so employees you mentioned, do some of them have a favorite watering hole?" he asked.

"Yes, and unfortunately the whole community knows about it. You'd do well to visit the Over the Fence Sports Bar at four thirty on a Friday afternoon." Ms. McPhaiden stood to indicate that the meeting was over.

Lapointe pulled his laptop from under his car's seat and opened the Northbridge file. From the three tabs marked Internal, Report to Client, and Observations, he selected Internal and entered:

Met with client 11:00–11:45 a.m. 05/28/06. Principles: Charles Wainwright, district supt, Claudia McPhaiden, chair school board. Client displeased with specific employees' lack of loyalty, stirring discontent, profiteering on land purchase. Client intends to terminate subjects, wants actionable info to build case for dismissal. Observation: Clients may be acting out personal feelings. Clients not realistic about possible negative fallout. Note: Clients' complaints were sufficiently vague to suggest that inv. might not yield definitive results. Inv. of subjects will certainly come to notice. Clients' expectation of secrecy unreal.

His next meeting with school district brass left him no more confident of his purpose than the first. The woman was late in arriving, missing the first question he put to Wainwright: "Though you indicated there were two suspects, the only name you gave me was Clausen. What about the other?"

"The other situation resolved itself," Wainwright replied.

"Good, that simplifies things. Next, we need to discuss the hours you want Clausen observed. Also, how essential is it that he doesn't know he's being investigated? Overt investigations are quicker and far less expensive." Figuring he'd laid enough on the table for the moment, Lapointe settled to take notes.

Wainwright drew from his personal well of paranoia. "He's not to know he's under suspicion, is that clear? And about your so-called basic package, can you assure us we'll get more than the image he's built for himself? We need to know what goes on under the surface of his life. Is that clear?"

"Yes, but I can find only what's there."

"Oh, come now. You can't be that innocent. There aren't all that many pitfalls to corrupt a man's life—gambling, women, alcohol, drugs, money, deceit. Find out what it is, and go from there."

"Once again, only if it's there. You're telling me that the subject is, in some manner, corrupt, and you want me to dig into his private life, collecting information until offenses against the school district are confirmed. Correct?"

"Yes, that's the essence of it. Think real estate; that's where you'll find the dirt." He looked to McPhaiden for agreement.

"Just a moment, Charles. Why are you limiting this to Mr. Clausen? What about Mr. Runyon?" McPhaiden had just arrived and was still adjusting to her chair.

"When you and I talked, I thought we agreed that he'd taken himself out of the picture."

"No, no, no, not soon enough. In the end, we might have to work around Clausen, but I refuse to leave one stone unturned as long as Runyon is on the scene. I read his contract and couldn't find anything to rid us of him. Nothing was fast enough."

"Don't worry; Runyon's toast."

Lapointe waited for the superintendent and board chairperson to sort Runyon's fate. Neither yielded so both names stayed in. He said, "Fine, as long as we're all on the same page. My next step is to draft a confidential authorization for your signature." Let them think its standard procedure, Lapointe thought. He'd sized up Wainwright as a highly placed flake, the worst kind, and should things work out not to the flake's liking, Lapointe didn't want him with grounds to complain about the service he got.

Lapointe was completing his second year with Seattle's Dern McComber and Sessions, specialists in security and investigations. After a three-year hitch with the MPs, followed by earning an associate's degree in criminology, he signed with the Seattle Police Department, only to be saddled with grunt work. Toward the end of his first year on the force, a friend with DMS Security dangled an offer before him that was too good to turn down. The Northbridge High gig was his second assignment without the supervision of a senior agent. Gordy Sessions, his supervisor, backed him from the home office. Jimmy Corbin, an old hand with the firm, was ready to cover extra hours of observation if needed. Having reviewed LaPointe's initial reports, the only positive DMS Security saw in the yet-to-be-signed contract was unlimited billable hours.

Lapointe was dressed to blend with the teaching staff. In his late twenties, he wore his hair in a short, blow-dried shag. His brown horn-rims, black loafers, and casual jacket and tie fit the scene. The only thing setting him apart was the blue trim of his security pass that marked him as authorized by the head office. It was eleven fifteen on Wednesday when he helped himself to a cup of coffee in the faculty lunchroom where early-lunch cliques took no note of him. His other hand closed over two portraits copied from last year's yearbook; both were now lab assistants for Runyon. He entered the lunchroom to take a position across from Terri Weatherby, a counselor who drew first lunch supervision on Tuesdays. Ten minutes of the lunch break remained when his eye caught a girl chatting with three friends at a half-occupied table. Aside from multiple earrings, black lipstick, and lime-green bangs, it was the Karin Torstad of one of the photos.

Lapointe began weaving a pattern among the tables, which piqued Terri's interest. Sensing her attention, he gave her a wave and pointed to his pass, which only heightened her curiosity. She watched as he caught his foot on a bench leg, slopping tepid coffee onto his wrist. Karin Torstad pivoted to catch him wincing.

"Oh jeez, man. You get scalded or something?"

"Wow, hot stuff," he said, blowing on his hand. He set the cup on her table and said, "May I sit?"

Karin pulled back and asked, "What are you, a sub or something?"

"No. Just fact-finding for the district office."

Karin tossed her head, throwing green bangs aside to give him a once-over suitable for a horse auction. She said, "Hey, if it hurts, get some lotion or something at the nurse's office. It's down that hall." She turned away.

Lapointe fanned one hand with the other. "No, it's okay. Can you tell me how to get to the biology classrooms?"

"Yeah. Out that door, straight ahead to the E building. That's it."

"That's where Mr. Runyon's classes are held?"

"Biology, yeah. Whaddya wanna know for?"

"Have you had a class from him?"

"Uh-huh."

"Good teacher?"

"Yeah. At least he tries to make it interesting, which is more than I can say about some people. So what are you? An auditor or something?"

"No, just a fact finder. Tell me, you like his style of instruction?"

"I just said so, didn't I? He's not standoffish, and he doesn't get all bent out of shape when dumb kids ask stupid questions."

"Is he more sympathetic to one group, say males over females?"

"I think he helps the girls more, but that's just because the guys think they're better at lab work."

"Has he helped you?"

"Sure, all the time."

"That's great, especially since girls don't typically pick off top scores in science classes. We could use more teachers who stimulate girls."

Karin inhaled deeply and stood. "No more. I don't like where this is going." She turned away and poked a number into her raspberry-colored cell phone, which sent Lapointe into full retreat toward the faculty lunchroom. The call had to be about him, but if so, to whom? He'd know soon enough if the person on the other end was connected with Wainwright's office. Terri Weatherby watched his retreat from her position by the serving line and made mental notes to have a talk with Karin Torstad and check on passes issued by the central office.

Runyon looked up from a stack of test papers. "You're early, Karin; what's up?"

"Look Mr. R, it's none of my business, but you know, there's been all this talk."

Sensing trouble, he turned back to his work and said, "There will always be talk. Is there something I can do for you?"

"I don't mean to butt in, but there's this guy who came into the lunchroom and started asking questions and stuff."

"What sort of questions?"

"About you." He laid his marker aside. That got his interest, she thought.

"Have you seen him before?"

"No. He was lots younger than you, sort of a college prof kind of dresser, and he had a security pass, but it was blue, not red and laminated like yours."

"Anything else?"

"He had sorta long wrists, or maybe it was short sleeves. And when he smiled, his cheeks lifted way up like this." She pushed at her face. "He was just sort of a medium kind of guy. His skin was a little dark but not like he'd been tanning or in the sun. Oh yeah, he had dark-rimmed glasses, and his hair was like he paid more for haircuts than teachers do."

Runyon couldn't help but smile at the comparison. He mumbled, "Thanks, kiddo. Check the prep area. You'll see a list of things for fifth-period lab. Two test tubes per station. One of everything else. Okay?" He turned on his way to the door and added, "Once again, thanks."

The rest of his day passed in a blur. Most of his students caught his remoteness and granted him space; others turned petulant when he didn't give them the attention they craved. Constant reminders that he was still the focus of the school's rumor mill had him backing from his parking stall at the earliest permissible time to drive upriver for twenty minutes to a stretch of shoulder where fishermen parked. He threaded his way down through salmonberry and devil's club to where seasonal high waters swept the bouldered banks free of rank growth. He sat on a rock watching crystalline water sluice by, welcoming its hypnotic effect as shadows lengthened.

Jane was at the mailbox scooping out a stack of flyers when Lapointe's Jetta pulled to a stop in front of Garnie's gate. With Dogwood Drive dead-ended five houses to the east, so few nonresident vehicles passed that each stranger was a matter of interest. The driver didn't budge. Probably cell phoning, she thought while riffling through junk mail for something worth opening. Across the street, Lapointe was listening to a KVI talk show debating a rumored reinstitution of the draft. As a veteran, anything military caught his ear though thoughts about returning to the military had dimmed with the Iraq thing dragging on. He pulled himself back to work by switching to Public Radio's classic jazz and noted the time in his expense register.

He angled his mirror to watch the woman. Her economy of features, build, and grooming made a package that was…natural, the one word that seemed to fit. He gave up trying to peg her age closer than between thirty-five and fifty. Soccer players and runners looked like that, but the ones he'd met were younger and not the type to live in suburban Cape Cod homes.

Jane watched the driver's head bob to a rhythm. White, with no bumper stickers, the car could be a company car, maybe real estate. On her way into the house, she crumpled a handful of flyers into the recycle bin in the utility room where she had yet to finish folding clothes. On her next pass by a window, the car was still there. After some minutes more, neither it nor its driver had moved. In fact, Lapointe was logging addresses on his laptop to check against real estate values. Jane watched as he pulled along the curb to another house, and another, until he disappeared from sight into the cul-de- sac. Five minutes later the Jetta idled past Jane's window and drove away.

Midway through third period on Thursday, an office assistant delivered a sealed envelope to Dale. The message was pure Wainwright. He was to "upon receipt of this message, arrange with the principal's office to exit the campus and report to the superintendent's office without delay." Having expected it, he wasn't shaken. Instead, he was angry that Wainwright would kick him out so close to end-of-the-year testing, putting punishment ahead of what was best for students. He stuck his head into the biology prep room. "Liz?"

His teacher's assistant looked up from a Harry Potter book. "Yeah. Whatcha need?"

"Can you watch things until the end of the period? You okay with that?"

"Not a problem." She watched him move to his demo table from where he surveyed the environment he'd developed: the posters and cartoons, the quick-reference charts, and the technology he'd scrounged and wired over years of tight budgets. The room was so much a portrait of his educational vision that it was impossible for him to envision anyone taking his place. He stood a moment too long, drawing quizzical looks from students. With his bag in hand, he walked to the door with half the class's eyes following him, opened it, and turned one last time with a lump in his throat to silently mouth, "Goodbye."

He walked straight past Alice and into Tom's office. When he spotted Cal Staehli, head of district security, he sat and asked, "You here for me, Cal?"

Staehli nodded.

"Nice touch. You want to cuff me?" He held out his wrists.

Tom spoke. "Knock it off. Cal is as upset as we are. He asked if you would leave on you own. Just so you know, Wainwright ordered him to take you off the campus."

Dale shrugged. "Sorry, Cal. I'm understandably a little upset right now. Has it occurred to you that you work for a piece of shit?"

Staehli nodded, drawing a thin smile from Tom.

Dale clapped his hands together to break the tension and said, "Well, you guys both have jobs to get back to. Let's get this over with. Bye, Cal. See you around, Tom. I'll be in contact about getting my personal stuff boxed." He wheeled and was out the office's back door before either could offer a parting handshake. When Tom rushed to catch him, Dale turned on him amid a hall full of students and blurted, "Go back. No more now. I'm out of here." He carved a path through the crowd and was gone, leaving Tom rooted like a post, sick at heart in the midst of streaming traffic.

Runyon nursed a remnant of his fabled cool as he approached the school district's central offices. He took a visitor's parking stall and presented himself at reception, seemingly as upbeat as ever. "Dale Runyon to see Dr. Wainwright. I think he may be expecting me." Time dragged by. He expected the wait, hoping that Wainwright, only a few steps and one door away, was equally discomforted. When noon came, he pulled out his phone and a loyalty card for Alfie's Pizza. He called in an order for a small Canadian bacon and pineapple to be delivered to the district head office. Time passed. His pizza arrived, and he sat munching while passersby threw curious looks at his lunch. At twelve forty he scribbled a note and asked that it be delivered to the superintendent immediately. It said, "Returning to my classroom. Call when you have time to see me. Runyon."

Wainwright flew out of his office in seconds to stop short at the sight of Runyon, pizza box on his lap, munching contentedly.

Wainwright growled, "Inside," and stalked back to his office, Runyon following in his tracks. The superintendent took a position facing the window, his back to his desk. Runyon laid the box on a corner of the big desk and took a seat. When the superintendent turned, his eyes went wide. "Get that off my desk!"

"That?" Runyon shrugged and retrieved the box. "One slice left. Have you had lunch?"

Wainwright pointed an unsteady finger at him. "You impudent... you impudent..."

"You need a noun to go with that." He took a bite and chewed slowly, staring unblinking at the superintendent.

"Listen closely to me. You're fired!"

Runyon replied in a honeyed tone, "And you listen closely to me. I will not say anything to you that's actionable, so if you have a recorder going, it won't do any good. First I want you to know that the entire school district knows you as a vindictive son of a bitch." Runyon cut off Wainwright's bark of complaint. "That was not slanderous, nor was it petty name-calling. It is pure and accurate description."

Runyon would never know how much of his short speech Wainwright took in, occupied as he was with shouting threats that failed to stem Dale's flow of acidic logic and protections under board policy. "You shut your mouth and get out of here!" He punched his intercom and shouted at his secretary, "Send Staehli in! Out of the building? Then call nine-one-one...I don't care. Tell them we have at trespasser."

Runyon pulled a sheet from his jacket pocket. "Bad move, boss. What'll they say when they find out you invited the trespasser. Now back to business. As to my being fired, you may relieve me of my duties, you can deny me access to my classroom, and you can even restrain me from contacting students, but if you take time to read district policy, you'll find that the best you can do is recommend to the board that I be terminated. In the short term, your best shot is to put me on administrative leave, or whatever you call it."

Though Wainwright's voice was cracking, he was far from out of ammunition. "I'm going to make you sorry you were born. You're a disgrace to teaching, you, you, you...you're going to regret you ever stepped into this office. You'll see; you'll see."

"Oh, stuff a sock in it, and do try to control your bleating and listen. Now here's your situation: Until you put together a compelling case for dismissal and push it through channels, I'm still drawing salary, boss. For my part, what really bothers me is that I gave the likes of you an opportunity to hurt me. I really pity little people like you who get their kicks by bringing their betters down." Runyon put the empty pizza box back on the desk. "You take care of this. I'm late for my tee time."

"You come back here!"

Runyon was chuckling mirthlessly as he turned at the door. "Was that a change of heart? Does that mean I'm hired again?" Something in Wainwright's murderous scowl told him he might be pushing him too far. Brushing through the cluster of staffers whispering excitedly beside the superintendent's door, he stopped by the reception desk and said, "Try to stay clear of the boss if you can. He seems a little peckish."

He plopped into his car, shaking. Never before had he taken someone down verbally and was disturbed that he enjoyed doing it. When his mind quieted, he wasn't surprised to feel thankful that Wainwright, trusting in his conceit, had ordered him to appear for a last scourging. The mistake Wainwright made was thinking the difference between their ranks could make him crawl. Dale felt no regret for forcing him into revealing himself as more bluster than substance. The bonus was watching him witness his own undoing. Runyon had his number, and whether he was fired or not—or whether Wainwright continued as superintendent or not—he would always know he'd been bested, something bullies don't easily endure. The thought left Dale feeling a little lighter than when he had arrived.

Dale pulled a Diet Pepsi from the fridge and stepped out into his backyard. The starts he and Betty had planted seven years ago had grown into maturing shrubs and trees. Evidence of his planning and labor, much of it with Roger's help, lay in every direction: a concrete retaining wall, landscaping timbers, the eight-by-eight garden shed, and raised beds for a token vegetable garden big enough to supply summer salads. The carbonated Pepsi sat poorly in his nervous stomach. He poured it into the lawn on his way to the garage where he surveyed walls and rafters hung with possessions. He wouldn't need much, certainly not the tire chains for a car they no longer owned or the canoe paddle that lacked a canoe. Aside from his golf bag, the whole collection could stay put for the time being.

He was searching for a missing sand wedge when Betty's car turned in. From the garage's side window, he saw the kitchen lights go on. And the ski stuff. Two pairs of used-up skis, bent poles, and a ski rack that fit the same car as the tire chains. He watched her pass the kitchen window. Shelves of half-used cans of paint filled a quarter of one wall. So many off-whites had collected dust that it was a chore to find the right match when a blemish needed covering. Why hadn't he labeled them? When the kitchen light went off again, he steeled himself for Betty's contempt and entered the house. He found her standing by the dining table.

"Hello. I hope your day went reasonably well." Inane, measured.

"I managed."

"We're going to have to discuss changes. Is this a bad time?"

"Lately, any time is a bad time. What did you want to talk about?"

"First, you. What do you plan to do?"

"That's my business. As far as you're concerned, nothing having to do with me is open for discussion."

"Fine. Next, I'll need to use the spare bedroom for a couple of days. After that the house will be yours, along with whatever else you want."

"No contest?"

"No contest."

"And the children?"

Dale walked to the fridge for a glass of milk to soothe his stomach. He called back, "They haven't been children for years. They'll make up their own minds."

"I suppose so."

"Good. Before we try to deal with anything else, I need to know something. How long have you known you didn't love me?"

It was Betty's turn to walk to the kitchen. Dale heard the microwave click shut as she reheated breakfast coffee. She returned to sorting mail at the dining table. "Interesting. I'm not sure I ever did. There were times I thought I did, and there were times when I was sure I didn't, but even then I was never unfaithful. Unlike you, unlike this last indiscretion."

"You know there were no other indiscretions."

"Do I? Anyway, beyond this recent indiscretion, I have been so very disappointed in you."

It was not what Dale expected. "Disappointed?"

"Yes, disappointed. You never turned out to be the man I thought you could become. You're no more than another Bill Clinton."

"Thanks. You've made this easier for both of us. You just admitted that you didn't marry me for who I was but for what you thought you might shape me into. Sorry that your grand plan didn't work out to your satisfaction. We should apologize for tying each other up in a marriage that should never have been."

Betty thrust her chin up and snapped, "Don't you ever expect me to apologize to you!"

"I don't, but it would help if you could."

Betty put the mail down to study him. "You're acting quite strangely. In fact I've never heard you quite like this. What's going on?"

"End of a career, end of a marriage, shopping for a new home. That combination can cause a person to act a little strangely, don't you think?"

"Your job's gone? Are you sure?"

"All the way gone. District security came to Tom's office to escort me out, but it didn't come to that. Then I stopped for a nose-to-nose with Wainwright during which he left no doubt that I was persona non grata. But that's not the big issue here." He walked to the mantle to retrieve a crystal award he'd received for excellence in teaching. He held it out. "Do you mind?" She shook her head. He pocketed it and continued, "What matters is that I'll be out of your life. You're still a beautiful woman with a lot of years and a world of possibilities ahead."

"You put me in a difficult position. The last thing I want to do is concede that you might have a point. Aside from being unfaithful, you do still seem to have some small grasp on logic."

"For whatever that's worth. Enough for now?"

CHAPTER 9

Tom slept poorly, discomforting dreams jarring his rest. He and Dale were in an inflatable boat drifting down a quiet river. Fishing was involved. The river morphed into a Galilee-type storm during which Dale fell over the side and paddled about, swimming toward or reaching out to the boat. The scene changed again, this time to whitewater and boulders. When Tom grabbed at Dale to pull him aboard, he shook loose and pushed the raft away. Afterward, he lay wide-eyed and sweaty. Jane snuggled against him, her hand tracing down his arm to find his hand and lace her fingers with his. She put her face near his ear and whispered, "After yesterday it's no wonder you're sleeping poorly. Think about us, and maybe your mind will clear. May I have a hug?"

The morning following Dale's disturbing exit, Tom called Wainwright's office to book an appointment. Sheila told him the superintendent wasn't taking appointments for the rest of the day but called back within the hour to tell him he could have fifteen minutes at four o'clock. He arrived early, sat, and tried to quiet the ache that had dogged him since his friend walked out of his school and maybe from his life. He was feeling no better and sensed a disquieting irregularity in his pulse when Sheila announced, "The superintendent is ready to see you now."

Wainwright leaned back in his chair. "Well, Clausen, I've seen to one of your main problems. With Runyon out of the way, I'm hoping you'll be able to focus your full attention on improving test scores." His smug jibe at Dale's situation shook Tom's fragile self-control.

"Dr. Wainwright, before you removed Runyon, did you consider that the tests you're concerned about are next week, and that every one of us has to do everything we can to help students' minds to be focused and ready—that is if we're committed to getting the results we'd like?"

"What on earth are you talking about?"

"In pulling Runyon off the job, you traumatized five classes. The only thing those kids will be thinking about is the loss of their favorite teacher. Advanced biology and computers? You must know a combination like that is practically irreplaceable."

"That's hogwash. No one's irreplaceable. Not Runyon, not you."

"Nevertheless, you should consider the possibility that a serious mistake has been made. It may well be that you had grounds for dismissing Dale, but there's a right and a wrong way to go about such things. We're nearing the end of a school year. In the interests of education, he should have been kept on until the end of the semester or at the least until dismissal proceedings were completed."

"Mr. Clausen, I'll say this just once: This is not your business. Your responsibility does not extend to hirings or dismissals. Is that clear?"

The rest of the conference went no better. Tom left the head office to drive to Dale's house, where he found the driveway empty and the curtains pulled. He was about to call from his cell phone when a low-slung Honda Civic with thundering speakers pulled up behind him to drop off Roger and speed away. Roger ambled to his window and said, "Hi, Uncle Tom. I expect you're here about 'the situation.'" Tom nodded, clicked the door lock, and invited him to sit.

Roger slid his seat back and pointed to a fence. "It's not like it came as a complete surprise. Mr. Kingston, our neighbor over there, had cancer for so long that we never knew him when he was well. Anyway, when he died, his family didn't go into shock. When you can see something coming, you're prepared. Ellen and I have talked about it. The way she put it was that Mom and Dad spent more time walking around each other than walking together. We thought they'd stick it out together until we were out of school like most dysfunctional parents do. They almost made it. Mom seems okay. It's Dad I'm worried about. I know that guys are supposed to be less sensitive than women, but not Dad. He feels everything. I wish there was something I could do."

"Me, too." Tom reached to give Roger's shoulder a squeeze. "I guess those of us who love him are going to have to wait for the hurt to die down."

"I don't think 'hurt' is the right word. He's mixed up."

In his preoccupation, Tom hadn't understood that Roger didn't yet know about his dad and Wainwright. He said, "Roger, 'hurt' is actually too small a word. The superintendent fired your dad."

Roger slammed a hand against the glove box. "No. I don't believe it. He could fire Mrs. Markowicz and so what, but Dad? Teaching is his life. You know how good he is. You can't be serious." Roger read his face. "You mean it. It's true then. Couldn't you do something about it?"

Tom told Jane about his day. She stayed close as he picked up the phone again and pressed redial to get the same recording, "Please leave a message." "It's Tom again. Please call." He tried TV, he tried reading, but nothing covered the sour taste of the day. Jane brought him a glass of wine, but it tasted harsh. At eleven thirty he gave up and crept into bed, layering an extra pillow to keep an expected bout of acid reflux at bay. Sleep came at length.

Tom wakened to the fumes of greasy, cholesterol-laden delights that rarely graced the Clausens' kitchen. When he padded downstairs tousle-headed and still in pajamas, Jane shooed him off for a shower while she butchered a grapefruit. Carbos and cholesterol aside, Jane was working a therapy on her man that, as he later forked another sausage from the platter, seemed to be working. "Doing better, dear?" she asked.

"Trading one issue for another. Eggs, waffles, sausage, coffee—one more bite and I'll need a stomach pump." He eyed the remaining quarter waffle and said, "Tell me to quit while I'm still ahead." He rose, rubbed his stomach, and rounded the table to plant a sausage-flavored kiss on her lips. "Delicious. Just the thing for chasing the blues away." He took her plate. "You sit. I'm on dishes."

Jane was off running errands and Tom was under the kitchen sink tightening a leaky drain trap when the phone rang. He thrust himself out to catch it before the call switched to the recorder. Rising from the floor left him light-headed. It was Garnie.

"Thomas, whatever you're doing, you simply must lay it aside. Aunt Sigi needs you."

"What's going on, Garnie? Her ankle acting up again?"

"No, no, no. She's at the police station. It seems she backed into a car and then drove away. The driver of the other car followed her, and, well, she called the police, and they arrested Aunt Sigi for hit and run. They arrested her! She's probably at her wit's end. You have to bring her home."

"Why me? Why not you?"

"Oh, balderdash. Why did I even call you?"

"Out with it, what's the matter?"

"Oh, I let my blood sugar go a little out of balance. Nothing to worry about, but I don't think I should drive quite yet. I'll find someone else."

"Where is she now?"

"At the police station. Didn't I already say so?"

"At least she's safe there. As soon as Jane gets back, we'll go together. What if there's a fine or ticket to pay?"

"Oh, for heaven's sake, I suppose that would be possible. Look, come over here and I'll give you a signed check. All you'll have to do is fill in the amount."

"And if they question me for floating someone else's check?"

"You needn't worry about that. The police are well-acquainted with Aunt Sigi's driving habits. They've handled my checks twice before."

Tom saw his Saturday eroding away to nothing. "Okay. I'll be over to pick up the check. We'll take care of it."

"You're a good friend, Thomas."

"Sure I am. Will she find you in good shape when we deliver her? If she comes home to find you on the verge of diabetic collapse, it won't be a pretty scene."

"Don't talk to me as though I were a child. Just bring her back in time to start dinner."

"You're impossible. Goodbye."

Jane put a hand on Tom's arm as he released his seat belt. "It might be better if I take the lead, girl to girl. Being arrested and hauled off to jail must have been a shock, especially at her age. Just imagine if you were in your eighties and dragged off by the police. Lights flashing, breathalyzer, Miranda rights—she couldn't handle that. Come on. Let's see if we can rescue her before they do any more damage." He followed her to the police department's high-security information window where a touch on a push-button brought a uniformed clerk. "Jane and Tom Clausen to see a detainee, Sigrid Halvorson."

A female officer appeared at a door at the end of the corridor. "Mr. and Mrs. Clausen? Please follow me." Officer Carerra led them to the door of a first-floor conference room. Through the window they saw Sigi sitting with a Styrofoam cup in front of her, apparently at ease and engaged in lighthearted conversation with a middle-aged officer.

Jane's jaw dropped. "Well, how about that. Next time, remind me to keep my anxieties under control." She turned to Officer Carerra. "She's not upset? No shock, no tears?"

"Nothing of the sort. Once we got her to realize she'd bumped another car, she had a moment of worry about what her car's owner would say—according to the registration its owner is, let me see here, Garnet Pittman. She's a dear. All our collars should be so sweet." Aunt Sigi brightened when they entered the room but kept still while Carerra updated the officer with her. "Arnie, Mr. Pittman called in. Mr. and Mrs. Clausen are friends of Sigrid's. Can you coach them through what needs to be done?"

Sigi put on a distressed face. "Oh, Mr. Clausen, I'm afraid I'm in a terrible fix. Is Mr. Garnet coming?" She reached to put a hand on the officer's sleeve. "Oh, my stars! Where are my manners? Mr. and Mrs. Clausen, I'd like you to meet Arnie Steffanson. Arnie is my friend Karl's nephew. Isn't this a small world?"

Officer Steffanson rose to shake hands. "Has anyone filled you in?" When Tom said, no, he patted Sigi on the shoulder. "Our public enemy number-one here tagged a nearly new Lexus when backing from a parking stall in the Safeway lot. Her car was barely moving when it crunched the rear light cluster on the driver's side. The owner of the Lexus witnessed it and called out for Ms. Halvorson to stop, but she drove away. The owner called 911 and gave the route the hit-and-runner had taken. We alerted officers who gave pursuit with lights and sirens at all of twenty-two miles per hour for the couple of blocks it took to get her pulled over. She claimed she never hit anyone until we pointed out her scuffed quarter panel. According to the report"—he passed Jane a police form—"you can see here that she said, 'Oh, my stars. Look what's happened to my car.'"

Jane asked, "What do we have to do to get her home?"

"Well, the Lexus's owner's pretty upset, her car being less than a year old. Mr. Pittman's insurance will certainly cover repairs. If it will cover a rental for the time the Lexus is laid up, it may help to soothe feelings. And since the collision occurred on private property, the incident report doesn't have to carry a traffic citation. The big issue here is since this was her third incident in four years, Ms. Halvorson will have to appear before a judge to discuss the future of her driver's license. It's important that someone talks with Mr. Pittman about this. Can you do that?"

"Sure. What about her car?"

"She understands that once the impound fee is paid, it can be picked up from the lot any time, but we advised her that it would be best if someone accompanied her. It also might be wise for Ms. Halvorson to stay off the roads until after the hearing. Is there anything else you want to ask?"

Jane reached for Steffanson's hand. "Thanks for the way you handled this. We'll do what we can to see that the right thing is done." She offered her other hand to Aunt Sigi to help her up. "Time to go home, Aunt Sigi."

The centerpiece of Tom's fishing equipment was Rusty, a 1964 Ford half-ton pickup that slept under the trees near their back fence. Rusty's space between a pair of needle-shedding firs was well-shaded, which encouraged algae. Tom tried to start it once a month and even power-washed it once a year to monitor the rust metastasizing upward from the lower margins of riddled body panels. Two things separated it from the dead hulks abandoned behind nearby sheds: its current license tabs and twin arcs of transparent glass on its windshield.

Another owner might have called Rusty "the pickup" or "the Ford," both mere descriptions. Rusty was family. Tom owned it before he and Jane married. It once hauled materials to remodel and landscape their home, and it had taken them camping. Tom loved Rusty not only for its utility but also because it linked him with the era of wrench-and-screwdriver auto repair. Now in an advanced stage of decay, Rusty's duties were limited to annual runs to the dump and hauling Tom's boat to a nearby launching ramp on the slough.

A ten-foot aluminum skiff, dented and creased from years of rough landings, nestled bottom up in a carpet of fir needles in Rusty's bed. Rusty and the boat testified to Tom's disinterest in fussy maintenance. In the right light, its interior glistened with fish scales.

Fishing was an excuse. In truth, Tom ventured into nearby sloughs and creek mouths to gain the company of solitude, that rare and enveloping friend no human company can provide. Herons, eagles, red-winged blackbirds, surface-skimming swallows, and the colonies of doves that nested in trees high on the north bank observed his visits. Rising mist and reflections sometimes lent the illusion that he was drifting in space where solitude and nature were free to work their restorative magic. Not capable of being entirely idle, Tom found the simple demands of fishing to be the perfect foil to the slough's otherworldliness. With all of that, he might have tired of the slough experience were it not that tidal cycles require frequent adjustments to navigation and fishing tactics. And every year was unique in that spring runoffs repositioned the bars and shoals that determined where the elusive cutthroat trout might rest. This time there would be a new variable: Jane was going with him.

He asked, "Did you load the thermos?"

"Aye, aye. Are you sure one tie-down is enough?"

"For as far as we're going." He checked the strap over the bottom of his upended skiff, snugging it tighter.

"Sandwiches and life jackets?"

"Behind the seat."

When he pried her door open, Rusty's deformed passenger door grated against fender metal with a raucus scraaawk. Jane rolled her eyes as he handed her in and said, "You really know how to impress a girl, Mr. Smooth Operator."

He was rounding to the driver's side when her cell phone chimed. "Yes, this is she. Oh, I'm so glad you called. We were hoping to hear from you. You haven't? Well, of course, I'd love to have you stop. When? Would it be possible to make it later? No, that's all right, I'll be here. See you soon." She pocketed her phone and gave Tom a somber look. "I'm sorry. That was Ellen Runyon. She hasn't been able to raise anyone at home. Betty phoned to tell her it would be best if she stayed in Seattle for a few days, and you can imagine how she took that. She wants to stop by this morning. What could I say?"

"I'll stay, too."

"No. you need downtime more than worrisome conversation. Besides, it'll be better if it's one-on-one. She needs a girl to talk with." Jane stretched on tiptoe to nuzzle his neck. "I'm sorry, sorry, sorry. Should I have told her to bugger off?"

"Not your style, Mrs. Mender. You have to do it because it needs doing. Besides, you can be replaced. Wheeeet." At Tom's whistle, Buster dashed to waggle against his leg. When he patted the passenger seat and said, "Up!" Buster clawed and wriggled onto the seat where, aside from his dripping tongue and broad dog smile, his posture was almost human.

Jane followed Tom to the driver's side. Addressing Buster, she said, "You boys be careful." And to Tom, "For your information, I plan to make up for this—candles, wine, the whole nine yards. You go get your R&R while I take care of Ellen. Come back to Momma, and together we'll figure some way to put distance between us and the world's problems. A deal?"

"A deal." He shifted into low and called out, "Don't plan anything for dinner. I'll bring fish."

She shouted after him, "I've heard that one before."

The tide had passed low ebb when Tom dragged his boat to the water. Once afloat, he pulled it broadside to the ramp to check his gear. Satisfied, and with Buster aboard, he pushed off, yanked the starter cord, and moved downstream to carve a bow wave that set perfect reflections of the far bank in motion.

Lapointe watched from a finger pier of the marina immediately upstream from the boat launch. In his short career, he had endured the boredom of hundreds of hours surveilling suspects from cars or afoot, but with this boat thing, he was ready to pencil in a number for however many hours it would take Clausen to get back. The scene was beautiful, but if he had written the script, he would be in the boat and Clausen would be on the dock.

He thought about Wainwright and the McPhaiden woman. Just yesterday she'd relaxed her animosity toward Runyon, saying, "Yes, the Runyon situation is solving itself. You have only to investigate the real-estate link between Clausen and Pittman and provide a record of where he goes and what he does when he gets there." Lapointe looked at the calm water, the reedy opposite bank, and the clear sky and muttered, "So here I sit. Some surveillance. Hours to bill for doing what?" He walked back down the dock to where a small dinghy with a tiny motor lay dry moored on the dock beside a converted seiner that radiated soft rock music. He called out, "Anybody on board?"

"Hi there. Whadja want?" The woman was in work clothes, a black T-shirt, and bib overalls. Sinewy and weathered, she greeted Lapointe with a gap-toothed smile.

"Is that little boat yours?"

"Yeah, why?"

"Could I rent it? I mean right now. I'll pay you well."

She took in his clothing: street shoes, slacks, and stylish cruiser jacket that might have been Pendleton. "How much you pay?"

"Twenty-five an hour, and I'll need gas."

"Make it thirty-five. First hour upfront."

He pulled out his billfold, peeled off some bills, and handed them up to where she reached over her rail.

"And your driver's license," she added. "It'll be waiting when you bring the boat back. Not after dark, you hear?"

"What about gas?"

"The motor don't burn much. You got three, four gallons in the red plastic tank. Any more 'n that, you're on your own."

One bend downstream, Tom shut down his motor to drift. He tied on a green and white crocodile spoon, pinched on two split shot sinkers three feet ahead of it, set his rod in its holder, and cranked up the Evinrude again. The engine's soft puttering was all but blanketed by the roar of traffic rumbling across six lanes of freeway bridge a half mile upstream, yet the mirrored slough possessed all the other qualities of quiet.

The shores were pocked by inlets bounded by walls of reeds, marsh grass, and loosestrife that drank up the freeway din to grant space for the "check-tee-eer, check-tee-eer" call of red-winged blackbirds. He followed a row of rotting pilings, reminders of when rafts of logs destined for mills were once tethered there. Ahead, near the right bank, a heron stood motionless against a background of tall reeds. Tom watched as it switched its head to a new position, freezing again until his approach sent it flapping slowly off to find a more private fishing spot. He read a change in light and motored into slack water where he cut power to free both hands for switching to a brighter-colored croc. His boat drifted to where a creek with no perceptible current entered from the north before wetting his line again.

Under power again, he nosed into the current and set his eyes on his rod's tip to watch for the quiver, indicating that the crocodile was jiggering as it should, thirty feet astern. His fishing was a matter of reading the water while holding a course as close to the bank as possible. Tom worked favorite stretches for a half hour without a nibble before reeling in to run downstream to give the slough's mouth a try. After two fruitless passes there, he switched to a brass and silver Canadian Wonder and trolled back upstream.

He was abreast the garbage dump when the fish hit and took line. He punched the engine's kill switch and set about the careful business of keeping the small hook set without horsing the fish. After three frisky runs, it all but swam into his landing net, a bright, fourteen-inch, sea-run cutthroat trout. Hoping that where there was one there might be another, he motored back a hundred yards for another pass through the same water.

The dump, closed for some years, was euphemistically termed a landfill. During its years of operation, unclassified garbage barged from Seattle had been spread across a marshy island between sloughs. Layer by layer it rose, each one capped with fill dirt until it became the highest land in the estuary. From its top, one could trace the slough from saltwater to the freeway bridge near Northbridge. As Lapointe drew closer to it, its top looked like a perfect place for surveilling the slough. If he could get up there, he would list his time as "investigative initiative."

He nosed the dinghy onto the dump's reedy shore where, with his bow aground, he tied his boat's painter to a stubby branch protruding from a driftwood log. He pocketed his socks, hung his shoes around his neck by their laces, rolled his pants above his knees, and stepped over the side, only to sink to his waist and momentarily lose track of his shoes. By pulling at the boat and its mooring log, he levered himself from the mucky bottom to slog onto firmer footing among reeds where he drained his shoes and slipped them on without socks. He routed his climb up a rainwater-cut cleft to reach the top, soon learning to be watchful for hazards when painful contact with a protruding piece of plastic pipe opened a small gash on his ankle. Once on top, he moved to the shelter of a parapet of soil bulldozed to the landfill's brink, where the grassy depression he crouched in trapped enough sun to abate his chill. When he propped his elbows atop the parapet, he spotted Clausen's boat moving slowly upstream from the lower reaches of the slough. The panorama was lovely: the reflections, far-reaching marshes, and Puget Sound stretching to distant blue-gray shores. Aside from the dunking, he congratulated himself on discovering a perspective he suspected few others had enjoyed.

He checked his watch. Seven hours on the clock already. One more and he could choose to log overtime or call Jimmy Corbin for backup. On weekdays, he'd used Clausen's work hours to check the man's credit report and record of arrests, ferret out investment information, and generally see if he lived within his means, and so far Clausen had come up squeaky clean. While tugging on a soggy sock, he reflected that the Northbridge gig had definitely turned out to be the weirdest assignment he had worked, stranger even than the wife who was certain her husband was sneaking off to meet a lover when, in fact, he drove to Tacoma weekly to spend an evening with cross-dressing friends—not gays, not transvestites, just guys who liked women's clothes.

After it became clear that Wainwright and McPhaiden had sent him on a fool's errand, he'd called the office to try to get the contract canceled, but Howard, his boss, told him, "Look, Tim, we blocked out ten days on your calendar for Northbridge. In other words, there are no other files on your desk. You've got five more days up there, so do what you can to stay with it." He was doing just that.

With his socks and shoes back on, he pulled out his cell phone. Luckily it was in his jacket that didn't get soaked as badly as his pants. He thought the guys at the office might get a kick out of where he was, so he tried dialing. No signal? Maybe it did get dunked. No matter, it would keep. Water squelched from his hundred-and-twenty-dollar shoes when he shifted weight. Damn, what a waste. As he tied his laces, he thought about how he might educate his clients regarding their errors without calling them stupid. Wainwright, what a butthead! Cover every waking moment, he'd said. Impossible. Wainwright and McPhaiden were all over Clausen like flies on a cow turd, except that Clausen checked out as a decent, all-American guy. Oh well, it was going to cost them. And the McPhaiden woman, what a bitch. He pulled out his notebook and jotted some numbers on a dry interior page: $105 for the boat, another $100 for getting dunked. And one way or another, they'd come across with $120 for his shoes. He watched the boat inch upstream. "Fishing. Let 'em make something of that." He sniffed. "Man, this air stinks."

His attention to his subject heightened when Clausen jerked his rod's tip upward and began playing a fish. From his distance, Lapointe saw the flash of silver in his landing net. "Well, how about that," he said to himself. "Nice fish." He kept his eyes on Clausen until the boat turned downstream again, at which time he ducked back into the sun-warm depression at the parapet's base. Unaccountably headachy, he rubbed his temples for a moment before lighting a cigarette.

Tom felt a change of pressure on his eardrums as though suddenly changing altitude. The slough's surface riffled as a single breath rushed across it to send birds into flight. At the event's epicenter atop the landfill, an invisible fireball of ignited methane bloomed around Lapointe's lighter flame with a soft suddenness that said whoooomp! Had he held his breath and closed his eyes, he might have suffered no more than singed body hair, but he gasped, inhaling a pint or two of the chemical reaction. And because that breath brought him little oxygen, he gasped again.

Panic set in when more deep breaths failed to satisfy his bloodstream's demand for oxygen. He mustered his remaining strength to struggle over the parapet and tumble head over heels into brush at the water's edge. Panting to make up for his seared lungs' diminished capacity, he looked for his boat, but both it and its driftwood mooring log were moving upstream on the incoming tide. And then he heard Clausen's motor putt-putting beyond a brushy shoal. He tried to shout but produced only hoarse croaks. He stood and waved, but the effort left him light-headed. He caught glimpses through the reeds of Clausen trolling beyond the shoal, heading upstream toward the boat launch, and taking his only chance for help with him.

Lapointe picked up a driftwood stick half the size of a baseball bat and threw it with all his might. It splashed down to send out a considerable ripple. He saw Clausen turn to look for its source before resuming his course. Lapointe grabbed up the next thing available, a waterlogged piece of cedar shake, not so heavy or aerodynamic but it was at hand. Mustering his last strength, he heaved hard, but it flew high and short, fluttering like a bad Frisbee.

The shake flew into a corner of Tom's vision. Having spent countless hours plying the same waters, he was quick to note changes or events. He throttled back and swung toward the landfill, wondering if kids might have taken to playing on its top. Not good, he thought, what with the methane problem and the real possibility of stumbling into toxic hospital waste. Following the focus of Buster's yipping and whining, he inched toward a screen of reeds where turbidity marked action, his propeller churning a muddy trail from the rising bottom. He was holding Buster's collar to keep him from going over the side in the direction of his interest when the motor bit into the bottom and died. He raised it and poled forward, following Buster's lead into a patch of reeds he parted with his oar to find a man sitting waist deep. His eyes pleaded as his head bobbed in rhythm with convulsive breathing. Tom leaned over the bow to seize the man's collar.

Holding on to him was one thing; getting him aboard was another. Tom thought of climbing out to thrust the man's weight over the gunwale, but when he tested the bottom with a hip-booted foot, it proved too soft. With his boat half-lodged in reeds, he found it impossible to swing broadside to do his work. Time was wasting. He pulled with all his might, roaring and grunting to inch the man's body from bow to beam where, at risk of capsizing, he grasped two handfuls of his coat and lunged backward, forcibly drawing his top half aboard to collapse face-first against the boat's bench seat. Rolling his legs aboard was a smaller problem. He positioned himself in the bow to reach for handholds on both sides of his collar and lunged back again, straightening him along the boat's length. After rocking free of the bottom and poling from the shallows, Tom reached a depth where he could lower the motor and yank it into life. He slammed the throttle full open.

Tom and Buster leaned into the breeze, stirred by their passage. The motor's little pistons pushed the boat at upwards of ten miles per hour, cutting the mile-and-a-half run to less than ten minutes. He shouted for help when skirting the marina's finger pier, incautiously nicking a sailboat when rounding up against the dock where he screamed at two zombie-like onlookers to call 911. The entire incident—finding the man, getting him to the marina, calling for help, and being questioned by police—lasted no more than forty minutes of surreal confusion. He thought he might be in shock.

Tom motored slowly from the marina's pier to the boat launch where he rolled the little boat on its side to slosh out mud and bits of marsh greenery. With his outing cut short, he took time to be methodical about rinsing, loading, and securing it. He wanted to give Jane plenty of time with Ellen, and he wanted to feel more settled when he saw her. He thought of how, evening after evening, Jane had absorbed so much of the impact of his recent issues. And now this. Better to let it come out naturally, which would happen soon enough. He considered the dishonesty of holding back, which she would see through in an instant anyway. He strapped the boat down and drove to the marina where he pulled a pencil from his tackle box and left a note for the owner of the sailboat he'd scratched.

Jane turned from putting groceries away, took one look at Tom, and demanded, "What happened?"

He raised his hands as in submission. "Please, finish what you're doing, get changed, and then we'll talk, sort of like we lead a normal life." He stepped to the fridge and pulled out the two cleaned trout. "Tell me they're pretty fish."

"They're pretty fish. Now what happened?"

"Please, hon, give me a minute. Tell me about Ellen. Did she know anything about what Dale's doing?"

"Okay, you get your reprieve, but don't think for one minute that you're off the hook." She waited until he gave her an acknowledging shrug. "Dale has a new cell with a new number, so that's why you're not reaching him. Ellen has it, but he made her promise not to give it to anyone else. They've talked twice, but he didn't have much to say about what he's doing, just tried to assure her that he's fine. As to where he's staying, all he told her was that he's found a place near Moraine. He said he wanted to see her but vetoed her driving up from Seattle. They arranged to meet at a coffee shop near the Seattle Pacific campus yesterday. She said he looked older. He apologized and said it was all his fault, that she should remember that Betty was blameless, which lit Ellen's fuse. She told him that she loved her mom, but that didn't alter the fact that she sometimes acted like a passive-aggressive terrorist. Isn't that a terrible thing for a daughter to say? Must be studying psychology."

Jane said that Ellen and Roger were in agreement that it would have been easier on everyone if their mom and dad had fought a little to relieve the everlasting pressure. "Can you believe that children talk about parents that way?"

"Unfortunately, we have no way of knowing, but it does seem the Runyon kids have grown up all of a sudden."

"How true. And she said that she and Roger are working up a plan. At least they think they are. They're looking to redefine the Runyon family—still a mom and dad and two kids but with the lines drawn differently. Ellen's focused on her parents' welfare, not her own. If you could have heard her, you'd have been so proud of our levelheaded goddaughter. But oh, my goodness, what a talker! The rest of it was padding, you know, conversational filler to keep things from getting too intense. And speaking of things getting intense, you're going to learn a new definition of the word if you don't open up. Out with it."

It had been only ninety minutes since the police worked to penetrate the shock that tied Tom's tongue. They were able to extract enough to fill a report but not enough to keep him from having to give a more complete statement the next morning. At home with Jane beside him and the confusion of the scene at the marina behind him, he sucked in a deep breath and said, "Let's walk." The words had barely escaped his lips before Buster scrambled to waggle and whine between them and the door, his slobbery excitement peaking when Jane reached for his leash.

Tom took the leash since Buster pulled toward his side during their walks. They walked the three-quarter-mile round trip from the cul-de-sac to the intersection twice before Tom finished his story with "And then they hauled him away, leaving me to wonder what it was all about."

"You say he spoke your name?"

"Sounded like it, but it was hard to tell with the motor running wide open."

They walked on, hand in hand, separately searching for cause or meaning in the events of a disturbing month.

"This has been some month." Her calm concern was a match for Tom's deliberate description. Reflecting on gale-force winds that once toppled trees in the neighborhood, Garnie once commented, "You lack sensitivity, Thomas—human responses, that is. While your more normal neighbors rush about in a state of panic, you and Jane fly into deep calms."

Back in the kitchen, Jane said, "I can't keep pouring wine to soothe your ruffled nerves, or we'll both be flaming alcoholics. Do you suppose we've done something that's put us in the midst of all this bother?" She bustled nervously from one task to another, wiping out the sink, repositioning countertop appliances, and dabbing at spots with a dishcloth.

Tom intercepted her and set the cloth aside. "Come with me." He led her to the living room to pull her down onto the sofa beside him. "I suppose one of us had to ask that question, but look at it this way: The world is full of bad stuff. Everything that's happened, happened to other people, not us. It wasn't me who got fished from the slough. Phil got canned, not me. Dad took a tumble, not me. The Runyons are splitting, not us. I'm losing a teacher, but I still have my job. Garnie's sick, not me. My boss is an even bigger jerk than I am. No, Mrs. Worrywart, it's been business as usual with the Clausens. Aside from what you'd expect from a husband who works for a tyrant, nothing out of the ordinary is happening here. How about you? Any unusual blips on your screen?"

She toyed with his fingers for a moment. "It probably doesn't mean anything, but the day before yesterday a man in a white Jetta was cruising our neighborhood. Probably a real estate salesman."

Tom barked, "A white Jetta?"

"Yes. What's special about a white Jetta?"

"There was a white Jetta parked by the marina. The police checked it out and found it was registered to an investigator named Lapointe, the guy I pulled out of the water." With their faces pressed so close, he couldn't focus on the gray-green pools of her eyes he asked. "How badly do you want to find out what's going on?"

"Does that mean you have a plan?"

"No, it means I'm about to do something, probably something stupid. Grab your purse; we're headed for the hospital."

Northbridge Police Chief Larry Tuininga and Tom had once shared the same workout schedule at the Y where Tuininga worked with free weights while Tom and Dale played racquetball. The give-and-take of locker-room banter had tested and cemented a friendship that allowed Tuininga to ease police procedure for Tom's interview. Rather than a sterile interview room, they met in Tuininga's office over bottled water.

"How's he doing?" Tom asked.

"Guarded condition, whatever that means. If he'd been shot, they'd tell me where and by what, but with the medical privacy thing—and, as far as we know, he's committed no crime—all I get from them is that he suffers from diminished lung function. We were hoping you could add something."

"Is this for the record? You want a nothing-but-the-facts rendition?"

"Uh-huh. I start the recorder, give the date and time. Then you state your name, et cetera, say what you were doing, and give the circumstances that led to finding him, that sort of thing. Try to keep the time line running straight."

It took Tom almost ten minutes to relive the incident on the slough. Tuininga penned notes as he spoke, once stemming an impulse to interrupt when Tom remarked that he thought the man, now known as Timothy Lapointe, had called him by name. The most difficult part for Tom was relating his slow race back to the boat launch and marina, cursing the little motor for not pushing them faster. He spoke of his lingering image of Lapointe, glassy-eyed and puffing, unresponsive to questions as though comatose. He recounted his reckless approach to the marina, scraping against an immaculate blue Ranger sailboat, and yelling at everybody within earshot to call 911. He recalled the boat owner who couldn't stop gawking and asking stupid questions to make the emergency call, the wail of sirens, the wonderfully efficient EMTs, the police and their questions that for some reason he had trouble dealing with, their search of the man's billfold, and his eavesdropping on the police discussion—Timothy Lapointe, cards from a Seattle private investigation company the cops didn't recognize, Lapointe's notebook with dates and times. He remembered the police scouring his boat for anything meaningful and an officer commenting, "Nice fish," as he hoisted them for his partners to see. And then they were gone. Tom tried to explain how he felt standing there alone, except for a foul-mouthed woman who wouldn't stop carrying on about losing her boat.

Tuininga touched the pause button. "Anything else you want to add?"

"Like visiting him in the hospital?"

"You did? Let's hear about it." He touched the pause button again.

"Jane and I drove into Port Gardner, figuring he'd been taken to General Hospital. That was about four thirty yesterday. It took some doing to get in. The attendant at the south desk turned us away after asking if we were family. Funny, because when we checked with the information desk at the north side, they gave us his room number. It must have taken time to get him stabilized because a team of three was still in his room when we cruised the corridor. As soon as they finished and cleared out, I ducked into his room." When Tuininga looked up accusingly, Tom said, "Hey, there's no law against visiting patients, is there? He definitely recognized me, no doubt about it. He wasn't up to talking with a breathing tube in the way, but he sure wasn't pleased to see me. How's that for gratitude? Anyway, his expression and body language, like turning away from me, said it all.

"I tried talking to him, introduced myself, and said I hoped he was doing all right. Still nothing, so I asked what he wanted done with his car. I kept at him in a low-keyed sort of way until he rolled back toward me and made a writing motion in the air. There wasn't any paper handy so I handed him my pen and the bottom of his Kleenex box. He printed 'no comment' and turned away again. Do you know anything about this?"

Tuininga shut off the recorder. "I'm as stumped as you are. As far as I know, there's been no crime committed. The only things we know are that, according to what you say, he might know who you are, and he might have been checking out your neighborhood. And he'd rented the woman's boat, but since it was picked up and returned, there's no issue there, which leaves me wanting to have a heart-to-heart with his boss. All I can suggest is that if you and Jane come up with anything more, you could try hanging a restraining order on him, not that he's going to give you any trouble for a while."

Lapointe's next visitor was Howard Sessions of Dern McComber and Sessions. Sessions, florid and overweight with a crew cut, pulled the TV remote from Lapointe's hand and punched Mute before taking a position behind the brown, plastic-cushioned guest chair Tom had occupied two hours before. He pulled readers from his jacket pocket, laid a notebook open against the back of the chair, and began, "Sorry about this, Tim, but we have issues to settle. Can you understand me?" Lapointe nodded. Reading from notes, Sessions proceeded to tick off points: the firm had severed relations with the Northbridge School District; the district would be charged for all hours up to but not including the day of the accident; the firm required that he have no further contact with the school district, Clausen, or Runyon; and they would provide transport to a Seattle hospital as soon as his release could be arranged. He emphasized that Lapointe would enjoy the firm's medical coverage as long as he said nothing about the Northbridge contract. Sessions stepped to the bed to pat Lapointe's arm. "Rest well. We'll be in contact." He left, leaving Lapointe to restore the din of NASCAR racers orbiting a subtropical course.

CHAPTER 10

It was Dana's second day back at work. Though her injuries proved superficial, the cosmetic damage of dozens of rashy punctures had kept her housebound until boredom became harder to bear than fear of being seen in public. Her father, Martin Koutac, who stayed with her through the first night, showed uncommon sensitivity by having a three-inch round button made that said, "Don't ask." She wore the stark, yellow-on-black button pinned to her denim jacket. Most of the children had been either kind or too self-absorbed to notice. A few shied away as though thorn cuts were contagious. All in all, it was easier than she expected, and each morning the inflammation was noticeably less than the day before. It was on that second morning at work that she accepted that there might be light at the end of the tunnel.

Grandma Marie picked up Pip from school, keeping her for the hour and a half it took Dana to finish her last run and clean her bus, ninety minutes during which Pip was supposed to do homework—time her grandpa cut into for games or trips downtown that spoiled Pip's appetite for dinner.

Dana bounded into the Koutac kitchen and called, "Mom?" It was reflex. From the time they could reach the doorknob, Dana and her sister, Trish, had barged in that way, and as adults, neither showed signs of giving it up.

"Gone shopping," Martin shouted from the den. Dana walked to the den to find Grandpa and Pip competing in a silly computer game where penguins dived in front of a Yeti with a club, the object being to get the Yeti to bat a penguin across a snowy waste. Martin said, "One more turn, the kid has me by five yards." After triggering the Yeti's swing too early, causing the penguin to do a header at the Yeti's feet, he gave his desk chair over to Pip. "You take over, honeybunch. Your mom and I will be in the kitchen."

Martin pulled down two mugs and poured tepid breakfast coffee from a thermos. "How did it go?"

"Not bad, considering. Kids can be nice when you need them to be."

"Are you ready to talk yet?"

"Maybe. Don't expect me to lead off."

"That's to be expected. My concern is that, while you're nicely stitched up on the outside"—he inspected her, touching a spot at her hairline—"the hurt inside might stay raw for too long. It needs to be looked at."

"Are you suggesting a shrink? Not this time."

"Okay, honey. We'll work it out. Is there a chance that you might accept that you did something dumb and that you're disappointed in yourself? Would I be off the mark to suspect that you don't want Pip to be disappointed or influenced by this situation?"

"Of course not, Dad! It's just that this whole business hurts so bad in so many ways that I don't know what to do next."

"Then don't rush to do anything. Forgive me for being nosy, but how did you and Runyon happen to hook up?"

"Softball. It was all perfectly innocent. At first."

"Mm-hmm. Right up to when he made a move on you."

"No, Dad. You've got to understand that...may I say this my way?"

"Shoot."

"You have to understand that no matter how pissed I am with him, it wasn't his fault. I led him on. I made the first moves. He was so proper and reluctant, and yes, I knew he was married, but he seemed...lonely. What got me going was how he seemed to focus on me like he couldn't get enough of talking with me, and that felt good. Do you know how long it's been since I've been out with a guy? My history with men—present company excluded—made Dale seem like Prince Charming. He was so nice, and I felt great about the little things he did for me. I mean really little things like holding a door for me. It was all so new and wonderful. After so much time of nothing much happening in my life, I felt like a nun who'd just broken out of a convent. And then Prince Charming showed me his ugly side. I know, he was married and was afraid to be seen with another woman. I get that. But he sent me out in the dark while he walked out under a light. That was wrong. I can't help believing that he was ashamed to be seen with me. I may be patched up, but the hurt from that's not going away."

Martin took her cup, set it aside, and wrapped an arm around her shoulders. "I wonder… I wonder what it'll take to patch up Runyon."

Dana pushed away to give him a hard look. "What's that supposed to mean?"

"Maybe this isn't the time, honey."

"You started it. What's to patch up with Dale?"

"What I said was patch up Runyon, not patch up with him. But since we've taken that detour, give this a thought: You led him on; he let you down. Judging from the penalties you're both paying, that sounds like a wash."

"That's easy for you to say. I'm the one who had to be patched."

"Outwardly. Runyon, though, was removed from Northbridge High, is being terminated, and will probably never find a job in education again. Claudia will see to that."

"She can't!"

"That's what lots of people have said about her, but she's proved most of them wrong. As long as she can muster two more votes from the board, it seems she can do anything. Shall I go on?"

"There's more?"

"Unfortunately, yes. Marriages seldom survive this kind of publicity, especially if the injured party, in this case Mrs. Runyon, claims the moral high ground. The fall may be too much for her to accept or forgive."

"Why are you doing this to me?" Dana collapsed against the table, sniffling and dabbing at her eyes.

Martin stepped behind her to lay his hands on her shoulders. "I told you this might not be the time. But as to why I'm saying these things, it's because you're a good person and because I love you. You're too good to let yourself wallow in self-pity any longer than necessary."

"And?"

Martin dumped his untouched coffee into the sink. "You didn't go through this alone, so you shouldn't expect to be the only wounded party. An important step in pulling yourself out of it is facing up to the whole of the reality, and that includes what's happening with your tarnished Prince Charming. You have to face this because the goodness in you won't let you heal if you don't."

She reached to cover one of his hands with her own. "What makes you such an expert?"

"Let me put it this way: a situation in your father's distant past had enough similarities to allow him to say, 'Been there, done that.' That's how you get to be wise. That's why they call what you're going through wising up."

"Well, forgive me for not feeling wise yet. Where do I go from here, Dad?"

"Home. Give Pip more than enough love to quiet the anxieties she must be suffering. Her classmates, as you well know, can't be counted on to be as understanding as your bus kids. Forgive yourself. Try to forgive Runyon; it'll help his chances of finding his way out of this. See if you can make a success of tomorrow. And come back soon, honey. Anything you're in, I'm in. Helping you helps me, too."

Dana began sniffling again. "I'm sorry; I really screwed up. I'm so sorry, Dad."

"Of course you are, honey. That's a good place to start."

Roger's call to his father's new number clicked to an answering service again, and again he left a message. "Dad, I understand you want some time alone, but this is getting ridiculous. Since you're obviously screening calls, I'll call again tonight at eight. Please pick up when it rings. Ellen and I love you."

Dale was avoiding not only telephone contact but also all contact with his past life, preferring the solitude of his car or his weekly rates room at the Travelodge. The distance between him and his well-wishers wore on him like a migraine, but he found it impossible to face anyone, believing he had earned exile. Roger's eight o'clock call caught him finishing dinner at Denny's, his phone's chime turning the heads of neighboring diners. He agreed to meet after the three o'clock exodus from campus thinned, which left enough daylight to do what he'd planned. Seeing no other course than hiding until the rumor mill found a new target for its speculations, he parked on the street below the school's tennis courts where he was less likely to be spotted.

Roger jogged to the car and jumped in. Dale said, "Hi, son," and drove south to join early commuters merging onto Highway 2. Dale broke the silence. "How's it going?"

"Okay, I guess. Ellen and I are dealing with it."

"I'm sorry. It must be upsetting. Your interview for the CWP scholarship, is this going to affect it?"

"It could have, until we found out you weren't dead in a ditch somewhere. You've been somewhat out of touch, you know."

"My fault. You'll let me know if there's anything I can do to help?"

"You can start by answering calls." Roger steeled himself to ask the question he'd been sitting on. "About that night, is it true? I mean about another woman? You don't have to say anything if you don't want to."

His father let a half mile go by before answering. "Yes and no. Yes, very briefly there was. No, I'm not with her. It was all very sudden and traumatic—for both of us."

"I'm not surprised, not about the trauma but that you were seeing someone else."

Roger's comment shook him down to his foot, which slipped from the accelerator, causing traffic to stack up behind. "You think that little of me?"

"No, it's not that. I just…I just thought that, well, not all your friends had to be guys. What I mean is that you and Mom never hit it off like most couples."

Dale muttered, "Do me a favor and let me know where you're going with this."

"Don't be so touchy. What I mean is you're entitled to a life, too. I suppose it would have been tidier to end the old one before starting a new one, but that's the way it goes, I guess."

They turned south at the Moraine intersection instead of north, which would have led them into the new city. The access road led through the partly developed but architecturally attractive Moraine Industrial Park to where banners on the first phase of a three-floor apartment complex advertised for tenants. The exteriors of the buildings, dubbed Cheshire Hills, were simulated half-timbered Tudor. New, old-fashioned gaslight fixtures glowed sodium yellow in the late day, and driveways were surfaced with simulated cobbles.

Roger asked, "Jeez, Dad, do they have garages or carriage houses?"

They parked in a numbered stall, and Dale led the way to the rear where he skirted a dumpster to reach a ground-level door opposite a wall of landscaping stone. "I talked them out of a key for the afternoon. Come on in." He pulled the curtains to admit afternoon light. "Well, what do you think?"

The air was thick with new-carpet smell, so new that fluff left by the laying crew hadn't yet been vacuumed away. Manufacturer's labels on windows and kitchen appliances carried user warnings and energy-consumption ratings. A bundle of simulated wood baseboard on the living room floor indicated that the unit was still some days from occupancy. Roger surveyed the kitchenette and living-dining area. "Kinda small, Dad. Are you sure you'll survive in a place like this?"

"It's seven hundred square feet. I like to think of it as a good fit, not a step down. Actually, I could do with a studio, not a one-bedroom. The main thing it has going for it is it's close to technology. Some of my ex-students work here. Who knows, I might end up working for one of 'em. And get this: this one rents for ninety less than identical units that lack views of dumpsters. Let me show you something." He pointed to a wall jack. "I have my choice of DSL or cable—free. I pay the phone bill, but internet service is included with the rent, which brings me to a problem: Do you think your mom would be upset if I retrieved my PC?"

Roger looked up from inspecting the under-the-counter refrigerator. "Dad, I think you've dumped a major guilt trip on her. She's not comfortable knowing she ran you off with nothing but the clothes on your back. I think she'd like to talk—no, I think she needs to talk with you again. Soon."

"That would be good. I'm still a ways from having the right words, so it won't be right away. But I'll do it; I'll do it. I'll call her. She's a good person. I'm determined not to cause her any more pain."

Roger stepped close to look his father squarely in the eyes. "Dad, stop. That's enough of that. What you're leaving out is that you're a good person, too. You and Mom did a fantastic job of toughing out a lot of years together, and all for Ellen and me. If either of you decides to stay miserable, you'll be dumping a guilt trip on us. Try looking at it from our point of view: How do you think it makes us feel that you invested so many of your years in a dead-end marriage, for us? Do you want us to feel responsible for messing up the rest of your lives, too?"

"How long have you known?"

"A long time. There's a big difference between knowing you guys were wired differently and knowing you had serious issues. I guess we began to know when we started visiting friends' homes. It isn't hard to tell the difference between natural affection and the forced kind, and there wasn't anything easy or natural about you guys. The first time I saw Jason Kohler's mom and dad kissing, I mean compared with you guys, they were making out. I got so embarrassed seeing how they held each other that I had to run outside. It took a long time to figure out that they had it right, and you didn't. What's really weird is how knowing that made me feel guilty—like if I hadn't recognized it, everything would be fine. Ellen felt pretty much the same. She and I never talked much about it until you came back from the New Orleans trip."

Dale was far from easy about having his marriage analyzed by his son, but he saw no good way to stop it. "That transparent, huh?"

"Well, duh. You didn't have to draw us a map. One thing I have to say for both of you; you were always civil and never fought, though it might have been better for everybody if you had yelled at each other a little. When you got home from that trip, you split from each other so fast that we were scared one of you wouldn't come back. And then things settled down to the Runyon version of normal. Cold but civil."

"Rog, how did you get to be so mature in so few years?"

"Promise you won't laugh?"

"Promise."

"You saved the best of yourselves for us. Good parenting. While you were hard on each other, you were wonderful to us." Leaving his father speechless, Roger turned to the gas fireplace to check its controls. "The place does have a few bells and whistles. Are you serious about taking it?"

"Yes."

"Good. It'll be a relief to know where to find you. Ellen said to get a promise from you."

"And what might that be?"

"She and I need to know for sure that you'll call Mom because she's not going to call you. We want a promise. The longer you put it off, well, you know, it might never get done. You two have things to talk out like our role in this. We'd kinda like to know where we fit into the new order of things, whatever that is. Do we have your promise…like before the end of the week?"

"Consider it done. Now I have one for you: Were you serious about moving out?"

"If I can work it, yes. I have enough in the bank to carry me for a while and a few hundred a month in programming fees coming in. No apartment, just a room."

"What about the university? You picked up more than a thousand in scholarships."

"Seed money. With student loans I should have it covered. I'll need your signature as cosigner, though."

"Rog, don't do this. It's like you're trying to drive a wedge between us. You know that your mother and I still stand ready to support your education. What's eating you?"

"What's eating me? So much is up in the air right now, like who lives where to who pays for what. I'm just making sure I stay on track. Let's just say that there was a time when it was a good thing a military recruiter wasn't handy when you guys were sniping at each other. No, make that when you just sat there and let Mom walk all over you."

"You just crossed the line, Rog. You'd do well to rethink that criticism. Think it over. When it comes to your mother, you, Ellen, and I did whatever it took to keep the peace. Fortunately, you have no idea of what might have happened if I got confrontational with her."

"Okay, okay, I'm sorry." Roger slumped against the kitchen bar with his eyes shut before snapping upright. "You want to get something to eat?"

The Northbridge library was one of few public places where Tom could count on not being disturbed. No Alice to break his concentration with "Call on line two." No Jane with "Sorry to interrupt, but if you're going to take off to play golf, you'd better hop up and fix the kitchen light switch like you promised." But social rules found no traction where Garnie was concerned. Tom's chair afforded a view of the main aisle where his neighbor was bearing down on him, wearing a pugnacious scowl that said there would be no games.

"Thomas, come with me." Garnie's brusque manner was one of many social flaws that Tom had set aside as irrelevant. The celebrated curmudgeon stalked off toward the periodical racks with Tom following in his wake. He withdrew a back issue of the *Tribune* and rattled through pages until he reached page two of Local News. "There it is in black and white. Well, what do you have to say about that?"

"What are you talking about?" Tom knew perfectly well that he had homed in on a report citing Northbridge's unflattering test scores.

"Hmm. Feigning ignorance doesn't become you. I am asking you as nicely as I can why you are lounging in the library instead of doing something about your school's abysmal scores on the WASL test." The Washington Assessment of Student Learning (WASL) was a battery of rigorous tests given at different grade levels that, contrary to its intended use, had become a convenient way of comparing schools.

Tom smiled benignly. "My friend, I hate to disappoint you, but having been worked over by experts recently, you have zero chance of irritating me. However, I have taken note of your low blow. Even by your standards, tagging me with responsibility for mediocre test results is a little shallow, don't you think?" Tom held a balled fist two inches from Garnie's nose. "Tell me, considering your endearing conversational style, how do you keep from getting your lights punched out?"

Pittman's eyes sparkled mischievously. Easily bored, he delighted in prefacing conversations with verbal bombs to shatter conversational partners' self-control. Once he gained an edge, he set about destroying hapless victims until they capitulated or fled, but he had yet to put Tom on the defensive. Tom called his bluffs, once letting him know that he was behaving like a mean-spirited, ill-tempered, bottom-feeding boor. Garnie loved it.

"The test scores, Thomas. Why the disparity between Northbridge and other districts' scores?"

"Back when dinosaurs roamed the earth and you went to Northbridge High, you knew what the problems were, and they're much the same today. In lots of homes, the fiction that a college degree must be every kid's goal hasn't taken root, thank God. Kids from the reservation get good counseling and are pretty much guaranteed jobs if they want to work. No diplomas required. And there are homes that don't subscribe to a single newspaper or magazine and voters who couldn't tell you how to get to this library. It's a mix. Did you know that the density of newspaper deliveries in any school's attendance area correlates with test results?" Garnie flapped his hands to indicate he accepted the point. "Don't forget that Northbridge's population averages fewer university grads than Moraine or Port Gardner. Parents who haven't picked up college credits are less likely to expect their kids to, either."

Tom tapped the newspaper. "Comparing Northbridge with Moraine is unfair in a lot of ways. The demographics of the two districts couldn't be more different. Moraine's a yuppie town with lots of high-tech jobs; Northbridge is more blue collar. The value of the average home in Northbridge is about two hundred twenty thousand, while Moraine's average is over three hundred thousand. Average household incomes in Moraine are enough that parents pay for their kids' educations while our graduates have to take out student loans." Noticing that Garnie's eyes had wandered back to his newspaper, Tom asked, "Am I boring you?"

"Not at all. Um, you seem to have a rather adequate command of the situation. Do go on unless you've run out of wind." He pushed the paper aside.

"All right. Northbridge's issues are rooted in history, all the way back to when your grandfather was active in the community. Northbridge was a mill town that in some ways still thinks of itself as a mill town. It was people like you Pittmans that donated land for parks, built the churches, funded special projects, and spearheaded school issues. You're the last of them. Aside from you, the breed's died out and the working population hasn't yet figured out that it's now up to them to keep Northbridge's institutions healthy. People need to pick up where you guys left off by accepting responsibility for their kids, their schools, and this town."

"Better teachers would help."

"Yes, that's a problem. But until we improve our image, Northbridge should consider itself lucky to have the staff it has. We have some awesome teachers."

"Would you agree that weeding out ineffective ones would help?"

"I work at that."

"Oh really. And how many teachers have you dismissed in your years as a principal?" Garnie overrode Tom's attempt to reply. "I know what you're going to say. I don't mean terminations for grand larceny, murder, moral turpitude, or whatever. I'm referring to ineffectual teachers, the drones. How many of them have you dismissed?"

"To be precise, one."

"Is that to say that you only had one ineffective teacher? I should think not. Pray tell, how long did it take you to dispose of that one teacher?"

"Just short of two years. It was a fast-track situation."

Garnie harrumphed and shook his jowls. "Disgraceful! The idea that tax money and children's futures are squandered to protect do-nothing teachers' jobs is extremely upsetting. Why, it borders on criminality."

"Due process, not criminality. First, a supervisor, that's me, is required to document incompetence. You don't measure what a teacher does or doesn't do in a day, or even a month. They have their styles, so you have to figure out what they are and why they don't work. Is a teacher not teaching, or teaching ineffectually, or maybe teaching the wrong things? If it's a simple matter of absenteeism, you have the problem of finding out if absences were justified. You don't want to come down hard on a mom who takes her child to cancer therapy. Once you have a handle on it, you go over it with the teacher. Out of that comes a plan for improvement and a warning.

"Anyway, there's a period of time allotted for shaping up, and if at the end of the period things haven't changed for the better—of course it takes more observations to find that out—there's another conference where options are presented. By the end of that next period, significant changes in teaching practice and student achievement must be demonstrated or the teacher's contract isn't renewed. Of course, that means the ineffective teacher stays until the end of the year. But that's not the end of it. Maybe the teacher files an appeal through his or her union. In that case, I'd better have all my ducks in a row because it could end up in court."

"Preposterous. I rather like a system where you confront the offending individual and say, 'You're fired.'"

"Don't have to. Once they know their days are numbered, most make it easy by opting for a career change. If the wrong people are doing the measuring, really good teachers can get slapped down for teaching more than what's required. They just quit. I just lost two of my best that way, and I truly do mean the best. Another was fired but not by me. Unless leadership is truly enlightened—no it's more than enlightenment. Leadership has to accept that good teachers break molds, defy traditions, exercise vision, and dare to ignore mentally lethargic critics. Instead, we work in a climate where teachers are at risk for caring and daring. If they're not terminated, they quit out of frustration."

"So I've heard."

"Sorry, Garnie, but I'm too close to the issue to be comfortable discussing it further. Anyway, you ought to study up on the WASL test. It's really not bad if used for the right purposes."

"Never mind, I found out what I needed to know."

"And that was?"

"Later, Thomas, later. Today's my dialysis day. I must run."

A figure of speech, Tom thought, as he watched Garnie waddle toward the library's main entrance.

CHAPTER 11

The email message from the head office was terse. "Principals Clausen and Nielsen are to report to Dr. Wainwright at 10:00 a.m., June 8. Subject: Standardized test results." Sent and received on the sixth, the directive forced Clausen to reorganize his schedule. Phil Krause, he thought, would have given more lead time and said something like "bring your ideas" or "I'm looking forward to your input." He ran a copy to show Jane.

Wainwright greeted Tom jovially. They talked as minutes passed about the time required for administering the battery of WASL tests. At five past ten, he asked, "Was there any confusion in your mind as to when we were to meet?" Tom said the message was clear. "Then what could be keeping Nielsen? Ten minutes late. Doesn't she understand that there are such things as telephones?" Wainwright's joviality was slipping. By a quarter after, he was up and pacing.

Tom laid out a series of graphs. "I brought some data about trends over the past three years that show gains and losses. See what happened to reading? It looked good in the newspaper, but I'd sure be happier if we could take credit for it."

Wainwright stopped pacing. "That's a strange thing to say. A gain is a gain. Why on earth would you deny your school credit for a gain?"

"We're all happy when test results show improvement. It's just that we didn't do it. It was J. K. Rowling's doing. Her Harry Potter series has kids who never got past Dr. Seuss digesting three-hundred-page books—and discussing them with friends. I suppose we could take the credit, but we sure didn't earn it."

"Another of your theories, I suspect. Without hard evidence to the contrary, the district will accept credit for the change without comment."

The ensuing discussion of teenage reading tastes held Wainwright's interest until, at ten twenty-four, Petra Nielsen rushed in breathlessly and tossed her notecase in a chair.

Wainwright leaned back in his tall, oxblood leather chair and stared balefully at her. Satisfied that his silent scrutiny had her suitably discomforted, he said, "Ms. Nielsen, you're going to have to accept that punctuality is a priority in this school district, whether for students, teachers, or administrators. Are we clear on that?"

"Excuse me. You haven't asked why I was late. May I tell you?"

"Excuse you? Ms. Nielsen, evidently you are not clear on punctuality. When I call a meeting for ten o'clock, I expect it to start at ten o'clock. No excuses."

"Whatever. You'll read about it in tomorrow's paper. Let's get to business so I can get back to school." She pulled her copy of the comb-bound WASL document from her case. "Looks like you're ready, Tom. Let's get on with it."

Wainwright's gaze flicked furtively between his agenda and Nielsen. She had said, "Let's get on with it, Tom." Who does she think is in charge? The comment about tomorrow's newspaper had stopped him for a moment, but he wasn't going to give her the satisfaction of inquiring into it. She had ruined it. The jovial mood and the new goals he'd engineered for his secondary principals faded like a distracted lover's ardor. Made uncomfortable by an upsurge in reaction to his management style, he had really tried to prepare himself, even to shelving his distrust of Clausen for the moment. The plan was to receive them with warmth, chat them up a bit, and then hit them with the expectations he and Claudia had talked over. It had seemed a small thing, a simple message for two principals, yet no thanks to the Nielsen woman, it slipped from his control. She sat there expectantly, having said, "Let's get on with it," as though he was supposed to jump at her command. The least he expected from her was contrition for arriving so late, but no; instead she attempted to gloss it over with take-charge brassiness. Since she wasn't aware of how out of line she was, her inappropriate conduct marked her as in need of correction.

Wainwright handed Tom and Petra copies of his expectations for improvement in test scores. The district called for a gain of 4 percent in math next year, 3 percent the second year, and 2 percent the third year. Demands for other test areas were similar. They spent a quarter hour talking over the new expectations that, if realized, would put Northbridge slightly above state averages, but only if state averages held still.

Tom said, "They look like reasonable targets. What happens if we fall short?"

"Reaching the new standards is your job. We feel so strongly about them being reachable that if you can't, quite frankly we'll be looking for someone who can deliver. In terms the public understands, you are the coach. Your contract will be renewed if you win games. If that seems harsh, look at the positive side. No one can be expected to perform without clear-cut goals, so actually, you might consider these targets as clarifications of your duties. You now know what you have to shoot for."

Petra said, "Or we could do like they did in Texas and Florida."

"And what might that be?"

"They purged their rolls of low-achieving students before testing. At the same time, they boasted of lowering dropout rates. Amazing, huh?"

"Ms. Nielsen, are you suggesting that we break the law and deceive citizens? Is this the example you would have us set for children?"

"Oh, please. That was what we used to call banter. I'm okay with punctuality, but do we have to do without occasional jokes? Sir, if you want to get top performance out of me, you're going to have to let me have some fun along the way."

"On your own time and in your own work environment, Ms. Nielsen. I enjoy a good laugh now and then, too, but you're going to have to restrain yourself from cluttering my time with your asides. Fair enough?"

Wainwright felt in charge again, which gave him room to smile. "I believe we've covered this well enough for now. Good day." He swiveled to his computer, ending the meeting.

In the parking lot, Tom asked, "Okay, what'll we be reading about tomorrow?"

"Gas leak. I had to evacuate the building. But with a meeting scheduled with His Majesty, maybe I should have let the place blow up, kids and all. How much you want to bet I don't get an apology?"

"I don't do sucker bets. You know, his numbers aren't bad, just about what I'd shoot for if it was up to me. His percentages are doable if the community supports them. If they don't, like the man said, we're unemployed."

Buster wagged his body while drooling happily on his favorite toy, a well-chewed Frisbee. Tom bent to wrestle it from his jaws and flipped it into the dining room with Buster scrambling in pursuit. Jane looked up from emptying the dishwasher to grumble, "That is why I refuse to waste money on fancy carpets or furniture."

Tom, having rinsed his hands of dog drool, shelved a stack of plates before cornering her by the microwave. She put up a token struggle and then pressed against him to receive a long, intense kiss. No words, just his arms and the press of his body rocking slowly. Tom's homecoming greetings said more about how his days went than the talk that came later. A pat on the behind and an "Anything in the mail?" signaled an easy day. But whenever his embrace stretched as this one did, she knew something had happened to put him in need of human warmth.

Her breathy whisper tickled his ear. "Who twisted your tail, Claudia or Wainwright?"

Tom was wiping down the counters after the breakfast cleanup. It was Saturday, almost midmorning, and a bright day beckoned through the kitchen window. The *New York Times* crossword had him stumped, and he was too restless to battle it into submission. Jane was deep in the Home and Garden section, leaving Tom to wipe up toast crumbs and finish loading the dishwasher.

"Hey, can you come out of the paper for a minute?" he asked.

She slid her readers to the end of her nose and stared over her lenses at Tom to convey that whatever he had in mind had better be good enough to justify the interruption. "Yes?"

"Let's get out of here, go visit somebody."

"Okay. Who?"

"How about Phil and Sarah?"

"Uh-uh, you'll end up talking school."

"Alice and Jerome? We haven't set foot in the Michaelsons' house for more than a year."

"Negative."

"Okay then, let's give Dale a jingle to see if he'll give us a tour of his apartment."

"No. Lovable as he is, I don't have it in me to sympathize with his plight today."

"Then let's drive up to Bellingham to see how Dad's getting along."

"Better, but still not good."

Tom slapped his washcloth into the sink. "Would you mind telling me what's going on?"

"You tell me. Everybody you suggest is messed up somehow, and you haven't touched on Garnie yet. I'd like to get together with whole people for a change."

"What's the matter with Alice?"

"Do you really want to listen to Jerome hold forth on neck braces, physical therapy, the ups and downs of painkillers, and the latest herbals he's on to keep himself regular? Once was enough for me, thank you."

"But they're our friends."

"I know that, but we're too young for this. When our time for creaky joints comes around, we'll probably get chatty about ailments, too, but not now. All this misery and sickness and job loss and divorce and pain makes me feel like we're living in a critical-care ward. Where are the well people?"

"Right here."

"Meaning?"

"Us. And since staying home isn't helping your gloomy outlook, let's get you a change of scenery. We really should check on Dad. On the way up, we can stop for a latte and a low-fat sticky bun in a sit-down bakery and maybe drop by Costco to impulse-shop and graze food-demo stands—that kind of stuff. We can discuss things along the way."

It was a call from Tom's mother that put them on the northbound freeway. His eighty-four-year-old father had taken a tumble, not the first, and though he broke no bones, he was bruised and stiff. More important was his anger at a body that was letting him down, even during everyday rituals. Her call was a plea to come as soon as he could, leaving Tom to understand that old Walt Clausen, grown irascible in recent years, was driving her to her wits' end.

While Tom drove, Jane opened a book, but every change of speed or passing vehicle had her looking up. He asked, "What's the matter?"

She closed the book and turned to searching FM stations. "Oh, nothing."

"That cloud you're under is nothing? Come on; out with it, girl. What's nagging at you?"

"It's so silly. You'd laugh."

"Try me."

"I know there's probably nothing to it, but, well, it shouldn't be worrisome. Anyway, you got veiled threats from Wainwright, Phil was squeezed out, Dale and Betty's situation, your adventure on the slough and the possibility that we're being investigated, Garnie's health, your dad's fall, and at the latest count, you've lost three top teachers. What's next? I thought trouble came in threes."

"So?"

"It doesn't take a genius to connect the dots. It's like we're at the epicenter of something ugly."

"But..."

"No buts. I know it's irrational. It just seems like there's too much going on to be coincidence. Lately, it's like if we didn't have any bad luck, we wouldn't have any luck at all."

Tom laid a hand on her thigh. "Sorry you're down in the dumps, hon. Times like this I wish we still had the old Chev wagon—bench seat, no seat belts. I'd pull you over for a snuggle." She patted his hand

and held it against her. As they coasted down onto the expanse of the Skagit Flats, he said, "You may have a point. All this hospital stuff. All of a sudden I'm in there twice. Me, the guy who hates hospitals. Before all this started, I hadn't set foot in a hospital since…" He caught himself. Before five weeks ago, he hadn't set foot in a hospital since November 1987 when the doctor who dealt with Jane's last miscarriage delivered the bad news that she would never be able to carry a child full term.

She squeezed his hand. "It's okay. Hospitals can't help but bring it to mind. I deal with that, too."

"Yeah. And tell me why it seems like work isn't fun anymore. I ask myself if I'm becoming clinically depressed and answer no, just discouraged. So, to buck myself up, I do the platitude thing: it's always darkest before the dawn, every cloud has its silver lining, and for every door that closes, another opens."

"There's light at the end of the tunnel." Jane added. "Do you actually find comfort in that dusty old stuff?"

"Not a bit, especially not around hospitals. People in hospital beds aren't in control, especially if they're caught in downward spirals, but that's them, not us. If I had to pick a next-worse place to be, it would be the district office. Wainwright's sucked all the joy out of the place, and unless I can do something about it, he'll screw up my school, too. And Petra's.

"When I get to thinking about good times on the job, they're when I'm not worrying about losing control. Not that I'm a control freak, but I do need to have a grip on things to feel peace. If that slips, my controller side yells at me to pull up my socks and make order of my universe. And then Wainwright comes up with something new to mess things up." He patted her thigh. "Anyway, I've got a funny feeling that everything's going to work out okay."

CHAPTER 12

Garnie phoned shortly before eight o'clock to ask for help with a problem. Tom started the dishwasher and strolled over to find him in the solarium with the local weekly on his lap. His problem, he said, stemmed from an editorial exposing an unhealthy concentration of bacteria in a local pond where children fished and waded. Midway through his tirade about the city's inaction to cure the problem, he uncharacteristically dropped it to get what he'd called Tom over to discuss.

He said, "Thomas, why is it that you have such a disinterest in silviculture?"

"Silviculture? Is silviculture the hors d'oeuvre you're serving before the main course today? What's up, Garnie?"

"Ah, what an odd gastronomic metaphor. You really do have quite a knack for corrupting language. The issue today is trees, Thomas, specifically management of forests. The *only* business at hand is silviculture. There will be no inconsequentialities."

"You mean growing trees."

"Of course, isn't that what I said? But as a supposedly educated person, you should know that responsible foresters do far more than let trees grow willy-nilly." Garnie tried but failed at putting on a contemptuous glare. "Growing trees, indeed!"

Tom muttered, "So you called me over to educate me. Go ahead, but try to make it more interesting than your last lecture."

"You do know that we prefer to plant trees rather than depend on natural seeding, don't you?" Tom nodded and cranked his hand in a circle to tell him to get on with it. "Well, the fuss and bother and expense don't stop there. Say it costs one dollar to plant one tree, and that tree costs another dollar in maintenance, administration, tax, and whatever every year for the rest of its life. We do that every year."

"Okay, you plant trees every year—maybe fifty years to harvest. Let's see, your forest averages twenty-five years in age so if you start from scratch and plant a thousand each year—"

Garnie cut him off. "That's enough. Now assume that I plant ten trees each year, and, for the sake of simplicity, the trees mature in ten years. How much will I have invested in ten years?"

"Ten years plus one, um…" Tom ran the numbers in his head. "If you planted ten each year and all survived to soak up ten years of costs, plus a dollar for planting at the head end of the process, the newest ten cost no more than the one dollar for planting. C'mon, Garnie; where are you taking me?"

"Into reality, my boy. You see, growing trees isn't that simple. A forester must consider that some seedlings won't take root, and those that do will be subject to deer browsing on their tops and disease and drought and lightning and beetles. You see?"

"Except for why you're leading me down this road. You're the one with a history of forestry to draw from. What do you want from me?"

"How insightful, Thomas. As usual you've seen through me. Clearly, I've met my match. One last question: assuming we have just those first ten trees, how might we best protect our investment?"

Garnie, as usual, gave no hint to his cryptic purpose, leaving Tom increasingly impatient. "Garnie, you're playing games with me again. If I answer your latest riddle, will you tell me what's actually on your mind?"

"Don't I always?" In fact, Garnie never divulged his private intentions, especially when touching on his secret areas of expertise. Though Tom usually enjoyed prying his way through Garnie's misdirections to ferret out his purposes, this wasn't turning out to be one of those times.

He said, "Here we go again. As usual, you want my opinion on something I know less than nothing about. Try this on and then change the subject: There's only one way to see it. It's a matter of cutting your losses as quickly as possible, and that means early detection of whatever's diseased or damaged beyond redemption. Now, are you going to tell me what the point is, or do I go home?"

"Thomas, Thomas, Thomas. You take everything so seriously. Why does there have to be a point? Why can't we simply enjoy hypothetical discussions?"

"Because you don't have a hypothetical bone in your body, that's why." Tom picked up his jacket and walked to the door, followed by Garnie's half-chuckling entreaties. "Oh, do stay a bit. No need to rush off in a huff. Thomas, you're not being polite. Thomas?"

The door closed on his voice.

Dale had family records, documents, deeds, and certificates of ownership arranged on the dining table when Pastor Gene Larsen of Lutheran Counseling Services rang the doorbell. Dale and Betty had known Gene for years. Not a divorce attorney, he had balked at Dale's proposal to mediate estate matters until Dale scaled back his role to answering questions if asked. After some cajoling, he agreed to meet with them to explain how other couples had approached their breakups. The estate was uncomplicated: a home with furnishings, two cars, two mutual funds, five acres of undeveloped land, an insurance policy, and a little-used membership in a recreational condo chain. The estate was debt-free except for nine years remaining on the home mortgage. After a delicate first meeting that accomplished no more than agreeing that by focusing on being civil with each other they stood their best chance of resolving issues without rancor, they felt ready to work toward an amicable split. Though their past pattern of resolving issues had Dale bending to Betty's will, they ended their second meeting by assuring one another that they would work toward giving each other a chance at a future, whatever that might be.

Two keys to the harmony were Dale's readiness to yield whatever points of contention surfaced and Betty's sizable inheritance that, along with the house, he was quick to concede to her. In turn, Betty granted Dale their mutual funds and the deed to five undeveloped acres. While they approached decisions about material things with painstaking caution, discussion of Roger and Ellen's needs brought outpourings of generosity. Dale described the austere budget he'd set for himself so any overage could go to college expenses. Betty commented that his budget might be too austere, reminding him that she could start drawing on her inheritance at any time. Larsen looked from one to the other, wondering what he might possibly add to a resolution that, compared with other divorcing couples he'd counseled, appeared to be shaping up nicely.

In the days that followed, Dale and Betty went to war over trivia. He asked for the toaster oven because it would fit his apartment, an appliance Betty said she couldn't do without, having memorized the minutes and seconds it took to cook a perfect freezer waffle or put the right complexion on a cheese sandwich. She recited a list of things it did better than a microwave like thawing bread products. And since it was she who used it most and understood it best, it was silly of him to want it. When he laid claim to the office chair that served his computer desk, she reminded him that it was the only chair in the house that held her in a seating posture that eased her occasional back pain. Of course it was Dale who instigated friction because each of his wants called for taking things from her home.

In less than a week, the harmony Larsen witnessed devolved into bickering that poisoned Betty's telephoned updates with Ellen. It was after her mother's second round of complaints about her father's small-minded acquisitiveness that Ellen called Roger to plan a strategy. They set a date for a family council to be held at Betty's church.

Roger took over when Pastor Larsen was late in arriving. When Betty asked, "What's this all about, dear?" Roger unloaded, charging his parents with behaving like children.

Dale replied, "It may seem childish to you, but we're doing our best to work things out,"

Roger cut him off. "If you keep on in the direction you're headed, you're going to ruin not only your own lives, but ours, too." Chastened, Dale and Betty settled themselves to discuss whether the house would be sold, who would receive Grandma Marta's estate upon her death, and what Dale might need to set up elsewhere. It went smoothly until he suggested that he'd like to stop by to pick up a few things.

Betty asked, "When and what exactly do you want?"

"My pillow, a set of sheets, a couple blankets. I want to go through the bookcase and box up what's mine. You can have the photo album, but I'll have to remove it from the house long enough to get copies made."

Betty interrupted, "Just one pillow? Does that mean you're sleeping alone?"

Ellen jumped to her feet. "Mom, stop it!"

Betty turned on her. "You don't understand your father like I do, dear, and besides, the pillows are matched pairs. If he needs one, he can buy a new one."

Dale folded forward to stare at the floor and sighed. "Okay, okay, forget the pillow. I'll be over Wednesday evening to pick up the rest of the stuff we discussed."

Still speaking to Ellen, Betty snapped, "You see? He chose church night to pick up his things. That means I either forgo church or give him free rein."

Roger's proposal was simple. "Mom, knock it off. You've got Grandma's money, which is more than you'll ever need. If Dad says he needs something you can't part with, give him the price of a new one. Dad, make a list of what you want to carry away. Make sure everything you want is on it because she'll throw a fit if you go back for seconds."

Betty's snappishness about small matters undid Roger and Ellen's plans for détente. Dale ended the meeting with "I give up. We're not getting anywhere." He thanked Roger for giving them food for thought.

Betty told Ellen that she appreciated her input but that she should understand that, ultimately, only she would be making decisions in her own interests. At that point, Roger said goodbye and headed for the door.

Dale called after him. "Wait a minute. Where are you going?"

"Who knows, maybe to join the Marines."

Betty screeched, "You can't be serious."

"Mom, you couldn't have chosen a more wrong thing to say to me right now. Just watch me."

Dale entreated, "Hey, cool down a little. This passion for becoming a Marine came on rather quickly. What happened?"

"What happened is that I love you both, but I'm not going to hang around to watch you chip away at each other. I'd rather be dodging roadside bombs in a desert than be party to this bullshit, and that's the truth. I'm not trying to talk you out of ruining each other's lives; I'm simply stating that if that's your choice, don't expect me to stick around to watch it happen."

Ellen took her brother's hand. "Mom, Dad, that goes for me, too. If this is what our family has come to, you can keep my tuition money. I'd rather spend my life working for OmniMart than taking a dime from dysfunctional parents."

"Ellen, you don't understand —"

"No, Mom, you don't understand. With all your religious education, you still think the world revolves around you. Grow up."

Dale was slumped over studying the floor between his shoes. His voice was soft. "Please, Ellen, if you need to vent, do it at me. We wouldn't be in this situation if it weren't for me."

Roger said, "Dad, I appreciate why you keep saying that, but don't. Just don't. I don't want to hear any more of that crap. Ellen and I have been talking with people, Pastor Lervick for one. Sis is in touch with a clinical psychologist at Seattle Pacific. The message we get comes down to this: You guys spent years screwing each other up. At least now, if you can manage to give each other some space, you stand a chance for new starts. Instead, look what you're doing." He turned at the door to say, "Mom, since the house and everything in it is so precious to you, I'll be looking for another place to crash."

"But where will you go? What about school?"

"No need to sweat the small stuff. You've got toaster ovens to worry about."

"Roger, Roger, what's gotten into you? That was unnecessarily cruel." Though her chin was still high, tears streamed down Betty's cheeks.

"Think about it." Roger reached for Ellen's hand. "Come on, Sis; I'll buy you a Coke."

After the door shut behind them, silent seconds stretched, the only sounds those of breathing punctuated by labored exhalations and gasps betraying inner turmoil. Betty cleared her throat and said, "We've been given an ultimatum. What do we do?"

"Stop the war."

"Talk sense for a change! I'm not at war with anyone."

"Roger and Ellen would disagree. Until we both accept that they're right, we're not capable of doing anything constructive. Maybe it's time to invoke their godparents' responsibility."

"Tom and Jane? None of this was their doing. I won't have them brought into this."

"Even considering what we stand to lose?"

Tom tipped Garnie's riding mower onto its side to expose a thick cake of clippings clogging the chute. He attacked it with a spackle knife, clearing all but the scraps he hosed out with a hard spray. He tipped the little John Deere onto its wheels and turned the key. After a few oil-fuming pops, it started. Tom stuck the knife in his jeans pocket. "No charge this time. Keep it clean and I won't have to come back."

"Well done, Thomas. You're such a wizard with practical things. But why the hangdog look?"

"With free mower repairs, you don't get to pry. Tell me, why on earth are you mowing your weed patch when you should be resting?"

"Because I am alive. Because the air out here is fragrant. Because I refuse to let nosy neighbors dictate how or when I should do what. Because the grass was tall. Is that good enough for you?"

"Oh, don't get all prickly. What I mean is, since you're obviously not in tip-top shape, why not be smart about playing the cards you have left instead of pretending you have a full deck? Cutting out some of the physical stuff might leave enough gas in your tank to propel your brain to warp speed, which, unless I'm mistaken, is your favorite private delight."

Garnie clouded up. "Cards, gas consumption, rocketry—my goodness, you're mixing metaphors today, but you've done worse than that. You crossed a line; don't you ever again dare to presume that you understand what you call 'my private delights.' You would be surprised."

"Come off it! All I'm saying is that if you push yourself beyond your limits and croak, who would I have to insult me? You'd be leaving me in an inane world of platitudes. Now hop on and drive this thing back to the garage. Your complexion says you've had enough for the day. I'll follow along."

"What for? Do you expect me to fall off? What would you do, give me mouth-to-mouth resuscitation? Disgusting! Now you listen to me well: I am going to die, just as you will in time, but then I've always been faster than you when it comes to reaching conclusions. What you must understand is that though I intend to die one day soon, I don't intend to do it all at once. In fact, I expect to be the liveliest deceased person in the Pittman burial plot. You'll see; you'll see." He gave Tom an impish grin and twisted the ignition key, but nothing happened.

Tom lifted the cowl and pulled and wiped the dipstick. "When was the last time you added oil? There's hardly a bead on the stick." He slammed the cowl shut and said, "Look, I know a really good Vietnamese landscaper who could shape the place up and keep your mower serviced. What do you say?"

"What I say is, in case you haven't noticed yet, you are on my turf, so I'm entitled to decide what to do and how to do it." To illustrate his command over his domain, Garnie picked at his nose and scratched his crotch. "Now, lest you think you've escaped my concern, I ask you again, why the hangdog look? Or in other words, tell me what went wrong with your day. Though you may not believe it, I am truly concerned about what transpired in the halls of learning to mute your normally sunny smile."

Tom marveled at Garnie's jumps from indignation to petulance to insistence to saccharin faux sympathy.

Garnie sat Buddha-like on the mower's seat while Tom checked its tires. "Believe me, you wouldn't understand. Your left rear tire is seriously low."

"Lacking understanding, am I? That's rather unkind. However, I choose to overlook it because the generosity of my heart calls me to help you lay your burdens aside. Throw your cares on my shoulders. Speak, and let my ears bear the brunt of your pain. Yes, I insist. It will make you feel ever so much better, and once you—"

Tom cut him off. "Garnie, knock it off. If I'm less than jolly, it's because the everyday, ongoing, you-can't-get-away-from-it issue of too much of me being spent on bending to mandates from people who don't understand education leaves me with too little energy to help kids who truly want to learn. There, will that shut you up?"

"Thomas Clausen, ever the idealist. You'd go insane if you weren't besieged by parents and discipline problems and nonachievers. It's in your blood now."

"You couldn't be more wrong."

"Are you saying that, should the right opening come to your notice, you might move away from all of this?" Garnie's arm swept across the stunning view of the Sound and distant islands.

"Point of reference: you're talking about your backyard, not mine. You ever read John Updike?"

"Fiction?"

"Yep."

"A waste of time. You should read history."

"I do. If you weren't so fixed in your narrow-mindedness, you'd find there's truth in fiction, too. Anyway, when Updike's character Rabbit Angstrom was asked why he quit teaching, he said something like 'I didn't want to end up thinking it was the only thing I could do.' You dig deep enough, you'll find a little of Rabbit Angstrom in everybody, me included."

"So where is your spirit of adventure? So little time and so many worlds to conquer."

"Being three years short of early retirement, I think I'll stay put."

Garnie eyed him speculatively. "Time will tell; time will tell."

"Will tell what?"

"Will tell that we are all subject to unpredictable fates." Garnie signaled the end of his interest in the topic by asking, "What do you think of the Chamber of Commerce shutting down for lack of funds?"

Tom continued poking about the mower, looking into its grass bins and delivery tube. "They earned it. When you don't deliver services that count, you can't expect dues to keep rolling in."

"Bravo. You handled that deftly. Now get out of my way." He twisted the key again with the same lack of results.

On his way to the street, Tom called back, "Raise the blade, and step on the clutch." The mower popped and putted into life. With Garnie bobbing unsteadily atop, it lurched across the walk to disappear around the far side of the house.

"Phone. It's Sigi."

"Okay, I'll take it in the garage." It was Wednesday evening, and with Thursday being garbage day, Tom was weeding out items that were too far gone from the load he was readying for the church's rummage sale. The call caught him staring at a garden sprayer with leaky seals.

"Hi, Sigi?"

"Mr. Clausen, I think you ought to go visit Mr. Garnet. He's in the hospital again, and he refuses to have visitors, even me. He was real bad this time. I called his room, but no one answered the phone. I know he'll put up a fuss to keep visitors away, but I was thinking that you, being the only one who sasses him when he acts terrible, might not pay attention to what he says. I'm sorry to bother you, but I wouldn't know what to do if something happened to the house."

"When did he go in?"

"I found him on the bathroom floor about two o'clock. Nothing I did helped much so I called for help. An aid car came and got him. The men were so nice."

"You said he refuses to see anyone. Any ideas?"

"Honestly, I don't know what goes on inside that man's head. He called from the hospital to tell me he wouldn't see visitors. And then he gave me his room number. Isn't that just like him?"

"Rest easy. Jane will be over to stay with you until I get back with a report. You girls get your heads together to figure out what you'd need from him to carry on if he's out of commission for a while, okay?"

The circumstances were very different from Tom's visit to the hospital the week before. Then, he had come driven by curiosity. This time he was concerned about not only his friend but also Aunt Sigi's uncertainty about her future—having no idea of what tomorrow might bring, other than the possibility of being put out of the house. His mind was full as he rode the elevator to the fourth floor.

A sign where the corridor split pointed to rooms 404 through 423. Tom found "Pittman, Garnet" in the name slot of Room 419 and knocked. Garnie's voice rang out strongly. "I'm busy. Go away."

"Okay, I'll be in the waiting room." He retraced his steps as Garnie's voice dwindled. "Thomas, Thomas, Thomas." Tom knew that barging in would push Garnie into the blustery defensiveness he raised when pressed to yield control. He retreated to a waiting room, hoping for a better opening to lobby for Aunt Sigi's needs. He suspected it would be a short wait.

He was right. Alone in a family waiting room, he slouched half-asleep watching the Channel 7 news. He awoke at the feel of change trickling from his pocket. He pulled himself erect to shake his remaining coins into place and reached behind his seat cushion to retrieve what he'd lost. He was surprised to pull back a few quarters, a small handful of lesser coins, and a ballpoint pen. Along with what he collected from under nearby cushions, it would make a sizeable donation to the Ronald McDonald House collection jar in the hospital's lobby. He was counting the money when an expensively barbered and shined gentleman in a double-breasted suit strode out of Garnie's corridor with a briefcase in hand. Moments later a nurse's aide summoned Tom.

Garnie's complexion was sallow. Propped up against pillows, he held an oversized clipboard on his lap, and a loose stack of documents was at his side. Tom mustered a smile. "Hi, neighbor, how are you feeling?"

He was sitting up. His hair was tangled, and his eyes had sunk into dark recesses. "Tip-top, Thomas. Aside from my kidneys, I'm A-one, and we'll do something about them. Mark my words."

"Who was the lawyer type?"

"Lawyer? I have no idea what you're talking about."

"Okay, I won't push." Tom angled a bedside chair so he would be eye to eye with Garnie. "Good thing Sigi found you. Do you remember anything about your ride in the aid car?"

"Just impressions. You know, faces hovering, motion, low voices, that sort of thing. They tell me it was a close call. It seems that I must become more careful."

"About time. You may be over-the-top bright in some ways, but when it comes to maintaining your body, you're a remarkably slow learner."

Garnie shrugged. "I don't live in my body. I live in my head." Before Tom could rebut him, he added, "Oh, all right. I made a mistake, but it's still my body."

"No, it's community property. If what you let happen to it affects other people, you and your body are other people's business."

"Not likely. Name one."

"Aunt Sigi, Jane, and me. Do you realize what state Sigi's in? She needs assurance that she'll be taken care of if you happen to not survive one of your episodes."

"Thomas, why is it that you persist in underestimating me? Of course she's provided for. If she chooses, she will live like a queen, go on cruises, live in a palace, and have servants if she wants them."

"Is that why the double-breasted suit was here?"

"I don't know what you're talking about."

"Goodbye, Garnie. Rest well." Tom pushed himself up from the chair and turned to the door.

"Oh, all right. I did have a visitor. Now come back and sit down."

Tom sat again. He asked, "Does Aunt Sigi know you'll provide for her, just in case? Or if she is in your will, does she know what provisions you've made for her welfare?"

"Hmm. Well, she certainly should since she hasn't lacked for anything so far. Hand me the water, please."

Tom adjusted the straw and handed it to him. "That's a first."

"What's a first?"

"You said, please. Let's get back to Aunt Sigi. Have you ever, ever, ever spoken to her about her finances, a pension, a medical plan, or what might happen to her if you die?"

"Why are you harping on this? Of course she'd be taken care of. She ought to know that."

"She doesn't. She's terrified about the uncertainty. Let's say you have a program set up to take care of her. Don't you think it might have been more humane to discuss it with her, maybe ask her what she'd choose to do if the decisions were hers to make?"

"Well, I'm certainly sorry if I caused her a bit of uncertainty."

"Uncertainty? Garnie, the poor old lady is scared—worse than monsters in the closet, alligators under the bed, things going bump in the night scared. She imagines that she might be turned out to live on the street."

Garnie fidgeted with his blanket and fussed with the tape holding his IV port. "For God's sake, Thomas, I'm hospitalized. Did you come here to sympathize with my condition or to kill me? I'm not well, you know."

"A person can put off doing the necessary when in good health, but you're not doing too well. I pray that you'll return to better health so I might continue your education, but until you do, don't you think it might be wise to comfort the lady who has cleaned and cooked for you all your life?"

Garnie put his hands to his face. "I wanted to surprise her."

"My friend, I know you have a big heart, but you need to understand that while surprises might be fun for children, security is an oldster's cup of tea. You've never had to worry, but Aunt Sigi started life without the tools or experience to deal with the world outside your house. She's worried. You could help her with that if you would. And before you answer, think about setting her up with the wherewithal to do what's needed to keep the house in shape."

Garnie had turned to surfing channels with the volume muted.

"Were you listening to me?" Tom asked, peevishly.

"Hmm, oh, yes, every word of your lecture." Garnie relaxed back into his pillows with his fingers laced across his stomach, the remote underneath. He closed his eyes and said, "Dialysis tomorrow and then I'll be home again, fit as a fiddle. I'll have a talk with her then. I think I'll have a little nap now. Turn off the light on your way out."

CHAPTER 13

Aside from Tom, the office was vacant. Alice, usually the last to stay, had gone home to Jerome, leaving the offices and halls eerily quiet for anyone used to their daytime bustle. Tom eyed the depth of paper in his in-box and dialed home. "Hi, sweetheart."

"What happened? I thought you'd be home by now."

"Pat Markowicz stopped by. With a lawyer."

"Why would she even fight it? She's too much of a complainer to enjoy teaching."

"Oh, she knew she was facing nonrenewal. She's just sore at herself for letting it come to termination."

"Are you on your way home?"

"That's why I called. I think I'll take a catnap here. I'm tired. Need a little downtime."

Jane sensed a flatness to his voice as though he spoke from a place more distant than the other end of a telephone line. "Tom, you listen to me. You don't sound well. You stay on the line and keep talking while I call nine-one-one. Keep talking, do you hear me? Tom? Tom, say something, please!" Her alarm went off when she heard the single gravelly syllable, "Uhhh," followed by a clunk and three rhythmic scraping sounds, each shorter than the last.

Jane couldn't know that seconds after her call to 911, Matt Lindahl, a custodian with a habit of stopping by the empty office to play solitaire on the one office computer lacking password protection, veered toward Clausen's office to see why the lights were still on. He found Clausen slumped forward on his desk. Though Lindahl had thought it a waste of time to lump custodians into the district's CPR training program, he thanked God for preparing him for what had to be done and went to work.

Though slight of build, Lindahl easily horsed Clausen's body into position on the floor where he loosened his tie, checked his mouth, and tilted his head back. His training flooded back as though given yesterday: pinch the subject's nostrils closed, take a deep breath, and immediately exhale, but not too forcefully. He opened his mouth wide enough to seal around Clausen's and exhaled. He had two impressions: a lack of back pressure and peanuts; Clausen must have been eating peanuts. He moved to apply chest compressions, his hands held just so, centered and below the nipple line. One, two. Lindahl was preparing to inflate Clausen again when the prone body spasmed with a great snorting gasp and inhalation, startling him so that he toppled backward from his crouch. Lindahl put his ear to Clausen's face to detect breathing. It was there. Clausen was breathing on his own.

"Wow!" One word summed up Lindahl's appraisal of his work. He'd done it, every technique he'd been taught except for the big one, calling for help, because making the call had been an instruction, not part of the drill. He looked for Clausen's phone and found its handset dangling off the side of his desk. Who had he been talking with, an emergency operator? He knelt to check his respiration again before calling 911. Better to give them up-to-the-second conditions. He made the call, gave his name and location, described the situation, answered questions, and hung up to wonder what else he should be doing. There had been no instructions on what to do after pulse and respiration were restored. Could more chest compressions help? Should Clausen be prone or should his head be elevated? No more than a minute after his call, sirens wailed onto the campus. Were they really that quick? he wondered. When a commotion erupted at the office's back entrance, he sprinted to the door and hit the crash bar to admit the EMTs who were hammering at the door's unbreakable polycarbonate window.

Lindahl parted the office's closed blinds to find the schoolyard ablaze with strobing emergency lights. While one EMT checked Clausen's condition, another quizzed Lindahl and gave his shoulder a congratulatory squeeze after he explained what he'd done. While dodging a gurney as firefighters wheeled Clausen from the office, he asked, "Should I call anyone? What should I do?"

The lead EMT took his name, thanked him for his help, and told him they would make the necessary calls once they had Clausen situated. As soon they roared off with lights blazing, he called his wife, MaryAnn who worked Thursday through Saturday at Tresses by Tess, a four-chair salon. MaryAnn finished her last customer of the day and rushed home to pass the news to as many of her friends and clients as she could reach during commercials.

Tom was vaguely aware of his state of drift in which no impression was anchored. Faces hovered to shadow him from overhead glare, and a bright point of light probed one and then the other eye. All the while his consciousness rose and ebbed, the whole of it surreal as though he was both object and observer—in his body and watching from without. He willed his arm to move without success, which sent a vague message that he might be paralyzed, but that impression, like everything else, was fleeting. He tried to stay awake for fear that if he slept, he might not wake up.

He was pleased that he had only been sleeping when roused by fresh jostling. There were faces again, and a confusion of voices that hauled him out of a vehicle and into cold air. Automatic doors hissed open, endless lights scrolled by above him, rolling and rolling, turning, dizzying; he felt the beginnings of nausea. Hands gathered him up and laid him on a table. It couldn't have been a bed; beds are never that hard or cold. When the motion halted, he drifted away again. Time meant nothing. Things kept happening, but it was all beyond his control or understanding. He was drifting, drifting, until a voice burrowed into his consciousness as though exhuming something buried. "Mr. Clausen, Mr. Clausen. Can you hear me? If you can, I need you to respond. Can you hear me, Mr. Clausen?"

Jane jogged the distance between the elevators and the acute cardiac care nurses' station. Her voice was unsteady and pitched half an octave above normal. "I'm Jane Clausen, Thomas Clausen's wife. Is he here?" She scanned a board of patient listings. "There, his name is there. He needs me to be with him. Please tell me where he is."

A large dark nurse lumbered around the counter to take both of

Jane's hands. "I'm Marvella. Now you just get yourself calmed down first, and then we'll go to see him. No need to fret. He's in good hands, and he's not critical." She squeezed Jane's hands. "We don't allow nothin' but calm around here 'cause it does our patients a world of good. Can you do that?" Her tag said "Marvella Johnston, RN," and the way she dismissed another nurse's approach with a glance said she was in charge.

Jane sniffled. "He's my husband, you know."

"Sure, honey. Easy, easy now. Take it easy. Get yourself under control. You okay now?" Jane nodded. "Okay, I think maybe you're ready now. Let's go but slowly." With Marvella's comforting thick hand on her arm, Jane let herself be guided to the second patient room on the right where Tom lay still with an IV drip taped to his arm. Marvella said, "You look like you could use a good sign. You see that nasal oxygen set hangin' loose there? Now that's a good sign around here. That means he's breathing and pumping okay on his own. Now you just sit yourself down at his bedside and do some therapeutic hand-holding, you hear?"

Alone with Tom, she pulled a chair against his bed. Before sitting, she leaned to kiss him lightly. His steady breathing showed no response to her touch. She was about to lay her head on his chest but pushed away for fear of what pressure on his heart might do. Of the room's two chairs, she picked the straight one. The other, a padded vinyl oddity more suited to napping than maintaining a vigil, would keep her beyond reach of his hand. She finger-combed his hair and stroked his arm, all the time talking softly.

Midnight came and went. Marvella looked in one last time before her shift ended. A male with none of Marvella's warmth checked Tom each hour. Jane's chair was too low or the rail was too high. No matter how she arranged herself, reaching to touch him cut the circulation in her arm, and she developed a backache. Her eyes were scratchy, and she felt a headache coming on. At 2:30 a.m., she walked to the nurses' station to ask for aspirin. For the next hour, she lay curled in the padded chair dozing fitfully. She woke and switched back to the straight chair, kneeling on its seat with her forearms braced on the bed rail. She resumed talking.

"I called for help. When you stopped talking, I knew you were in trouble. Anyway, I talked with your doctor, and he says you're going to be all right." She sniffed and pulled a Kleenex from the nightstand. "I love you. You know, you shouldn't scare me like this. I can't think of a time when I've been so frightened. Promise me you won't do it again? I promise I won't ever say anything about trouble coming in threes. Or fours or fives. Never again. I met a really nice nurse, a great big RN, who runs this floor. She's the one who helped get you settled, but I suppose you don't remember that. Anyway, her name is Marvella, and she's very big and very sweet and very black. You'll like her.

"She said that calm's the word around here, so don't get all upset when I tell you this: You and I are just getting started so don't you for a minute think of leaving me this way. Oh, I know, I shouldn't be lecturing you about don't do this and don't do that, but it's taken me twenty-two years to teach you how to love me just right, so there's no way I want to go through breaking in a replacement. Darn it, you're not replaceable—not at breakfast or dinner, but especially at night. I don't ever want to spend another night without you beside me. Remember this?" She began to sing, "and to feel in the night, the nearness of you." How's that for a golden oldie for my golden oldie." She dabbed at her eyes and blew her nose before resuming her grip on his hand. "It's not that you're so old; it's just that your musical tastes never evolved—stuck in the sixties. Or before. Maybe, sweetheart, that comes from not having kids around the house. But you know what? You've made my life full all by yourself. Maybe that's because you're just a big kid who never grew up. It's like I hit the jackpot. I got my man, and I get to spend my life raising a big kid. Like you always said, you have to grow old, but you don't have to grow up."

She pulled a glass with a flex straw close and took a sip. "I hope you don't mind sharing. As they say south of the border, *mis gérmens son tus gérmenes*. But if that's so, why is it that when one of us is down with the sniffles, the other stays healthy enough to be nursemaid? Oh, yes, about sharing, I found my baseball cap in your car. Again. That's my hat, and I don't appreciate you snitching it every time you run off to play golf. I'll make you a deal though: you come out of this in one piece and you can wear it any time you want. If that's not enough, you can have first shower every morning for a year. No, make that six months. And even though I prefer potatoes, you can have your precious rice with dinner any time you want. One more thing: I promise not to hog the front page. No more than five minutes before we trade sections, okay?" As if in answer, she sensed a flexing of Tom's hand. A slow smile was stretching his lips.

Jane hugged his arm, right up to the tape stabilizing his IV port. Prattling disjointedly and blubbering, she said, "You were listening! Oh, sweetheart, you're awake. You're going to be all right, but you shouldn't have been listening. That wasn't fair; I was just trying to make you feel good. Can I give you a hug? Would it harm you?"

In answer, Tom reached across with his free hand and patted his chest. Jane struggled with the bed rail, finally getting it to retract enough to let her lean in against him. He stroked her hair.

A quiet moment passed with Jane sniffling and Tom softly caressing her head before he said, "Shower, rice, newspaper."

Jane lunged and kissed him, harder this time. With her lips still on his, she said, "What about the hat?"

He looked puzzled. "What hat?"

"Never mind," she said. "Let's concentrate on getting you home again."

Charles Wainwright and Claudia McPhaiden sat across his desk from each other with the sun beaming in. Not wanting her discomforted by facing the windows, he rose and pulled the new curtains closed. She asked, "How are Jean and the girls?"

"Reasonably well, Jean's still struggling to accept Northbridge. I'm afraid she became spoiled by the southern Oregon climate. She complained all winter about the cold and damp, but then doesn't everyone? I think her problem is that with Meg at the university and Beth working for Boeing, her nest is suddenly empty." His eye caught on her necklace. "That's impressive turquoise. The silverwork is Navajo, right? And earrings to match. You certainly do know how to dress."

Claudia warmed to his compliment. It was a rare meeting with

Charles when he didn't have something positive to say about her. After Karl, her first husband, died, she married Bruce McPhaiden, a widowed high school classmate who began pursuing her at their class's thirty-year reunion. Having shared so much history, it seemed easy and natural that they should get together, go to dinner, watch videos, spend trial weekends away, and eventually marry. Bruce was a firefighter who rose to lieutenant by inching his way up the ladder for twenty-six years and was four years short of full retirement when they wed. After their wedding, Claudia foresaw fruitful golden years. She had a man to grow old with. She dreamed of travel, cruises, wintering in the southland, and getting to use the French she'd studied in high school and college.

When Bruce retired, he celebrated by buying a sixty-inch, high-definition TV and a new La-Z-Boy. When she spoke to him of other cultures, he said, "Why can't you be happy here? We live in the greatest nation in the world, so why spend money traveling to second-rate countries where they don't even speak English?" Her dream died one evening when she was watching a travelogue on Tuscany. Bruce asked for the remote and switched channels to a hockey game, saying, "I'm not going to watch any more of that foreign crap."

Disappointment with her children's unspectacular lives, Karl's early death, and now Bruce's couch-potato lifestyle depressed and infuriated Claudia by turns. Two years before, Charles Wainwright had caught her in a bout of depression at a school directors' convention. She had lashed out at him, saying, "What are you staring at, young man?" Apologetic, he said, "I'm sorry if I made you uncomfortable. It's just that you, (she recalled that he stammered a bit) stood out. The cut of your clothes, your hair. If you don't mind my saying so, it all works well together. Very effective." His words felt like balm on her distraught spirit. Bruce lacked the vocabulary and spirit to say such a thing.

That morning at the Red Lion was the beginning. They attended sessions together, discussed school issues, met for coffee, and talked about Northbridge's challenges and why he was attending the conference—that he had once been a county superintendent, put his career on hold while dealing with medical issues and that those issues had been resolved. She asked about his focus as an administrator, and his quick answer had been "responsibility." He said that he had chosen to hold his teachers to account and that they'd risen to the challenge. They talked about the necessity of shaping district staffs into loyal teams with the shared goal of giving children a better education.

Throughout, he was a perfect gentleman, attentive and complimentary, but he never crossed the line. After all, she was nine years his senior, ten during the month leading up to his March ninth birthday. Even so, there was one evening at the recent board retreat in Semiahmoo when, she had to admit, she wouldn't have minded if he had been a bit more forward.

Claudia lifted her purse from her knees to his desk, which, as Wainwright had come to understand, marked her switch to business. "You know, Charles, you were very fortunate to have engaged an ethical firm. They wrapped up the investigation so discreetly that no one will ever know he was here. And wasn't it considerate that they chose not to bill all his hours."

"That shouldn't be a surprise. I'm sure the fiasco could have hurt their image, too. Anyway, it's water under the bridge." He glanced to see if she picked up on his attempt at a play on words.

"It's strange how things work out as though providence is putting its stamp of approval on our efforts."

"You lost me, Claudia."

"First, Mr. Runyon set himself up for termination, and then Mr. Clausen had his well-timed heart attack. I don't think we'll have to worry about either of them again. When you think of it, what are the odds that both would self-destruct within the same month?"

"Off the charts, but I'm glad you reminded me. I should have Sheila send Clausen a card from the central office staff—sorry to hear of your problem, hope you have a speedy return to health. She'll make it sound right."

"And we'll need to pull someone up from the ranks to fill in till the end of the year, someone with credentials."

Wainwright had been studying Claudia's silver and turquoise pendant. He said, "Yes, that's nice," and leaned to lift it off her breast for closer study. She glowed, and her breathing quickened. He returned it to her breast, pressed it into place, and said, "Stop by again and we'll review the district's procedure for permanent replacements." Claudia stood for her ritual spine-straightening drill, palmed the pendant, and smiled down at it, then up at Wainwright as she turned to leave.

The remainder of Wainwright's day passed smoothly. Claudia was right. Problems evaporate, and things fall into place only when you follow the correct path. Clausen's fateful collapse helped to calm the insecurities that built as his critics multiplied. But they seemed to be quieting down lately. He looked back over his handling of opposition. Firing hadn't always worked. A few marched right back, accompanied by lawyers who dragged him through depositions and tedious court proceedings that cost him valuable time.

The pending settlements could still be expensive. That secretary, Trina Philips, now there was a piece of work—in her mid-thirties and wearing braces, for God's sake. Not a team player, full of herself, and free with opinions. It seemed she still had friends in the office; either that or she'd been an unusually meticulous recordkeeper. Otherwise, how could she have every word of her evaluations at her fingertips, even the poll results that won her Secretary of the Year? Wainwright bristled at his remembrance of how, after telling her attorney that she had been terminated for incompetence, he waved her awards under his nose, saying, "How are you going to explain these to the judge?" It wasn't pretty, but getting rid of her was worth the half-year's salary the court awarded her. What really galled him was being ordered to give her a letter of recommendation that reflected her past performance reviews. He soon found it more practical to demote troublemakers into positions they weren't particularly fond of. A semester or two in purgatory and they adjusted or quit. No doubt about it, he was getting the hang of things.

"Dr. Wainwright."

"Yes?" he barked at the intercom. He had been wrestling with how he would handle a scheduled report to the board on his "Vision for Excellence." It had run headlong into a program Phil Krause had put in place that had earned broad support over its first two years. The board had requested that Wainwright justify the proposed switch, which had seemed no great problem since he had just read a report that contained almost perfect support for his argument. The trouble was he couldn't find the document again. He'd already spent too much time trying to put it together. The key was missing, that motivational something that started on the lower half of a right-hand page in a journal, if only he could remember what journal it was in.

"It's Lauren Johansen, junior high librarian. She's been trying to reach you since Wednesday."

"Put her through."

"Dr. Wainwright, this is Lauren Johansen, middle school librarian."

"Yes, Ms. Johnson, what can I do for you?"

"That's Johansen, sir."

"Of course. Isn't that what I said?"

"Only approximately, sir. The reason for my call is that I'd like you to answer one question: how many parents' complaints does it take to make a book disappear from my library's shelves?"

"That's easy. One."

"You can't be serious, sir. You're joking."

"Look, who is this?"

"Lauren Johansen, junior high."

"Yes. I'll make this simple. While you have millions of books to choose from, I have only a few thousand voters to satisfy. Those numbers tell me that you're going to pull the book from circulation."

"Don't you want to know what book is being challenged?"

"I don't need to know, Miss Johnson. Think of it as pruning a hedge. Clipping a leaf here or there doesn't show unless you make an issue of it, and we wouldn't want that to happen, would we? The book won't be missed. If you want, you can store it in a back room in case a parent demands it. Now, I appreciate the good work you do, but should any other book be challenged, your first response will be to remove it from circulation until we have time to make a ruling. Is that clear?"

"Abundantly clear. Goodbye."

Since most phone calls end when a caller uses the handset to depress a switch in a phone's cradle, the person on the other end hears a click without knowing how forcefully the handset was dropped. But background noise continues if the circuit is still open. Lauren Johansen was seriously peeved when she slammed the phone down, startling two friends also holding handsets that kept the line open, all connected to the same call. Lauren popped up from her chair and took possession of the two handsets in turn, placing each in its cradle to dim the background in stages. Johansen and friends had called from the downtown office of the Northbridge Teachers' Association where Denise Macklin, one of the three conspirators, gave her a hug. "Oooh, that was marvelously mean. Here's a thought: Can you imagine the alarms you set off if the paranoid SOB caught the call not ending all at once? If he did, don't you think it might make him a teensy bit suspicious? How long do you think it'll take him and caller ID to figure out where it came from?"

"And to tell me I'm fired," Johansen said. "Frankly, I could not care less. Jobs in other districts beckon—places where smiles, trust, and happiness reign and there's singing and dancing in faculty rooms. Girls, you watch; I'm out of here."

Paula Bergdorf, a tiny kindergarten teacher from Adams Elementary, chirped, "Oh, Lauren, you're so full of it. Would you really trade working in a war zone for boring predictability? You might not have fun here, but you're collecting some great stories to tell."

"Patience, girls." Denise Macklin, association president, closed a blue notebook. "I have his whole dossier here, page after page of missteps. Believe me, he's going to take a fall. Hard! Seriously, Lauren, you really should stick around. It'll be worth it to be here when it happens, and I promise you won't have to wait long. At the rate he's burning bridges, his days are numbered."

Macklin said, "Maybe, but as long as McPhaiden runs the board, his job's secure. Only the board can dump him. Look, We all have the same choice Lauren does. We can sit around and wait for a new board, or join the exodus. Have you heard that Callie Wallace is leaving?" To their expressions of disbelief, she said, "Yes, she is."

Bergdorf's birdlike voice lost its music. "Well, if that isn't the worst. There goes my son's math teacher. Who's left to teach upper-level math?

Anybody? Or will we have to send our kids to the community college to pick up what we can't offer?"

Denise put an arm around Bergdorf. "Smile, Paula. Grit your teeth real hard and smile. We're going to get him. We're going to take him down and walk all over him. Missy Barnstable's sister-in-law lives in Lexington, and Missy has talked her into collecting everything she can lay her hands on about Dr. Charles Wainwright. And if he's still around in a year, think what'll happen if Trish Ostrander wins a seat on the board. She and her dad on the same board? Wouldn't that be a hoot? I wish we could support her without Claudia labeling her an NEA puppet."

Paula shrugged into her coat and retorted, "Yes, but that won't happen fast enough to keep tomorrow from being too much like today, and that really sucks."

CHAPTER 14

Tom was mired in a disabling passivity. He couldn't seem to want anything other than Jane's company. No thoughts about school, Buster, fishing, or Garnie lasted long enough to reflect on. A corner of his mind noted the oddity of accepting whatever happened to him without complaint about being cold or warm, thirsty or hungry. The fact that he wasn't a complainer by nature didn't mean he was easily satisfied but that he preferred to manage personal things by himself. So he found it odd to wake from any of the many naps he took each day to stare into bright daylight without bothering to look away; or if cool, not make the effort to pull up a blanket; or if thirsty, know that his mouth was dry but do nothing more about it than move his tongue to verify his condition. Like a side of beef, he was twice loaded onto gurneys to be hauled off for testing. There was the sting of a needle in a darkened room where he was off-loaded onto a hard table. Technicians peered at screens. There was some kind of X-ray or fluoroscopy and another battery of sensors stuck onto his chest, but he couldn't remember them being yanked off. Perhaps, he thought, they weren't stuck on with the same grade of superglue as before.

It was in the afternoon of his second day in the hospital that the fog cleared enough to open the way for complaining. He grew irritated at the inanity of daytime programming and thumbed angrily across channels for something worth his interest. When a nurse, responding to his plea for food, brought him a tiny container of applesauce, he snapped, "I asked for food!" Reports of his worsening disposition pleased Dr. Liu. Though Tom was ravenous, the food he was offered was bland and insubstantial. He asked Jane to go to the cafeteria for a sandwich, a slice of pizza, a burrito, anything to fill the hole. She took his request to Marvella, who by virtue of her size and her advantage of being vertical, loomed over him. She said, "Now you listen to me. I've taken a liking to your wife, so I wouldn't want anything to happen to you that would make her unhappy. Are you with me so far?" Tom nodded. "Then you'd better start thinkin'. Think about that poison you sent her for, how it'll clog your arteries and plug up your bowels. Think about how eatin' that stuff'll make you as big as I am. Are you scared yet?" Tom burst out with a quick laugh that Marvella's fierce glare stifled. "You laughin' at me, boy? You makin' sport of Marvella?"

"No, ma'am. You're the boss."

"Who's the boss?"

"You."

"Now that we got that straight, here's the menu choices for dinner. Sorry, but the chef regrets being out of prime rib." She laid a folded sheet on the bedside table.

Tom looked at her suspiciously. "Are you messing with me?"

Marvella stared hard enough to unsettle him. "I'm *caring for you.* You decide you don't like what I do, you're messing with me, and you don't want to do that. No sir, you don't want to do that." She gave Tom a quick wink and strode out, Jane following in her wake.

"Marvella, I thought calm was the word around here."

"Oh it is, honey. Think Galilee. Our Lord taught us that you've got to put the waves down to get some calm. You gotta look beyond the miracle to see the why of what he was teaching. So here I am, big and brash and on the scene when storms are brewing. Storm control's part of my calling." She pinned Jane to the wall with a finger on her sternum. "And while I'm on the subject, this experience might be wasted on your man if he doesn't read Psalm 116. And I do mean soon. You gonna remember that?"

Jane leaned into Marvella's bulk, wrapping her arms most of the way around her. "You've been a wonderful friend. I won't forget any of this."

Calm didn't come easily to Tom. Dr. Liu stopped by near five o'clock to tell him testing wasn't complete and that he'd have to spend at least one more day in the hospital. At least one more day? Did that mean one more day or what? After his drug-induced torpor dissipated, he was allowed to walk and, aside from feeling weighted, couldn't sense any significant weakness. Thus far, no one had shared anything beyond blood-pressure readings with him, and even then he was made to feel he was prying into state secrets. He was peeved that Dr. Liu—he heard her accented voice down the hall—spent her time checking records at the nurses' station, looking in on him only briefly. He said, "Now that you're here, Doctor, I need to know two things: first, when are you going to discuss my condition with me, and second, when am I being discharged?"

She picked up his hand, held it, and turned it to examine both sides. Then she looked into his eyes, behavior he took as peculiarly Asian since none of his other caregivers showed touchy-feely inclinations. She said, "All right, I'm releasing you after tests are completed tomorrow. You should plan to be here through lunch. As to your condition, I've been in touch with two of my favorite consultants who think you're quite an interesting case. Today is Thursday. I want you to have a quiet weekend at home and then be in my office at ten thirty on Monday. We should have our opinions fairly well formed by then. Have your wife drive you."

"But she's working."

"She didn't work today, did she? I think you'll find she's willing to take a few more days off. I'll see you Monday."

A receptionist called out, "Mr. Clausen, may we see you at the desk?" Tom dropped a *Science Digest* onto Jane's lap and stepped to the counter where he filled out yet another privacy form. The clerk took the form and said, "I see you have your wife with you. The doctor would like to see you both. Please follow me."

Their first stop was an EKG lab where Tom was wired up for still another test, not counting the continuous signal collected by the chest strap monitor he'd been wearing. He sat still, the only sound in the room from a printer churning out tape. When satisfied, the technician said, "All done, you can talk now." She popped the wires from his patches and said, "Would you rather pull them off yourself? Some say it hurts less if they do it."

Tom was tugging at the last patch when Dr. Liu knocked and entered. She greeted Jane with "I'm glad you could join us," took a moment to study the EKG tape, and slipped it into Tom's file. "You can put your shirt on," she said. The diminutive cardiologist touched a stylus to her tablet and said, "Now let's go over your results."

She explained that since blockage appeared to be moderate, they were looking to other causes and that her diagnosis still had an element of educated guesswork to it. She pulled his electrocardiogram from his file. "Look at this," she said. "This line shows a normal trace. See here? Now see what's going on here; the difference is irregular enough to be of some concern. It indicates probable weakened contraction of the middle and upper portions of the left ventricle. People live with that all the time, but it achieves significance after one suffers an event such as yours. I've talked with colleagues about this, and they tend to agree that you most likely experienced what's called stunned heart syndrome."

"Is that good or bad news?"

She closed the folder. "On balance, good. One thing you should know is that stunned heart usually occurs in women, which makes your situation a little unusual. Another is that your heart is relatively undamaged, which will allow you to recover nicely in a stress-free situation. The more important piece of information is that research connects stunned heart with levels of stress that produce surges of adrenalin, often stretching over days or weeks. Some people can take it. You can't because of two things: the way you are wired to handle stress and the amount and type of stress in your daily activities. The persistence of the fatigue you complained about is a clear indicator of that. But since you're the one who needs to be convinced, I'd like you to verify that with your own web search."

She paused and tapped his chest. "Do I have your full attention?" When he nodded, she said, "In nontechnical terms you should accept that what you experienced was a breakdown. You must understand that if you go back to what you've been doing, it can and probably will happen again. And that could kill you."

With her warning hanging between them, Tom lost his stare-down with the doctor. He swallowed hard and said, "I'm fairly flexible. Whenever there's a need to alter course, I think I adjust pretty well. Bottom line, tell me if there are warning signs I ought to be watching for. Most of all, I want to know if I can go back to work."

Dr. Liu laid her data device aside and said, "We still have a few minutes. Let's talk about that. Why do you want to go back to work?"

"It's what I do. It's what gives meaning to my life."

"What about your wife? What about your health? Do they have meaning?"

"Of course, but at the risk of sounding vain, I think I'm a round peg in a round hole, and I truly believe that Northbridge High is well served by having me as its principal."

"Mr. Clausen, get this straight: You're gambling with your life. You might find yourself leaving Northbridge High horizontally, carried out again, and much sooner than you expect if you go back to your old routine."

"Doctor, you can't know the psychic rewards of my job or how they keep me afloat. Nothing else I might do with my time could compare."

"So, if you couldn't go back, it would be the end of your world, so to speak. Are you telling me that your job is necessary to, as they say, float your boat? Tell me, what do you like most about your work?"

Tom launched into a litany that included kids, ideas, change, creating hope, nurturing new teachers, meeting people he would never meet otherwise, and networking with bright coworkers. He said, "I get to support good ideas and run interference for my teachers. I play an important role for a good school in a very good town."

Dr. Liu raised her eyebrows.

"Okay." Tom continued, "call it implementing. Then there's tracking graduates. It's deeply satisfying to follow the careers of students who go on to do good things and to feel that I might have played a small part in their successes. On the trivial side, unlike classroom teachers I don't have to wait till a bell rings to go the toilet. That may not sound like much, but with the amount of coffee in a principal's day, it can be a big deal."

Dr. Liu interrupted, "But you're not going to be drinking coffee, at least not caffeinated coffee. Now tell me what you don't like about your job."

Tom looked puzzled for a moment. "Well, budget cuts drive me nuts. They cut into programs so they generate friction with the staff. I'm not the best detail man, so spending half my time compiling reports is sort of soul deadening. There's always at least one teacher who is such a screwup that they cost me time straightening them out or, if worse comes to worse, laying the perfect paper trail to get them to resign. That's the easy stuff. Parents can be headaches. Of course to make a school work, you have to have rules, and of course kids are programmed to test rules, but that's another headache you learn to accept. Try keeping three unions happy. A couple of weeks ago, the fire marshal stopped by to set off the alarms and time our evacuation. The next morning a shop steward was in my office complaining that the disruption cut into his people's guaranteed twenty-minute break. Uh-huh, give me a break!"

Dr. Liu noted his passion about the negatives.

He continued, "Here's the worst part: Moms and dads get so upset when we hold their kids to school rules that they hire lawyers, and the lawyers drag me into court, together with a counselor or coach or whoever else might have been involved. It costs us a half-day minimum when that happens. No, the worst part is getting undermined by a superintendent and school board. If the wrong people get into those positions, they can micromanage you right out of town." Emptied, he sat back and shrugged. "Schools are institutions, so we have institutional-type problems. It's expected."

The tiny cardiologist stepped closer to look him hard in the eyes. "Then being a principal isn't the perfect job you claimed it is. From what you've told me, you maintain your good attitude toward your work by accenting the affirmative and downplaying the negative. You don't have the perfect job. You have a job setting that nurtures your creative side. You obviously need to have an element of mission in your life's activities, and that's all to the good, but please don't delude yourself into believing it's the perfect job, even for you, especially in your present condition. If you plan to stay under my care, you're going to have to choose between two courses. Your best choice is to find low-pressure employment that involves more physical exercise, and if you won't go for that, then take a sabbatical, after which we'd see how you're doing.

"In the meantime," she said, scribbling on a pad, "I'm setting you up with some meds. If you behave yourself, I won't see you again for two weeks. Stop at the counter and Becky will schedule your appointment."

He shook her tiny hand, and she slipped out. He was always amazed how she floated wraithlike into and out of rooms with never an audible footstep and never a click or thump when she placed objects on counters, and how her subdued voice somehow carried authority. Tom had come to believe that her light precision was the perfect touch for one who worked on hearts and that it would be worth his while to do whatever it took to keep her on his case. He looked at Jane and said, "Well?"

Jane, who had sat silent throughout, stepped over to fasten his top shirt button. She said, "You heard the lady."

"Dad, I know you're out of the loop, so you might not know that Uncle Tom's in the hospital with heart trouble. Gimme a call to let me know you picked up on this, would you?" Roger folded his phone, buckled his helmet, and pedaled down Commerce and past Burger King toward the tracks. The bicycle, a hybrid with a second set of wheels hanging in the garage for off-road use, was Roger's way of getting about while burning off excess energy. Cars were to tinker with, not to own—yet. The closest he'd come to owning a motor vehicle was a wrecked Honda Helix scooter he hoped to make road worthy. With two cars in the family, he'd had little trouble borrowing wheels in the past, but with his dad up in Moraine and his mom touchy about her things, getting a car when he needed one had become a problem.

What Roger didn't know was that Tom had been released only hours before his call and was settling into his recliner at home. He tried calling Jane's cell while she was at Tom's bedside but couldn't get through. His father was busy with job interviews, his mother too absorbed in her plight to be concerned about anyone else's condition, and Ellen, once he'd alerted her, was relentless in pressing for updates on her Uncle Tom's condition.

A street cleaner working on Walnut caused Roger to brake for an oncoming pickup. He banked around the corner at Dogwood where a late breakthrough of sun penetrated the arching canopy of maples to dapple the street. The approach was familiar to Roger, who mowed the Clausens' lawn when they were out of town and fed and walked Buster if they were away for an overnighter. Following the disastrous meeting at church, he had enjoyed a three-night stay in the Clausens' island of peace that might have lasted longer if the police hadn't rousted him out to explain why he wasn't living at home. His mother had filed a missing person report on him, though he had attended school and bicycled openly about town. When rounding the bend that brought the Clausen house into view, he saw both cars parked side by side in their usual places. Curtains were open. His tension slackened as he coasted to the Clausens' back door.

"Roger, come in." Jane rose on her toes to give him a hug. "It's so nice of you to come by. I'll bet you're here to see Tom. Go on in; he's in the living room."

Roger hesitated. "Are you sure it's all right?"

"If you're not going to take my word for it, go see for yourself. He'll be delighted to see you." She gave him a nudge. "Go on. Get in there."

Hearing conversation in the kitchen, Tom was on already on his feet. Two days of enforced rest had left him with a backlog of nervous energy, something one of Dr. Liu's pills was supposed to counter, but since their stop at the pharmacy was little more than an hour before, Tom's first dose hadn't taken effect yet. He lapped an arm around his lanky godson and led him into the living room. "It's great to see you. How are your mom and dad?"

"That's something else. The big question is how are you?"

"I'm in pretty good shape for the shape I'm in, which is to say, there's nothing seriously wrong with me."

"That's great. Maybe I shouldn't be asking, but are you going to take the rest of the year off? All that's left is tests, graduation, and closing up."

Tom hesitated, giving Roger a searching look, and said, "You're getting to look more like your father every day." He paused. "This might not be what you were after, but it's all I have to offer in that department. It seems that a lot of us are facing changes of plans. As you've recently discovered, course-altering stuff does happen." He moved toward the kitchen. "I'm going for some water. Can I get you anything?"

"A can of pop if you have any."

Tom returned with the drinks and flopped into his chair. "Well, to make a long story short, I'll be looking for another job. My doctor believes that I'm not cut out to be a high school principal, at least not after the incident that landed me in the hospital. In a way it was a wake-up call. I like my job, and I thought I fit it pretty well, but—"

Roger injected, "So does everybody—I mean, want you back."

"That's nice to hear, but it seems that parts of me can't keep up with it. So my body sent a message that enough was enough. The good news is that as long as I keep the stress down, I should be as good as ever."

"What'll you do?"

"I'm just now beginning to wonder about that. One option is to stay in this chair while Jane brings home the bacon, be what they call a kept man."

"Oh sure. Somehow I don't think that's going to fly."

"Or if I can get out of the principal mode, start thinking outside the box. I may be facing something like molting or a chrysalis change. A new life, so to speak." Neither spoke for a moment. Then Tom asked, "How's your dad?"

"Were you talking about yourself or him?"

"Him, me, plenty of others. It seems a lot of us are in the same boat, looking for a friendly shore to wash up on. The difference between your dad and me is that he's lost way more than I have. I'd really like to see him. Do you know we haven't talked since his last day at school?" Again, Tom gave Roger a probing inspection. "What the heck, you're a big boy. I'm thinking that if I clue you in on some choice bits of your dad's past, and he gets wind that I'm educating you along those lines, we can count on him surfacing." He leaned toward Roger and grinned. "Here's one that's sure to set off his alarms: It happened one night when we were having a few beers in a bar across the state line in Idaho. Your dad and I met these girls we thought were unattached..." Tom spent the next half hour regaling Roger with stories about his father that bounced him between disbelief and roaring laughter. And then the pill began to take effect, dulling Tom's delight in reliving college escapades. Sensing the change, Roger patted him on the shoulder and left, stopping to give Jane another hug and tell her how great it was to see his Uncle Tom looking so well.

Roger rode home in fourth, his gear for climbing mild slopes. He was lightened. His Uncle Tom, fresh from a life-threatening event, had been in rare form, philosophizing, story-telling—the same reliable friend he'd always known him to be. And with the storytelling, Roger felt welcomed into the adult world, no holds barred. Yet so much was still going on that had to be worked out. Uncle Tom had emphasized that there are worse things than losing health, which had to be pointed at his dad. And his mom. Uncle Tom certainly made it clear that he didn't need to be told much to understand a lot. Reimagining Uncle Tom's stories, Roger weighed some ways of dropping hints about that night at the bar in Moscow. That just might do it, he thought. His mind was full as he cruised homeward.

Tom owed Phil Krause a call. Krause had called the day before when he was napping, and he had returned the call as soon as he awakened, only to find that Krause was out. He'd reread the Krauses' newsy get-well card and was eager to talk with him about two nearby districts that had posted openings for superintendents. If Krause landed one of them, he and Sarah might avoid the agony of moving, a personal cost superintendents experienced more often than teachers. "Hi, Sarah. It's Tom Clausen. Is Phil home?"

"Yes, but he's tied up in the den with our real estate agent. I'll have him call you back. No, wait a minute; I think he's breaking free."

So much for not having to move, Tom thought, chafing at the phone's open-circuit beeping that only commercial phones once had—one more tiny irritation to confirm his need for work that would occupy his mind. Sarah clicked back on. "Tom? Give me the number where you'll be in half an hour and he'll call back."

Her assumption that he might be running around town threw Tom into a fresh spasm of cabin fever. It had been ten days since the "incident." His morning bouts with the *Times* crossword proved he was as alert as ever—or nearly so. Yesterday, he'd gone until three in the afternoon without dozing off, and then he slept for only twenty minutes. The lure of coffee was such that he rummaged up an old jar of Sanka, brewed a cup, tasted it, and poured it into the sink.

He and Jane had argued the evening before. After dinner she brought out the vacuum cleaner and roared about the house during a CNN special report. When the din drew too close, he stepped to the wall and disconnected the cord. When flicking the switch did nothing, Jane turned to find him holding the cord's end. He said, "Please. We'd agreed that you'd vacuum when I'm out of the house, didn't we?"

Jane teetered somewhere between throwing the vacuum at him and stalking out of the house. She screeched, "Out of the house? You're never out of the house. How do you expect me to get anything done if I have to wait until you're out of the house?"

"Like it's my fault I'm stuck here? The days are bad enough without having evenings cluttered with vacuum cleaning. I volunteered to take it over. If you'd just let me add vacuuming to my chore list, we wouldn't be having this discussion."

"No, we'd have a dirty house. I'm not going to sacrifice cleanliness for a few less decibels, and that's final. If that's a problem, you can use some of your hours doing more of the housework—but not vacuuming. You never get all the dirt up."

"And that's final" was a familiar end to their arguments. Once said, there would be no communication until the triggering event was put to rest. He knew it was his fault and that there would be no negotiating about what channel to watch, when to turn the lights out, or anything else until he made amends. He'd started it. He would have to put it to rest, or at least try. As a start he plugged the vacuum cleaner's cord back into the socket and shut himself in the bathroom with a *National Geographic.*

They should have grown used to these tiffs, but that would mean they accepted them. Over the years, their arguments had always been over inconsequentialities. Serious issues they reasoned out together. Their days progressed in reasonable harmony until some small thing like vacuum cleaning rose up between them. They regretted their fights but learned to accept them as now-and-then purgings of pent-up tensions, punctuations in their life together, like cats coughing up hairballs.

He sat on the toilet trying to concentrate on an article titled "King Tut Revealed," while outside the sound-permeable door, Jane's jerky manipulation of her industrial-strength vacuum cleaner betrayed her agitation. Working her usual pattern, she ended in the den, shut it off, and rumbled it across the kitchen floor to the utility room. Silence descended while each wondered what the other was thinking. He heard the television come on in the den and was about to emerge from his retreat when she called out, "Tom, are you all right?" He flushed the toilet to suggest he had been doing more than hiding out, opened the door, and put his arms around her. "Jane, honey, we're gonna have to work up a plan to get me out of the house. And, if you'll let me, I'll try to make the carpets as clean as you like them."

CHAPTER 15

"I'm home!"

Jane's announcement set Tom, still peckish, to wondering why, after opening and closing doors and clunking her bag onto the kitchen counter, she belabored the obvious with that announcement. Of course she was home. Not that he wasn't glad for her company, but he suspected that at the next moment she might barge into the den and say, "Here I am, standing in front of you." He cursed the cranky state of mind that grew from his enforced idleness. She defused his mood by stepping behind his computer chair to wrap her arms around his neck and lower her face into his hair. Her breath was warm on his scalp as she murmured, "Whatcha doin', sweetie?"

He leaned back against her. "Organizing dinner. Documenting a life change. How does this sound?" He handed her a freshly printed sheet.

May 23, 2006
Dr. Charles Wainwright
Superintendent of Schools
Northbridge Public School District

Dear Dr. Wainwright:

Dr. Liu, cardiologist with the Port Gardner Clinic, advises me it would not be in my best interest to return to duty as principal of Northbridge

High School for the remainder of the current school year and possibly for the entire ensuing semester. I hope, but am not certain, that I will be able to return to duty for the second semester of the 2006–2007 school year.

Please note the terms for medical leave in my contract. The wording contained therein allows for a semester of leave with assurance of returning to the same position. Should my condition require absence from my office for the entire school year, there is no stated prohibition to the same wording applying..

Because my unplanned exit left a number of issues unsettled, it is my intent to make myself available to assist whomever you select as my replacement. My recommendation for short-term interim principal is Darrel Van Horn, whose firm hand and familiarity with the school and its issues qualify him as transitional leader.
My cardiologist recommends that I not only temporarily vacate my office, but that I also limit my exposure to school issues. I recognize that this may work a hardship on my replacement, so I will be open to phone contact with Northbridge High's head secretary, Alice Michaelson, for one hour per day.

Though being absent from the work I love causes me deep regret, I am confident that my chair will be filled with someone sufficiently qualified to serve the school well. My best wishes to you and your staff as you make adjustments for my absence.
With regrets,

Thomas D. Clausen
Principal, Northbridge High School

"Well, what do you think?"

"Aside from two periods at the end of your second paragraph, it should do. Content-wise, I think he should be happy that you want to come back. Other than that, it sounds a little stiff, like the guy who's going to read it. It should be well received."

"We'll see." He pushed away from the computer and led Jane into the kitchen to have his handiwork approved. "Chicken breast, broccoli, and rice tonight. That suit you?" He glanced out the window. "Looks like company. Omigosh, it's Dale!"

Roger's call to his father about Tom's cardiac event left Dale with a fresh load of guilt for not answering his calls. He recalled the time in Tom's office when, after explaining his ill-fated evening with Dana, he'd asked Tom if he was all right, to which Tom had said he was just tired, very tired. He should have seen it coming. All the warning signs were in place: the fatigue at the golf course, his need to catch naps, the heaviness to his step. Until his best friend's heart stopped, he'd been free to wallow in his own problems, but once it happened, the series of screwups he'd heaped on Tom connected too directly with his collapse to dismiss. He did mail a card that could arrive the next day in which he wrote, "Words can't express how sorry I am. Please, recover fully and soon." It had been thirteen days with no contact which, given their history, was a lengthy silence.

Tom answered the door. "Hey, Dale, I've been wondering when we might hear from you. Been out of town?"

"No. As a matter of fact, I've been busy mustering the courage to stop by." He stood rooted at the far side of the welcome mat, his body language apologetic. "Tom, Jane, I am so sorry. I know apologies can't undo anything, but I hope you can forgive me for the pressures I heaped on your overload. And now it seems there's nothing I can do to help make things easier for you."

Jane squeezed his arm and pulled him in. "No more of that, you hear? We're delighted that you've come. Now I'll get out of the way to let you two do some male rebonding."

Tom propelled him through the kitchen. "That guilt bit was eloquent but not necessary. You have your problems, and I have mine, so let's agree to let the stuff we've been through connect us, not set us apart. Now come on in here and sit down." Dale perched on the couch without touching the backrest.

Tom opened with "We've sort of lost track of each other with all that's been going on. So where are you living? What's happening between you and Betty? How are the kids handling the change? Are you working? I'm all ears; fill me in."

With Tom prompting, Dale began to soften while telling how Roger took over whenever his or Betty's suggestions grated on the other. He wrapped references to Betty and "her house" into one package. Like Aunt Sigi, he found himself imbuing a house with values hoped for and values lost. Aside from memories, some that he wished would dim, the house contained few things he wanted. He was confident that with Betty's money, it would be well maintained. He described his apartment near Moraine and that he'd already broken his vow not to have a TV, which set them to trading comments on *West Wing* plots. Tom inquired about Dale's job prospects, how the interviews were going, and which of the openings he felt best about. The discussion stayed focused on Dale's changing situation until, when most of an hour had passed, he commented, "Odd, isn't it? I came over here to ask about your health, and we've talked about nothing but me." He called after Tom who had disappeared into the kitchen. "Am I that self-centered?"

Tom returned with two bottles of amber ale. "That has nothing to do with it. With me, what's to wonder about? I had a problem. I'm getting well. Besides that, I'm still living with the same old wife in the same old house. Boring. Face it, you're more interesting. Compared with me, you're living a soap plot."

May 26, 2006
Mr. Thomas D. Clausen
6541 Dogwood Lane
Northbridge, WA

Dear Mr. Clausen:

Your many friends in the district are saddened by the news that you will not be able to continue as principal of Northbridge High School. Everyone at the school and the staff of the central office join to wish you a speedy recovery.

Thank you for volunteering to assist in implementing a smooth transition. I am sure that Mrs. Michaelson would agree to your suggestion, but it would be more practical for you to communicate through us here at the central office. Of course you understand that it might cause difficulties should you advise the high school directly while another principal is trying to settle in. Therefore, Mr. Mike Crowley, our new human relations director, will be your designated contact should you wish to comment to the district on pending issues.

About the terms of your amended contract (enclosed), you should note that the provisions for medical leave have been amended. You are quite correct that one semester is covered, but you will see that medical leave is not extendable. Had you applied for a sabbatical leave and had it been approved by the board prior to your leaving office, there would have been no problem. Also be advised that your medical coverage will extend through your last contracted day with the district. We look for your rapid recovery.

Sincerely,

Dr. Charles Wainwright
Superintendent of Schools

Tom stood at the mailbox rereading Wainwright's letter. He folded it and slipped it into a pocket before setting off for Garnie's. Aside from his visit at the hospital, they hadn't talked. Garnet Pittman had never been one to accept sympathy, but with his worsening condition now requiring three days of dialysis each week, his starchy rejection of sympathy wasn't going to keep Tom from his friend's side. Besides, it felt good to be out and about.

Visitors were dropping by the Clausen house daily. His mother, Jeanine Clausen, had driven down twice from Bellingham to find him, she said, more relaxed than before the incident and much better company than his father. Old Walt Clausen had recovered from his tumble only to pick up a stubborn attack of pneumonia. Alice Michaelson stopped to check on him his second evening back from the hospital, giving him the opportunity to send a handwritten note to post in the faculty room, telling his staff how he missed them and asking that they give him a week before dropping by. Aside from a drive to Bellingham with Jane at the wheel and an appointment with Dr. Liu, his stroll across the street was his first social outing.

The day was clear with a slight breeze, while overhead a dappling of high clouds signaled a change of weather. He threaded through Garnie's thicket of azaleas and rhododendrons where honeybees worked the shaded late blossoms. For all its impact, the letter weighed lightly enough that Tom's senses held on to the beauty of the day. When his thoughts reverted to the letter, he found himself unbothered by Wainwright's wordy animosity and happy to not particularly give a damn.

Feeling energized, he mounted the steps at a trot and banged three times on the massive doors that Garnie preferred not to answer. Bolts and latches clacked before Aunt Sigi pulled it open. "Mr. Clausen! Oh, how nice to see you." For an instant she seemed ready to throw the emotional reserve of the Pittman home aside to give him a hug. Instead, she said, "I do hope you've come to visit. Come in, come in. Mr. Garnet is resting in the den. You go right on in. I'll have tea ready in a jiffy."

"Thanks, but I'm off caffeine. Could you make that herbal? Is he feeling all right?"

Aunt Sigi sniffed. "Who knows. You'll find him playing possum. That way he gets to scold me for disturbing his sleep or trying to sneak around him if he's awake. I get it either way; you'll see."

Just as she said, Tom found Garnie slumped in a chair, his head lolled to one side. Tom spoke softly. "Garnie?" Not an eyelash flickered. He tried again, a little louder. "Garnie, are you awake?"

One of Garnie's eyes sprang open as he righted his head. "Well, if I had been asleep, you certainly shouted me out of that state." He rubbed at his eyes and rearranged himself in his chair. "Hmm. To what do I owe this auspicious honor? How many days has it been since you last made the long trek from your house?"

"Come on, Garnie; you know we've both been out of commission."

"Oh yes, I do recall something to that effect. So tell me, do they say you're going to live or die?"

"Not only live, but I'm also planning to outdo you across the board. Having been given a new lease on life, I plan to surpass your records in ill temper, bad manners, intolerance, and petulance. In fact, if they ever erect a monument to Northbridge's foremost grouch, it's going to be for me, not you. How do you like that?"

Garnie perked up. "Oh, Thomas, it is indeed a joy to have you sniping at me. Once you got past that insipid mewling—Garnie, Garnie—why, for a moment there I thought I'd have to call pest control to have you swept out. And yes, I did hear you hammer on the front door. What were you trying to do, beat it down?"

"Yes, but since we don't feel a draft, I must not have succeeded. You first: fill me in on your condition and what's being done for you."

Garnie's descriptions slandered every doctor and nurse who played a part in his care, maligning everything from their ancestry to their training. When Tom asked who he would recommend to anyone who might find themselves in the same fix, Garnie named the same people he had just trashed. His weight was down. His color was off, and his hair and nails needed trimming. The den table's stacks of papers and periodicals, though not disorderly, were unusually misaligned. Clearly, Garnie's energy was low. Yet he managed to muster his normal vitriol for Tom's visit. "And you? You look absolutely in the pink. Are you taking up malingering as your next career?"

"Ah, Garnie, no sense in trying to hide anything from you. I'm luxuriating in semi permanent sick leave, but you must promise not to blow my cover. Your right-wing extremist friends might go postal if they hear that I'm still drawing pay for, as you so aptly described it, 'having both front feet in the public trough.' My only remaining problem is that my heart flies into fits of dangerous irregularity when disagreeable people focus stress-producing remarks in my direction."

"Then it's a good thing you're with me. When do you go back to work?"

In reply, Tom pulled the letter from his back pocket and passed it to Garnie, who pointed to the table. "Hand me my glasses." He rearranged the smudges on his lenses, perched them on his nose, and mumbled, "Blah, blah, blah. Mmm, nice enough. Ooh, that's nasty of him. Oh, what a rascal; that's not called for."

Gesturing with the letter, he said, "What we have here, Thomas, is a small man in a big chair. I know because I can't count the times I've had to separate such creatures from their seats. Truth be known, I'm still plagued with some of them. What this person shows is incompetent mean-spiritedness. You see, people gifted with inspired nastiness, and I claim some expertise in that department, can defame those they despise without getting personal about it. Cutting people down should be done with such surgical precision that they don't know what hit them. This Wainwright fellow can't help but stamp his personal brand on whatever inhumanity he's about." He shook the letter. "Oh, how I'd love to get him in my arena. This popinjay—French cuffs and pocket hankies, really! That twit would never make it in the big leagues of troublemaking. Mark my words; he doesn't have what it takes to survive the trouble he causes."

Garnie folded the sheet and handed it back. "Dear boy, in the course of our recent discussions, you made mention of your antagonists. Do take a moment to balance that account by telling me a bit about your friends."

May 29, 2006
Dr. Charles Wainwright
Superintendent of Schools
Northbridge School District

Dear Dr. Wainwright:

My proposal to work through Mrs. Michaelson was predicated on years of partnering with her in accomplishing the work of my office.

I understand and appreciate her many organizational talents. She respects me, and our relationship has been the most stress-free aspect of my work with the high school. Since I have been advised to keep stress to an absolute minimum, my offer of assistance with ongoing issues can only apply on the terms laid out in my last letter. Actually, my doctor would have preferred no contact.

As to the extendability of a medical leave, I took the liberty of discussing the pertinent paragraphs of your letter with an attorney friend. He knows little about the harmony educators enjoy with each other, so his suggestion that I might not wish to return to a hostile work environment may have been excessive. Further, he pointed out that your wording was such that, on balance, a court might interpret it in sympathy with a claimant over the wishes of district administration.

As I explained above, the only source of calls from the district that I will be able to answer will come through Mrs. Michaelson. She has indicated that she will be happy to relay any issues that require my input. Thank you for your understanding.

Sincerely,
Thomas D. Clausen

The reply came four days later, a small miracle for snail mail. Its content and tone were what he expected.

June 1, 2006
Mr. Thomas D. Clausen
6541 Dogwood Lane
Northbridge, WA

Dear Mr. Clausen:

We are pleased to inform you that you may recuperate in peace. Fortunately, we had no trouble replacing you with an experienced administrator who is successfully correcting the issues you left for your successor. Since Northbridge High now has a full complement of administrators, it should no longer be necessary for you to have contact with Ms. Alice Michaelson or Northbridge High School.

Dr. Charles Wainwright
Superintendent of Schools

Jane plopped groceries on the counter and asked, "What's the latest from the Grinch?"

"Would you like me to read it to you—expressively?"

She ducked inside the loop of his arm to follow him as he read, "Dear Mr. Clausen, we are pleased to inform you that you may recuperate in peace…" When finished, he asked, "Why don't I feel bad about this? Why don't I want to kill him? I'm supposed to be devastated. Instead, I'm totally placid. Do you suppose…do you suppose that I missed my calling, that maybe I was cut out to be unemployed and that I might be hardwired for lolling about the house watching soaps?"

"Could be." She reached up to pat his cheek. "According to my limited data, househusbands do make better lovers than overworked principals." She checked her watch. "The Michaelsons want us there by six-thirty. You think you're up to driving, or do you want to doze?"

"Drive. There's a fresh pot of decaf. You pour. I'll give Alice a call."

Tom slowed as traffic backed up ahead. The problem proved to be drivers lifting their feet from accelerators to goggle at a horse trailer minus a right-side wheel. Its passengers, two haltered Holstein heifers munching grass in the median swale, were being watched over by a woman in denims. The tow vehicle was gone for parts or help. Once the heifers appeared in rear-view mirrors, speed picked up.

Tom reset the cruise control and continued. “Here’s the odd thing: You know how survivors can feel guilty about their sense of relief when a dependent husband or wife dies after a long illness?”

“I’ve never thought about it. What are you getting at?”

“They’re expected to mourn, not feel lightened by no longer having to carry the load. That’s the way I feel—at least sixty percent of me. I can’t bring myself to feel all that unhappy about not going back to work. Every day it’s getting harder to act all broken up when well-wishers ask when I’ll be back on the job. Is that a good sign or a bad sign?”

CHAPTER 16

Harry Morgan, the last board member to arrive, closed the conference room door. It was seven o'clock on Tuesday evening, and displeasure at a second night of board business dimmed the group's usual chatter. Claudia had called them into executive session, which kept them from transacting official business or even debating toward a consensus. They could discuss but not decide. The issue before them was the Northbridge Teachers Association's bombshell vote of no confidence in Wainwright's administration.

The teachers' union, known as the Northbridge Education Association or NEA, had so irritated Wainwright that he'd redefined NEA as Negate Every Advancement. The conflict between Wainwright and the NEA began shortly after he took over when Denise Macklin, association president, presented the NEA's position to the board: "The NEA, the district's major source for educational knowledge and practice, requires that it be furnished with transcripts of board plans and decisions." He'd listened as she recited the contributions her organization made, and he even stayed silent through her naive suggestions about directions the district might take. While Wainwright understood that Macklin, a veteran teacher, had seniority on him, he was convinced that his short but intensive study of new directions in education put him light years ahead of her in planning and administration. He believed that once his programs were in practice, their success would blow her away. Copies of his position paper were in board members' hands, and extras were ready for board members who showed up without their packets.

Claudia's voice rose over the murmuring. "Let's get to business so we can all go home. What we're here for is to get some sense of where the teachers' union was coming from in calling for a vote of no confidence. Who'd like to lead off?" Board secretary Nancy Corbin tested her pen on the margin of her steno book and turned on her recorder.

Wainwright took the lead. "It is all too easy to look on this as a bad thing. In fact, we should be looking at it as an opportunity. The union's vote of no confidence opens a door for change. First off, you hired me to implement change, to increase test scores, and to enhance the image of the district. When I took over, I found myself faced with a traditional faculty—not that tradition is bad, but we all know how it can get in the way of change. Teachers build little empires based on outmoded ways of teaching, and when we called for change, we asked them to give up something of themselves. It's painful but, like Harry Truman said, you can't make an omelet without breaking eggs.

"Every proposal we've made has been greeted with hostility, so we've had to remove certain people from cherished positions because they refused to change. They abused their positions by squandering opportunities to do their jobs better. Look what they've done. It took only one or two to incite the whole faculty to a vote of no confidence. What that tells me is that we struck a nerve.

"We find ourselves in a position where it's easier to do what's wrong than to do what's right. Think about the sports page: How long does it take for a new coach to build a program? The first thing he must do is overcome loyalty to his predecessor. The next is to bring in new talent. The last is to blend the new with the old to come up with a winning team, and that's what we're in the midst of doing. What we need to realize is that change requires the breaking of old molds and the shelving of useless traditions. If we're not up to that, it'll be business as usual—low standards, high dropout rates, and lackluster test results. Frankly, I can't settle for that."

Wainwright's approach that the best defense was a good offense came to him when he gave up searching for the key document he'd lost. Sheila had left at five, leaving only a computer tech and two custodians roaming the administration building. He was alone in his office, pondering—as he did when a child, hiding out to invent new personas before entering new schools. Solitude was his creative condition. He pulled the curtains and locked his door. Secured, Wainwright studied the NEA ballot he had requested from Macklin. Under a scrawled "Void. Sample copy," it said:

The current district administration demonstrates sufficient leadership skills and knowledge to increase student achievement and build support for schools across the community. [ ] agree [ ] disagree

Should a majority of votes from certificated staff be negative, the association's votes will constitute a Declaration of No Confidence.

Harry Morgan growled, "Yeah, but that doesn't explain the lopsided vote. Seventy-six percent negative? From where I sit, that's like being down fifty-zip deep in the fourth quarter."

Cutting off Wainwright's rebuttal, Mary Chesterton added, "Maybe we're looking at only one side of it. I'd like to be brought up to date on what's positive. Surely what the district's been put through over the past year has brought benefits." Her eye caught Martin Koutac's quick wink.

"Indeed." Claudia McPhaiden gave Chesterton a grateful smile. "That's a much better place to start. Charles, would you summarize the initiatives that have born fruit?"

"I'd be happy to. As you know, our new Reading Across the Curriculum program has boosted middle school test results four points and junior high scores over six points. That's huge progress for one year."

Koutac interrupted, "We've been over that. Our gains are about what other districts posted. The consensus is that gains in reading are more due to Harry Potter and Lemony Snicket books than curriculum changes. I'd like you to point out just one test result that shows gains relative to the districts around us, just one."

Wainwright turned on him. "You want positive change? I'll give you positive change. How about what's happened to the factors that provide a background for improvement? How about the drop in on-campus violence and theft? And how about the reduction in dropouts?"

"Thanks for reminding me." Koutac fanned a comb-bound report before him. "Could decreased violence have something to do with doubling campus security? Might the reduction in dropouts have something to do with expelling almost three times as many students as the year before?" He turned to McPhaiden and added, "But maybe those dots don't connect."

The undercurrent of unease with Wainwright spread from Koutac and Chesterton to include Harry Morgan. Nate McCollum chose to sit back and let the others spar. Claudia kept a wary eye on Wainwright who, as she had reason to suspect, didn't handle criticism gracefully. After most of a fruitless hour passed, she said, "Well, I know we all would like to go home. Now that we've had a chance to air our thoughts, let's agree to bring some positive thinking together for the benefit of the district the next time we meet. Do I hear a motion to adjourn?"

It was clear to Koutac that the fat was in the fire. He felt sure that the others, even tight-lipped Nate McCollum, had seen Wainwright for what he was: a fraud. The notes he'd penned didn't begin to identify the positive thinking Claudia called for. Instead, he had printed a list of adjectives, some underlined: uneasy, evasive, recalcitrant, defensive, shifty-eyed. The meeting was clearly a watershed event. Toward its end he smiled when Wainwright's eyes met his, the effect of his far-from-innocent pleasantry scoring a hit. Koutac sensed that Wainwright's reign had just ended, and he relaxed, sensing that over the days to follow, Wainwright would be taking on water and sinking until some terminal event put him under. And his body language said he knew it.

Claudia called for order. "One last detail. Assuming we'll all be present for graduation, we'd better know what we're going to do. Who wants to be first to hand out diplomas?"

It was graduation night. Jane returned to find Tom sprawled in his chair watching for the fourth or fifth time—she had lost track—*All That Jazz.* He thumbed the Pause button and asked, "Did I miss anything?"

"About two hundred well-wishers asking how you are. I told you it was a dumb idea for me to go alone. Now everybody thinks the worst."

"Sorry about that. If I'd have shown up, it might have been five hundred. Not that I'm all that popular; it's that people can't help being insensitively nosy about others' misfortunes. I'm not ready to run that gauntlet." He climbed out of his chair to stretch. "So tell me about it."

Jane led Tom's mind's eye into a grandstand filled with families, a scene he had presided over for nine graduations. He asked, "How did Van Horn do?"

"Just fine. Took care of the technical stuff and managed crowd control."

"You mean he wasn't on the podium?"

"Not even close."

"But he's the principal. He's supposed to be up there helping hand out diplomas. Damn good thing I wasn't there. I'd have made a scene, probably gotten arrested, cardiac arrested."

"Not funny, but speaking of scenes, do you want to hear the most interesting part?"

"Let's have it."

"It started normally. Imagine sunlight flickering off a blue sea. Well, that's what we saw looking down on the graduates under blue mortarboards, the flicker being faces turning to see if they could spot their parents. Claudia ran the show. She gave the usual instruction that everyone should refrain from applauding until the last graduate received a diploma—as if no one knew the diploma folders were empty—and as usual, the audience ignored her and broke into family cheering sections before the first dozen graduates crossed the stage.

"Wainwright was third to pass out diplomas, which included the Rs. The announcer read Roger Runyon's name, followed, of course, by quite a list of honors and study grants. So Roger walked up to Wainwright, who had his diploma in one hand and the other ready for the ritual handshake. Well, Roger just stopped. The announcer called the next one up, but he was stuck behind Roger with no place to go. Roger whispered something to Wainwright that upset him, and then Roger stayed put like the two of them were locked in a stare-down. Stopped the proceedings, he did. Wainwright leaned toward him, probably telling him to move it, at which time Roger took his diploma in both hands so he could avoid a handshake. It was quite dramatic. All the other graduates had their little cheering sections, but with Roger walking off while brushing Wainwright's touch from his diploma, the entire grandstand hummed with murmurs. Believe me, anyone who didn't know what it was all about knows by now."

Thong Phan won the CWP Scholarship, which left Roger and the other runner-up, Jen Ostrander, to commiserate. Though they had never dated, parallel schedules of advanced placement classes had coupled their minds for enough shared challenges to get to know and admire each other. Being serious young people, neither was expected at the rumored parties, which left them wondering what to do on graduation night. When their paths crossed during the confusion of turning in caps and gowns, Roger said, "Jen, one of these evenings, if you're not totally booked up, do you think we might spend some time together?" She said, "Sure, how about tonight?"

Jen inherited her father's height, which helped her to star in her favorite sport, volleyball. While her mother was a beauty, Jen was a handsome young woman with angular features, good muscle definition, and a loping gait that kept her ponytail in motion. Until their senior year, Roger hadn't thought of her as especially attractive. She was Jen, a classmate and friend, until they partnered in Advanced Placement Chemistry labs where their friendship deepened. They took to meeting for lunch a day or two each week. They met at the public library to prepare for classes. For both, high school had been a time of discovery that so occupied their minds neither did much dating, yet their parallel paths left them innocently vulnerable to the force that was building between them.

Roger unlocked his bike and wheeled it to the parking lot where he folded it into the cavernous trunk of the tan Chevrolet Caprice Grandpa Koutac had given her. She hopped behind the wheel. "Where to?"

"I'm hungry, of course. How about a burger and then we'll decide? You pick the place. My treat."

With a background of soft rock from the car radio, they munched and talked about where their classmates might be—the kegger at the lake or the party at the Kittlesons that Jerry had advertised as "no adults allowed." Roger said, "I don't need more company than you. If you don't mind, let's cruise a little, maybe find a quiet place and just talk." It was near 11:30 p.m. when curiosity took them past the Kittlesons where the party had spilled onto the front lawn. Roger commented. "I bet cops are on the way. We'd better move."

Jen patted the steering wheel. "We're immune. This barge is so uncool that the police never give it a second look. Where next?"

"Mom sleeps like a log when I slam into the house and rummage for food, but try to sneak in and she's up in a flash. If you want, we could do popcorn and channel surf." They drove to Roger's home and parked. The old Caprice had a bench seat that offered Roger opportunity. He slid toward Jen and stammered, "I would really, truly like to put my arms around you. Would you mind?" In response, she took hold of him and buried her face in the hollow of his neck. They were careful with each other, neither wanting to break the spell that grew with gentle touches and caresses that prefaced their first kiss—and another. Roger's voice was hoarse against her ear. "You are so very, very special. I don't want anything to go wrong, so maybe we'd better go inside—if that's okay with you."

Betty awakened at one fifteen to go to the bathroom and noticed flickering light from the television in the family room. The first things she saw over the big high-backed couch were a commercial for erectile dysfunction pills and three beer bottles on the coffee table. And then she saw her son and a woman, their arms entwined, together on the couch. No matter that they were clothed. The scene with the beer bottles and the bodies all but joined brought back the night of her fall to enflame her aching conviction that once stained by sin, life afterward could never be more than a tawdry compromise.

This was worse because now it was not only Dale but also her son who was caught up in his sin. The message was clear: "For I, the Lord, am a jealous God, visiting the iniquity of the fathers upon the children to the third and the fourth generation of those who hate me." The bad seed had been passed to her son. Her legs almost collapsed under her as verse after judgmental verse careened through her brain, hammering home the full burden of the wages of sin—unto the third and fourth generation. An involuntary wail of despair welled from her throat. Jen and Roger who had been spellbound by the electric connection of their touching bodies, sat up.

"Hi, Mom. I'd like you to meet Jen, Jen Ostrander."

Ostrander? No, it couldn't be. From the time of Dale's indiscretion, the name Gustafson was so engraved in her brain that anything or anyone related to the Gustafson whore's wantonness was suspect; the father who served on the school board and his daughter, Trish Ostrander, the whore's brash sister who had her finger in every pie. And now her son was consorting with the Gustafson tart's niece in her own home. There was no mistaking her. It was the same girl who walked across the stage shortly before her son's shocking scene with the superintendent. Was there no end to it? Humiliation upon humiliation. What more could go wrong? Of one thing she was sure: this wasn't her son's doing. Dale had put him up to it. As if he hadn't hurt her enough, his slut's niece was lying with her son. Degradation and filth had permeated her house. Impurity.

"Mom? What's the matter with you?"

"With *me*? What's the matter with me? Until you come back with a repentant heart, this is no longer your home. Get out and take that tramp with you."

Back in the Caprice, Roger could find no words to apologize. Jen took his face in her shaking hands and said, "I know she's your mom, but after what she said about me, I'm entitled to an opinion. I'm more shocked than hurt because what we just witnessed was not someone in her right mind." Jen's hands steadied as she put her face close to his, her features soft in the glow of a street light. "That woman, your mother, just cleared something up for me."

"I'm so sorry, Jen. Of all the places to take you…this was a colossal disaster. I wouldn't blame you if you never wanted to see me again."

"Oh, stop that and listen to me. My family has really been down on your dad for what happened to Aunt Dana. You know, with him being a married man. But tonight changed the whole picture for me. Wow, if we'd had a clue about what he was married to—well, anyway, it looks like we might have been too harsh on him. After all, he's your dad, so there has to be a lot of good in him." For a second time she burrowed into the hollow between his neck and shoulder, quickening his breath. She murmured, "You know, she's in there thinking you'll crawl back, contrite heart and all."

"Not going to happen. It would only justify her tantrum. I won't stay there; there are places where I can crash."

"Then let's go get your stuff, you and me. I need to face your mother again because she has no right to think I'm the kind of girl that gets thrown out of places. Does that make any sense?" She pulled back into the Runyon driveway and opened her door. "Come on. I'll help carry your stuff. Are you sure you have a place to crash? Some place where I can find you?"

Her words, "some place where I can find you," gave him strength. "I think so. Uncle Tom—that's Mr. Clausen—is my godfather, not my real uncle. I think he and Aunt Jane will understand." They gripped each other's hands tightly on their way back to the house.

Betty, sobbing private tears in her bedroom, didn't reappear. What had she done? In the face of fornication, what else could she have done? It wasn't the end. She had instructed him on how to return, and once he was free of that Jezebel, he would—with a contrite heart. They had left her no choice. "As for those who persist in sin, rebuke them in the presence of all, so they may stand in fear." So what if there had been no multitude to stand as witness. But "why should not the son suffer for the iniquity of the father?" That can't be right. It's too cruel, but it is written. Her ears detected motion. Someone was in the house. Roger had come back but not alone. She was with him. Her spasm of rage might have carried her out of her room were it not for her condition—red eyed, disheveled, and defeated by her son's fall from grace.

Roger led Jen to his room where he began stuffing clothes into a duffel bag. She looked about, absorbing the many things she didn't know about him: framed quotes, book titles, the Yamaha keyboard, a guitar, a soprano sax, and bits of trivia that added layers to his substance. It took two trips to the car before his "essentials" were loaded. A laptop with a bag of CDs, a tattered Disney monkey, clothes to last between weekly washdays, and another duffel bag of things he would have had trouble explaining in his agitated state. From behind her door, Betty's hearing penetrated the soft electric hum of her home to detect footsteps and murmured conversation. She followed their second trip past her room to the front door and heard it close behind them. Car doors opened and closed. An engine started and faded. She cried the night away.

A motion sensor triggered a pole light when Jen turned into the Clausen driveway. Nearing 2:00 a.m. the house was dark, but inside Buster sounded his alarm, woof-woof-woofing without, it seemed, pausing to breathe. A patch of light appeared in a window. Roger knocked at the back door and whispered, "He might have a gun, you know. Or he might say, 'Come back in the morning.'"

Jen whispered, "Or, 'Roger who? I don't know a Roger.' How sure are you that this is the right house?"

"Trust me; it's more right than the last one I took you to. These are good people."

A light came on behind the Venetian blinds of the door's window. A finger pried slats apart followed by the lock clicking. It was a different Mr. Clausen than Jen had seen cruising the halls of Northbridge High. Tousled, puffy from sleep, and clad in robe and slippers, he seemed four inches shorter without the elevating authority of his office. He stepped aside. "Come in; please come in." Jane padded up behind him and said, "Roger? Oh, what's happened? Both of you, come in."

Roger handed Jen forward for introduction. "Uncle Tom, Aunt Jane, this is Jen Ostrander, my best friend. We've had a tough evening."

"We've met. Welcome, Jen. Do you want to talk with just one of us, or is it okay to do this as a foursome?"

Jen, an honor student and captain of the volleyball team, had caused a furor when, after starring in basketball as a sophomore and junior, she elected not to play her senior year because of a full advanced-placement schedule. She was well-known to Tom.

Roger inched into describing the scene they'd endured. "You know my mom pretty well and how she can get pretty rigid about things? Well, Jen and I didn't want to hit the after-graduation parties so we went to my house to watch TV. Being graduation and all, I pushed the envelope a little by helping myself to a couple of beers from the stash Dad left in the garage. We surfed channels and settled onto the couch to watch the last half of *Spaceballs*. About us being together, Jen's been a special friend for years, but tonight was the closest thing to a date we've ever had. Well, Mom woke up, spotted beer bottles, and caught us, well, with my arm around her. It wasn't any big deal; we weren't doing anything wrong."

Jane bridged Roger's pause. "How did she react?"

"She went nuts. I've seen her angry before, but she really lost it this time. Totally out of control. She spluttered a lot and threw a bunch of Bible verses at us. She kicked me out and said I shouldn't come back until I had a contrite heart. The worst of it was that she called Jen a tramp. I was so proud to be with her and wanted Mom to meet her, but she ruined everything. If she expects me to choose between her and Jen, she's out of the picture. Some family, huh?"

Jane took Jen's hand. "There's a phone on the kitchen wall if you need to check in."

"Thanks, but I have my cell. I've already called twice. They're anxious but not worried."

Jane turned back to Roger. "You know you're welcome to stay here as long as you want. The spare room is the same as when you last stayed there. Did you bring some things with you?" He nodded. "Then you'll need a key, just a minute." She padded into the kitchen, returning with two keys hung from a yellow smiley-face disk. "Here, consider these yours. Now come with me; we'll need to push a few things aside." Jane led Roger upstairs, leaving Tom with Jen.

"Thanks for helping out, Jen. I don't mean to butt in, but have you and Roger talked about why you, of all people, might have tipped his mom off balance?"

"Of course. And you should know that Roger and I have been friends for years. Nothing that happened between his dad and my aunt affects who we are to each other. His mom was so totally out of control…like unhinged. I can't imagine what she's going through after throwing her son out of her house. It's so sad. And about thanking me for helping, you're the ones we should be thanking."

"You said 'we.' Good. I'm sure you're the best medicine for him right now. Pardon me for asking, but how involved are you?"

"I really don't know. We just discovered that we're very close, maybe closer than we thought. Close enough that I don't think either of us is ready to give up the other because of this. I guess we're sort of blown away by finding out that we might be more than friends. Oh yeah, besides that, we were consoling each other for not quite getting the CWP award."

"Impressive. I knew Roger was in the running and that you've always been pretty much straight-A. You make quite a couple." Tom shifted back to his concern about the Runyon breakup. "Thanks for being so open with me. It makes it easier to share something with you. This is how I see it: I think there's something else upsetting Mrs. Runyon that you had no part in. It seems that Betty Runyon might be the kind of person who's been certain about what life was supposed to be from the time she was a child. It came from rigid Bible training—not the love and forgiveness part, but the hellfire and damnation part. She was taught that belief trumps reason like you see happening in politics. The people she encounters never shape up to her idea of biblical perfection so she writes them off as hell bound. I was surprised that her husband coped with it as long as he did."

"Was she married before, or do you mean Roger's dad?"

"Roger's dad, it was a first marriage for both. But a time came when his need to be loved bumped into your aunt Dana. And unless I'm mistaken, she had needs in that department, too."

"Uh-huh. No dating, just Pip. What a setup. And when Roger's mom saw me with him, I was the bad seed sent by the family that undid her husband." Jen inhaled sharply. "From the father to the son? Oh my God! That's what she was ranting about. She's really condemned her own son. The poor woman!"

"Yes. And that would account for the intensity of her blowup. Would any of this change things between you and Roger?"

"Why should it? I'm not Aunt Dana, and Roger's not his dad. I think its best that we live life based on who we are, don't you?"

CHAPTER 17

Dale bypassed Starbucks once before turning back to take a parking slot. He sat through the din of station-break commercials while his watch crept toward five o'clock. At one minute till the hour, he locked his car and steeled himself for an encounter he feared could leave him in a worsened state. Her voice at the hospital echoed in his mind. "Stay with me" and "Don't leave me," but he had fled from the security officer's attention. And it was Dale who had sent her into the darkness to "work her way around the house." It could go very badly, but he had no choice. He had to see her to tell her what filled his thoughts day and night. He entered and immediately spotted her at a window table from which she, no doubt, had watched his uncertain approach. She acknowledged his arrival with a neutral nod and a raised hand. He joined a short line at the order counter that, instead of giving him time to compose himself, heightened his anxiety.

Gina Troxell and her partner, Marybeth Rosenau, sat at a table bringing their books up to date when he entered. Gina was a whiz with a laptop, except she couldn't swing her gaze from the month's expense and income data to the screen without losing her place each time so the two met over lattes. Marybeth was reading data to Gina, whose fingers danced over the keys to match Marybeth's input, until her typing stalled when Marybeth went silent.

"Guess who just walked in." Both Gina and Marybeth were born and raised in Northbridge, graduated from Northbridge High, and co-owned a Merry Maids housecleaning franchise. Little happened in Northbridge that escaped their scrutiny.

"Oh yuck, Runyon the Butcher running around loose." Gina

sneaked another long look. "Too bad, but even a hunk like him isn't worth bleeding for."

"You got that right. Don't look now, but guess who he's sitting with."

Gina turned to watch Dale approach a booth. "Oh, wow! Some people are certainly slow learners. You'd think she'd be more careful after being married to…what was his name?"

"Gus Gustafson. Anyway, I read an article about victimology that said some people are wired to link up with losers and that losers can spot them. Too bad. Gina, you're staring!"

Equipped with a short Americano, Dale took the chair across from Dana. He found curiosity when their eyes met, a better greeting than what he'd feared. He said, "Hello."

With arched brows Dana asked, "Just hello?" She might have said "Hello to you, too," or "How are you?" However, that would have been too open, too welcoming when unsure if the score had been evened for the hurt he'd caused her.

"Call it caution. I'm afraid of making a mistake."

"That's understandable." She kept her responses terse. It was he who had called so she was prepared to hear him out, not entertain him with social chatter. Yet each time she opened her mouth, she regretted the harsh tone she was powerless to control. "You've made some big mistakes."

"Yes, but this is now, and if I come off a little stiff, it's because I'm afraid that you might take something wrong when I mean no offense. I don't want that to happen."

"Why?"

Dale had resolved to stay on safe ground, yet her single syllable probed the core of his distress. "I don't want to dodge your question, and I don't want to drive you away with ill-timed declarations. I need a little help here. Would you please tell me if you're at all interested in why I called you or why we're sitting here together?"

"Yes, I'm interested. I'm actually somewhat concerned about you."

"Then here's the situation. I dream about you. Most times the dreams are good, but when I wake, there's the empty realization that you're gone from my life. Sometimes I see you bleeding and wake up terrified. When that happens, it takes hours to get back to sleep. You're on my mind, and I can't want to get over you." Dale, who was turned toward the window, sneaked a glance at her. Their eyes locked briefly.

Dana said, "What do you plan to do about your situation?" She had come to hear him out, not to concede points. She knew when she agreed to meet that being alone with him might, like a drink in the hand of a recovering alcoholic, open a regrettable response. Yet she hadn't been able to not want to see him. After his call, she counted three reasons for agreeing to meet. First, with her father's help, she had come to realize that neither fault nor fallout had been one-sided. While she knew he was married, she expected him to act like he wasn't. Second, by asking around, she knew that, more than her cuts and punctures, he was losing critical elements of his life. Third, her niece, Jen, had taken her aside after Sunday dinner to tell her about her meeting with Dale's ex, whom she had described as dangerously loony.

"I don't know," he said. "That's not entirely up to me. It's been more than six weeks since we last talked, but it seems longer than that."

She conceded to herself that yes, it did seem a long time, which thawed her defense enough to ask, "Are you well? Are you working?" She had watched women's heads turn, which brought back her first impressions when they met at softball league sign-ups. How long ago had that been? He was and wasn't the same person. Damaged as he was, he still had what it took to distract two women she knew from their work session. He had lost weight. Something more was missing, a buoyancy, something about how he carried himself.

"Yes to the first. About work, it's been irregular, short-term stuff. I signed on with Delta Biometrix as head of information technology. They have about a hundred employees on a net of eighty stations. They had linkage problems, which was right up my alley. When they gave me an office and lots of responsibility, I thought, this is it, a new career. I was in the middle of bringing their systems up to speed when a Canadian outfit bought them out. They took a look at my plan, which had taken two weeks of unpaid overtime to develop, and decided to finish it themselves. The short version is that in rushing to please, I worked myself out of a job."

"Oh? As I recall you weren't such a fast worker." Dana clenched her eyes shut, regretting her brain's lack of a delete key. She had come to the meeting not wanting to appear either too familiar or too remote. If only there was a way to take it back.

"No comment." But he added, "I think we both realize that too much happened between us to pretend we're the same people we were, so I'll say what I came to say and then get out of your way. You don't have to respond. I'll just leave." He pushed their cups aside to open a clear path across the tiny table. "I miss you. Through most of my adult life I'd come to accept that being with a woman was hard work. Until you. But dammit, the way it worked out, it seems I traded the drudgery of my marriage for pain for both of us. After what's happened, I can't expect much, but the one thing I do want to see happen after mucking up your life is you and Pip pulling things back to normal. That said, I'd better go now. I hope you'll let me see you again."

"Why? Why me? You could have your pick. Behind you on your left—don't look now—two women I happen to be acquainted with have been salivating over you ever since you walked in. So I'm asking, why me?"

"There's no one else in my mind. I've given you more than enough reason to shut me out, and I have to live with that. It's a question words can't answer. If you don't mind, I'd rather leave it on the table for now. The tension's pretty heavy, and that's not good for, you know, constructive talk. It's like we've been jockeying for position more than talking."

"So it seems. You're right; this hasn't been easy for me either, but I do think that it might be healthy for both of us to meet once again, not right away, just to clear the air."

"You'd do that? Wonderful. That's what I was hoping to hear, and please understand that I won't push for anything more. There's a lot on my heart that needs to stay there for now. Thank you, and by the way, you look great. I was worried about that, I mean how well you'd heal."

"Makeup does wonders." She stuffed her napkin in her cup. "I'd better go."

They rose together and walked out, Dale holding the door for her. She had started toward her car when she turned to say, "Your son's nice. Do you know he's been seeing Jen?"

Wainwright left his office after taking a call from Claudia who had just spoken with Nate McCollum. He had called to tell her that after the executive session, he'd come to suspect that Koutac might have been right all along about Wainwright, and it might be worthwhile to reexamine their support for him.

Wainwright stormed from his office and drove home. He slammed the door from the garage to the utility room closed, dropped his attaché case, and went straight to the wet bar to pour two fingers of Glenlivet. He shouted up the stairwell, "Jeanne, Jeanne, where the hell are you? "I know you're up there. Answer me, dammit! Don't make me come up there to get you."

Jeanne Wainwright appeared at the top of the stairs with her hair bundled in a towel. "I'm here." She was grateful for the flight of stairs separating them after what he did the last time he used that tone with her. When she'd tried to soothe his anger, he slapped her hard enough to make her nose bleed. The second time he exploded, she tried telling him that she wouldn't put up with such hostility in her home, which didn't work any better. Ranting that as long as he paid the bills, he made the rules, he threw her out into the night. The incidents weren't many—six if she counted the flare-up when a hotel clerk told them they would have to settle for a lesser room than the one he had reserved. Feeling threatened, the clerk called security. Security called the police. The police gave Charles (then William) the choice of leaving peaceably or going to jail. Jeanne spent that night cowering against the passenger's door of Charles's Pontiac while he drove the night away at reckless speed. The lesson she absorbed over her years with him was that he might turn anything she said against her and that "I'm here" might have been two words too many.

"You're moving back to Oregon. Call the renters and tell them to get their asses out of the house. I'll have a mover here in ten days—do you hear that? Ten days! Don't even think of camping in front of your soaps because you're going to be too busy getting things packed and ready. Is that clear?"

"Yes." She held her position, hoping he had run out of venom. Jeanne found herself teetering between staying rooted and retreating, which hadn't worked any better for her. She recalled him charging her from behind, shouting, "Don't you turn your back on me!"

"What the hell are you standing there for? You've got work to do. And don't touch my side of the closet; I'll take care of that." Wainwright turned and threw down the scotch incautiously, hitting the wrong pipe, which set off a coughing fit. He was still gasping when he slammed out of the house.

It was the moment Jeanne had been preparing for. Throughout the first years of their marriage, she was captive to a belief that life for her and her daughters could be livable only by staying married to a steady income. That perspective changed with Meg newly married and Beth working at Boeing. Jeanne's lesbian sister, Jan, and her paralegal partner did everything in their power to rescue her from the marriage in the beginning, but their well-intentioned intrusions failed to take Jeanne's insecurities into account, causing her to defend against helpful suggestions with a ferocity that was quite out of character with her normal timidity. But Jan's advice had taken root. Incident by incident and year by year, it percolated up to erode Jeanne's valuation of her marriage.

Jeanne had been readying herself since the move from Cottage Grove, collecting scraps of information about Charles's financial affairs. He assumed that, by ordering her not to touch his mail and throwing a scare into her now and then, he had built a fire wall that would stand against her curiosity about his affairs. Not having been married before, he had no idea how naive that was. In fact, Jeanne had organized photocopies of every scrap of information she could lay her hands on into folders that also contained copies of Charles's mutual fund holdings, bank account numbers and past balances, insurance policies, and warranty deeds.

Her complacency ended with Charles's insensitivity to how happy she'd been in Cottage Grove. It wasn't that Moraine was an unpleasant place to live; it was how he dragged her there, coming home one day to announce, "We're moving." Upset about the loss of friends and the home she had come to love, she called Jan who, after hearing her out, put her partner, Kelli, on the phone. Kelli took an interest in Jeanne's plight, coaching her on legal options and giving tips on how to protect her interests, including procedures for freezing Charles's assets.

Charles wished he had changed his Brooks Brothers suit and tie, which trapped heat from the afternoon sun on the Moraine Mall parking lot. He entered the mall's air-conditioned glitz and hype where the young and not-so-young dressed and carried themselves to mirror their fantasies. He felt himself changing, as though molting. With each step down the mall's concourse, his Charles Wainwright persona crumbled away as he became just another face without an identity.

McCollum's defection had been the last straw, crumbling his control to let Koutac's gang depose Claudia. He saw it in their eyes. The last week had been an unmitigated disaster. Time to move on. Charles fancied himself a good judge of character, but lately people he trusted to be loyal had dared to question his decisions. And Claudia—he'd groomed her to support him through thick and thin, but even she was wavering. Jeanne, though, was no mystery. Reliably afraid of her own shadow, she knew how to take orders and would take care of the move. Having whined ever since leaving Cottage Grove, she'd be happy to do whatever it took to get back there, leaving him free to reorganize.

He had only a week until the scheduled closing of his office for the vacation month of July. Better check with finance tomorrow to see if his check would be ready. Two months' salary would tide him over while he sought out something new, a low-pressure single act with none of the bureaucratic crap he'd endured here. Maybe just disappear for a while, go fishing, tell Jeanne to stay put in Cottage Grove. That should keep her happy. The district would figure out soon enough that he was gone. Once they figured out that he'd jumped contract, they wouldn't be inclined to mount a search for him. They, too, would just as soon forget the whole thing.

Wainwright's shirt was stained with sweat when he reached Jamaica Joe's Espresso. Equipped with a vanilla latte, he settled in with his notebook to do some planning. He had little to do but plan until the day before the district offices closed, and then it would be full speed ahead. He'd already arranged to have the proceeds from the sale of the house, whenever that happened, deposited in his account in the Bahamas. And he'd hired an investigator to remove a special box from his closet and forward it to an address in Bakersfield. Of all his gigs, he wished this one had let him walk away with his head held high, but what the hell. At least he'd be up a few dollars. Thanks to the inflated housing market, he might clear forty thousand on the house. It would have been smoother to wait till he was gone to list it, but that had a downside, too. So far no one had asked about the sign in the yard.

Under the guise of packing, Jeanne boxed everything she wanted: her mother's china and crystal, artwork, and valuables she cherry-picked from their belongings. Furniture for a two-bedroom apartment was locked in a local storage unit. She did check his side of the closet, not to pack his things but to go through his pockets, and when she got to a box on a top shelf marked "Personal: Do Not Open," she pulled it down. Leaving its seal intact, she razored it open from the bottom and arranged its contents on his bed.

The time for serving papers on Charles was coming up. Kelli had advised her on how to freeze his assets to keep him from looting their accounts since Jeanne had no experience in such matters, but she rightly suspected that the contents of the box, together with her files, might yield enough reason for an attorney to stop his withdrawals, credit card charges, or sale of assets. She found certificates and college degrees, all phony. Covering the king bed, they could paper a small wall, about thirty in total. She found evidence of her husband impersonating, or considering impersonating, a gemologist, a California real estate broker, a physical therapist, an insurance adjuster, a hotel manager, an Oregon building inspector, and of course, a Kentucky superintendent of schools. She carefully repacked all but a few of the papers, sealing the box's bottom with Magic Mending Tape and returning it to its shelf. Kelli had advised her that timing was all important and that she should rent a storage unit—two, if her looting of the house called for more space. She would use Charles's last day at his office to wrap up her divorce attorney's to-do list. He would come home that evening to find her gone and the divorce papers, with copies of documents she kept to restrain him from contesting the divorce, set out on the kitchen counter. He would go wild when he realized what she had done but she didn't plan to be around to witness that. Jeanne and her unmarried daughter, if she opted to join her, would be on their way to Branson, Missouri, to take in some country music. Or maybe Hawaii. Despite what she'd done to lock up her husband's assets, Jeanne wasn't a vengeful person and was surprised to hear herself whisper, "He's earned every bit of it."

CHAPTER 18

"Tom, phone. It's Aunt Sigi."

Tom swung to look at the patches of stone and brick peeking through spreading foliage that would one day mask the mansion from sight. Jane handed him the phone.

"Hi, Sigi. What's up?"

"Mr. Garnet's dead. Could you come over? I don't know what to do." Her tone was matter of fact, the same voice that had called to say, "Mr. Garnet's lawnmower won't start, can you help?"

"Are you sure?"

"Of course I'm sure. He fell out of his chair, and he's lying on the den floor all bent up. I need help straightening him out."

"Did you call nine-one-one?"

"No, Mr. Garnet always told me that nine-one-one was for emergencies. He's through having emergencies. Will you come over?"

"Be right there."

Jane took the phone. "You look terrible. Another emergency?"

"Not according to Aunt Sigi. She said Garnie's dead. She's over there alone with his body."

"Oh dear. Just like that. I wonder if anyone other than us will care."

He nuzzled her forehead. "I have to go. Would you come with me?"

Roger, just back from walking Buster, read their expressions. "What's up, Unc?"

"Hold the fort for us. There's been a death across the street. No telling how long we'll be."

Both big front doors were open. Tom knocked and called, "Aunt Sigi?" The atmosphere was changed. Every curtain was pulled back, allowing a flood of daylight to draw out colors from the Persian carpets that segmented the entry and living room. The house was cool from a draft sweeping through the open solarium door that rustled the parted curtains. In the presence of death, Tom and Jane were stunned by how the play of afternoon light brought the house to life. As light and shadow sharpened the effects of design features, they felt they were witnessing the architect's intent for the first time. Aunt Sigi's emergence from the kitchen with a cup of coffee echoed the living room's luminosity. Her silver hair, normally tied in a neat bun, fell in shimmering disorder over the shoulders of a blue and silver training outfit, a surprising change from her usual cotton dress and cardigan. She said, "This way. He's in the den."

They found him face-down in front of his chair, his jowly face flattened against the oak plank floor. One arm was flung out as if to arrest his fall, the other folded awkwardly under him. Tom took a toppled stack of back issues of *The Economist* as evidence that he had grasped for support before going down. He asked, "When did you find him?"

"Oh, about three o'clock. I gave him a squirt of honey, but it didn't do any good. I yelled at him and pushed at him with my foot—more like I touched him with my toe—but nothing worked. After I decided he was dead, I called my friend, Mr. Steffanson—you remember him—and he said to call you." She sipped her coffee and tried to tame her hair with finger combing. She put her cup down and stepped to Garnie's feet. "Here," she said, "I'll take his feet. Help me straighten him out."

Tom handed her cup back to her. "No. People will need to know how he died. It's better to leave him just as he is. Would you like to call nine-one-one, or do you want me to?"

The starch went out of Sigi. "But after they take him, what'll I do?" The prospect of living without Garnie to battle with struck her like an avalanche. Though neither had held much affection for the other, they were fixed navigation points for each other's lives. Without Garnie to work around and to clean up after, and without his thoughtless snide remarks to complain about, Sigi's roadmap for life had lost its main reference point. Aside from Inger, Arnie, and two brothers and their families, her world had been defined by Mr. Garnet and The House for so many years that she no longer possessed the will or flexibility to consider a different life. Tom picked up the den phone and made the call.

The Pittman family burial ground occupied a twenty-by-forty-foot plot at the northeast corner of the thirty-six-acre Marine View Park, donated to the city by Waldo Pittman in 1940. The terms of the gift that bound the city to mow among the few gravestones and keep the iron fence in repair had been ignored for so long that no local could recall seeing it groomed. Garnie's sister, Alicia Morrison, visited the plot the day after his death to find her parents' graves overgrown by thorny creepers. Without consulting the city, she hired a team of landscapers to strip it to soil and lay new sod. Her pleasure with the seamless perfection of the new turf earned a bonus for Nguyen and Sons Landscaping Services, the firm she hired at Tom's recommendation.

The burial plot, on the opposite side of the park from public parking, was reached by walking around a playground and crossing a swath of grass posted with "Dogs must be leashed." Tom and Jane arrived to find Aunt Sigi's plain-dressed nieces and their husbands in one group, their stair-step children having broken away to race about the park like a pack of wild dogs. A second group, identifiable by its dark suits, consisted of the money men, dealmakers hoping that parts of the Pittman empire might need their services. Tom recognized the lawyer he saw leaving the hospital, but the rest were strangers whose glances glossed over him without a nod. Locals and business associates milled in separate eddies. No one dress code prevailed, though enough color was worn to suggest that, other than the suits, the guests anticipated a celebration of life, not a funeral.

Two rangy elders joined Aunt Sigi, the taller, her friend and dancing partner, Karl Steffanson. The gentleman in the plaid Pendleton cruiser jacket and bolo tie was Garnie's erstwhile mill manager and confidante, Chet Tovson, who worked for Pittman timber operations from his seventeenth birthday until retirement. The men closed ranks around

Sigi and best friend Inger for warmhearted chatter, frequent touches, and laughter. Jane spotted Mildred Gunning standing alone. Mildred, long-retired head librarian and grande dame of Northbridge's book clubs, suffered bouts of confusion. Jane excused herself to shore her up.

Tom spotted another loner studying the social action. He approached and introduced himself. "Hello, I'm Tom Clausen. You must be from out of town." The man was near to Tom's height of five-ten but much heavier. He had arrived in the Lincoln town car parked in a handicapped zone near the playground, its liveried driver lounging against its passenger side. Everything about him marked him as a stranger: the tailored, double-vented suit jacket; the detailing on his shirt—not items one could buy off the rack. His dark complexion, wavy gray hair combed back to fall over his collar, and Italian shoes marked him as from a far place. The bulky traveler gave Tom a measured smile when greeted.

"I am Dr. Kostadin Paunov, from Bulgaria. I'm sorry that I have come too late to visit with my friend, Timberman."

Tom cut in. "Pardon me, but the man being buried is Garnet Pittman. Are you sure you're in the right place?"

"Yes, I knew him by another name. Many of us who play international chess on the web use other names. Mine is Odessus," and he gave Tom a brief account of his dealings with Pittman.

"Forgive me for asking, but where did you learn English? If you have an accent, it's very American."

"Moscow. I was sent there to learn, and what you hear is how they taught me, idioms and all. Then I studied in Germany and France. How do you know Timberman?"

"I live across the street from his home."

"Then you are his beloved educator, the one who loved to irritate him."

"Yes, that would be me. Pardon me, but I have things to do right now. We're to reconvene at the mortuary and then move to Garnie's home. I'll have someone help your driver find his way if you like. You will come, won't you? We have a lot to talk about."

Ranks of white folding chairs were arranged in a garden setting at the mortuary. The air was still and the sun intense. Alicia caught Tom by an arm. "Oh, Thomas, we've been talking about you. We hope you will do us a great favor. You see, we've all been at such a distance from poor Garnet's last years that we scarcely know what to say about him. Do you think you could say a few words?" Tom looked to Jane. She nodded.

"Of course. But given your brother's, shall we say, interesting approach to life, I can only speak of the Garnie I knew. Promise you won't take offense if it doesn't come out right?"

"Then we can count on you? Excellent."

To Tom's knowledge, Garnie had never leaned toward Christianity or any other form of worship, so his curiosity was high when Reverend Wilson of Northbridge's Soundview Presbyterian Church approached. Wilson threaded though chairs to reach him, greeting and back-patting his way until he dropped into a vacant chair. "Warm day for a burial, Mr. Clausen. Just to make sure, did Mrs. Morrison ask you to speak? Or maybe I should ask, would you be comfortable speaking about Mr. Pittman?"

Tom, who had been sorting through the bizarre anecdotes that filled his history with Garnie, smiled. "Not a problem. I'm pretty good at thinking on my feet. You'll find it interesting."

Wilson stood and cocked his head. "Okay then, the ball's in your court." He glanced at his watch. "You're up in ten minutes." There had been no church service, only document-signing at the mortuary attended by Wilson, Alicia, and two representatives of Pittman Pacific, Inc.

Never having met the deceased, Reverend Wilson was spared characterizing him. In fact, he would have referred Alicia to another minister had his secretary not reminded him that Garnie's father had contributed almost half the construction money for Soundview Presbyterian. After Alicia left his office with the date and time locked down, he spent a few minutes googling popular funeral and interment verses and readings.

With the sun scorching his scalp, Wilson intoned, "O God, great and all-knowing, all-powerful judge of the living and the dead, before whom we all will appear to render accounts of our thoughts, words, and deeds, let us be reminded by the passing of our friend, Garnet, to be mindful of our own mortality and to live each day for—live each day, each day for what it is, a gift from God. Let us always walk in His wisdom and be obedient to His commandments so that when we also depart this world, we may experience a merciful judgment and rejoice in everlasting happiness. Father, we ask this through Jesus Christ, our Lord. Amen."

Wilson wakened to his error halfway through the prayer, stumbling when he found himself giving his closer. He sought relief by announcing, "The family has selected Garnet's friend, Tom Clausen, to say a few words. Mr. Clausen?"

Tom, hands empty of notes, stepped forward to settle himself and scan the group, making eye contact where he could. Including children, fewer than eighty were in attendance. He began, "To give a picture of what my neighbor, Garnie Pittman, meant to us, I offer good news and bad news. The good news is that in recent years I had more personal contact with Garnie than anyone here, except for Aunt Sigi." He blew her a kiss. "The bad news is the same, that I knew Garnie Pittman better than most. Some of you won't be surprised when I say that he could drive people nuts." He waited for the nervous chuckle to subside. "And I expect he managed to offend every one here at some time. To explain Garnie, I'll begin with the ridiculous and work toward the sublime, but I must confess that Garnie Pittman left me with way more material on the ridiculous end of his spectrum."

Tom pointed into the audience, "Ardis. Ardis Swenson, I couldn't pass this on to you while Garnie was alive, but please consider the tale you are about to hear as a bequest from Garnie Pittman, something to remember him by when you look across the fence to the big house to the south of you: the case of Pittman versus Swenson's dog, Digger." Tom was in rare form as he drew on memories of incidents with Garnie. His droll monologue rolled on for fifteen minutes through which he had every adult teetering in hysterical laughter on their unsteady chairs. When he role-played Garnie's antics in the public library, a cheerful screech burst from Mildred Gunning, drawing a hug from Jane who had stayed by her side. The younger children, clueless as to what the laughter was about, giggled at their parents.

Tom paused for the laugher to subside. "That was one side of Garnie—his mask, his protective layer, his shell. The real Garnie was a multifaceted wonder who had difficulty relating to the world. Garnie was impressively intelligent, frustratingly devious, and, in certain ways, deeply insightful. I say in certain ways because, while he was blind to the needs of people closest to him, he was up on issues of regional and world importance. His mind was busy with complex thoughts that most of us couldn't follow and that prevented him from relating to the people around him. It's what often happens to people who are too smart for their own good.

"Garnie was powerful. He wielded his economic clout with the subtlety of a mule skinner's whip but always with the welfare of Northbridge at heart. He was born to power. His father and grandfather were the godfathers of Northbridge in their times. If you look into how the institutions of our town came to be, you'll find Pittman fingerprints all over them. I saw Garnie go up against OmniMart and win to help our public schools. With Garnie, it was always the schools. How many of you know that he was once a college teacher?" Only Alicia and Sigi's hands went up. "With Garnie, it was once an educator, always an educator. Not only was he a constant school supporter here in Northbridge, his reach was international. We might never have known how far his interests ranged had Dr. Kostadin Paunov not traveled all the way from Bulgaria to pay his respects." Tom nodded to Paunov. "Thank you for joining us. We are honored that you chose to travel such a distance to be here with us today. Garnie helped Dr. Paunov establish a new kind of university in Bulgaria. Isn't that amazing?

"Garnie was a student of social and economic change, especially here in Northbridge, his town. He was raised by a family that built and supported so much of it that he thought of Northbridge as his town. When he saw harm headed its way, he acted to head it off. I once saw him change the character of a commercial development when cut-rate promoters tried to cheapen it. And yet the people who benefited from him saw him as the town character, an oddity, a curmudgeon. In truth, he was all of that. But the strange man who dressed oddly, insulted people right and left, and lived like a hermit was a giant. It is hard to assess his impact on the people of Northbridge, but believe me, it is huge. He did leave us one final gift—if only we have what it takes to pick it up. What he left us is this: Through all his giving, and because of his giving, he is our exemplar, a model for civic generosity. Despite his peculiarities, Garnie Pittman was always a giver, never a taker. Day by day he left our world better for having walked in it. I will truly miss him. Farewell, my friend."

A hush followed Tom as he returned to his chair beside Jane and Mildred. Reverend Wilson reclaimed the lectern to let the thoughtful moment stretch. At length, he said, "Thank you, Tom. Now please join in the closing prayer printed on the last page of your Order of Service."

By the time Tom and Jane pulled into their driveway, the circular drive across the street was filled with cars, leaving the overflow to rank up along the curb in front of the Pittman and Swenson homes and on to the cul-de-sac. They spotted Roger, the event's volunteer valet, taking the keys to L. H. Terhune's Audi. Terhune, publisher of the *Northbridge World*, never passed up a free lunch.

The paths to the house were freshly groomed and the stairway and porch cleaned, but the grand old home and its grounds showed their age. The main entry doors were latched open to give guests views through the oval entry hall with its curved stairway and out through living room windows to sun-flecked water. It was the first time Tom had seen the elegant rooms free of clutter. The den had been cleared of Garnie's papers, and having lost a battle with Alicia Morrison, Aunt Sigi's fabric clippings were elsewhere for the day.

Little other than surface cleaning had readied the house for caterers, who set up near the solarium in the post-Victorian great room where visitors could imagine costumed couples waltzing to a string ensemble. Tom linked up with Paunov again. "Come with me. We can talk in Timberman's home office."

"Speaking of offices," Paunov said, "I wish he could have known that the building that houses my university office is named Gorska Sgrada, or Forester Building in his honor." He stepped behind Pittman's desk to lay a hand on the closed laptop computer and murmured, "Then this must be where he sat for our chess matches."

While Paunov scanned titles on the shelves, Tom pulled down the first of three leather-bound journals and opened it. The first page bore a photo of a girl, captioned in handwritten cursive, "Lillian Mardesich, Valedictorian, Northbridge High School, 1953. CWP winner in the amount of $5,000." Short entries filled more than half the page, the ink color changing with updates.

Graduated WSU, chemical engineering
Employed Scott Paper, 1958–1961 and 1970–1991
Port Gardner City Council, library board, UGN
Married, Richard Thiele, 2 daughters, Rose and Ella Thiele

The next pages held four more entries dated 1954, ten for 1955. He tucked the journal under his arm and waited for Paunov to complete his inspection.

Downstairs again, Tom steered Paunov toward Alicia. In her early seventies, Alicia's elegantly coiffed white hair was tinged platinum-gold. Like Garnie, her weight had gone to her hips, one of which she favored as she limped toward them. Aside from her build, everything about Alicia Morrison contrasted with her deceased brother's Spartan lifestyle. For his burial, she had draped her weight in a flowing, navy-blue silk gown that set off gold and onyx accessories. He passed Paunov to her, saying, "Alicia, Dr. Paunov would like to speak with the sister of his friend, Garnet Pittman." She linked arms with Paunov to prevent his escape and led him onto a flag-stoned veranda that commanded forty yards of weedy lawn that sloped to an untended, view-obstructing laurel hedge. Sigi's nieces and nephews, who knew the lay of the land from previous visits, scampered through a gap in the hedge to clamber down subsided sections of a stone stairway to the beach.

Alicia reappeared after ducking away to trade her navy dress for a sparkling sari-like gown in peach, maroon, and gray. "Thomas, I always knew you were a dear, but your talk, every word was precious. I know perfectly well how little time you had to prepare. How did you do it? I mean how did you do it so perfectly? I must tell you that your performance put me in total agreement with Garnet's assessment of you." She sipped her drink and said, "Oh, how impolite. Dr. Paunov, come with me, and we'll find a beverage of your choosing." She marched heavily back to the bar to pass him off to a bartender and launched off to greet latecomers.

"She's enjoying this," Jane observed.

"Maybe a bit too much," Tom said. "The cleanup, the rearranged furniture—I don't know her well enough to speculate, but it might be that she's putting her brand on the house, which might not work well for Aunt Sigi."

Jane pinched his ribs. "Knock it off, Mr. Meddler. That's Pittman family business. Now, intentionally changing the subject, did you check out the label on your wine? I can't read Spanish, but I'll bet this Grand Reserva 1984 didn't come from the grocery store."

Tom sipped appreciatively. "Nor the lobster-sized prawns or the single-malt scotch or the Perrier for teetotalers. Think about it: What if Alicia and her obvious zest for material living took up residence here? Like they say, there goes the neighborhood." Jane gave him another pinch and said, "What's that you're hiding under your arm?"

"Something we should look at together. I'll see if Roger can run it across to our kitchen."

They strolled back into the house where Tom spotted Paunov, again standing alone. "Dr. Paunov, would you like to see the library where Timberman spent his time?" Tom led him to the second of the two bedrooms that made up Garnie's private suite. He pulled the heavy gumwood door open to reveal a wall of library shelves loaded with stacks of periodicals. Only three vertical sections adjacent to his desk contained books, mainly hardbound reference books: dictionaries, *Bartlett's Familiar Quotations*, a thesaurus, outdated almanacs, a Merck's manual, and the Columbia two-volume encyclopedia. Tom was surprised by the number of theological books, some apparently quite new. "This was his private place. I'll show you the den where he and I talked. It was the only other room he cared about. Did he write to you about his turf war with his housekeeper? They had an ongoing battle for supremacy over space here. But this room was sacrosanct. What you see here is pure Timberman. Do you have any questions about him?"

"No, Tom, I'm content remembering him from working with him. You spoke about his father and his father's father, a dynasty. Do you know anything about its size or holdings?"

Tom patched together what he knew of Pittman history as they moved to the den and on to the veranda. "The Pittman estate includes a lot of land, most of it in forest. There are other assets, though the only one I'm sure of is an interest in the Port Gardner Savings Bank. It's all his sister's now." Tom guided Paunov to the bar. "I'm still impressed that you traveled such a distance to see him buried when some of your many friends in Bulgaria might be close to death."

Paunov ordered a brandy and held it up to the light. "As we say in Bulgaria, a single death is a tragedy, a million deaths is a statistic. Salud!" He downed his drink.

Tom replied, "I wonder if the person who came up with those words considered that every individual in a million deaths is a single death, a tragedy."

Paunov signaled the bartender for a refill and scoffed, "Of course not. It was Josef Stalin." With a fresh glass in hand, he bowed slightly and said, "Thank you for inviting me to your home, but I cannot accept. Tomorrow I am tied up with a banker about transferring money to the Pittman estate. Then I'm scheduled to appear at the University of Washington. You see? Thanks to Timberman I am successful, and once successful I lost control over my time." He downed his drink and shook Tom's hand. "I think we will meet again. As a matter of fact, I am sure of it." He walked from the house.

CHAPTER 19

Freeway traffic had returned to normal summer congestion following the Fourth of July crunch. Cars and vans laden with kayaks, bicycles, and clamshell carriers streamed northward toward the relative peace of British Columbia. Motor homes and pickups towing boats vied with commercial truckers for space in the turgid stream, moving at a stately fifty miles per hour. The day was warm and still with the faint pall of civilization's exhalations blanketing the landscape. Tom loosened his tie against the heat, thinking that the Northbridge exit sign was taking an unusually long time to come into view. It was his first day dressed up since his stay in the hospital, and it would have been longer if Phil Krause hadn't lined up an interview for him with a suburban district east of Seattle. The spot he interviewed for was director of secondary education.

He was barely through the door when Jane thrust an envelope at him. "You got a mystery envelope in the mail. I didn't dare snoop, it being registered and carrying a real sticky stamp. Here's the opener; go for it."

Tom studied the return address, McAfferty and Malcolm, Attorneys at Law, names he'd never had dealings with. The name Malcolm rang a bell. The funeral. He dropped the envelope by the telephone and said, "Later. How about a cup of tea?"

"Don't you dare! You're as curious as I am. Rip it open."

The letter was short and to the point:

The executors of the estate of Garnet Franklin Pittman (deceased) request your presence at the offices of Pittman Pacific Corporation in the Port Gardner Savings Bank building at 5:00 p.m. on the afternoon of July 22, 2005. It is further requested that your wife, Mrs. Jane Clausen, also be in attendance. Should you find it impossible to attend at the time and date mentioned above, please advise Ms. Darci McClellan, LLD, of McAfferty and Malcolm who will arrange another appointment at your convenience. It is further requested that, in respect for your long-standing relationship with Mr. Pittman, that you hold this communication in highest confidence. We cannot overemphasize the need for discretion in this matter.

Dennis Malcolm
Attorney at Law

"What do you make of that?" he asked.

"Read it again," Jane said. "Especially the part about bringing your wife, Jane Clausen. If he had to specify which wife, how many others do you have stashed around the county, Mr. Bigamist? Or is it trigamist?"

"I've given up keeping count."

After a third reading, he put the letter down and took her hands. "The last time I helped Garnie with his mower he said he wasn't going to die, at least not all the way or not all at once. Or something like that. I was blunt with him about letting Aunt Sigi know she was secure so this could very well be about her. What do you think?"

"No idea," she said. "It's the tone that interests me. This isn't an invitation you can turn down. Whatever they're up to can't happen unless you're there. It could be about selling the house. You know, it's not inconceivable that he mentioned you in his will. When you think of it, outside of you, who else put up with the old goat?"

"He wasn't that bad if you didn't take any crap off him. You were pretty hard on him."

"He brought it on himself, dressing like a bum and chewing with his mouth open and insulting everyone he met. He smelled bad, too. With all that money, he should have taken better care of himself."

"Then he wouldn't have been Garnie. His trouble was being too smart for his own good. He wasn't the only genius to turn out goofy, you know. Call it unbalanced if you like, or a bubble or two put of plumb. When it came to art and music, Garnie was living proof that nobody's a genius across the board. And socially?"

"About the letter, do you think we're the only people who got one, or do you suppose other people got letters like this? And the bank closes at five o'clock so this has nothing to do with regular business. Did you think about that?"

He opened the refrigerator. "Good, there's iced tea left. Let's finish it on the patio and let Garnie rest in peace." Jane's frown deepened. "What's the matter?"

"I don't know. It's such a strange letter. I just know I won't be able to put it out of my mind." She pulled away to reach for glasses.

July 22nd was clear and windless with afternoon heat welling up around the few who hadn't sought shade. Tom and Jane found a vacant meter a block from the sweltering young man in suit and tie who stood at the bank's door as they approached. "Mr. and Mrs. Clausen?" He inserted a key card and opened the door for them. "They're waiting for you. Take the elevator to the fourth floor and turn right. The room is at the end of the hall."

They entered a conference room with a view of the Sound. One of four men at the window was Dennis Malcolm, sixtyish, gaunt, and hunched, as though he carried a disease. The others were of similar age but fit—a graying trio of gym members, all in dark suits ranging from Malcolm's pinstripe gray to navy. All four shirts were white and the ties conservative. People who think alike, Tom thought.

Malcolm led the trio to them. "Mr. and Mrs. Clausen, let me introduce you to some friends of Mr. Pittman. This is Gene Boatman of the bank; this is Andy Markovic, our CPA; and this gentleman is John Hodges who represents the board of directors of Pittman Pacific. Let's be seated so we can begin."

The Clausens were directed to chairs across the table from the four suits, who each had a thick blue folder before them. Malcolm took charge. "I'm sure you're wondering why we've asked you to attend. As we progress, you'll appreciate why it wasn't appropriate to give you the full substance of our meeting in a letter. It has to do with certain provisions in Mr. Pittman's will that named you, Mr. Clausen. You will be asked to accept a position of some responsibility you may or may not choose to accept. Of course you are under no obligation, but either way, I hope you will hold the content of this meeting confidential."

Tom reached across the table and pulled Boatman's folder to him, saying, "May I? If what we're here for is that weighty, I'm sure you agree that we should be fully informed." He pulled his chair closer to Jane. The cover read "Last Will and Testament, Garnet Franklin Pittman."

Malcolm said, "Yes, certainly, but since your reaction to what you hear today will tell us whether you need or want what Mr. Pittman offers, we were in agreement to withhold your copy until you declared yourself." He looked right and left and got affirming nods. "You should know that we are understandably concerned that what the will asks of you might be outside your comfort zone, but being bound by Mr. Pittman's wishes, we must pass his exact request on to you." Malcolm paused as though weighted by his responsibility. "You should carefully consider the complexity and scope of the proposal you are about to hear, and please understand that Pittman Pacific's board of directors is capable of continuing to bear certain of the responsibilities that would fall on you should you decide that Mr. Pittman's plan needs more experienced advisors.

"Now, without further comment, we'll turn the meeting over to Mr. Pittman." A technician activated a projector that splashed a rectangle of light on a screen behind the Clausens, causing them to stand and turn their chairs. The screen showed the logo of ERS, Evidentiary Recording Service, secure and bonded.

Pittman appeared on the screen seated between Boatman and Markovic at a table. He was drawn and pale, and his collar gapped around his shrunken neck. Oxygen tubes looped over his ears to his nostrils. The camera zoomed in to frame him while a microphone moved into view, clunking and rattling as Boatman's hand and arm offered it to Garnie, who snapped, "Give it here, dammit." He was sweating.

Garnie glared right and left, cleared his throat, and spoke straight to the camera. "I am Garnet Franklin Pittman, of sound mind and deteriorating body. The declarations and instructions that I make here are to be carried out exactly." He glared again to his right where Markovic was seated. "Through my years of voting the majority of Pittman Pacific's stock, I have directed a fixed percentage of Pittman Pacific's corporate profits into a fund to benefit regional education, and by regional I mean jurisdictions in which Pittman Pacific's interests pay wages and taxes.

"My time is running short, so it is important that I ensure that the education fund is perpetuated, and to do that I have chosen as my successor, Mr. Thomas Clausen, and should more Thomas Clausens come out of the woodwork, I am referring to the former principal of Northbridge High School. This is the Thomas Clausen who was never cowed by my belligerence, a man whom I counted as a friend, and one whose mind is up to the tasks I leave to him, should he choose to take them on.

"While Pittman Pacific's operations supply cash to the fund, which operates under the name of the Charles Winston Pittman Fund, administration of the fund should rest with a person or persons of integrity who know the local educational landscape. In the past, recipients of the awards have been chosen by me to enable the higher education of worthy students and teachers. These scholarships have been known only as CWP scholarships, a choice I made to preserve anonymity and family privacy that suited my style. However, upon my passing, I hereby instruct the fund's administrator to redesignate the scholarships as Charles Winston Pittman Scholarships in memory of my brother who lost his life during the Korean conflict." Pittman turned to his left and muttered, "What'd you do? Pinch the tube? Give me more oxygen, dammit." He breathed deeply for a moment before addressing the camera again.

"Um, ownership of my majority interest in Pittman Pacific is being transferred to the CWP trust account, which is being restructured to allow the executor of the fund to vote those shares and operate as I have done. To make a long story short, that also means exercising oversight of Pittman Pacific's operations, authorizing audits, and tapping off thirty percent of the corporation's net profit to fuel the fund." Pittman paused and closed his eyes for a moment. A hand slid a glass of water into the picture, which he swept away before fussing with the fit of his oxygen tubes. Looking to the left, Pittman said, "This is for your own good, Dennis." He swung back to face the camera. "Thomas, should you choose to accept this challenge…you should engage your own counsel. Should you choose to decline, you are hereby empowered to select someone from the world of education to serve in your stead. Time is of the essence. Either way, you have six months from the time of my death to assume or establish new directorship of the fund. One hundred thousand dollars has been set aside to cover expenses you might incur during that period. After that, the new director of the fund—I'm trusting that it will be you—will receive an annual stipend of one-hundred seventy-five thousand dollars, no more except for cost-of-living adjustments. Though not a princely sum, it is beyond what I ever took for my own purposes as you all well know.

"I'm tired now, so I'll wrap this up quickly. Thomas, you are to be provided with the necessary papers…to understand the history and scope of Pittman Pacific and the fund. Make sure that you're furnished…with a copy of my written will, all twenty-six pages of it, complete access to the fund's files…the minutes of Pittman Pacific's board meetings beginning one year ago…and current and past financial statements and tax reports." He paused to look both left and right. "Yes, that's right, current and past, especially the past five years. To make sense of all that you'll have to…engage a corporate CPA of your choosing. With legal counsel…and a new accounting firm on board, you'll be amazed…how fast that hundred thousand will disappear. Goodbye, Thomas, and good luck." Pittman turned, knocking the microphone over to produce a loud pop. He turned sideways, and in a voice that carried without the microphone, he called to someone behind him, "Get me out of here!" The screen turned blue except for the white ERS logo.

Boatman broke the silence. "Well now, it's certainly going to be a different world without him." The four smiled among themselves as though sharing a private joke.

Malcolm said, "I understand you were neighbors so you undoubtedly picked up hints of what we've been through with Pittman." He looked around to confirming smirks from Boatman and Hodges. "Well then, he left plenty of room for us to take care of you. We'll certainly honor that."

Hodges waved his copy of the will at Tom. "He certainly threw you a challenge, a world of responsibility to manage for a hundred seventy-five grand. I'm assuming you'll need time to think about it."

Malcolm walked to the window where he rubbed his jaw thoughtfully. "Things could go on as before. We have a good team in place, and if we check out to your satisfaction, we could handle it for you, except the scholarship program. We'd need you for that of course, and it goes without saying that the hundred seventy-five thousand is yours. It's what Mr. Pittman wanted for you."

Tom looked to Jane, who gave him a small nod. With Tom holding Boatman's copy of the will, they stood and shook hands with the four. Tom said, "I believe this meeting is over. You'll have an answer tomorrow. In the meantime, Mr. Hodges, Mr. Markovic, Mr. Boatman, and Mr. Malcolm, you should be readying the documents according to Mr. Pittman's instructions. All of them. Thanks for your time. You'll be hearing from my attorney shortly after I hire him."

Once in the car, Jane leaned over to deliver a peck to his cheek while dropping a pocket-sized recorder in his lap. She said, "Well done, darling. Let's get out of here; I feel unclean."

They drove to the freeway in silence, broken when Tom said, "Tell me, why did I do that?"

"You mean serving notice on the sharks, of course. You read them for what they were and didn't like what you saw. You left them wondering."

"Did it show?"

"No more than the mismatched fender on your Subaru, but what difference would it make? They were reading you, too, Mr. Inscrutable. Or at least trying to. For a while there, they thought they had you in the bag, but they were overmatched. When it comes to getting inside people's heads, you can be downright scary like a science-fiction worm that burrows into brains. Like at that Northbridge-Fircrest wrestling match. You remember, I had to poke you to stop you from staring that poor man into leaving."

"That was different. He was cursing a referee in my school, in my gym."

"And now you've graduated to psyching out lawyer types. Do you remember what you told me after the Fircrest match was over, that you could tell a lot about people by how contained they were? You said you prefer wrestling fans who lunge about as if they're the ones on the mat to the ones who sit like they're watching a movie. So what did you see at the meeting?"

"Just that. They were too contained. It was scripted, who would say what and who would pick it up from there. They should have opened by asking Alicia and me how we wanted to handle things? They didn't. She wasn't even invited. Instead, they insinuated an inside takeover out of the goodness of their hearts. When they proposed to continue managing the estate's assets, they made their second mistake because they've never been in control of Pittman's entire assets. At least that's the impression Garnie left me with. The third error was telling me what I'm not able to do and that I ought to turn down the salary offer. When they laughed at a hundred seventy-five thousand, I thought that anybody who can afford that kind of attitude is someone Pittman Pacific can't afford. Sure, it's small by CEO standards, but I don't plan to be a standard CEO."

"Tom, do you realize what you just said?"

"Just speaking hypothetically. What I meant was Pittman Pacific doesn't need a standard money-grubbing CEO."

"Do me a favor and keep your lip buttoned until your mind catches up. You might be digging yourself into a hole."

"Or envisioning a new future. What's the matter with that? How many people get a chance to even consider such a thing? This is heady stuff. Why not savor the moment? Carpe diem!"

"Let's go straight home, Mr. Highflier. You need some energy drained."

CHAPTER 20

When Tom and Buster returned from their Saturday walk, Jane handed him another envelope and waited for him to open it. Again, the sender was Dennis Malcolm, Attorney at Law. He ripped it open and stepped into the living room with Jane in his footsteps. When he folded it after a brief glance and looked across the street, she said, "Well, are you going to tell me what it is?"

"You're not going to believe it."

"Try me."

"Here's a clue. It starts, 'Dear Thomas…'"

"It's from Garnie?"

"Shush and listen." He unfolded it again. "Dear Thomas, Since your employment situation shows no signs of resolving itself, and in keeping with your usual sluggishness, you probably haven't yet formally accepted my offer, I have a small job for you. A party is to be held at my home on Saturday, October 2, but the house is in no condition to receive guests. Therefore, I want you to assemble tradesmen to do whatever is possible to restore the old barn to entertain up to eighty people. And tidy up the exterior. My inquiries tell me that necessary improvements may be effected for no more than $400,000, a sum you will agree is totally outrageous. As overseer, of course you will be entitled to ten percent, and if you don't muck it up by procrastinating, the project shouldn't occupy more than your spare time.

"Get your man, Nguyen, if you like, to fix the grounds. I want the house cleaned in and out and what's broken repaired. One caution: Do not let anyone apply a pressure washer to the stone and brick. Steam cleaning will do nicely. The rest I leave to you, hoping that my faith in your abilities isn't misplaced.

"Since I have relaxed my control over my affairs, there is no way for me to know with any certainty the exact day when you will receive this letter. That shouldn't matter as long as you 'fill the unforgiving minute with sixty seconds full of distance run. 'Ready or not, the party must take place on October 2. Rest assured that all other arrangements have been placed in the hands of competent service agencies.

"Mr. Eugene Boatman of Port Gardner Savings Bank is authorized to disburse funds against your signature as needed. It should be a grand party with enough surprises to assure a certain liveliness so don't let me down on this. I look forward to seeing you there, G. W. Pittman."

"Dead but not gone," Jane said and sighed. "What are you going to do?"

"First, check with Aunt Sigi to see if she knows anything about this."

"Well, of course she wouldn't. You can't think that by dying, the old goat became sensitive about her feelings. And speaking about sensitivity, don't you feel a tiny bit like you're being manipulated?"

"That's Garnie. He knows, or rather, knew how to get me on the hook. He knew that I respect the house enough to be concerned about its condition. Fixing the place up is the best thing that could happen to the neighborhood. Besides, as you well know, I'm getting bored out of my mind with nothing to do."

"Like ten percent of four hundred thousand has nothing to do with it?" Jane moved to the kitchen to count days on the calendar. "If you're going to do it, you'd better get jumping. Do you realize you have less than seventy working days?"

"If you think like a schoolteacher, sweetie. Add Saturdays and it should be enough. You care to help?"

Charles Wainwright was still at his desk at five thirty collecting personal things, including a district laptop and the fake Remington bronze he had billed to the district. Only he knew it was his final day. The day had started with a budget meeting and then a conference about staffing issues. He attended a Rotary lunch before sparring with the district's bus mechanics' unhappy representative. The workday ended with staffers dribbling out between four thirty and five, leaving him to consider who and where he might be tomorrow. After a stop at the bank machine, he would kiss Northbridge goodbye, no forwarding address. The benefits of lifting his personal file from Personnel's records and disappearing were twofold: Should the district choose to come after him, it would have less to work with to pick up his scent. Secondly, considering the changed mood of the board, he was reasonably sure its members wouldn't care to have anything more to do with him. In ten hours he would far enough away that Northbridge would be nothing more than a memory he intended to erase. Good riddance. He still had to get final instructions to Jeanne, but by email. Yes, if he went to the house before leaving to remind her of where she stood, she might try something to hold him in town, as she did before he pried her out of Cottage Grove. His bags were in the car.

On July 13th, with half of the district office's staff vacationing and the rest dreaming of having August off, business was reduced to summer maintenance projects, job interviews, grant writing, and a shopping list of small tasks. The only department operating at full speed was Purchasing, where orders for materials for the fall term were being processed. A meeting was in session in the small conference room.

"Please, may I have your attention?" The board members looked up from a four-way discussion and sat back with arms folded across their chests. Claudia McPhaiden and her gavel were at one end of the table; Morgan, Chesterton, Koutac, and McCollum were at the other end. Chairs to McPhaiden's left and right were vacant, marking the board's new orientation. The board was in "executive session," where rules of order were relaxed to allow the give-and-take of creative discussion. Informality was aided by meeting in the small conference room that seated no more than ten. Nancy Corbin, the board's secretary, readied herself to capture discussion points.

Claudia asked, "Has anyone heard from Dr. Wainwright?"

Mary Chesterton blurted, "What does that have to do with anything? He's history, gone, out of our lives. Thank God."

"Really, Mary, we shouldn't jump to judgment. He's entitled to a vacation like everyone else. In case you haven't noticed, half the administrative staff is vacationing."

Harry Morgan jumped in. "Half the administrative staff didn't arrange with finance to collect their July and August paychecks at the same time, and half the staff didn't clean out their offices before they left."

Nate McCollum chimed in. "People normally don't carry their personnel files away to read on vacation. If we could lay our hands on his laptop, we might know what he's been up to but that's gone missing, too."

Mary Chesterton said, "We could go on all night like this. The point is he's gone. Water under the bridge. Did you know there's a RE/MAX sign in his front yard? I stopped by Monday to find Jeanne packing. When I asked if she could help us to contact Charles, she said, 'I have no idea where he is, and furthermore, I don't care.' Now, do we want to keep on wringing our hands about something we should be grateful for, or should we figure out what's to be done now that he's gone?"

Claudia offered, "The first thing …"

"No, Claudia. The first thing we should do is elect a new chairperson. It was you who got us into this." McCollum looked about for agreement. "Martin, would you consider taking the gavel?"

"Sorry, Nate, but I think that'd be counterproductive. Now, before she was interrupted, Claudia was about to suggest a first course of action. I'm willing to hear her out because we don't have time for recrimination. There's heavy lifting to do that won't get done if we keep sniping at each other so, if, as you say, someone has been at fault, the best course would be for that person to resign their seat, but right now we have work to do. Claudia, what was it you started to say?"

"Thank you, Martin. The first thing we should do is develop a pool of names for a temporary or permanent replacement of our superintendent."

Chesterton shouted, "No, don't even think of it! There you go again, micromanaging school business. Get this straight, Claudia: It is not our business to come up with a list of candidates. There are people who know how to go about such things, but we're not them. You tried it once and look where it got us." Nancy scribbled to keep pace.

"Oh, no you don't." McPhaiden was poised between sitting and standing. "Don't try to put it all on me. If you'll remember, we checked his background, and we all voted to hire Charles. Everyone was involved."

Chesterton smiled broadly and said, "Since it's come up, the vote was three in favor, two opposed." She looked around to measure support. "Let's take a moment to review the selling points that supported Wainwright's candidacy for the job. We saw degrees and certificates up the gazoo. We naively phoned the Meade County schools to ask if he was the golden boy he said he was. They said yes. We asked about his schooling and that checked out. We asked the *Meade County Messenger* for articles describing his activities. I gotta hand it to you, Claudia. Wainwright was everything you said he was. Trouble was the guy we hired wasn't the Charles Wainwright from Brandenburg, Kentucky."

"So it seems. He could have fooled anyone."

McCollum waggled a finger at Claudia. "Not the police. When they dusted his desk for prints to see who swiped his office stuff, the name they came up with was Lightfoot, not Wainwright. It seems you haven't gotten the message yet, Claudia. No, he wouldn't have fooled a placement service or a professional headhunter. We failed the district by taking on a task we weren't qualified to handle."

"But we checked on him."

Chesterton scoffed, "So you say. There's checking, and then there's checking. What did we get? A bunch of statements from Meade County saying what a peach of a guy he was and one grainy picture. Either they're all liars or the guy we hired was a fake. Anyone want to give odds?"

"Remember how he handled the picture?" McCollum asked. "He said, 'Look at that. It sure shows what a bout with cancer can do to a person.' All of a sudden our suspicions turned to sympathy. Damn, he was good."

Claudia raised her voice. "Yes, yes, yes. But that's all behind us now. We have to get someone in place to run the district."

"Slooow down a bit," Morgan drawled. "Back to basics. If you'll look on page three of your school board policy"—he stopped to weight his copy open with a book—"you'll see a list of the stuff we're supposed to deal with. Follow along with me: 'Formulate and adopt policies for the governance of the schools'—and you see that's to be done in concert with the superintendent. Next, 'approve the annual budget, approve negotiations agreements, require and consider periodic reports on the educational program, approve capital outlay, approve bills previously authorized, require an annual report on school programs, require adequate reports on school property and equipment,' and finally, 'act as final appeal for school personnel, students, parents, and other community members.' Boil it down and we have formulate, adopt, approve, require, consider. Anybody find anything in there about running a search for a superintendent?"

Claudia rapped on the table for attention. "If we can manage to set aside the finger-pointing, I wish to point out once more that there's no one at the helm of the district. We can't run schools without putting someone in the superintendent's chair."

Chesterton screamed, "Dammit, Claudia. Stop it. Just stop it! We can't run a search because we're not supposed to run a search."

When she saw she had everyone's attention, she went on. "Short term, here's what we do: Draft a statement to everyone on the organization chart who reports directly to the superintendent. Ask them for nominations from among their number to serve as interim superintendent until interviews of qualified candidates can be completed."

Martin Koutac sensed that they had reached a good time for his question. "If you were asked who in the world you would like to have carry us through this, what's the first name to pop up in your minds? Harry?"

"That's easy. Phil Krause."

"Okay, but after the shabby treatment our board gave him, I think we could write him off even if he hadn't taken the job at Moraine. Anyone have a different name?"

The remaining three shook their heads. Claudia sat staring at the tabletop. Martin nudged them. "Think of another leadership-type person who knows the district and commands a similar level of respect. Nate?"

"Well, until he had his breakdown, I would have said Tom Clausen."

"Exactly," Mary Chesterton said. "Martin and I were interested enough in their demise that we took it upon ourselves to look into the district's actions regarding them. Our request to Personnel for the year's entries into Clausen's personnel file brought up some stuff that was more shock than surprise. I have copies."

"Mary," Claudia shouted, "as Martin said, this is no time for recriminations. We need to move on."

"And we will." Chesterton slid packets to each board member and the secretary. She continued, "The first pages, marked 'Evaluation,' are copies of recent entries into Clausen's personnel file. Read them and tell me if they reflect the Tom you know." She sat back to enjoy expressions of surprise blooming around the table.

McCollum was first to speak. "Disloyal? Insubordinate? Lets personal opinions override district policy, objectives, and directives? Who came up with this crap? Listen to this: 'harbors private agendas that conflict with district policy.'" He tossed his packet toward the head of the table. "This isn't evaluation; it's character assassination."

Chesterton said, "There's more. Turn to the next page and read the highlighted section near the bottom."

Again, she and Koutac sat back while McCollum and Morgan digested the paragraph. Claudia sat with her eyes closed and jaws tight.

"I don't understand this. It's from the district's health insurance carrier about notification of Clausen's termination." He looked up and asked, "Termination? Wasn't he on sick leave? It says his coverage ends upon termination. What's going on here? It sounds like someone decided to cancel Clausen's coverage when he was down and out. That's mean." McCollum turned on McPhaiden. "Claudia, how much of this were you aware of?"

CHAPTER 21

Tom and Jane crossed the street to find Aunt Sigi ready with a surprise. She scurried to the den and returned with an envelope she shook at them. "Wouldn't you know it? Mr. Garnet is still at it. He had this letter delivered that told me I should be expecting you, and here you are. That man! I've been after him for years to fix the place up, but all he'd say was 'No, no. We're getting along just fine the way things are.' Now I'm going to have workmen crawling all over the place. He should realize that—"

Jane patted her arm. "Aunt Sigi, he's gone. He's stopped realizing things."

"Oh, fiddlesticks, I know that. It's just that I catch myself expecting to see him in the den or walking out for the mail. As disagreeable as he was, at least he was company. The big old place didn't seem anywhere near so empty with him in it. It's not the same anymore, and now he says you're in charge of it."

Tom said, "May I see the letter?" It took seconds to learn that Garnie had announced to Sigi that he, Mr. Clausen, would be managing repairs and renovation of her house. Time for a white lie. "We got a letter, too. Garnie said we were to help you. He said that you were the only one who really knew the house and that you would know what needs to be done. If you like, we could work as a team, pool our thoughts. It's a big house, and considering how much it needs, it might take all three of us to set it right. What do you think?"

"Oh, well…" Aunt Sigi seemed confused, then blurted, "I'm not used to a man asking for my opinion, at least around here. Maybe I could find some way to help."

Jane took her by the arm. "Then let's go put the pot on. From what Tom's told me, nothing ever gets done here without a pot of tea."

Leaving the women to brainstorm in the kitchen, Tom began his first intentional look at the house's needs. During prior visits, his admiration for the home's design features overshadowed its needs, but Garnie's commission to set things right changed that. His new viewpoint transformed the mansion into a collection of problems that needed attention: cracked plaster, gapped flooring, peeling paint, faulty wiring. The closer he looked, the deeper its needs, and he had moved only a few steps from where he started. He dropped into an Early American chair to think not about what had to be done, but how to get his mind around the project. He imagined Garnie sitting across from him, asking, "Thomas, despite your ignorance about such matters, suppose you had a fine old house, a house like this one, a house that had been neglected. How would you approach the overall problem of renovation?" The women in the kitchen were startled to hear him shout, "Garnie, this isn't fair!"

Jane gave him a quizzical look when he rejoined them. "And what was that all about?"

"Venting."

"At?"

"Garnie. You're right; he's pulling the strings, my strings. Are we sure we want to go through with this?"

Not privy to the ladies' discussion while he was being overwhelmed, he was taken aback at their firm "Yes!"

The conversation turned to the issue of Sigi living alone. She said she didn't like to cook for just herself. She suggested that maybe an apartment or condo might be best; she could move to Port Gardner to be closer to her friends, all reasonable options. Jane interjected that she wasn't entirely alone, that she had friends across the street, and with Ardis Swenson's husband, Linne, in a care facility, she could certainly use a neighbor's company. To which Sigi said, "Ya, ya. Two old ladies rattling around in two big barns. It doesn't make much sense."

Jane poured the last of the tea into Sigi's cup, saying, "It's the suddenness of change that's getting us. Will you promise me this? Let a few months go by before you decide on any big changes. We'll need you here."

Leaving Jane to help Sigi consider her next steps, Tom excused himself to continue his inspection.

Sigi considered Jane's suggestion about Ardis. "Ya, sure, it would be nice to have company. I'll talk with her."

"Then call Karl and Inger and anyone else you can think of. Fill the house with your people for a change. There must be tons of seniors who'd like to be less lonely. The house is yours to use, you know."

"Oh, I don't know. That's a hard thought to accept. I mean making decisions willy-nilly. I guess I'm not used to it, Mrs. Clausen."

"Jane. Get used to calling me Jane. And while we're changing things, remember that the path between our houses runs both ways. You're invited for dinner tonight."

"Oh, I couldn't."

"Since you don't have a good reason for not coming, we'll see you about six. Now here comes Tom again. From the look of him, we have work to do."

The trio spent the middle half of the day inspecting and taking notes. As with Tom's first survey of the living room, needs were apparent wherever they looked. On the outside, the bricks and stonework were secure, but two weathered sides needed new mortar. The original pine window sashes had suffered a century's weathering and would have to be replaced, but as Garnie specified, the work would necessarily be confined to the spaces needed for the party. The roof's French slate tiles would need a professional's inspection where the attic showed effects of a line of leaks. Their tour left them so overwhelmed that they jumped on Jane's recommendation to turn their survey over to professionals.

The most obvious outside problems were moss and grime. Deeper issues might lie beneath, but until the dirt, algae, and moss were stripped away, no one could know. Sigi said, "My mother told me to always start at the top. Her house wasn't much, but she kept it spotless, and she did it by starting at the top. You start low and work up; you catch all the dirt from the top on your already cleaned surfaces."

Tom and Jane found their suggestions either playing catch-up with Sigi's practical assessments or upsetting her. Situations arose when she complained, "No, no. You'd be patching it when it should be made right," or "That won't do. No, that won't do at all because that's not the way old Mr. Pittman meant it to be." The meeting reconvinced Tom that decisions shouldn't be made without the advice of somebody who knew what they were doing.

Jane returned from a coffee-shop meeting with her principal, Edgar Campos. She had asked for the meeting to lay out her uncertainty about returning to work for the fall term, given Tom's situation. Campos took it well and suggested that she take a leave of absence and to please, please, please return to Stevens Middle School as soon as possible. Lightened by shedding that concern, she returned home to find Tom vibrating with happy energy.

She said, "Wow, do you always get this happy when I'm away? Or did I just miss it when the elephants came by?"

"I just had a call from Alice. The new board had the administrative staff nominate one of their own to serve as interim superintendent. Guess who they picked?"

Jane stiffened. "No way. You call them right now and tell them you can't do it, or else."

"Relax. They tapped Petra. Can you imagine how much fun it'll be to teach and learn? She's the best kind of crazy, just what's needed."

"What's your name?" Wainwright froze as events attached to his past names rose to unsettle his gut. He was in custody. After an incident at a Utah restaurant, he had been chased down by a Utah highway patrolman, cuffed, and taken to the Washington County Sheriff's Department where, when asked for his name while being fingerprinted, he sighed and yielded up his true identity.

"Gary Lightfoot."

"You have identification?" The deputy was seasoned, all of fifty but still fit. He held himself cocked like a spring should his collar need to be taken down.

"I left it at my motel."

"I'm going to release the cuffs so you can empty your pockets. Lay everything in the tray on the counter. Larry, lend a hand here, would ya?"

A second officer, overweight in the way NFL tackles are overweight, stepped up to fix Lightfoot with a penetrating stare he chose not to challenge. Car keys, a sales receipt, coins, and a nail clipper rattled into the tray. "Watch, too." He stripped off the three-hundred-dollar Rolex he had scammed from the jewelry store in Sacramento. He had grown fond of the watch. "Back pockets." His heart sank as he dropped in his cordovan Swank billfold with eight hundreds, three tens, two ones, and Wainwright's identity. Damn the woman. After keeping her and her brats off the street for eleven years, this is the thanks I get.

His Chase Bank card had carried him through gas stops and a night at Boise's new Comfort Inn. It wasn't until a coffee and gas stop in Ogden that he suspected something was amiss. He had chosen the Pay Inside option at pump eight, topped his tank off with regular, and poured himself a cup of Columbia Dark Roast before swiping his debit card. The clerk said, "Sorry, it must be maxed out. I hope you got cash." Not possible. A mistake, they happen all the time. He pulled out his Chase credit card, which worked without a hitch.

He had two hundred-sixty miles until a dinner stop in St. George to think about it. A mistake, it had to be a mistake. He was still mulling the thought when he presented his Chase card to pay for his meal. As before, the clerk said, "Sorry, sir. Your card has been rejected." One might have been a mistake. Two had Jeanne's fingerprints all over them. Jeanne! If credit cards, then what else? The chubby boy behind the counter grinned crookedly at him as though he was another penniless deadbeat and said, "Cash, please." When the boy tried a tired joke about bad credit cards, Wainwright felt a roaring in his ears, and the scene became dreamlike. He and the smirking clerk were on a spot of island in a sea that didn't exist. He sucker punched the boy on the cheek, toppling him against a refrigerated pie display. Wainwright ran to his car, pursued at a respectful distance by outraged patrons with cell phones. A 911 operator relayed his license number to the Utah highway police, and he was pulled over before he reached the Arizona line.

The next morning, a detective named Merck visited Wainwright's cell to work him over with a slow-paced, cat-and-mouse interrogation.

Merck was everything Wainwright wasn't. Weathered and wiry, his shaggy straw-colored locks matched a drooping tobacco-stained mustache of the same hue. Fancy jeans, cowboy boots, and a snap-pocket shirt did little to dilute his cop-ness. Merck would intimidate if in a choir robe.

Merck described Gary's situation as shit out of luck, up a creek without a paddle—that he had screwed the pooch, messed his nest, sold the farm, and crossed over onto the dark side. He explained in more legal terms that he was facing assault and theft charges. And oh yes, speeding. Bail had been set at ten thousand dollars, mostly because of the faked documents investigators found under his car's battery. Merck told him he might be receiving a federal visitor, who would expect him to explain why he hadn't filed federal tax returns since 1991. And oh yes, Homeland Security might be around to ask what sort of work required so many identities. Merck turned at the cell door to say, "Oh, yes, if there's anything y'all want, anything at all, just ask. You probably won't get it, but there's no harm in asking."

The renovation consultant, Mack Groeninger of Bayview Construction Services, took one look and backed out saying it couldn't be done in the allotted time. But he did take time to offer suggestions about prioritizing the work, which was why the first piece of equipment to arrive was a cherry-picker truck capable of servicing the highest parts of the house. The worker in the bucket stripped off the rusted TV antenna and dropped it into the overgrown lilacs obscuring the den window before attacking moss with his pressure washer. His area of attack was north-facing surfaces where greenish-black hummocks covered and lifted the slates. From his boom basket, the worker blasted bushels of the stuff loose, driving it downslope to tumble over choked gutters and splatter malignantly across shrubs and walkways. Clearly, Aunt Sigi's mother knew what she was talking about.

On the sixth day, and two days later than scheduled, a different service truck with a two-man crew arrived to take over the cherry-picker. One handled a hose from the cage atop the boom while his partner regulated a propane-fueled boiler that fed live steam to a nozzle.

Tom monitored the progress from across the street while wrestling with the frustrations of construction scheduling. Had it not been for daily advice he bought from Jamie Cruz, a teacher-friend turned builder, the job would never have met its deadline. Aunt Sigi, watching the exterior work progress, said that if dressed for the job and not fearful of heights, she would have loved to be up there blasting away grime so thick that it scaled off in chunks. Working horizontal stripes downward, the steam jet returned dark-gray-brown quarried stone to its original light amber and burgundy-gray brick to dusty rose. A slurry of grime and moss spattered across the roof debris to create a sun-crisped apron on the lawn. The day the man from ReStore Cleaning Specialties turned his steam nozzle onto the marble porch and steps, discoloration washed away so effectively that, when Jane checked progress in the late afternoon, it looked like new stone.

When Tom cornered friends in the construction industry for referrals to the area's best finish carpenters, they reverently put Emil Shumacher at the top of the list, adding that he was retired and no longer answering their calls. With more money than time, Tom visited Schumacher at his home to offer him fifty dollars an hour to look at the house and give his opinion on what it needed.

Schumacher, short, barrel-chested, and taciturn, answered Tom's knock. His home was one in a row of 1920s mill worker's cottages he'd upgraded to stand among its neighbors like a polished agate in a bucket of stones. Schumacher absorbed Tom's proposition without comment, staring as though his decision might appear between Tom's eyes. At length he nodded and turned toward the back of the house to shout, "Annie, you tink you can get along vitout me for a couple hours?" A voice shrilled back, "Sure, hon. Make sure you're back by five. You hear?" Schumacher buttoned his cardigan and said, "Ve go now. Vut did you say your name iss?"

Schumacher warmed on the drive across the estuary, his accent fading as he adapted to Tom's questions. When they pulled into the driveway, Schumacher was all eyes, and his accent thickened again. "Dis iss it? Dis iss vot you call a house? Oh, ya, it's a honey for damn sure." After introducing him to Sigi, Tom said, "Have a look around.

We'll be in the kitchen." They waited while the craftsman prowled the house like a visitor in a museum. His broad, short-fingered hands ran respectfully along surfaces, moldings, a carved mantelpiece, and an ornate built-in bookcase. Tom found him hunkered down where the main bedroom corridor branched. He looked up and said, "You vouldn't notice it, but dese corners are mortised. I never seen such a ting in dis country."

When the Austrian agreed to look at the Pittman mansion, he didn't anticipate the effect the house would have on him. Tom waited until Sigi and Schumacher were seated and the tea poured before asking how he thought the interior's problems should be addressed. When their cups were empty, Schumacher said, "Come vit me." He led them from situation to situation, explaining what he would do if he were on the job, to which Tom said, "Then that's the way it should be done. Who can handle that kind of work?" Schumacher found himself on the hook, finessed out of retirement for one last job. But before agreeing to take it on, he asked if he might bring his wife to see the house, explaining, "I made her a promise. She von't understand. No, she'll be pissed for sure if she don't see dis place. She has such a gute eye for fine tings."

Schumacher agreed with Garnie's assessment that only the great rooms, stairway, main-floor bathrooms, and entry should be addressed before the party. Beginning the next Monday, he and a helper set a deliberate pace for work that might have seemed slow to observers, but with no waste of motion or material—and, as far as Tom could determine, never a need to redo work—he was on schedule. Task by task, they took on more than carpentry, resecuring light fixtures, vents, and towel racks and replacing doubtful electrical switches and outlets. Schumacher was laying his hands on quality he hadn't touched since apprenticing in Karnten, Austria, before emigrating in 1952. Some pieces he touched brought to mind images of the Bavarian artisans who had shaped the walnut accent pieces that had been designed by artists, not architects.

On Emil's first day, Tom pointed out where the mantelpiece had sprung loose at a corner and tipped. No more needed to be said. Emil's skill and respect for the old house allowed Tom to give him his head. His trust was more than confirmed when Emil showed up with a freshly carved pomegranate finial to replace one that once capped the upper end of the grand staircase's railing.

Once she accepted Jane's kitchen as the project's nerve center, Sigi spent as many daylight hours in the Clausen home as she did at the mansion. Tom managed to find someone to replace the rotten gutters but found that the best names in the building trades were booked through the summer. To get a painting contractor on board, he dipped into the fund to bribe a painter's client into postponing her house painting from the second two weeks in August until a month later. When Sigi insisted on a shade of blue that was an obvious mismatch for the stone and brick, Jane reined her in by asking, "Could you come up with pictures of the house in its glory days? I'd like to see what we're trying to resurrect."

Mr. Nguyen and his four sons committed to work one day each week and accomplished so much on their first day that it looked as though they might finish well before the October deadline. Tom wanted the lawn replaced, but Nguyen argued that August was the wrong month for that. Instead, he aerated, fertilized, and overseeded, rising early to drop his youngest son off to manage the watering.

Jane pushed the Start button on the dishwasher and took a seat across from Tom, who was hunting through a heap of notes and receipts. Patting a stack of papers, she said, "Are you so deep into this that you can't see how off-the-charts crazy this is?"

"What's crazy? I'm earning good money fixing a neighborhood eyesore. Do you have a problem with that?"

"Just as I thought. Being a man, you bury yourself in the nuts and bolts of the project without ever wondering why. You're not restoring a house; you're fixing it up so a dead man can host a party. Do you know anything about the guest list? Of course not. The dead man's sending out the invitations. How about catering, flowers, or beverages? No problem, the dead man is taking care of everything. That's what's crazy. Do you want to know what's even crazier? Since the dead man happens to be Garnie, you know perfectly well that he's setting the stage for, well, you know Garnie. It would be just like him to use his 'memorial party' to get the last laugh on everyone who annoyed him. You just wait and see."

"Does that mean you won't go?"

"Are you kidding? I wouldn't miss it for the world."

CHAPTER 22

The morning of the party dawned clear, except for a hint of ground fog—football weather. The last painters and cleaners had left before six on Friday afternoon, leaving the driveway free for caterers' and florists' vans. Tom and Jane stood at their bedroom window in pajamas admiring the fruits of eighty-five days of haggling and wheedling with stressed contractors. Though they felt drained, they were pleased with how the Nguyens' efforts changed the curb view of the aging mansion from neglected to majestic.

With the brutally raw effects of heavy pruning first to meet the eye, the facelift wasn't perfect. Touch-up painting had to be halted the day before. Nevertheless, the quality of workmanship wherever Emil Schumacher's relentless precision restored original grandeur, ensured approval from anyone who knew quality. It would have to do, for the guests' view would be limited to the public parts of the house.

Though Tom had no idea of who or how many Garnie had invited, he took it upon himself to add the Schumacher and the Nguyen families, and he made sure that Aunt Sigi's friends and the neighbors Garnie had alienated were included. He had no idea of the number of parking spaces that would be needed. The Pittman, Clausen, and Swenson driveways plus roadside parking in the lane would accommodate no more than forty to fifty cars and the three planners worried about the other issues that wouldn't surface until the last minute.

Jane complicated their concerns with "Like it or not, we'll be the hosts. You can't invite a hundred or so guests and not have hosts." Sleep did not come easily the night before.

At ten on Saturday morning, dog-walking time along Dogwood Lane, an extended van turned into the mansion's circular drive. After wrestling out a heavy platform dolly, they set about wheeling display plants into the house, followed by enough flowers to deck out a half-dozen funerals.

The caterer, whom the Clausens had met before, arrived in a Camry followed by a hired van. Tom and Jane watched from home as two commercial barbecue grills, beer kegs, cases of liquor, coolers, pallets of glassware, tables, folding chairs, and serving counters flowed from the truck. Tom, on edge since waking before five, said, "I can't take this any longer. Are you coming?"

Jane looked him over. "Yes, but only if you change from pajamas. Once we're across the street, we won't see home until the last guest is swept out. And since no one else volunteered, you're still head host, Mr. Big Cheese so make it your wedding and funeral suit."

"Nope, not for an afternoon mansion party. I'm opting for my Ari Onassis outfit."

Jane brightened. "If I'm partying with Onassis, I get to wear my slinky green pants suit. Let's get to it. Only four hours till showtime."

The near silence of the mansion's empty great rooms quieted Tom's pre-party jitters. He and Jane had attended enough fund-raising galas to feel comfortable rubbing shoulders with dignitaries, but with Garnie's ghost hovering in the background, Tom wasn't at ease. He could feel its presence taking charge, moving in the air, getting ready to upset guests' expectations. As Garnie's party, Tom had no doubt that it was engineered to expose pent-up animosities. Being dead wasn't going to stop him from consigning people to social trash heaps for willful ignorance or dimness of understanding. Of course there was a chance he might be putting on the party for no other reason than to honor his ancestors, but that would be foreign behavior. Of one thing Tom was sure: the guests would be as unsuspecting as he was about what Garnie had in mind for them.

The restored house was readied to serve not as a testimony to the deceased's life but as a catalyst for conflict. His spirit would somehow initiate moves that, if they reflected Garnie's style, would have his guests blundering through a social minefield. In part, Tom wanted to leave, to take Buster for a long walk and not return until the carnage was finished, but he knew he had to play out his role. And the slim possibility remained that he might be wrong.

A server polished glasses behind a portable bar in a corner of the dining room. Low voices drifted from the kitchen. Another server set Sterno burners under a row of chafing dishes and removed two florists' arrangements from the buffet table to replace them with candles. The portrait over the fireplace had turned out well. When Sigi was unable to come up with anything better than four-by-six group shots showing Garnie together with others, Tom picked the best and had a photo processor blow Garnie's image up to the grainy eleven-by-seventeen print he passed off to Northbridge High's retired art teacher, Dean Morgan, who, for $250 dollars, pumped up the size to twenty by thirty, photoshopped it with brushstrokes, and had a T-shirt shop transfer it to canvas, which he overpainted to produce what Tom hoped would be accepted as a commissioned portrait. The impressively framed and matted picture, while not flattering, caught much of Garnie's curmudgeonly essence.

Emil and Annie Schumacher arrived at one thirty, a half hour before the doors officially opened and early enough for Emil to show Annie his handiwork. Tom introduced Annie to Jane, adding, "Sorry to pull your man out of retirement, but we needed him. You saw the place before he started. What do you think of it now?"

Annie, already with a beer in hand, said, "What do I think? About the house, I understand beauty and quality, and you have them both here. About Emil, we're both coming to suspect that retirement might be overrated. Actually, the man's been a whole lot easier to live with since you hired him. What I mean is I wouldn't be sorry if you found more work for him."

Tom laughed. "I'd love to. Once I get a handle on the long-term provisions for the house, I can think of nothing better than keeping Emil on the job until it's done. Until then, get him to put the word out that he's available. From what I hear, your man's the go-to craftsman for special projects." He spied friends being received at the door by a liveried greeter and excused himself. "Emil, Annie, carry on and meet some people. I have to play host."

He greeted Martin and Marie Koutac at the door. Martin grasped Tom's hand and quipped, "This your place?" He looked around appreciatively. "My, my, what a departure from the principal business. But like they say, a change is as good as a vacation." When Tom turned to greet the couple behind them, Martin said, "I hope we don't get kicked out for bringing party crashers. You know my daughter, Trish, and this is her husband, Mel Ostrander. Mel's a builder. Once he heard we'd been invited to the Pittman place, he wouldn't stay behind. He tells me he's parked out front a few times over the years to admire it."

Tom took Ostrander's hand. "You folks are welcome. Mel, try to connect with the man in the brown suit. He's the Old Country craftsman who's putting the place back into shape."

Ostrander and Schumacher had already spotted each other and waved greetings. Still grasping Tom's hand, Mel called over his shoulder, "Emil, you want to take me on a tour?"

Tom passed the Ostranders off to Emil, who steered them toward the main fireplace, one of his more challenging projects. Emil caught Mel's eye dropping to open seams between flooring strakes and muttered, "Ya, ya, ve didn't have no time for dat yet. Come on, I show you the gute stuff."

Annie, her beer glass drained, took Trish in tow for a second run at the bar. Tom began to relax. Things were starting well.

By two thirty, the first wave of guests had exhausted their curiosity about the home and drifted through the solarium to the patio, where a rented gazebo gave relief from the autumn sun. Tom and Jane sipped apple juice and circulated, greeting and introducing the newly arrived, helped for a time by Aunt Sigi until she was cornered by her friends, Inger and Karl. With the temperature in the low seventies, the high-arched front doors stood open with a doorman at either side to check invitations. Tom kept an eye out for loners as guests eddied from group to group. Northbridge mayor Sarah Kenyon arrived, followed by William Dodge and Dennis Malcolm from the bank. Tom was able to identify most; for the few he was unable to supply with names, he made a quick study of a doorman's list of invitees. Seeing Wainwright's name freshened Tom's apprehensions about Garnie's ghost's plans. He stood alone staring out at the street to get composed.

Ardis Swenson, dressed in a rose-hued, sari-like gown arrived with her invalid husband, Linne, nearby guests boosting his wheelchair up the marble steps. L. H. Terhune, publisher of the *Northbridge World* and Garnie's longtime contender for the title of Outstanding Town Curmudgeon, turned heads upon entering. Terhune was identifiable by his girth and swagger that carried him straight to the buffet, where, disdaining forks and plates, he ranged the table with napkin in hand, treating each offering as finger food. Tom gave a hoot of delight when Darrel Van Horn and his wife, Toshi, entered. Alicia Morrison came clad in a verdigris tent and a collection of orange baubles. Stunned by the change in the home, she threw her arms wide and howled, "Beautiful, oh, how beautiful." She rushed to press herself against Tom. "I had no idea it could ever be like this again. You must take me on a tour." Her gaze froze on Garnie's picture. "Oh, his portrait. I've never seen it before. Who is the artist?"

Betty Runyon arrived accompanied by her daughter, Ellen. She latched onto Jane to tell her how nice it was to be so honored with an invitation and proudly displayed the embossed card, which read "In recognition of your contributions to Northbridge youth through church and education, you are cordially invited to an open house at the historic Pittman mansion…" Knowing Betty's peculiarities, Jane wondered about the thought behind the invitation. When, in the course of conversation, Betty chose to criticize the availability of "drink," Jane avoided responding by exclaiming, "There's Sarah Kenyon, our mayor. Come along, you two should get to know each other."

Jane was introduced to Chet and Doris Tovson, a pair of handsome elders. Chet introduced himself as former manager of the Pittman Pacific Mill before it burned. She greeted Andy, Pittman Pacific's witty CPA, while Claudia McPhaiden, in her trademark dark business suit, stood near, chatting amiably with a group of suits and ties. Jane wished for a chance to read her invitation.

Tom dropped out of a conversation when he spotted Phil Krause's head above the crowd. "Phil, Sarah…another wonderful surprise in an afternoon of surprises. You should know that Mr. Pittman did the invitations before he died, and I accept your presence as testimony to his good judgment. Come in, come in, we have some interesting people for you to meet—and observe."

Smiling mischievously, Phil replied, "Uh-huh, a real mixed bag—Claudia, Terhune, Martin, Van Horn, Chesterton. Why so many school people, and who are the others, the strutters and posturers?"

"Aside from friends, we have two mixed bags here from Garnie's two favorite arenas—school people and corporate big shots. I can't speak for the corporate bunch but look at the school people, both sides of the school board and enough unresolved grudges to start a riot. Does it seem strange that terminated teachers were invited to the same party as the people who canned them? I wonder if Wainwright's going to show. He's on the guest list."

Krause said, "You have to be kidding. If he did show up, which will never happen, it would be like throwing a match into a fireworks warehouse." Sensing Tom's confusion, he said, "You mean you don't know?"

"Humor me. I've been a little one-dimensional fixing the place up. What don't I know?"

"Oh, this is too good. I'm getting a feel for your friend Pittman's type of intrigue." Krause pointed to the patio. "There she is. Pittman would want you to put your question to her. No doubt about it. Go on, now."

Tom wove through guests to where Claudia stood under the gazebo taking in the view of the Sound. Smiling, he said "I hope you're enjoying yourself."

"Quite impressive, Mr. Clausen. It seems that you were destined for other than school administration, wouldn't you agree?"

"If you're suggesting that you did me a favor, no, I can't. But you can do me one now. I understand there's some new buzz on Wainwright. Can you fill me in?"

McPhaiden's features hardened. She snapped, "Read the papers," and pivoted to march into the house.

Tom rejoined Krause. "Thanks a lot. All I got from that was one very pissed-off lady. Would you mind telling me what's going on?"

"Of course you know he jumped contract and disappeared." Tom shook his head. Krause continued, "Well, he did. It seems he surfaced in Utah. Somebody with the LDS church here got the word through family connections. Terhune gave it space on page one, not much, because he didn't have much information yet. The story, if it's accurate, is that he was arrested in Utah and turned over to federal agents. Terhune's article said an authoritative source volunteered that Wainwright wasn't his real name. You'll have to read it to believe it."

Tom sucked in a lung-stretching breath and let it slide out. "On that note, you'll have to excuse me." He wove through the crowd searching for Jane and found her with Alicia at the base of the lawn discussing the need for a new stairway to the beach. He squeezed her hand. "I need you for a moment, please." He led her to a shaded brick path next to the Swensons' garden wall. "Wainwright's under arrest in Utah. It seems he was an imposter, a fake."

"Oh, dear. Who else knows?"

"Everyone but us. There was a short article about him in the last issue of the *World*."

Jane leaned her head against his chest. "Oh boy. I guess that accounts for some of the odd comments I've been catching." She looked up at him. "Then I suppose we'd better get back inside to referee. Oh dear."

A banker type in a casual gray suit and glossy woven-leather loafers accosted Tom as he and Jane returned. He introduced himself as Paul, no last name offered, and asked if he could have a minute of Tom's time. He directed Tom out the front door and onto the stairway. Indicating the grounds, he said, "Great job, Tom. I can't tell you how much you've improved the curb appeal. When this classic hits the market, given its view and lot size, it'll fetch top dollar. The only drawback is the neighborhood. If we could interest a developer in snapping up those cottages across the street, we could doze 'em, throw in enough fill to raise the lots for partial views, and put up some homes in the six- to seven-hundred-thousand range. Nothing too fancy mind you, just enough to jack up the value of the neighborhood. I just wanted to congratulate you for your good work."

He patted Tom on the shoulder and was turning to reenter the party when Tom grasped his lapel and pulled him back. "The Cape Cod across the street—do you see it?"

"What the hell do you think you're doing?" He pulled against Tom's grip.

"That is not only a house. That is my home." He relaxed his grip and pushed him away, saying, "Enjoy the party." Tom left the dealmaker at a loss for words and rejoined his guests, thinking, "Garnie, you old fox." He found Krause by himself, people watching.

Krause said, "You're right. I can feel it coming. It's in the air. From what you've told me about Pittman, I wouldn't expect anything less."

They looked about as the rippling background of voices turned strident. At the buffet, Aunt Sigi stormed up behind Terhune to smack his greasy fingers with a serving fork and order him to "eat like a gentleman or go home!"

Krause said, "Do you think your friend foresaw that?"

Tom said, "You were asking about the others, the ones with the expensive haircuts. They're not here for the free booze and food. Most, if not all, are angling to improve their connections with Pittman Pacific. So what do we have? Ambitious climbers, power seekers, abusers of office, victims, and revenge seekers. All under one roof.

"Here's another one for you: A moneyman just congratulated me for the work done on this place. The way he put it was…," and Tom told him about the scheme for demolishing his home. "I wish you'd known Garnie well enough to appreciate his flair for the theatric or his delight in manipulating people. Being a hardwired social disaster, he couldn't deal with people face-to-face so he pulled strings from a distance like a puppeteer." Tom's wave took in the houseful of guests, "Everyone here's a puppet—me, the guy who thinks he's going to bulldoze my house, Claudia."

"Do you think he's pulling my strings?"

"Maybe. Maybe not. But bringing you together with Claudia was no accident. Or you might think of your invitation as an honor, a counterpoint to the sleazeballs. When Garnie wasn't being insufferable, he liked to recognize talent and reward it." Jane caught his eye, her raised finger stirring the air. "Walk with me; Jane says I have to circulate."

The crowd topped out at well over a hundred. Tom's role as host was generally accepted, which kept him busy shaking hands and acknowledging the glowing comments about the house as though it were his. Terhune abandoned the buffet and, with pen and notepad in hand, shouldered Krause aside to burden Tom with questions for the next week's issue of his paper.

Tom rejoined Krause and looked back. "Terhune's back into the food, thinking he's got his story. I hope you and Sarah don't plan to leave; the really interesting stuff is yet to come."

"You're still convinced Pittman's staged a happening?"

"Without a doubt. It's like our demented genius created what our profession calls 'teachable moments.' Look around, antagonizers mixing with the antagonized and pain mongers with sufferers; something's going to pop. Follow me. If it's going to happen, I might as well prime the pump."

Tom led Krause toward a conversation group where Claudia McPhaiden appeared to be making a point. He accosted a dark-suited executive type. "Hello, I'm Tom Clausen, and this gentleman is Dr. Krause, new superintendent of the Moraine School District." He turned to Claudia. "Well, isn't it a small world?" He turned back to the men. "Dr. Krause and I share the distinction of having been canned by Ms. McPhaiden. Watch yourselves."

Claudia emitted a brittle laugh. "Oh, come now, you were both due to rise. Look what you've done with yourselves."

Tom replied, "Ah, yes. We should thank you for that. The question is does Northbridge thank you for it? Enjoy the party, Ms. McPhaiden. Gentlemen."

Krause pulled him aside. "Well, you just proved your point about Pittman. He jerked your strings, and you responded. That's not like you, Tom. What's got into you?"

"Me? What got into you when you sicced me on Claudia to ask about Wainwright?" He looked back toward Claudia who was enjoying a breezy conversation with a new listener. "Look at her. Criticism rolls off her like water off a duck. Am I sorry I ruffled her feathers? No, I'm mad."

Gene Boatman, CEO of Port Gardner Savings Bank, arrived, followed by Dr. Pennington who lived two doors east of the Pittman house. Linne Swenson tired early, so he and Ardis were first to depart. They left as Dale Runyon arrived with Dana Gustafson on his arm. Dennis Cray, head librarian of the Northbridge library, followed them in and was surprised to find one and then another of his junior librarians milling with guests.

Tom called Krause's attention to the newcomers. "Dale's here. This tops it all." He rushed to the door to grab him in a bear hug that Dale returned one-armed, maintaining a grip on Dana's hand. "Dale, you know Phil." He turned to Dana, "Have you met Phil Krause? Phil, I'd like you to meet Dana Gustafson, Martin Koutac's daughter." Krause, almost two heads taller than Dana, beamed down. "Very pleased to meet you. Did you know your dad and sister are here? Last seen, they were on the patio."

Phil and Dana chatted, giving Tom space to whisper to Dale, "Betty's here, but we'd have to ask Garnie why. No, considering that he invited Claudia along with the people she fired, bringing you and Betty together was intentional and mean-spirited. This'll be hard to forgive, filling his house with animosity and setting me up as referee."

Dale handed his invitation to Tom. "Read it. If this is an example, he custom-tailored each one to stroke an ego— a nice touch but putting Betty and me in the same room?"

Tom looked at the invitation: "In recognition of your invaluable service to Northbridge High School, both academically and athletically, you are cordially invited to an open house at the historic Pittman mansion."

"I figured that since it was my only thank-you since being fired, why not? So here we are." He glanced across the room to find Betty staring at him. He tightened his grip on Dana's hand. "And there she is. Tom, are you sure Caligula didn't make out the guest list?" Dale exchanged glances with Dana and said, "Excuse us for a minute, will you?"

He drew Dana into the solarium. "She's here. It might be best to leave before we have a confrontation. She can be vicious."

Dana gave him a searching look. "So Jen tells me. But it seems like a nice party, so I'm not going to let her keep me from enjoying myself. A time like this had to come. I didn't expect it to be so soon, and I didn't expect it to be fun, but here we are. Better to get it over with in a crowd where she can't go nuts. Let's do it."

"You're sure?"

"Yes, I'm sure. What's the matter, you chicken?"

"Yes, I know her." He looked back at his ex to catch her snapping her head away, unwilling to be caught staring at him. "Maybe you're right. Maybe it's best you find out what she can be. Let's go."

Upset by Dale's approach, Betty strained to maintain her conversation with Alicia Morrison. She was aware of him standing at the edge of her vision but pretended to ignore him until she saw he was holding a woman's hand. She made a sound like a hiccup and jerked around to face them, slopping Perrier and lemon on the floor. Alicia, not accustomed to losing others' attention, drifted away to fascinate someone else, leaving Dale and Betty locked in a stare-down while Dana watched demurely.

Dale broke the ice. "Betty, I'd like you to meet my friend, Dana Gustafson. Dana, Betty and I were married until recently."

Betty lifted her chin. "Your friend?"

Dale tugged at Dana. "Trust me, we should go. This isn't going to turn out well."

Betty, already six inches taller than Dana, threw her head back to look down her nose. "How old are you, child?" Nodding toward Dale, she said, "Did I hear him say 'trust me'? Aren't you the tramp who almost lost your life trusting him? A home-wrecker, and so young."

Ellen, along with other nearby guests, was alerted by her mother's strident tone. She stepped between Betty and Dana.

"Mother, stop it! Try to get control of yourself."

"God forgive you for siding with adulterers. It shames me that I brought you to where you could see the two of them together, shameless sinners that they are. Say goodbye to your father because he has forsaken 'the way' in choosing the sinner's path. Come, we're leaving."

Ellen shook her head. "No, I'm staying. We'll talk when you come to your senses."

Dale guided Dana away from the hubbub and into the den, where he said, "I'm so sorry that your family might have witnessed that."

She yanked her hand from his grip to jab a finger onto his sternum. "Well I'm not; I hope they did. Your ex just threw the Koutac family's doors open to you. And if they didn't see it, they've heard about it by now. You watch, after what she just did to another Koutac, they're gonna take you in like a starving refugee. She says there are two tramps in the Koutac family? You'll see."

Guests goggled at the high-decibel tiff as Betty wailed, "Godless, godless, godless." Challenging the onlookers, she shouted, "It will be no less painful for you who harbor adulterers and fornicators," and rushed out the door. Looking on with Phil and Sarah Krause, Tom whispered, "Like I was saying."

A few steps away, Claudia, who had lost the attention of her conversational partners to Betty, made another try at captivating a listener. She said, "Hello, I'm Claudia McPhaiden," to which the lady replied, "I'm so sorry about that; you'd do better to keep it to yourself. I'm Carol Hudson, wife of one of your victims. You might remember firing my husband, Ian Hudson? By the way, the tall blonde with the big voice is Betty Runyon. Her ex-husband is here, you know."

Claudia's rush from the house might not have been noticed had she not slammed her glass down forcefully enough to break it on the seventeenth-century Flemish sideboard and later ignored the parking valets to storm down the driveway, shouting, "What has been done with my car?"

The ripple of comments following Claudia's departure settled back to cocktail talk among the corporate contingent. A small man sporting cowboy attire took Alicia in tow to make an introduction. "Mr. Hodges? Remember me? I'm Merrill Smythe, stockholder in Pittman Pacific. Of course you know Mrs. Morrison." Alicia, halfway through her fourth Chardonnay, extended a languid hand. Smythe continued, "Considering the impact of Mr. Pittman's passing, we feel it would be in the interests of both the corporation and the stockholders to schedule a special meeting as soon as possible—that is, a stockholders' meeting."

Gene Boatman, CEO of Pittman Pacific, smiled paternally. "Not to worry, my friend. The company remains in the same capable hands that directed it for years. Isn't your annual meeting scheduled for January, as usual?"

"You know it is. You also know that your tame board of directors meets before then. What we want is a moratorium on board action until the stockholders meet. No, make that, we *demand* a moratorium."

Boatman's smile stiffened. "I don't understand where this is coming from. Do you have some reason to suspect the board? What is it you're afraid might happen?"

"We're concerned about what might happen without Mr. Pittman seated on the board. He was our advocate. He took it upon himself to represent us, fighting the board at every turn. Until we know who's voting his shares, we can't allow the board any leeway. I'm sorry, but that's the way it has to be."

Boatman's smile bent into a sneer. "You can't allow the board leeway? Let me help you out, Mr. Smythe. It isn't up to you to tell the board when it can or cannot meet. If you persist, you'll need the assistance of a stable of very expensive attorneys. Now I'm sure you have other people to greet, so if you'll excuse us…"

Boatman turned from Smythe only to collide with Alicia Morrison's tented bulk. Alicia, swaying slightly, tipped her glass toward his blue paisley tie and said, "Really, Eugene, you should learn to be more accommodating." With the front of Boatman's linen suit darkly wet and her glass empty, Alicia stepped away and chirped, "Oh dear, it seems I need a refill." She pivoted to plow a path to the bar, the billows of her sequined gown sparkling in the afternoon sun.

CHAPTER 23

More than two months passed since Garnie's party. Tom, Jane, and Smythe had met with Boatman, Malcolm, and Markovic at the bank each Wednesday morning to expand their understanding of Pittman holdings and operations. Sensitive to Boatman's hostility and the daunting challenge of spreadsheets and financial statements, Andy Markovic, Pittman Pacific's lead CPA, guided Tom, Jane, and Smythe through the labyrinth of numbers. When Malcolm sought to gloss over executive compensation, a tension arose that moved Markovic closer to the stockholders. In successive meetings, it was to Markovic, not Malcolm and Boatman, that Tom addressed questions, which left them fidgeting with concern.

Tom, Jane, Merrill Smythe, and Andy Markovic were gathered in Garnie's home office, where Markovic led them through his analysis of Garnie's hidden files. Upon arriving, he thanked Tom privately for excluding Boatman and Malcolm, tactfully agreeing that certain revelations about the estate might be more conveniently illuminated with them absent. The new person in the group was Martha Sperry, a taciturn corporate attorney who cut her legal teeth with a prestigious Seattle law firm specializing in the financial sector. Sperry's was the name that surfaced most often during Tom's casting about for counsel.

It had taken Markovic's accountant's eye to unravel Garnie's files. He displayed spreadsheets dating from 1993 that Pittman had highlighted to point out differences between numbers from internal records and those published in annual reports. While Tom was boggled by the weight of data, Jane was in the thick of it, taking notes and nimbly questioning issues that flew over his head. His struggle to grasp the broad sweep of Pittman affairs gave rise to his first question to

Markovic: "Andy, Pittman Pacific has forty-one million and change in the CWP scholarship fund. And you say that the fund is committed to dispense five percent per annum, which is a little over two million. If, as you say, I get paid a hundred seventy-five thousand plus expenses, that's pushing nine percent for me. Isn't that a little steep?"

Markovic turned the projector off. "Tom, the fund was originally set up to maintain itself at twenty-five million or more. Beyond its basic endowment, it gets income from Pittman land deals. What happens is that when urban growth rubs up against parcels of timberland, they now and then get rezoned to residential or commercial. Call it growth. The price per acre skyrockets. It's been a Pittman Pacific policy to maintain a constant balance of timber acreage by selling off rezoned land to developers and buying up equivalent acreages of forest. The upshot is that including logging—understand that we clear-cut the acreage we sell—we net an average of eleven thousand dollars per acre of rezoned land and pay out about fifteen hundred to replace it. Half the proceeds go to the CWP fund. You get to choose whether to disburse it or sock it away in the fund."

"How much are we talking about?"

Markovic turned on the projector again and called up an operating revenue sheet. He pointed to a line item. "That's the 2001 figure, nearly $1.4 million in land sales. The fund's share was around seven hundred thousand dollars, which brought the total amount that could have been disbursed last year to around three million. Based on that figure, your cut doesn't seem so exorbitant, does it?"

Jane said, "Interesting that Boatman and Malcolm never mentioned that land sales affect the fund."

"Well, yes, that is interesting," Markovic agreed, spacing his words. "Let's say it's been easier to deliver the big picture here rather than there and leave it at that."

Sperry interjected, "That's cool, unless something comes to light that might require further attention."

She and Markovic nodded agreement to each other.

Tom and Jane dined that evening at Tuscany on the Port Gardner waterfront. Jane touched his glass to hers. "I noticed you ordered the cheapest wine on the list, Mr. Miser. You can take the boy out of the country, but you can't take the country out of the boy."

"Do you really want us to change?"

"Nope. It's enough to know that we could indulge ourselves if we wanted to. Like a trip to Italy?"

"Could happen, maybe with a side trip to Bulgaria. Give me another month or two of throwing my newfound weight around, plus studying up on the board seats I've fallen into, or onto. Right now I'm having a blast exerting power."

"Like 'advising' Port Gardner Savings Bank to open a position for director of technology and to invite Dale to apply?"

"Something like that. After one accounting period, they'll know their IT contractor was costing more than an in-house specialist. You ran the numbers. You know. Give 'em a few months with Dale and they'll thank me. Or us."

"Or for convincing the other woman in your life, Alice Michaelson, to submit her resignation so she can resume her role of bringing order to your desk?"

"An extra six thousand a year, flextime, and a hand in choosing recipients did help some. And you, what's it going to take to ensure that your agile numeric mind is on hand when I need it? You know I can't do this without you."

"Keep that in mind, Mr. Highflier. Now that they're gone, I suppose you'll get your pick of Boatman's or Malcolm's offices. I can't believe how deep they'd reached into the cookie jar, and Garnie left it to us to cut them off. What a guy."

They sat back to ruminate privately.

Jane broke the silence. "You know, I really understood it when Andy led us through his spreadsheets. I can do this stuff."

"You've always been the numbers person. My mind doesn't work that way."

"That last meeting at the bank, will we ever forget Malcolm's reaction to Andy's report?"

Tom shook his head slowly. "You could see the wheels turning.

Disbelief into outrage. Boatman took it like a man, but Malcolm looked like he was going to burst a blood vessel. They'd been so contemptuous of Garnie, when all the time he was tucking their shenanigans away in one innocent-looking manila folder marked 'Priority.' No directions for where to find it, stuck it away in a file drawer to be found or overlooked. Testing us to the end."

"I'd say we passed, Mr. Big Shot. Have you held still long enough to realize how big a big shot you've become? You're firing a CEO and a corporate counsel, two experienced big shots. At least they thought they were."

"Not quite, sweetheart. They're not being fired; they're going to resign. If they're as clever as they claim to be, they'll understand that, in their circumstances, walking away with their freedom is a pretty generous severance package."

Jane held her glass out for another pour and said, "Do you find it interesting that nobody's mentioned the elephant in the room?"

"You mean why, with all that evidence, Garnie didn't take them down?"

"Yep. He certainly had the temperament for it."

"It had to be that he couldn't, for reasons that died with him—I hope. Whatever leverage Markham and Boatman had over him isn't doing them much good now."

Shortly after six o'clock, families seeking choice bleacher seats streamed into Northbridge's stadium for the school's ninety-first graduation ceremony. Though the ceremony wouldn't begin for another hour, preparations had been underway since noon. Staging, skirted with blue and white bunting, bridged a length of sideline at midfield. Ribboned-off ranks of folding chairs on the track and sideline area awaited the graduating class. The band was setting up in a strip of track in front of the bleachers instead of their traditional block of seats in the lower center of the grandstand. With graduating classes now topping six hundred, every available seat was reserved for graduates' families.

Thirteen months had passed since Tom Clausen had been carried from the Northbridge High campus, time enough for the school to achieve a new balance under new leadership. He was finding it difficult to imagine working there, though there wasn't a wall on campus that could keep him from knowing what went on behind it. Memories were his remaining link, not a lingering desire to return or ambition to complete projects left undone, and most importantly, he felt no sense of belonging.

The separation between his new reality and his previous life became clear when he stopped at the district office to request two tickets to the upcoming graduation ceremony. Sorry, they said. Tickets are reserved for graduates' families only. Citizen Clausen. No more special rights or privileges from School District 508. But though his old channels had closed against him, he judged rightly that his new behind-the-scenes role carried enough clout to gain entry. He called Martin Koutac, school board chairman, who assured him that two tickets would be made available to him.

He and Jane found the hidden parking slots behind the cafeteria still empty. They locked the car and walked a familiar path to the stadium. Despite his detachment, Tom found himself on the lookout for litter and graffiti as though readying a memo for the custodial staff. They entered the stadium and climbed through a gauntlet of well-wishers, friends they were happy to greet, until oft-repeated, well-meaning questions had them looking for cover. The questions were sincere and the questioners' concern buoyed him up through the first twenty encounters. He wasn't easy about fleeing, but he wasn't going to let himself become a center of attention on the graduates' night.

They reached the top, knocked on the press-box door, and ducked in. "Thanks, Duane," said Tom. "We need to hide out for a bit." Duane Hendrickson, Northbridge High's ubiquitous events volunteer, was setting volume levels on a mixer board. Band Director Gordy Taylor roved from microphone to microphone at track level, sounding a tone from a tuning gadget and speaking into the mic. The third member of the team, a young woman Tom didn't recognize, stood halfway up the bleachers to gauge each tone and signal the press box for needed changes.

Following the national anthem and an invocation, Van Horn was first at the podium. As though addressing an infantry battalion, he laid down the rules: The audience would be permitted to applaud only after the last graduate received his or her diploma. "No personal cheering sections are allowed. If you do, you'll only be embarrassing yourselves and your sons or daughters." He explained that while there were many outstanding students and award winners, only the alphabet would rule their order of appearance.

The valedictorian, a rotund boy named Seth Parsons—a boy Tom recalled as an articulate complainer—gave a politically charged speech that challenged the graduates to make the world a better place by, after their eighteenth birthdays, using their votes to give the nation's capital a housecleaning. Pointed and partisan, Parsons had the board and invited VIPs throwing nervous glances at each other. A lesser speaker might have been politely interrupted, but the young man was a spellbinder, a natural and forceful speaker who brought his political allies to their feet. At the end of his speech, over half the audience erupted in applause that drowned out scattered catcalls and booing.

Tom leaned to Jane's ear. "This is why I won't miss graduations. You plan and plan, but something always upsets what you hope for."

"But the boy's in your camp. Why aren't you supporting him?"

"I do, but I can't. No, make that I couldn't have—back then. It's a public school thing. Principals, teachers, students—it doesn't matter who; school people aren't supposed to speak for or encourage partisan opinion. Thank you, Seth Parsons, for helping me to be happily out of it."

Board members went through the ritual of trading handshakes for empty diploma folders. Twenty students at a time lined up to climb the stairs at the right, heard their awards announced, received their blue leatherette folders, and exited without a hitch. The tone changed after Charlie Perkins bowed deeply when handed his empty folder. Instead of moving off, he looked inside, showed the audience it was empty, and staggered crestfallen to the stairs. Perkins's physical comedy changed the dignified ceremony into a happening. Ignoring Van Horn's admonition, families cheered and whistled, and graduates competed to see who could pull off the most original passage across the stage.

Once the tide turned, there was no stopping it. A semblance of order returned for the awarding of special honors and scholarships. Midway through, board member Trish Ostrander called out, "Winner of the Charles Winston Pittman Award in the amount of twelve thousand dollars, an award she will use for tuition and expenses at Stanford University, is Deanna Longstreet. Congratulations, Deanna."

Jane hugged Tom's arm as she whispered, "What are you thinking?"

"How it feels to be part of Miss Longstreet's story and how many times Garnie must have felt the same."

She firmed her grip and said, "Yes, gone but not forgotten. Do you miss him?"

"A big yes and a little no. Being that close to a truly fabulous character was special, but I couldn't help suspecting that something might pop up to divide us. There were times when he was pretty hard to take,"

"No, no, no. Under the bluster, you two loved each other too much for that to happen." She turned his chin toward her and said. "Why so serious? What's going on? Out with it, Mr. Reticent."

"At times like this I don't know how to thank him enough. We owe him so much."

The grandstand emptied as families poured down to track level to join with graduates. With the band dispersed, an orchestral recording of "Pomp and Circumstance" floated on the warm evening air, repeating and repeating until it ended with a click. Duane flipped the press box's lights off, locked up, and waved goodnight as he passed, leaving Tom and Jane huddled on the top bench of an empty grandstand.

CPSIA information can be obtained
at www.ICGtesting.com
Printed in the USA
LVHW090328180720
661006LV00001B/5